DARK SHADOWS

THE COMPLETE ORIGINAL SERIES: VOLUME THREE

HERMES
PRESS

neshannock, pennsylvania

Published by Hermes Press
2100 Wilmington Road
Neshannock, Pennsylvania 16105
(724) 652-0511
www.HermesPress.com; info@hermespress.com

Cover image: Jonathan Frid as Barnabas Collins painted by George Wilson
Cover and book design by Daniel Herman
First printing, 2011
LCCN 2011929309
ISBN 1-932563-57-1

Image scanning and digital corrections by H + G Media and Louise Geer, Troy Musguire, and Alissa Ross, who all
worked above and beyond the call

From Dan, Louise, Sabrina, and D'zur for Gort and Maya

Dates of original publication: *Dark Shadows* #15, August, 1972; #16, October, 1972; #17, December, 1972; #18, February, 1973; #19, April, 1973; #20, June, 1973; and #21, August, 1973. All comic artwork by Joe Certa. All covers painted by George Wilson.

Acknowledgments

Hermes Press would like to thank Jim Pierson and the rest of the folks at Dan Curtis Productions for their help in supplying the many extras found in this book and the volumes to come. Also, a tip of the ole hat to Dr. Jeff Thompson who was kind enough to write the enlightening Introduction to this book.

Publisher's Note

As anticipation grows with the announcement of a big screen version of *Dark Shadows* there's been renewed interest in the original. Fans of the show are still loyal and enthusiastic about *Dark Shadows* and there's optimism amongst admirers of the series that cinematic treatment of the show will generate even more interest in Barnabas, Collinwood, and its residents. Volumes One and Two of our complete reprint and our complete overhaul of The Story Digest of our series met with overwhelming support and requests that we speed up production of these reprints, so we're obliging and Volumes Four and Five will be forthcoming shortly.

— *Daniel Herman*, Publisher

Printed in China

DARK SHADOWS

THE COMPLETE ORIGINAL SERIES: VOLUME THREE

contents

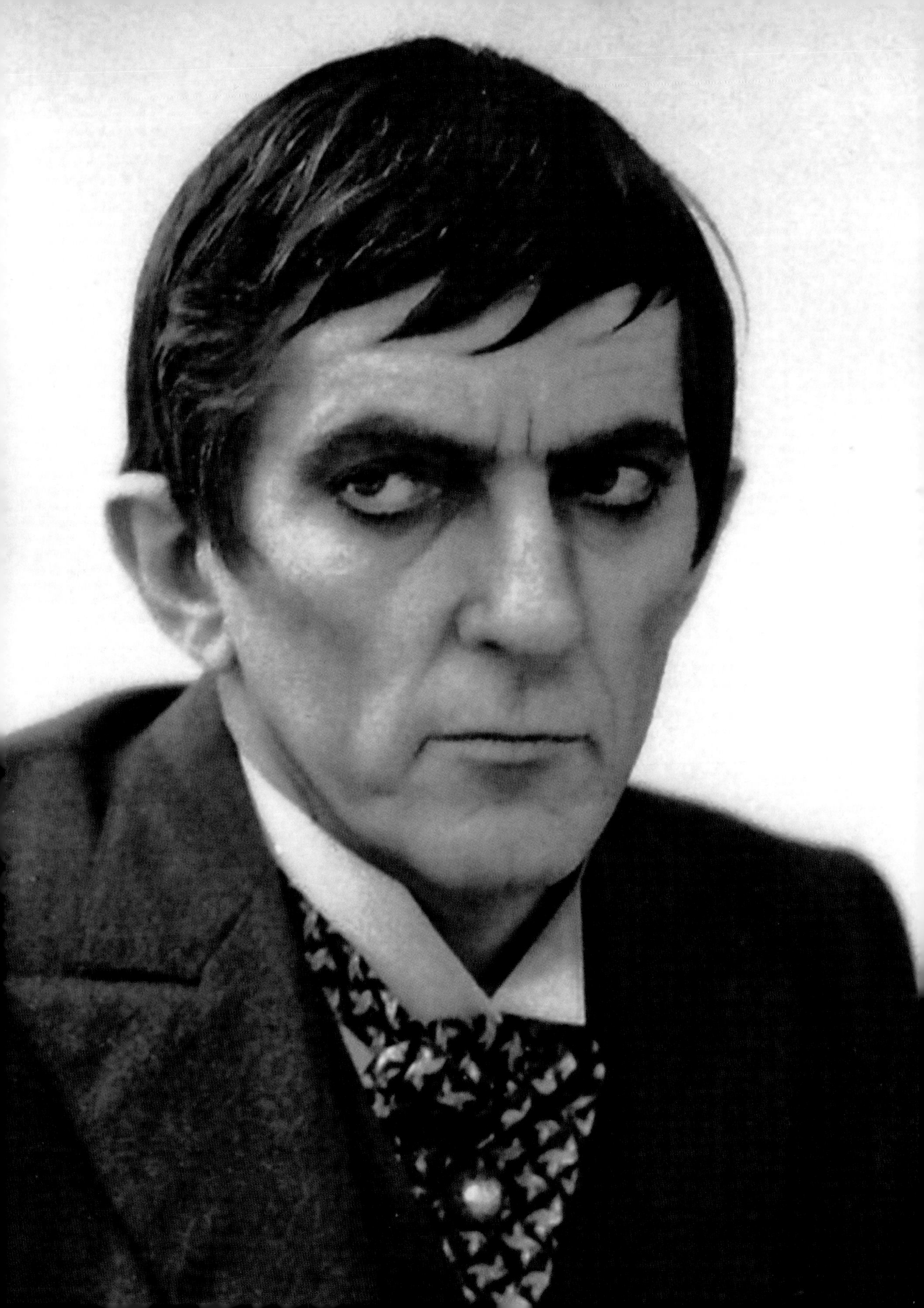

Introduction

Dark Shadows: A Look at the Comics

By 1972, the year that *Dark Shadows* creator Dan Curtis produced *The Night Stalker* for ABC-TV and began a decade of bringing horror to night time television, the bi-monthly *Dark Shadows* comic book had become a reliable seller for Gold Key Comics. By then, the comic-book series about Barnabas and Quentin Collins had outlasted the original television series on ABC (June 1966-April 1971), Dan "Marilyn" Ross's series of *Dark Shadows* novels for Paperback Library (December 1966-March 1972), and the *Dark Shadows* newspaper comic strip from Newspaper Enterprise Association (March 1971-March 1972). Indeed, Gold Key's *Dark Shadows* series would last until late 1975, a few months after the TV show had risen again in syndication on local stations.

Every issue of *Dark Shadows* was illustrated by Joe Certa, co-creator of DC Comics' Martian Manhunter, and edited by Wallace I. Green, Gold Key's managing editor. The uncredited writers included Donald J. Arneson and Arnold Drake. Throughout the comic book's 35-issue run (dated December 1968-February 1976), Green, Arneson, and Drake remained faithful to their basic

concept of the character of Barnabas Collins as "a romantic hero." According to Wally Green, "We thought of him as a sympathetic character with a lot of problems. That's the way we saw him. He had to be a hero despite the evil part of him which he was constantly fighting." The reluctant vampire Barnabas was a more sympathetic anti-hero than the title character of the Marvel Comics Group's *Tomb of Dracula,* which had premiered in early 1972 at the moment when Gold Key had shrewdly promoted *Dark Shadows* from quarterly to bi-monthly status. In the stories in *Dark Shadows* #15-21, Barnabas reveals his heroic, villainous, and even romantic sides. Here is an issue-by-issue look at the comic books reprinted in this third volume of *Dark Shadows: The Complete Original Series* from Hermes Press.

DARK SHADOWS #15 (August 1972). **"The Night Children."** Cali, girl queen of demons, and Andras, boy marquis of Hades, are called up from hell by Angelique to battle Barnabas and Quentin both at Collinwood and in the netherworld. In "the Black Pit," Barnabas battles "Zozos, the creatures which bear fallen spirits from above to this terrible place." Later, Angelique inflicts upon both Barnabas and Quentin "another, more horrible

Atmospheric publicity portrait of Jonathan Frid as Barnabas Collins from *Dark Shadows*.

fate—the Harppes." In this issue, Joe Certa draws Angelique with flowing russet hair and Quentin as a ferocious werewolf. Certa's Zozos are winged, ape-like demons, and his Harppes are flying shrouds with skulls for faces. Barnabas's wolf's-head cane plays a role in the story as both Angelique and the Harppes turn away from "silver, the cursed metal of purity!"

DARK SHADOWS #16 (October 1972). **"The Scarab."** This story begins *in medias res* as Potiphar, an immortal Egyptian sorcerer, tells an enslaved Barnabas Collins, "I have lived more than 4000 years! You a mere 200! But today our time in eternity has come! Today **I** will become master of the sun and lord of all earth!" After six action-packed pages, the unnamed writer's story goes back "only one short month ago" and reveals how Potiphar comes to Collinwood; hypnotizes Quentin, Elizabeth, Roger, Julia, and Stokes; and robs Barnabas of his will.

Potiphar orders the helpless vampire to steal the Double-Headed Crown of Senem and the Golden Girdle of Ibex. They are the only artifacts that remain to be acquired before the entire, lost Treasure of the First Kingdom is restored. Once all of the enchanted riches are in Potiphar's possession, he will be infused with enough energy to "rule the sun and the earth forever!" The world's only hope is that "the good in [Barnabas's] nature" will break Potiphar's unholy control of him. For this issue, Joe Certa draws pyramids, scarabs, sarcophagi, tanks, and Jeeps.

DARK SHADOWS #17 (December 1972). **"The Bride of Barnabas Collins."** In one of the best stories in the series, Barnabas slips through "the foggy mists of time" and emerges in "that dreaded somewhere which is nowhere…the place which has no past and no future…the place of eternal present"—Limbo. In this strange place out of time, Barnabas meets Hope Forsythe, a dark-haired beauty who

is being forced into marriage by the corrupt Tibourne. It is love at first sight for Hope and Barnabas, and they pledge themselves to each other immediately.

Barnabas defeats Tibourne with the help of Ward Forsythe, Hope's brother, who is also lost in Limbo. Barnabas tells Hope, "[Now] we can return safely to the real world together!" However, he and his beloved are of two different worlds that will never meet again, and "once he passes through the fogs of time, [he and Hope] will be separated forever."

Suddenly, Barnabas finds himself back at Collinwood—and Hope is gone. In the last panel, Barnabas whispers to the wind, "I will never forget you, Hope! You have shown me [that] the dream of happiness I long for may one day come true! Good-bye, my love—my Hope!" (Despite the catchy title of the story, Hope weds neither Tibourne nor Barnabas.)

DARK SHADOWS #18 (February 1973). **"Guest in the House."** This change-of-pace crime drama is another one of the best stories of the comic-book series. Erik Mica, New York's underworld kingpin, hides out at Collinwood and (as realtor "Erik Michaels") courts Elizabeth Collins Stoddard. He realizes Barnabas's secret when he does not see Barnabas's reflection in his cigarette case. Mica threatens to expose Barnabas as a vampire unless Barnabas joins forces with him in crime.

Both men are taken by surprise when Paul Robbor, Mica's arch enemy, follows Mica to Collinwood and passes himself off as Erik's "business partner." By the end of "Guest in the House," one criminal has fallen to his death from Widow's Hill, and the other has died, become a vampire, and perished at sunrise. Joe Certa's splash page of urban mob warfare—"the violence of underworld wars"—is impressive. Meanwhile, cover artist George Wilson's painting for the cover of *Dark Shadows #18* is especially striking as it depicts Mica, Robbor, Collinwood—and Barnabas's transformation into a bat ready to attack one of the mobsters.

DARK SHADOWS #19 (April 1973). **"Island of Eternal Life."** Barnabas's will is stolen by Captain Targut, the ghostly captain of a phantom pirate ship from 1609. Targut's pirates take Barnabas aboard the spectral vessel where Targut's confederate Farnsworthy performs a magical rite over him.

The phantom ship sails to the Island of Eternal Youth where Lani, a Polynesian ghost-woman, helps Barnabas stage a mutiny and reclaim his will. "Remove the curse which locks my will in that vial around your neck or pay the consequences!" Barnabas warns Captain Targut. The ghostly pirate's destruction frees the souls of the others, and Barnabas leaves the island. In the form of a bat, he flies back to Collinsport. "How strange," he thinks to himself, "that from her, my own hope for peace is renewed! Good-bye, Lani—forever!"

DARK SHADOWS #20 (June 1973). **"Quentin the Vampire."** Dr. Julia Hoffman injects the vampire Barnabas Collins with a blood serum which "only balances [his] system temporarily." She is unaware that her patient's cousin Quentin Collins also suffers from an unspeakable curse. When Quentin transforms into a werewolf in front of Julia, she stabs him with the closest weapon, a hypodermic filled with Barnabas's "blood serum." Now, Quentin becomes a *vampire* under a full moon!

"I have an idea," Julia tells Barnabas, and flies to Canada in an unresolved plot point that perhaps foreshadows the events of *Dark Shadows* #33 (August 1975, "King of the Wolves") two years later. Ignorant of the true nature of Quentin's problem, Roger sends Quentin "to New York City to see a specialist in brain disease," and Barnabas chases his cousin all the way to New York's Chinatown (in the last four pages of the story) before he can inject Quentin with Julia's serum which ends Quentin's vampirism but not his werewolfism. "His curse is as it was in the beginning," Julia later tells Barnabas, "but we know there is a cure somewhere." Barnabas, retiring to his coffin, holds out hope for both his cousin and himself.

DARK SHADOWS #21 (August 1973). **"The Crimson Carnival."** The arrival in Collinsport of Dr. Karl Ruthven's Carnival of the Occult coincides with the visit of Elizabeth's cousin, Constance Collins Harker, and her new husband Garry. The Harkers, who were introduced in *Dark Shadows* #13 (April 1972, "Hellfire"), return to Collinwood in order for Garry to use the Collins family library "to do some research on witchcraft for [his] psychology thesis."

Garry Harker is not the only one interested in that arcane library. Dr. Karl Ruthven craves the *Book of Eternity,* an ancient volume of powerful spells, and the last known copy rests in the Collinses' dusty collection. Barnabas's coffin is stolen—and Constance learns Barnabas's secret—in the course of this *Dark Shadows* adventure.

In the next seven *Dark Shadows* issues, Barnabas Collins will battle the witch Angelique, a cult of vampires, and a giant, two-headed dog while a shrunken Quentin Collins will face a "giant" cat *a la The Incredible Shrinking Man.* These next seven issues will include another nod to 1950s sci-fi—a *Dark Shadows* remake of *Invasion of the Body Snatchers* (in issue #22)—as well as one of the very best stories of the series (issue #24) and the most notorious *Dark Shadows* story ever published (#28). All seven will be reprinted in volume four of this collection from Hermes Press.

— *Jeff Thompson, Ph. D.*

Dr. Jeff Thompson teaches English at Tennessee State University in Nashville. He is the Rondo Award-nominated author of *The Television Horrors of Dan Curtis: Dark Shadows, The Night Stalker, and Other Productions, 1966-2006* (McFarland, 2009) and *House of Dan Curtis: The Television Mysteries of the Dark Shadows Auteur* (Westview, 2010).

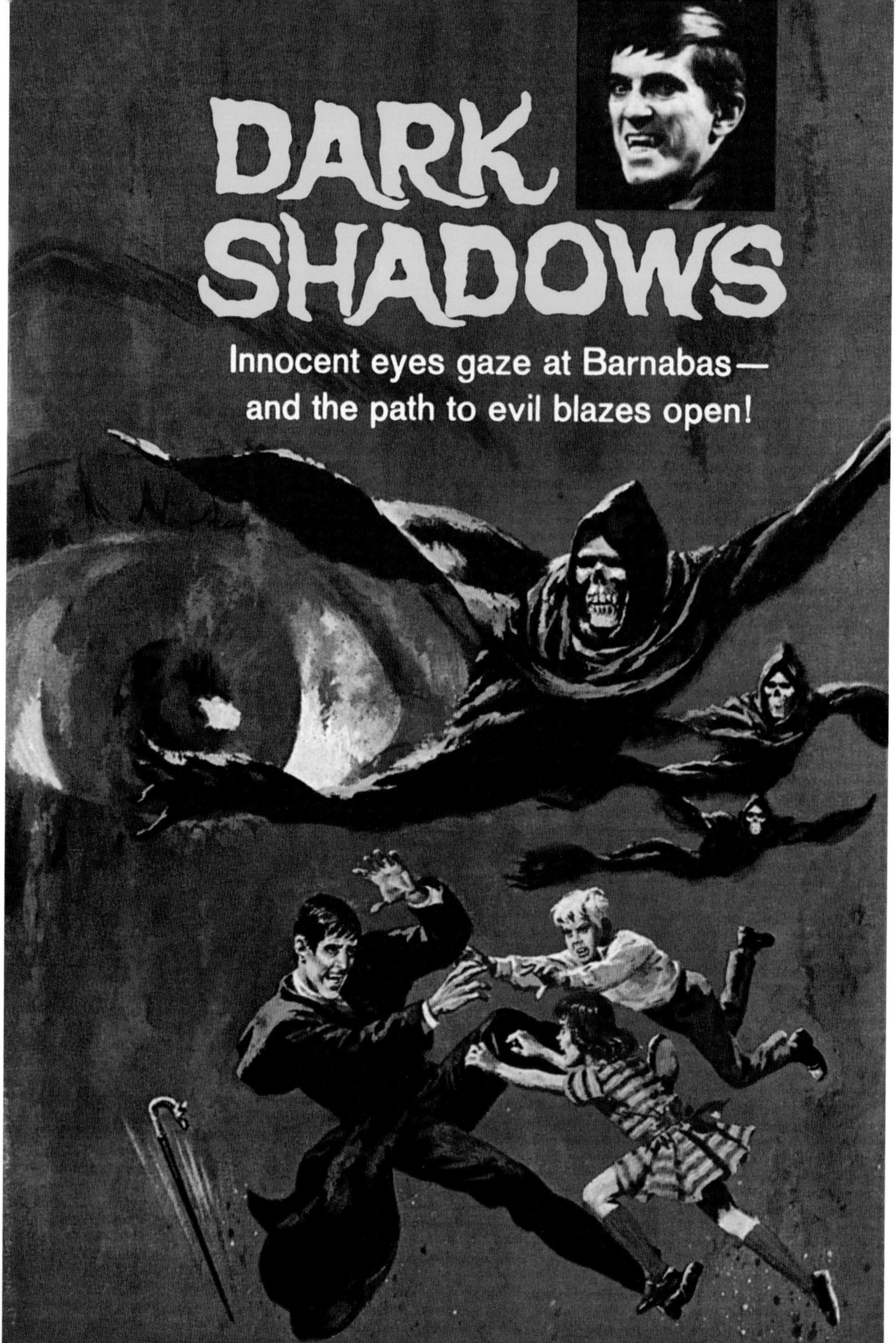
DARK SHADOWS
Innocent eyes gaze at Barnabas—
and the path to evil blazes open!

DARK SHADOWS

The NIGHT CHILDREN

PART 1: MASKS OF INNOCENCE

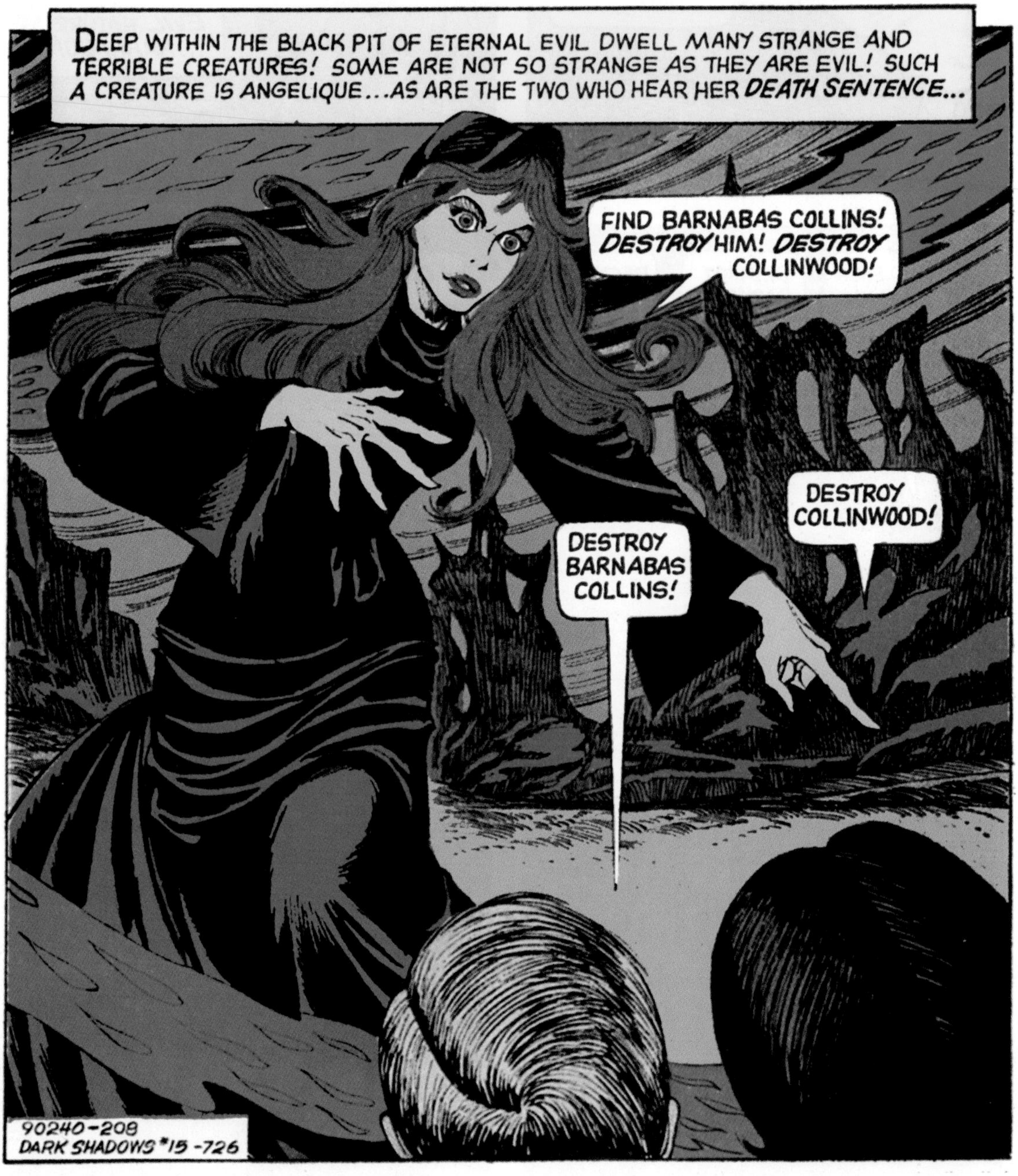

DEEP WITHIN THE BLACK PIT OF ETERNAL EVIL DWELL MANY STRANGE AND TERRIBLE CREATURES! SOME ARE NOT SO STRANGE AS THEY ARE EVIL! SUCH A CREATURE IS ANGELIQUE...AS ARE THE TWO WHO HEAR HER DEATH SENTENCE...
FIND BARNABAS COLLINS! DESTROY HIM! DESTROY COLLINWOOD!
DESTROY BARNABAS COLLINS!
DESTROY COLLINWOOD!
90240-208
DARK SHADOWS #15 -726

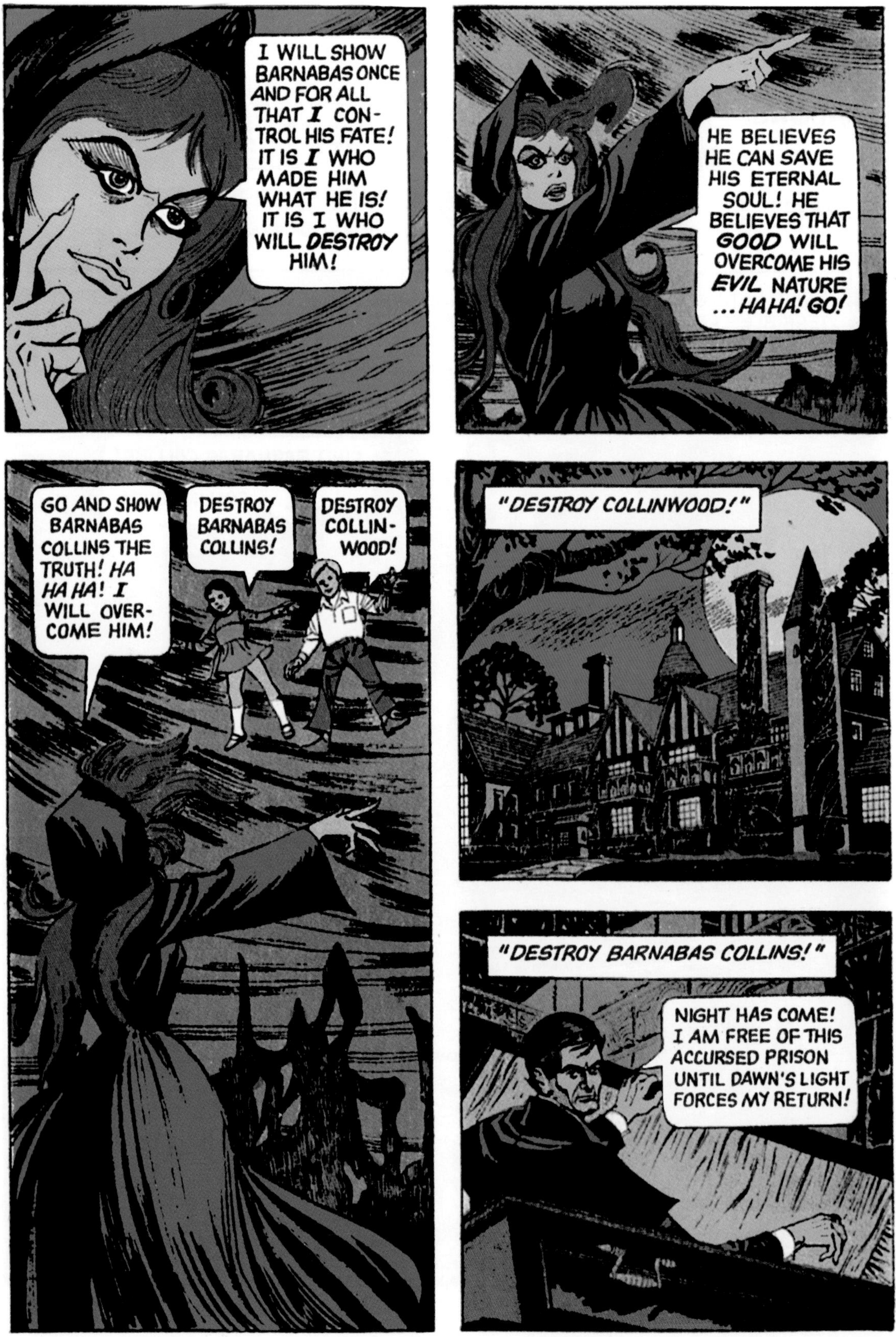
I WILL SHOW BARNABAS ONCE AND FOR ALL THAT I CONTROL HIS FATE! IT IS I WHO MADE HIM WHAT HE IS! IT IS I WHO WILL DESTROY HIM!
HE BELIEVES HE CAN SAVE HIS ETERNAL SOUL! HE BELIEVES THAT GOOD WILL OVERCOME HIS EVIL NATURE ...HA HA! GO!
GO AND SHOW BARNABAS COLLINS THE TRUTH! HA HA HA! I WILL OVERCOME HIM!
DESTROY BARNABAS COLLINS!
DESTROY COLLINWOOD!
"DESTROY COLLINWOOD!"
"DESTROY BARNABAS COLLINS!"
NIGHT HAS COME! I AM FREE OF THIS ACCURSED PRISON UNTIL DAWN'S LIGHT FORCES MY RETURN!

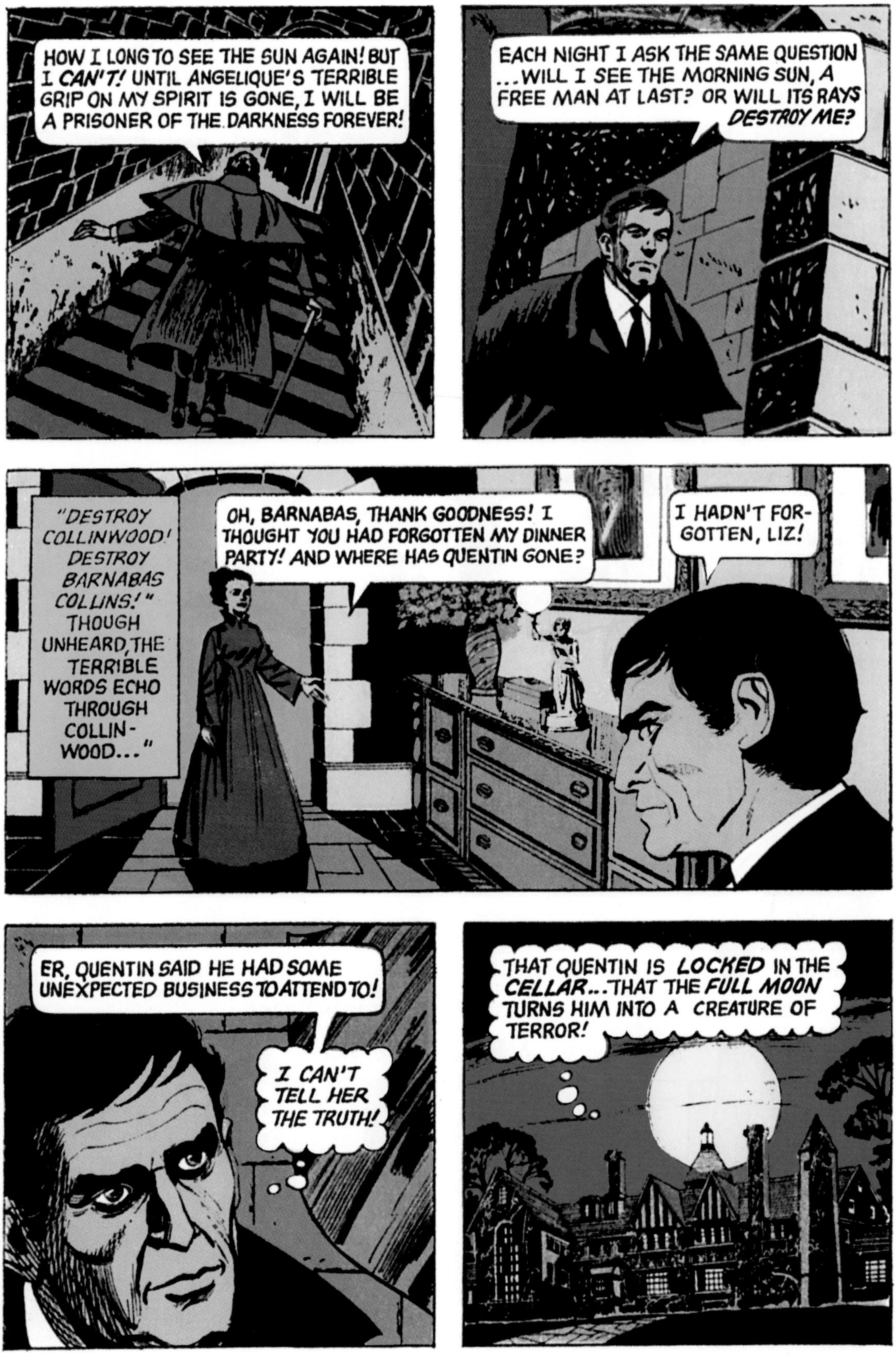
HOW I LONG TO SEE THE SUN AGAIN! BUT I CAN'T! UNTIL ANGELIQUE'S TERRIBLE GRIP ON MY SPIRIT IS GONE, I WILL BE A PRISONER OF THE DARKNESS FOREVER!
EACH NIGHT I ASK THE SAME QUESTION ...WILL I SEE THE MORNING SUN, A FREE MAN AT LAST? OR WILL ITS RAYS DESTROY ME?
"DESTROY COLLINWOOD! DESTROY BARNABAS COLLINS!" THOUGH UNHEARD, THE TERRIBLE WORDS ECHO THROUGH COLLIN-WOOD..."
OH, BARNABAS, THANK GOODNESS! I THOUGHT YOU HAD FORGOTTEN MY DINNER PARTY! AND WHERE HAS QUENTIN GONE?
I HADN'T FOR-GOTTEN, LIZ!
ER, QUENTIN SAID HE HAD SOME UNEXPECTED BUSINESS TO ATTEND TO!
I CAN'T TELL HER THE TRUTH!
THAT QUENTIN IS LOCKED IN THE CELLAR...THAT THE FULL MOON TURNS HIM INTO A CREATURE OF TERROR!

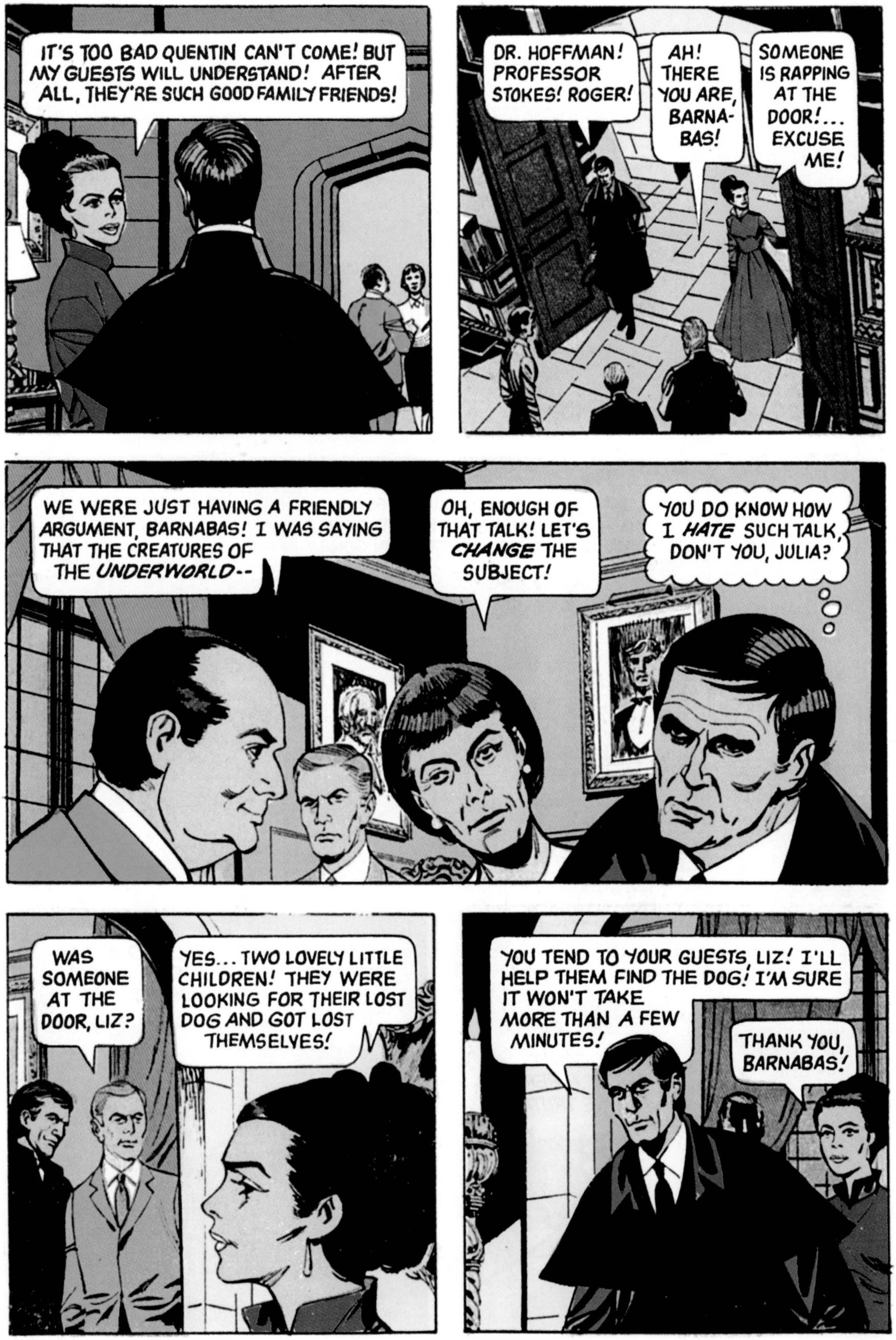
IT'S TOO BAD QUENTIN CAN'T COME! BUT MY GUESTS WILL UNDERSTAND! AFTER ALL, THEY'RE SUCH GOOD FAMILY FRIENDS!
DR. HOFFMAN! PROFESSOR STOKES! ROGER!
AH! THERE YOU ARE, BARNA-BAS!
SOMEONE IS RAPPING AT THE DOOR!... EXCUSE ME!
WE WERE JUST HAVING A FRIENDLY ARGUMENT, BARNABAS! I WAS SAYING THAT THE CREATURES OF THE UNDERWORLD--
OH, ENOUGH OF THAT TALK! LET'S CHANGE THE SUBJECT!
YOU DO KNOW HOW I HATE SUCH TALK, DON'T YOU, JULIA?
WAS SOMEONE AT THE DOOR, LIZ?
YES... TWO LOVELY LITTLE CHILDREN! THEY WERE LOOKING FOR THEIR LOST DOG AND GOT LOST THEMSELVES!
YOU TEND TO YOUR GUESTS, LIZ! I'LL HELP THEM FIND THE DOG! I'M SURE IT WON'T TAKE MORE THAN A FEW MINUTES!
THANK YOU, BARNABAS!

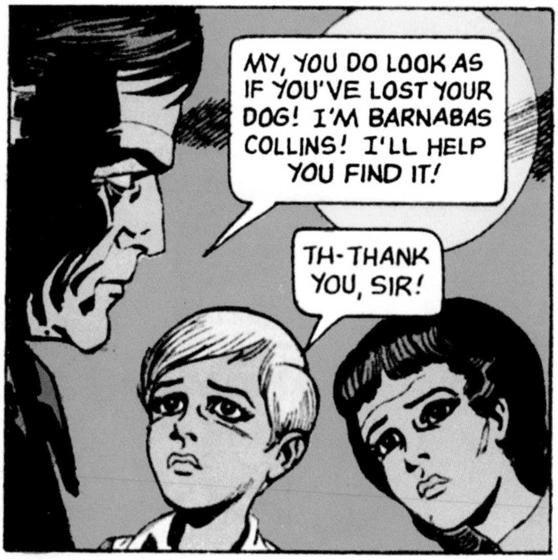
MY, YOU DO LOOK AS IF YOU'VE LOST YOUR DOG! I'M BARNABAS COLLINS! I'LL HELP YOU FIND IT!
TH-THANK YOU, SIR!

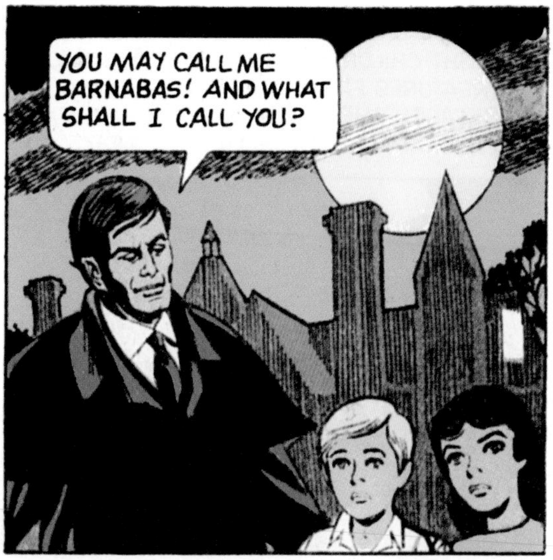
YOU MAY CALL ME BARNABAS! AND WHAT SHALL I CALL YOU?

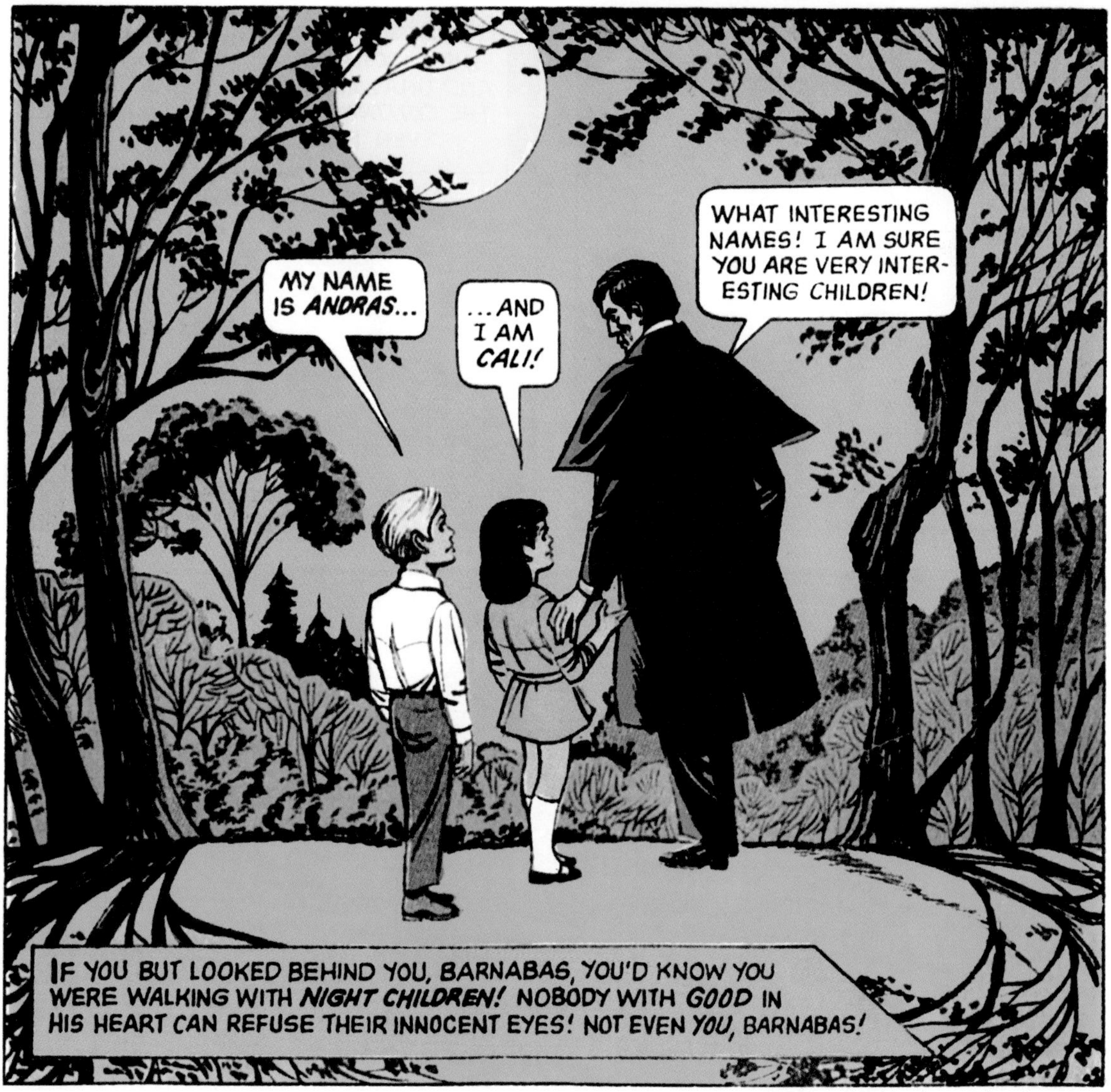
MY NAME IS ANDRAS...
...AND I AM CALI!
WHAT INTERESTING NAMES! I AM SURE YOU ARE VERY INTER-ESTING CHILDREN!
IF YOU BUT LOOKED BEHIND YOU, BARNABAS, YOU'D KNOW YOU WERE WALKING WITH NIGHT CHILDREN! NOBODY WITH GOOD IN HIS HEART CAN REFUSE THEIR INNOCENT EYES! NOT EVEN YOU, BARNABAS!

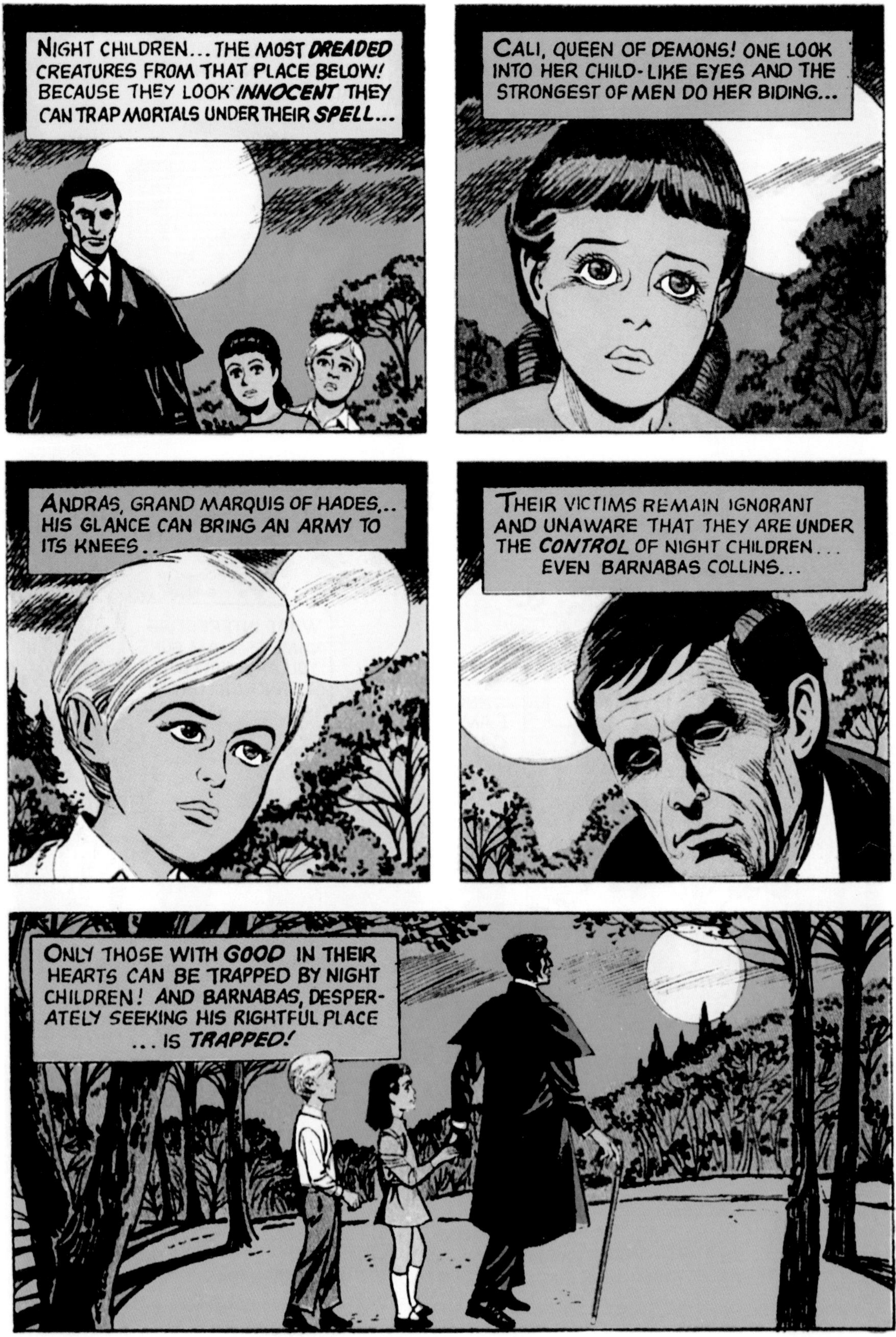
NIGHT CHILDREN... THE MOST DREADED CREATURES FROM THAT PLACE BELOW! BECAUSE THEY LOOK INNOCENT THEY CAN TRAP MORTALS UNDER THEIR SPELL...
CALI, QUEEN OF DEMONS! ONE LOOK INTO HER CHILD-LIKE EYES AND THE STRONGEST OF MEN DO HER BIDING...
ANDRAS, GRAND MARQUIS OF HADES... HIS GLANCE CAN BRING AN ARMY TO ITS KNEES...
THEIR VICTIMS REMAIN IGNORANT AND UNAWARE THAT THEY ARE UNDER THE CONTROL OF NIGHT CHILDREN... EVEN BARNABAS COLLINS...
ONLY THOSE WITH GOOD IN THEIR HEARTS CAN BE TRAPPED BY NIGHT CHILDREN! AND BARNABAS, DESPERATELY SEEKING HIS RIGHTFUL PLACE ... IS TRAPPED!

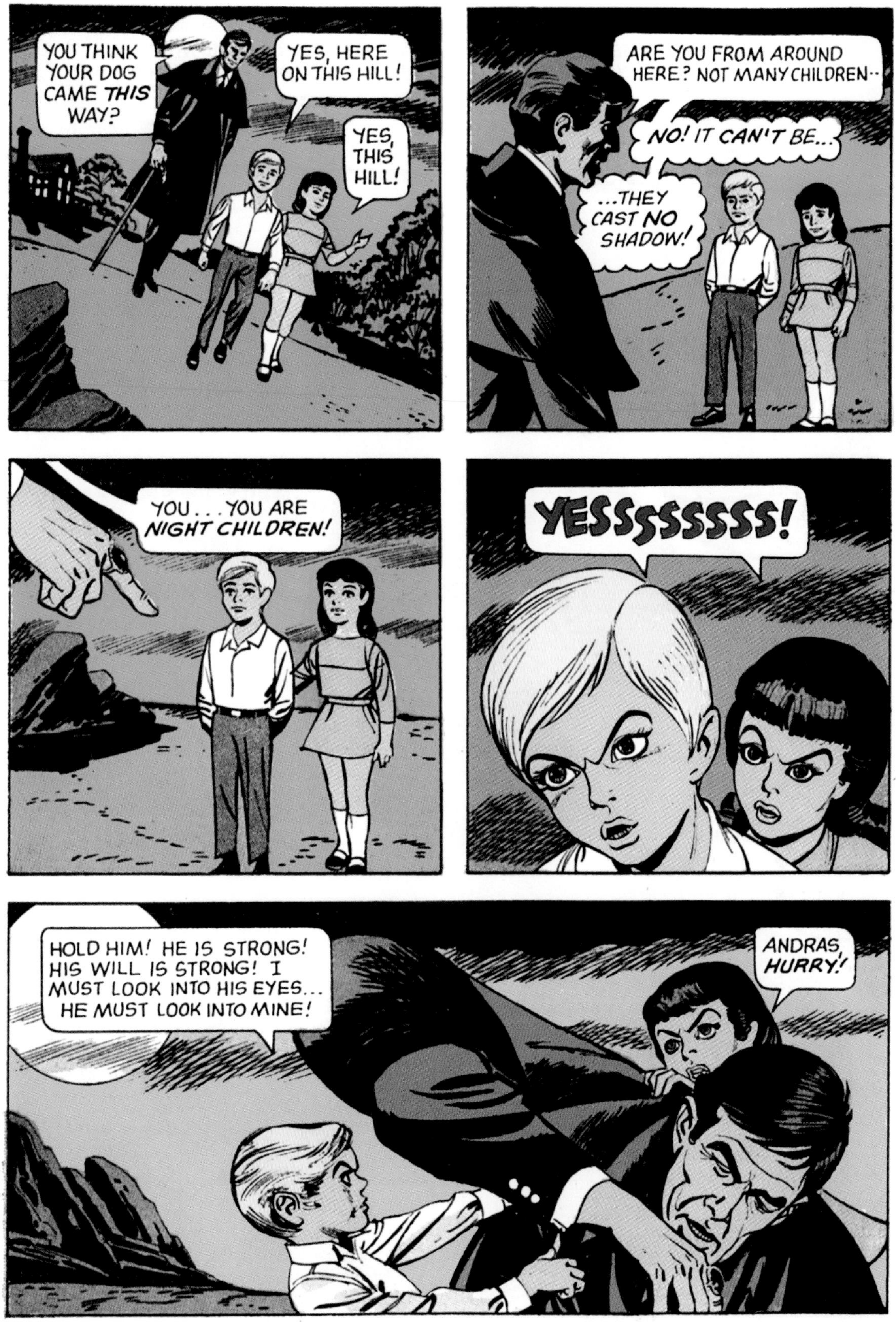
YOU THINK YOUR DOG CAME THIS WAY?
YES, HERE ON THIS HILL!
YES, THIS HILL!
ARE YOU FROM AROUND HERE? NOT MANY CHILDREN··
NO! IT CAN'T BE...
...THEY CAST NO SHADOW!
YOU... YOU ARE NIGHT CHILDREN!
YESSSSSSSS!
HOLD HIM! HE IS STRONG! HIS WILL IS STRONG! I MUST LOOK INTO HIS EYES... HE MUST LOOK INTO MINE!
ANDRAS, HURRY!

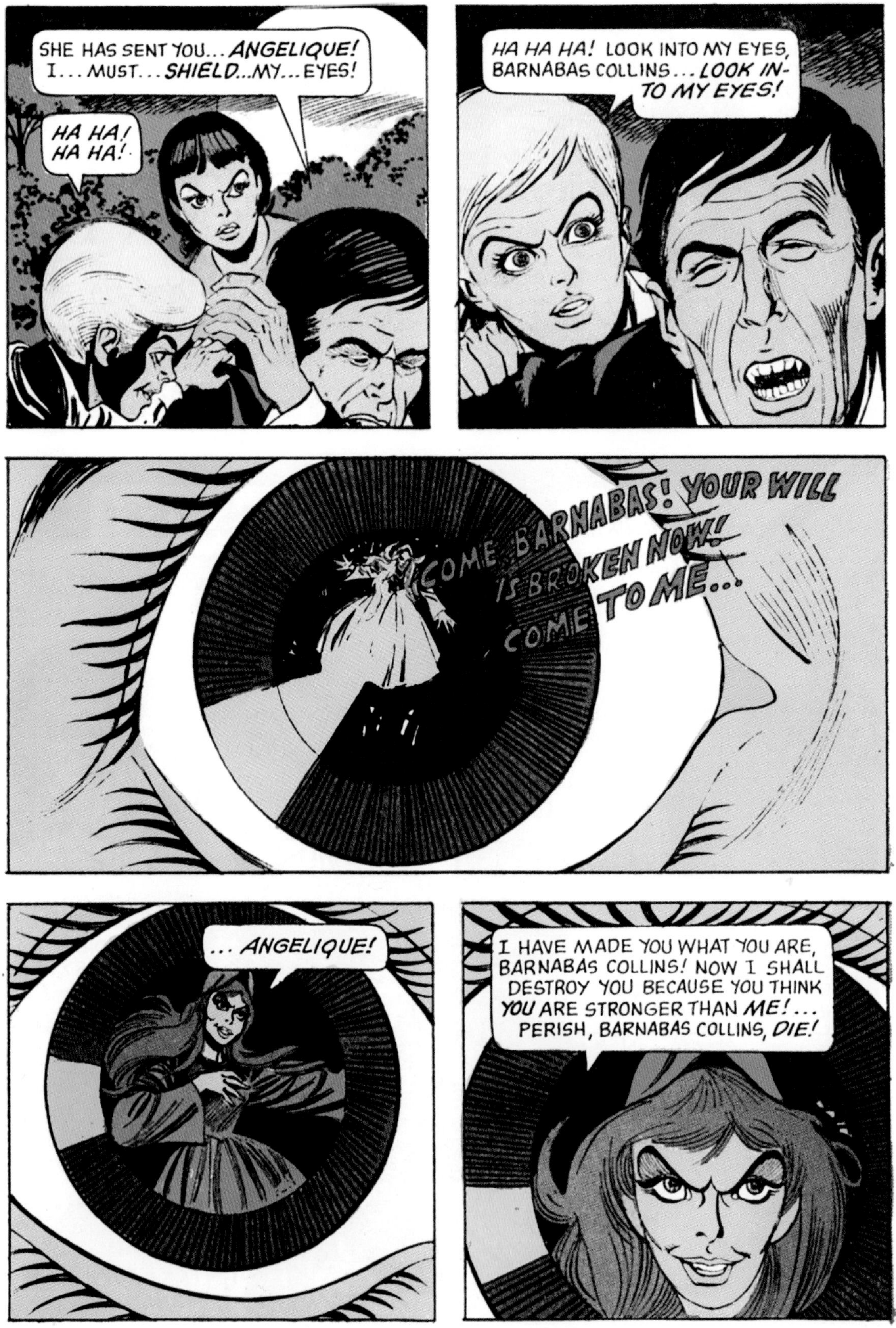
SHE HAS SENT YOU... ANGELIQUE! I... MUST... SHIELD...MY... EYES!
HA HA! HA HA!
HA HA HA! LOOK INTO MY EYES, BARNABAS COLLINS... LOOK INTO MY EYES!
BARNABAS! YOUR WILL IS BROKEN NOW!
COME, BARNABAS!
COME TO ME...
COME...
... ANGELIQUE!
I HAVE MADE YOU WHAT YOU ARE, BARNABAS COLLINS! NOW I SHALL DESTROY YOU BECAUSE YOU THINK YOU ARE STRONGER THAN ME!... PERISH, BARNABAS COLLINS, DIE!

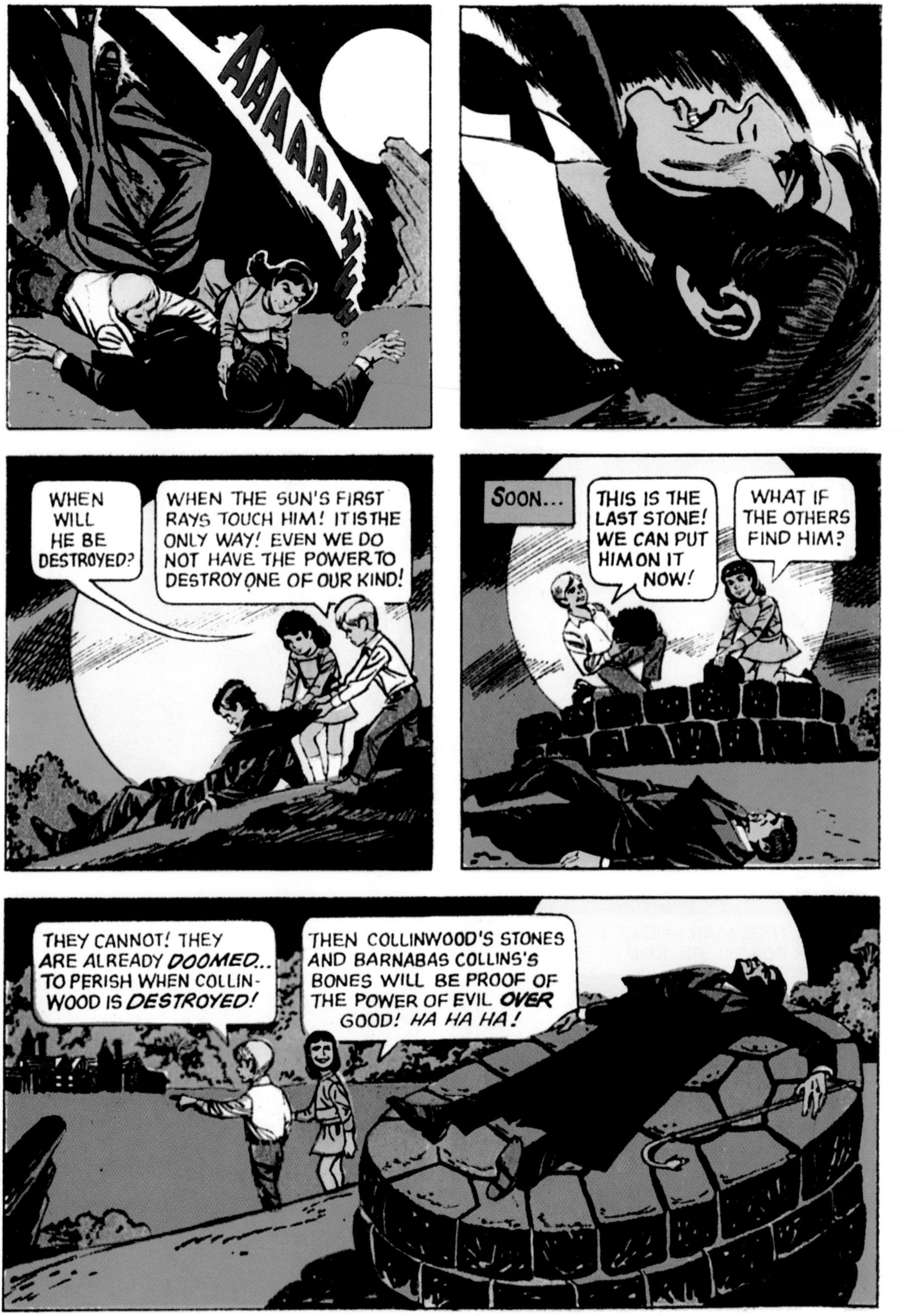
AAAAAAAHHH
WHEN WILL HE BE DESTROYED?
WHEN THE SUN'S FIRST RAYS TOUCH HIM! IT IS THE ONLY WAY! EVEN WE DO NOT HAVE THE POWER TO DESTROY ONE OF OUR KIND!
SOON...
THIS IS THE LAST STONE! WE CAN PUT HIM ON IT NOW!
WHAT IF THE OTHERS FIND HIM?
THEY CANNOT! THEY ARE ALREADY *DOOMED*... TO PERISH WHEN COLLIN-WOOD IS *DESTROYED*!
THEN COLLINWOOD'S STONES AND BARNABAS COLLINS'S BONES WILL BE PROOF OF THE POWER OF EVIL *OVER* GOOD! *HA HA HA!*

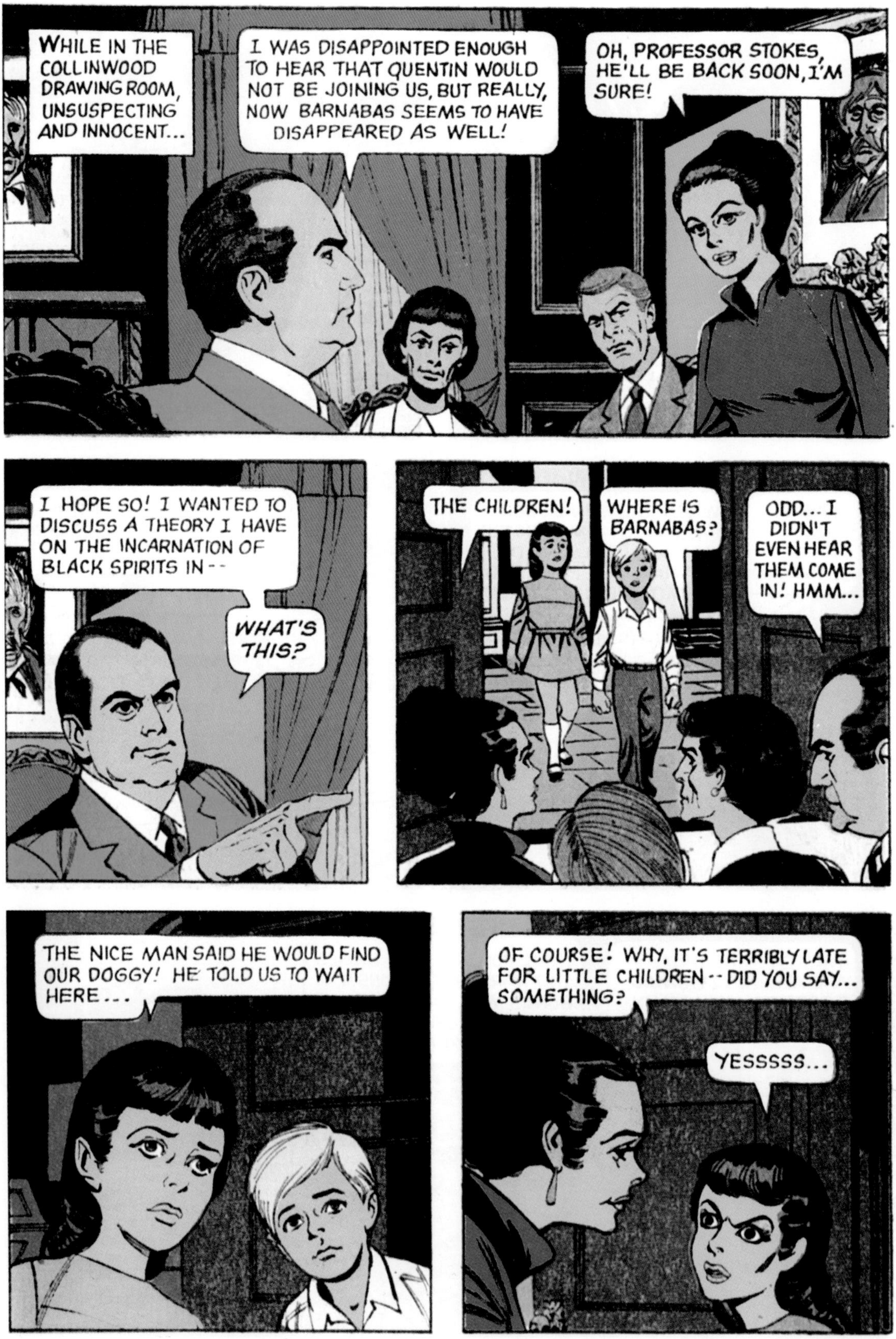
WHILE IN THE COLLINWOOD DRAWING ROOM, UNSUSPECTING AND INNOCENT...
I WAS DISAPPOINTED ENOUGH TO HEAR THAT QUENTIN WOULD NOT BE JOINING US, BUT REALLY, NOW BARNABAS SEEMS TO HAVE DISAPPEARED AS WELL!
OH, PROFESSOR STOKES, HE'LL BE BACK SOON, I'M SURE!
I HOPE SO! I WANTED TO DISCUSS A THEORY I HAVE ON THE INCARNATION OF BLACK SPIRITS IN--
WHAT'S THIS?
THE CHILDREN!
WHERE IS BARNABAS?
ODD... I DIDN'T EVEN HEAR THEM COME IN! HMM...
THE NICE MAN SAID HE WOULD FIND OUR DOGGY! HE TOLD US TO WAIT HERE...
OF COURSE! WHY, IT'S TERRIBLY LATE FOR LITTLE CHILDREN--DID YOU SAY... SOMETHING?
YESSSSS...

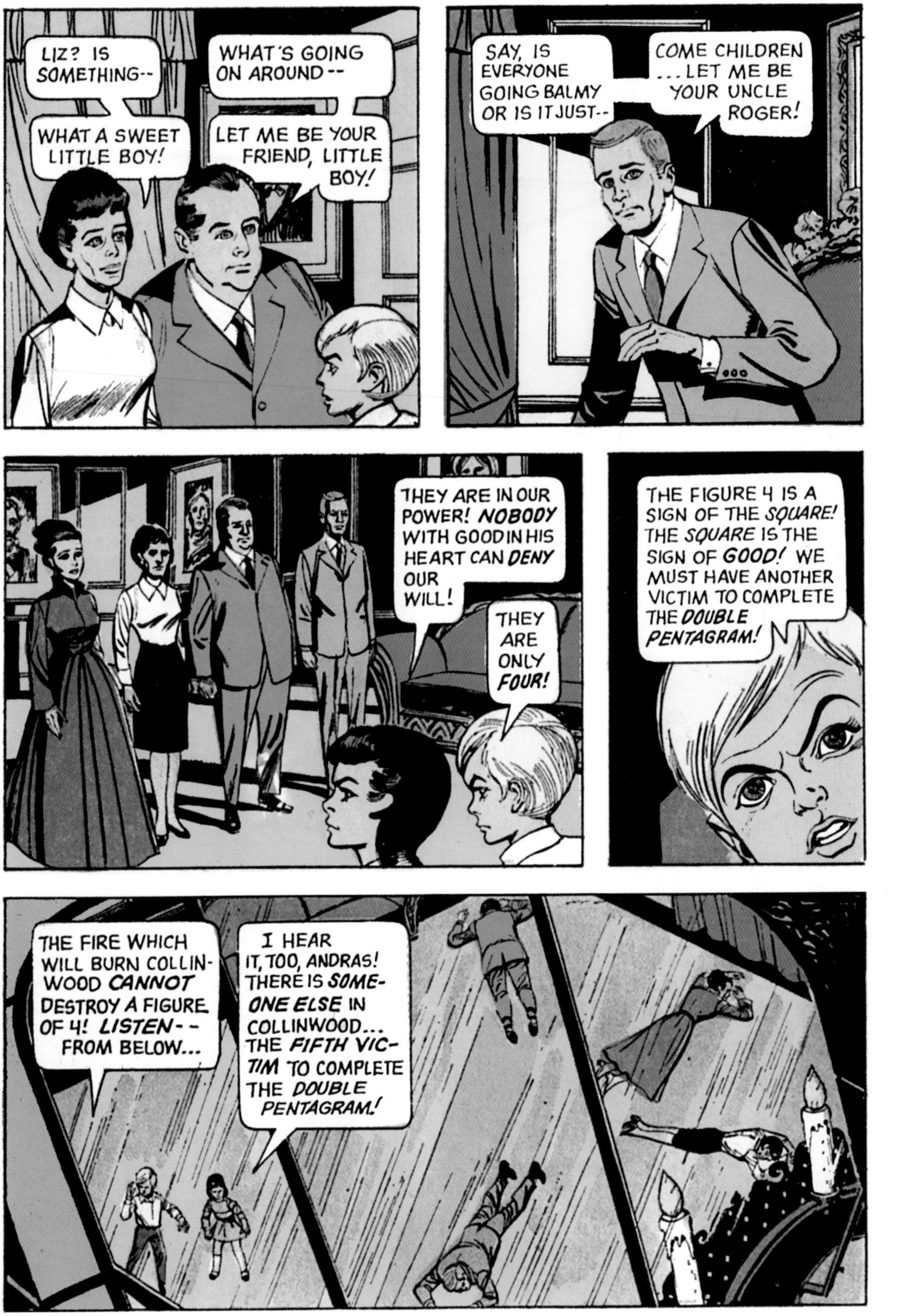
LIZ? IS SOMETHING--
WHAT A SWEET LITTLE BOY!
WHAT'S GOING ON AROUND--
LET ME BE YOUR FRIEND, LITTLE BOY!
SAY, IS EVERYONE GOING BALMY OR IS IT JUST--
COME CHILDREN ... LET ME BE YOUR UNCLE ROGER!
THEY ARE IN OUR POWER! NOBODY WITH GOOD IN HIS HEART CAN DENY OUR WILL!
THEY ARE ONLY FOUR!
THE FIGURE 4 IS A SIGN OF THE SQUARE! THE SQUARE IS THE SIGN OF GOOD! WE MUST HAVE ANOTHER VICTIM TO COMPLETE THE DOUBLE PENTAGRAM!
THE FIRE WHICH WILL BURN COLLIN-WOOD CANNOT DESTROY A FIGURE OF 4! LISTEN-- FROM BELOW...
I HEAR IT, TOO, ANDRAS! THERE IS SOME-ONE ELSE IN COLLINWOOD... THE FIFTH VIC-TIM TO COMPLETE THE DOUBLE PENTAGRAM!

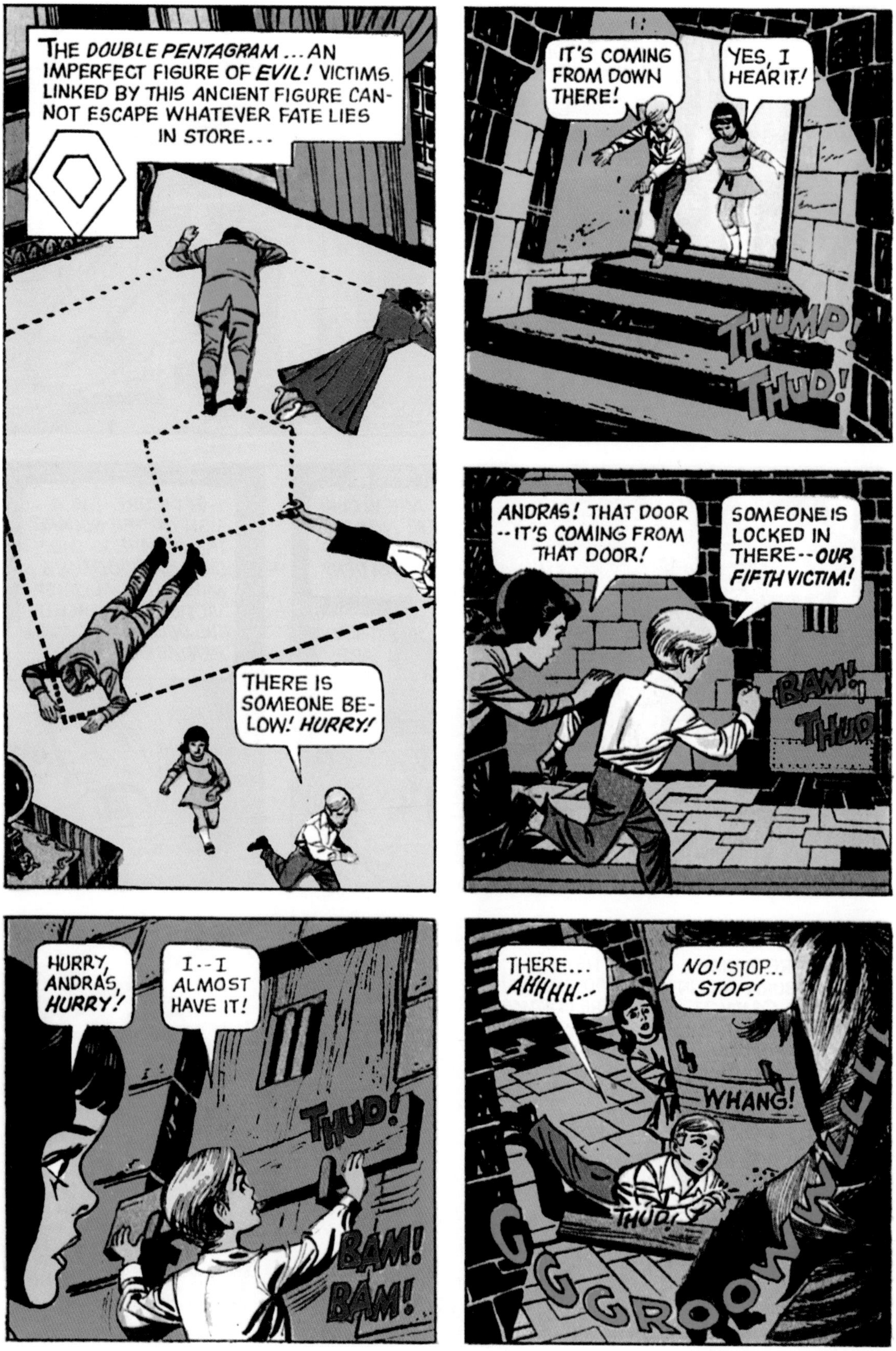
THE *DOUBLE PENTAGRAM* ... AN IMPERFECT FIGURE OF *EVIL!* VICTIMS LINKED BY THIS ANCIENT FIGURE CANNOT ESCAPE WHATEVER FATE LIES IN STORE...
THERE IS SOMEONE BELOW! *HURRY!*
IT'S COMING FROM DOWN THERE!
YES, I HEAR IT!
THUMP! THUD!
ANDRAS! THAT DOOR --IT'S COMING FROM THAT DOOR!
SOMEONE IS LOCKED IN THERE--*OUR FIFTH VICTIM!*
BAM! THUD
HURRY, ANDRAS, *HURRY!*
I--I ALMOST HAVE IT!
THUD!
BAM! BAM!
THERE... *AHHHH...*
NO! STOP.. *STOP!*
WHANG!
THUD!

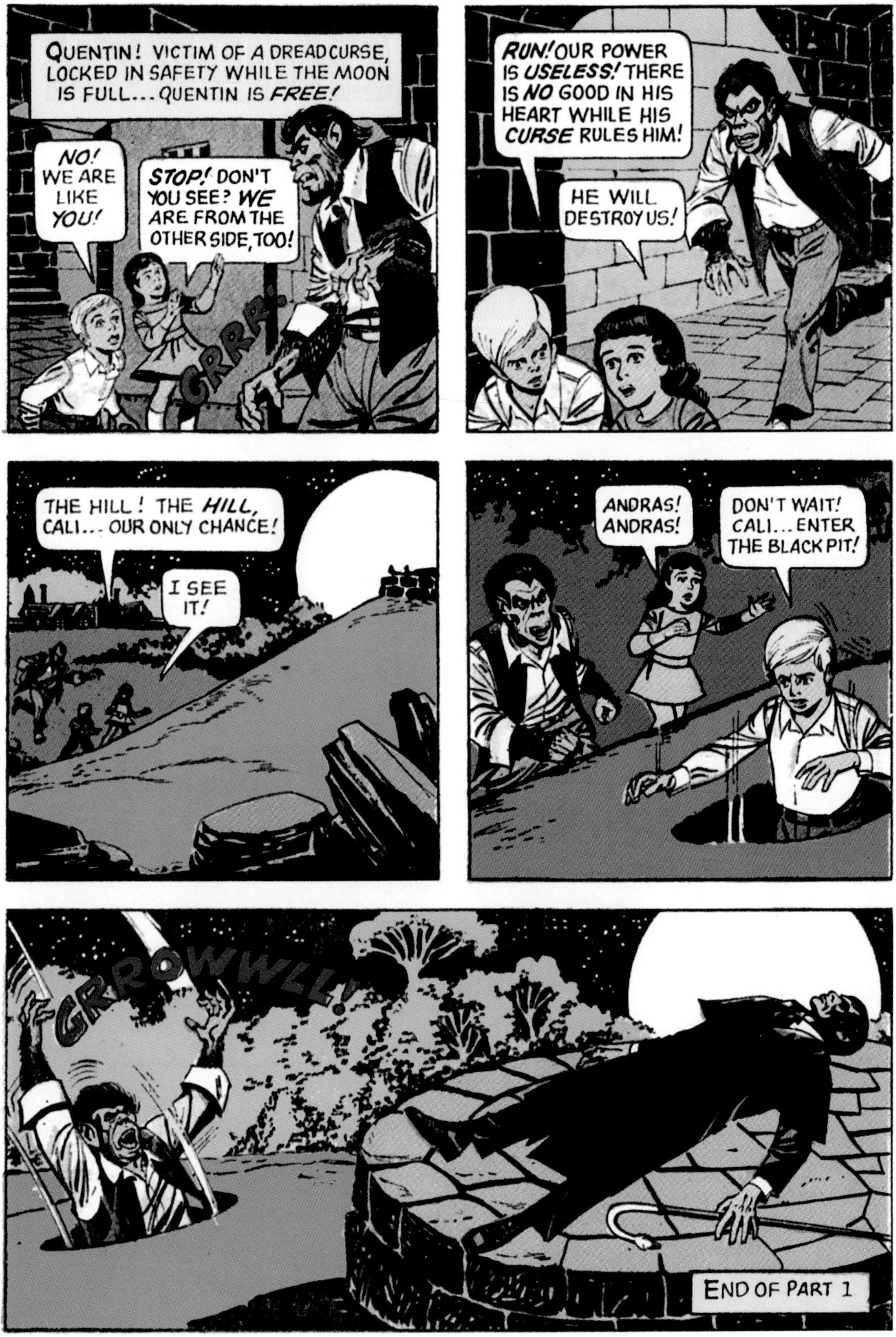
QUENTIN! VICTIM OF A DREAD CURSE, LOCKED IN SAFETY WHILE THE MOON IS FULL... QUENTIN IS FREE!
NO! WE ARE LIKE YOU!
STOP! DON'T YOU SEE? WE ARE FROM THE OTHER SIDE, TOO!
GRRR!
RUN! OUR POWER IS USELESS! THERE IS NO GOOD IN HIS HEART WHILE HIS CURSE RULES HIM!
HE WILL DESTROY US!
THE HILL! THE HILL, CALI... OUR ONLY CHANCE!
I SEE IT!
ANDRAS! ANDRAS!
DON'T WAIT! CALI... ENTER THE BLACK PIT!
GRROWWLL!
END OF PART 1

DARK SHADOWS' The NIGHT CHILDREN

PART 2: THE PURSUIT OF QUENTIN

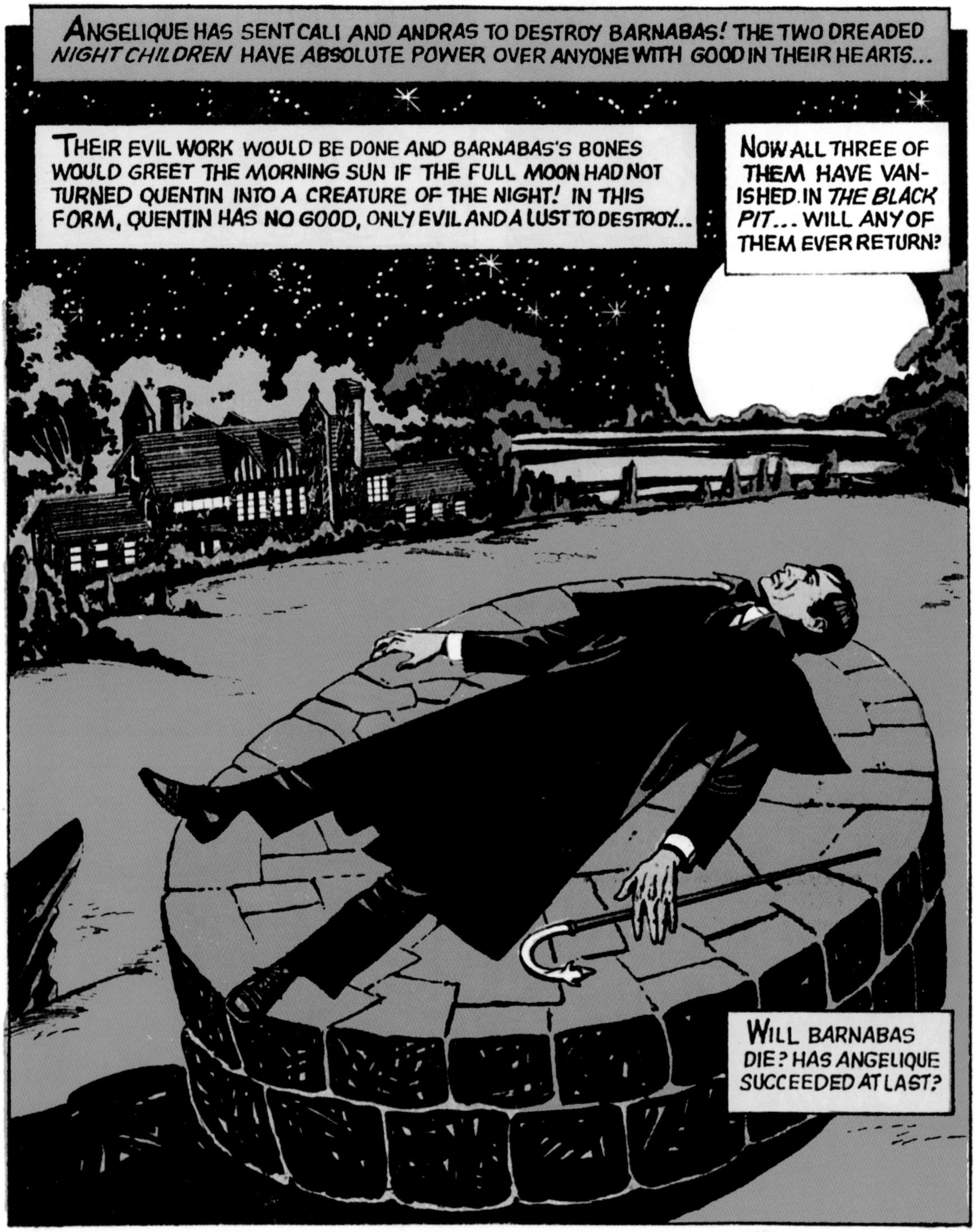
ANGELIQUE HAS SENT CALI AND ANDRAS TO DESTROY BARNABAS! THE TWO DREADED NIGHT CHILDREN HAVE ABSOLUTE POWER OVER ANYONE WITH GOOD IN THEIR HEARTS...
THEIR EVIL WORK WOULD BE DONE AND BARNABAS'S BONES WOULD GREET THE MORNING SUN IF THE FULL MOON HAD NOT TURNED QUENTIN INTO A CREATURE OF THE NIGHT! IN THIS FORM, QUENTIN HAS NO GOOD, ONLY EVIL AND A LUST TO DESTROY...
NOW ALL THREE OF THEM HAVE VANISHED IN THE BLACK PIT... WILL ANY OF THEM EVER RETURN?
WILL BARNABAS DIE? HAS ANGELIQUE SUCCEEDED AT LAST?

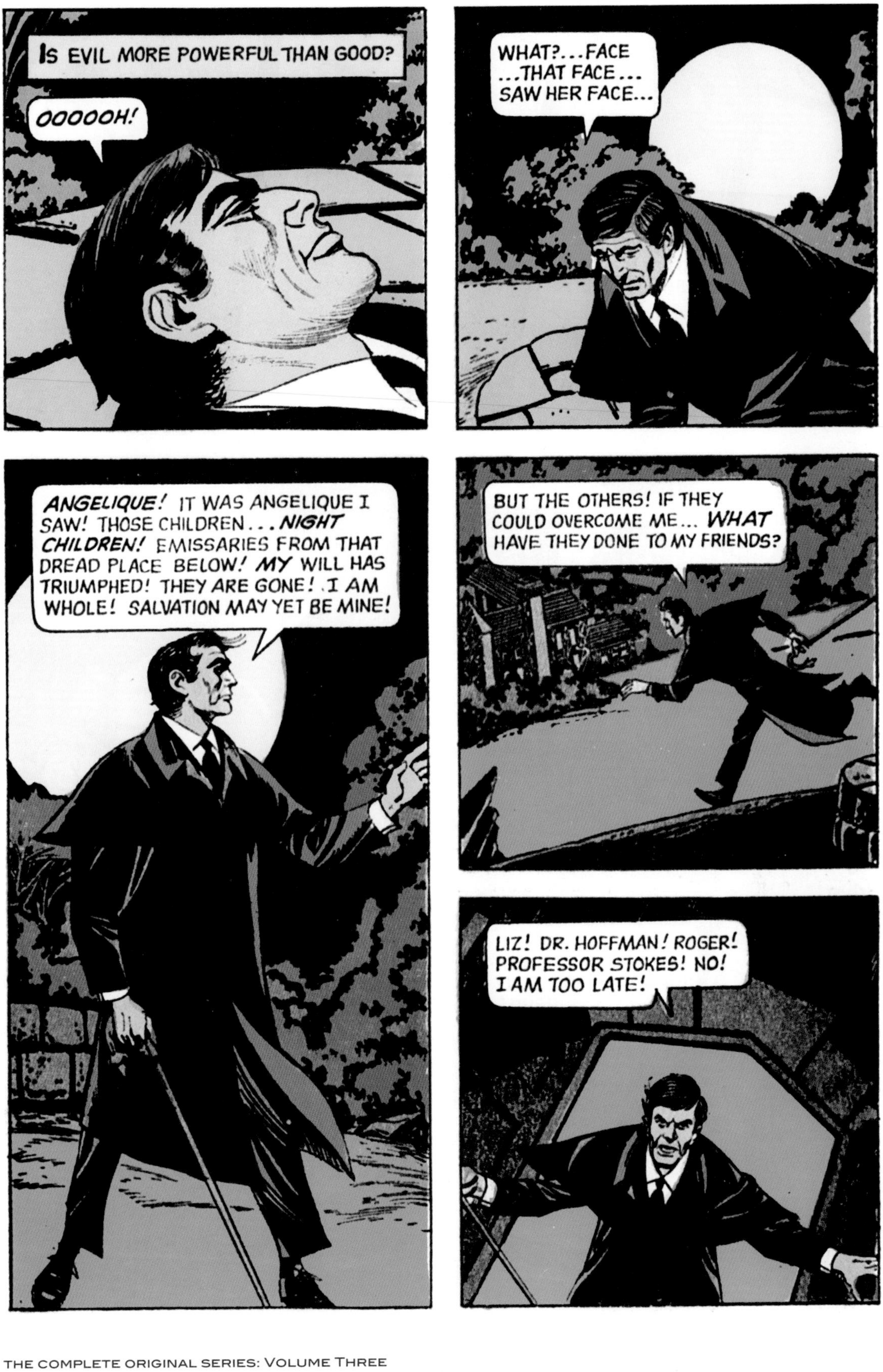
IS EVIL MORE POWERFUL THAN GOOD?
OOOOOH!
WHAT?...FACE ...THAT FACE... SAW HER FACE...
ANGELIQUE! IT WAS ANGELIQUE I SAW! THOSE CHILDREN... NIGHT CHILDREN! EMISSARIES FROM THAT DREAD PLACE BELOW! MY WILL HAS TRIUMPHED! THEY ARE GONE! I AM WHOLE! SALVATION MAY YET BE MINE!
BUT THE OTHERS! IF THEY COULD OVERCOME ME... WHAT HAVE THEY DONE TO MY FRIENDS?
LIZ! DR. HOFFMAN! ROGER! PROFESSOR STOKES! NO! I AM TOO LATE!

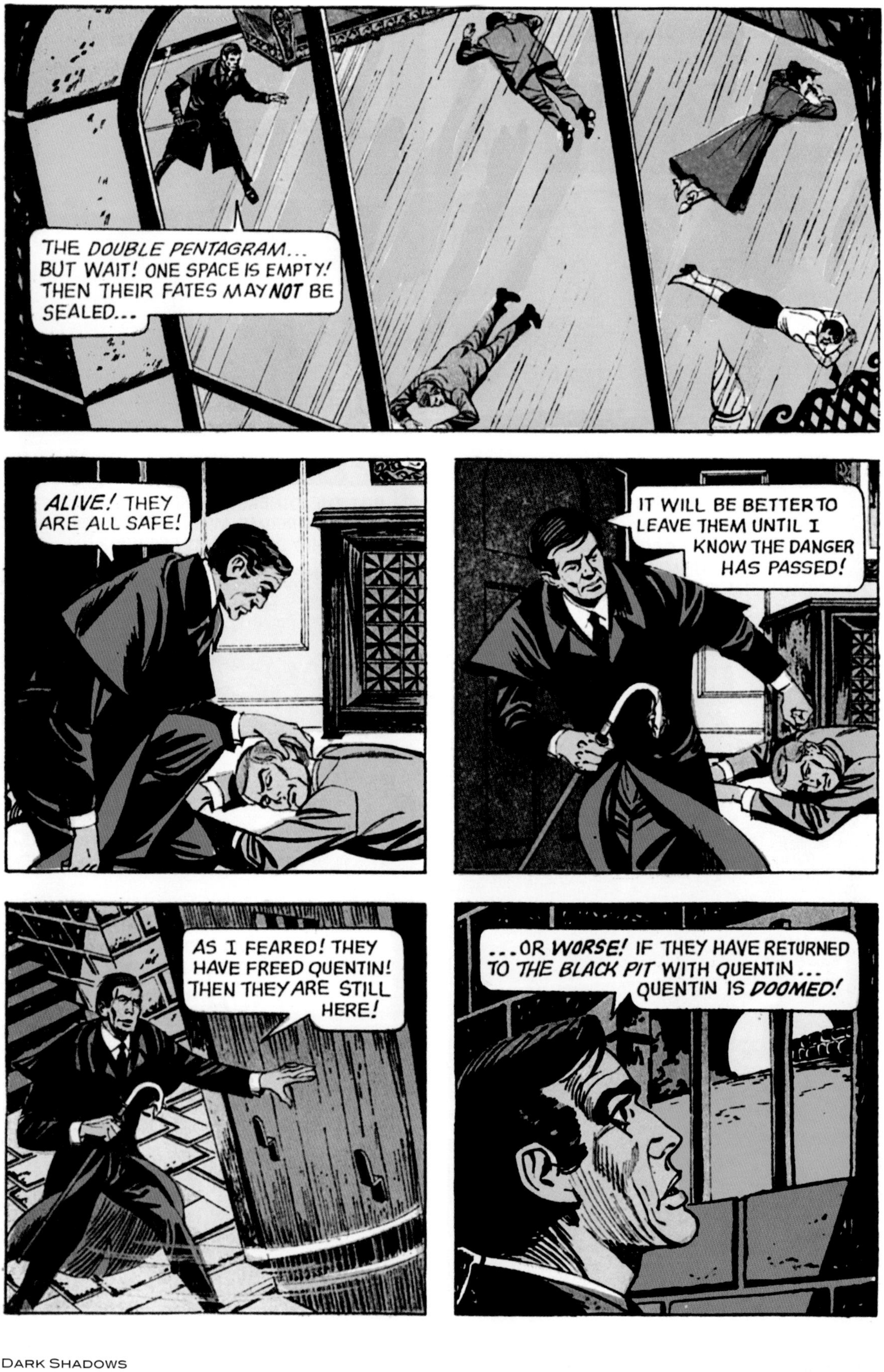
THE DOUBLE PENTAGRAM... BUT WAIT! ONE SPACE IS EMPTY! THEN THEIR FATES MAY NOT BE SEALED...
ALIVE! THEY ARE ALL SAFE!
IT WILL BE BETTER TO LEAVE THEM UNTIL I KNOW THE DANGER HAS PASSED!
AS I FEARED! THEY HAVE FREED QUENTIN! THEN THEY ARE STILL HERE!
...OR WORSE! IF THEY HAVE RETURNED TO THE BLACK PIT WITH QUENTIN... QUENTIN IS DOOMED!

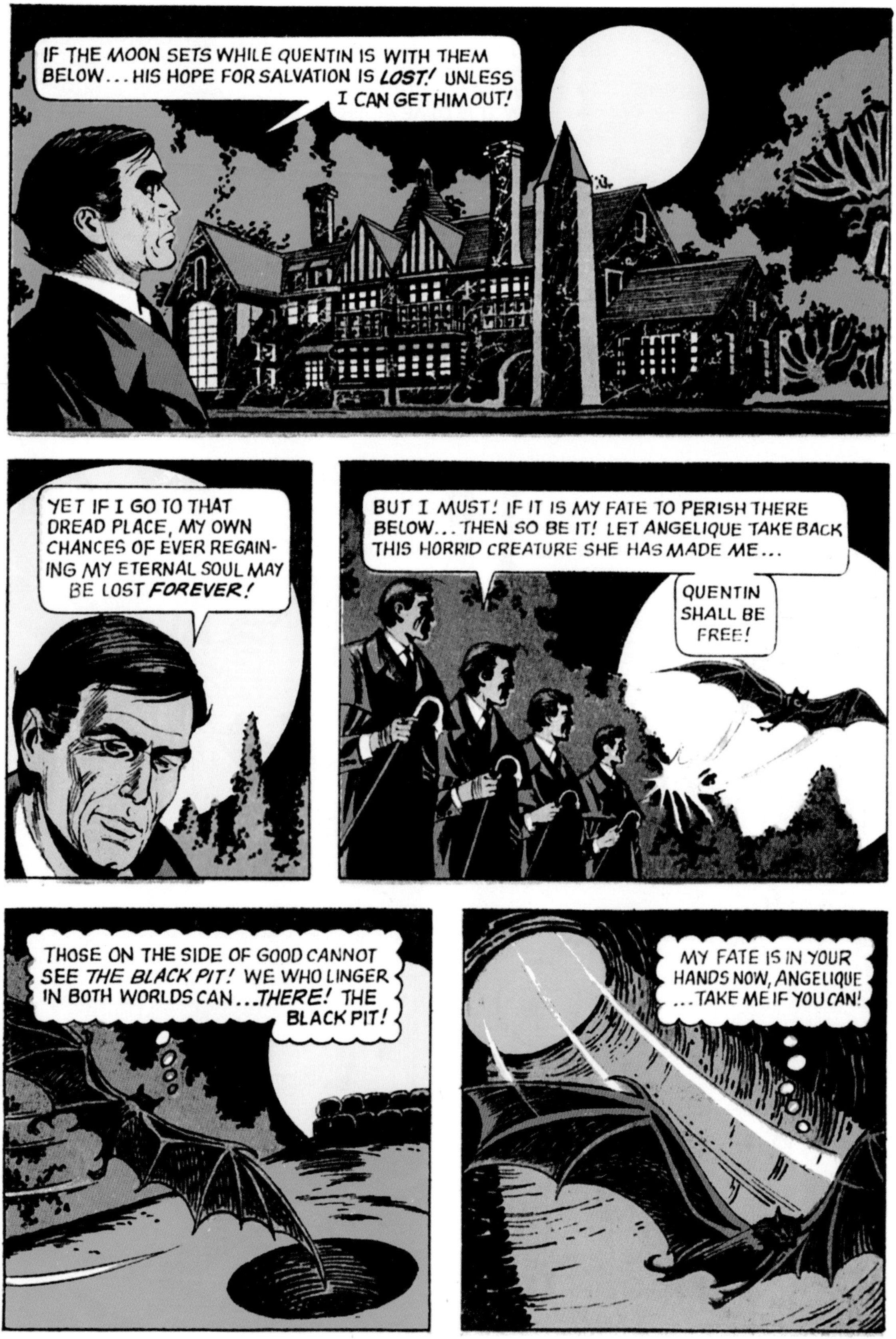
IF THE MOON SETS WHILE QUENTIN IS WITH THEM BELOW... HIS HOPE FOR SALVATION IS LOST! UNLESS I CAN GET HIM OUT!
YET IF I GO TO THAT DREAD PLACE, MY OWN CHANCES OF EVER REGAIN-ING MY ETERNAL SOUL MAY BE LOST FOREVER!
BUT I MUST! IF IT IS MY FATE TO PERISH THERE BELOW... THEN SO BE IT! LET ANGELIQUE TAKE BACK THIS HORRID CREATURE SHE HAS MADE ME...
QUENTIN SHALL BE FREE!
THOSE ON THE SIDE OF GOOD CANNOT SEE THE BLACK PIT! WE WHO LINGER IN BOTH WORLDS CAN... THERE! THE BLACK PIT!
MY FATE IS IN YOUR HANDS NOW, ANGELIQUE ...TAKE ME IF YOU CAN!

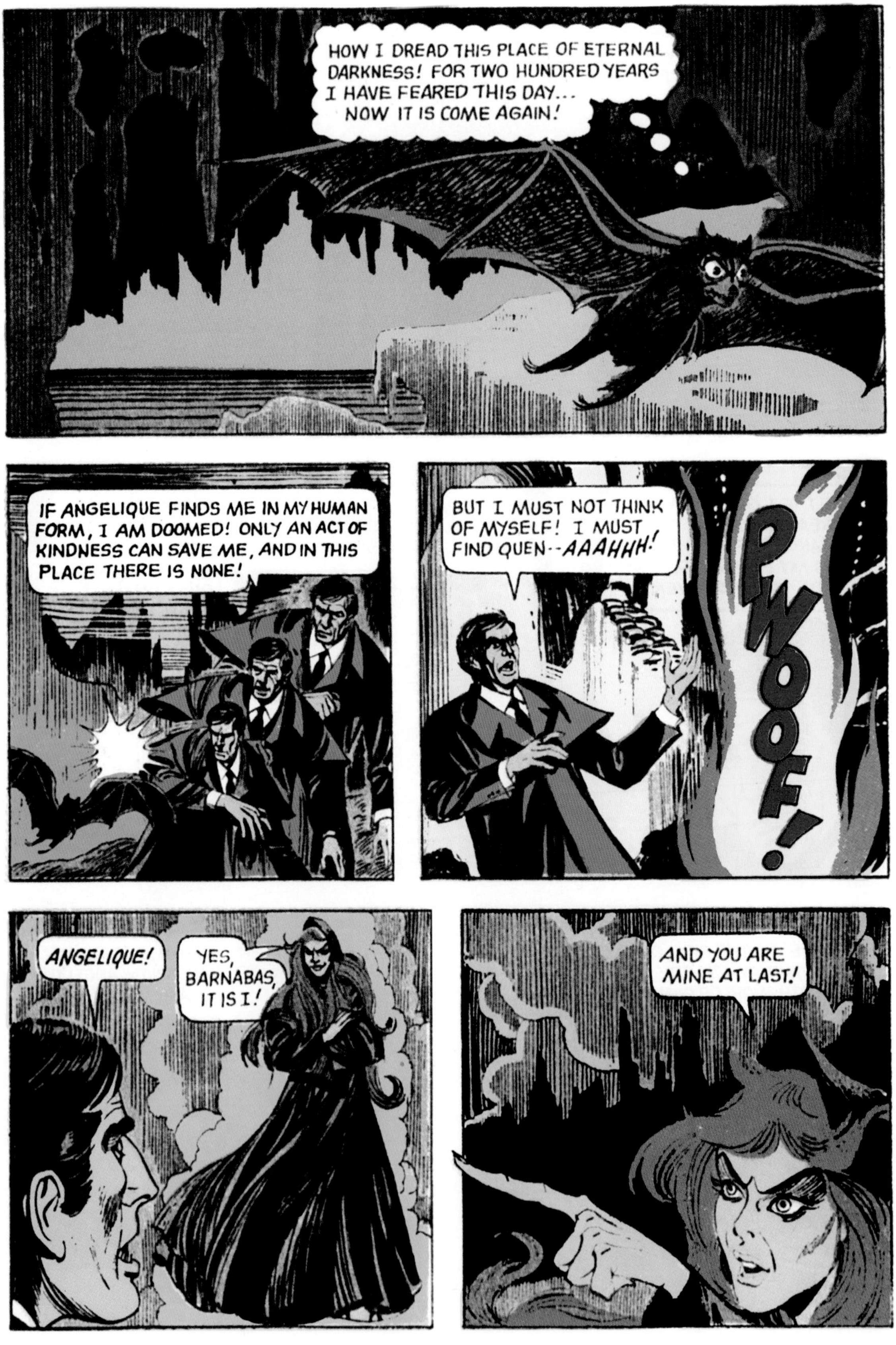
HOW I DREAD THIS PLACE OF ETERNAL DARKNESS! FOR TWO HUNDRED YEARS I HAVE FEARED THIS DAY... NOW IT IS COME AGAIN!
IF ANGELIQUE FINDS ME IN MY HUMAN FORM, I AM DOOMED! ONLY AN ACT OF KINDNESS CAN SAVE ME, AND IN THIS PLACE THERE IS NONE!
BUT I MUST NOT THINK OF MYSELF! I MUST FIND QUEN--AAAHHH!
PWOOF!
ANGELIQUE!
YES, BARNABAS, IT IS I!
AND YOU ARE MINE AT LAST!

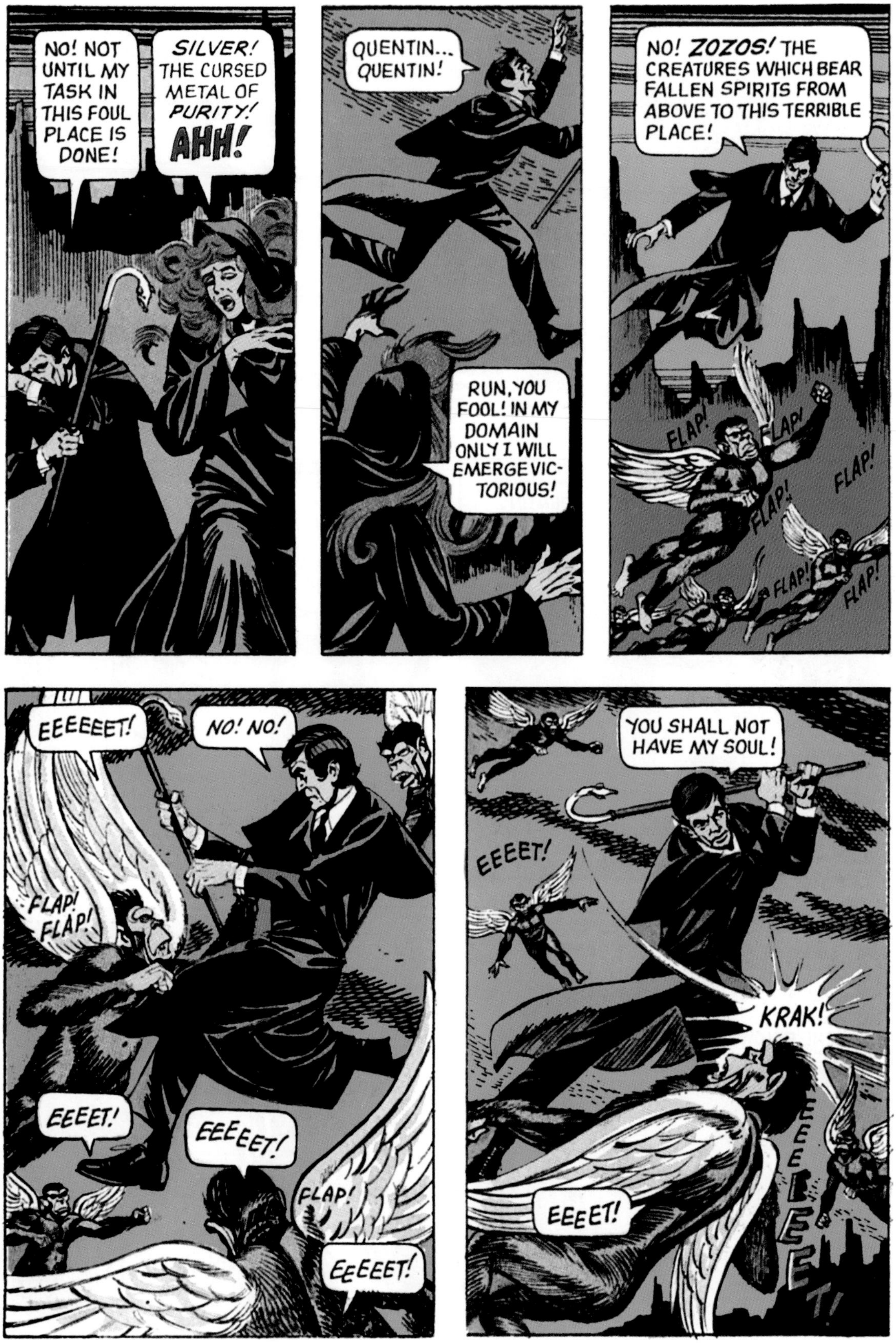
NO! NOT UNTIL MY TASK IN THIS FOUL PLACE IS DONE!
SILVER! THE CURSED METAL OF PURITY! AHH!
QUENTIN... QUENTIN!
RUN, YOU FOOL! IN MY DOMAIN ONLY I WILL EMERGE VICTORIOUS!
NO! ZOZOS! THE CREATURES WHICH BEAR FALLEN SPIRITS FROM ABOVE TO THIS TERRIBLE PLACE!
FLAP! FLAP!
FLAP!
FLAP!
FLAP!
FLAP!
EEEEEET!
NO! NO!
FLAP! FLAP!
EEEET!
EEEEET!
FLAP!
EEEEET!
YOU SHALL NOT HAVE MY SOUL!
EEEET!
KRAK!
EEEET!
EEEEEEEEET!

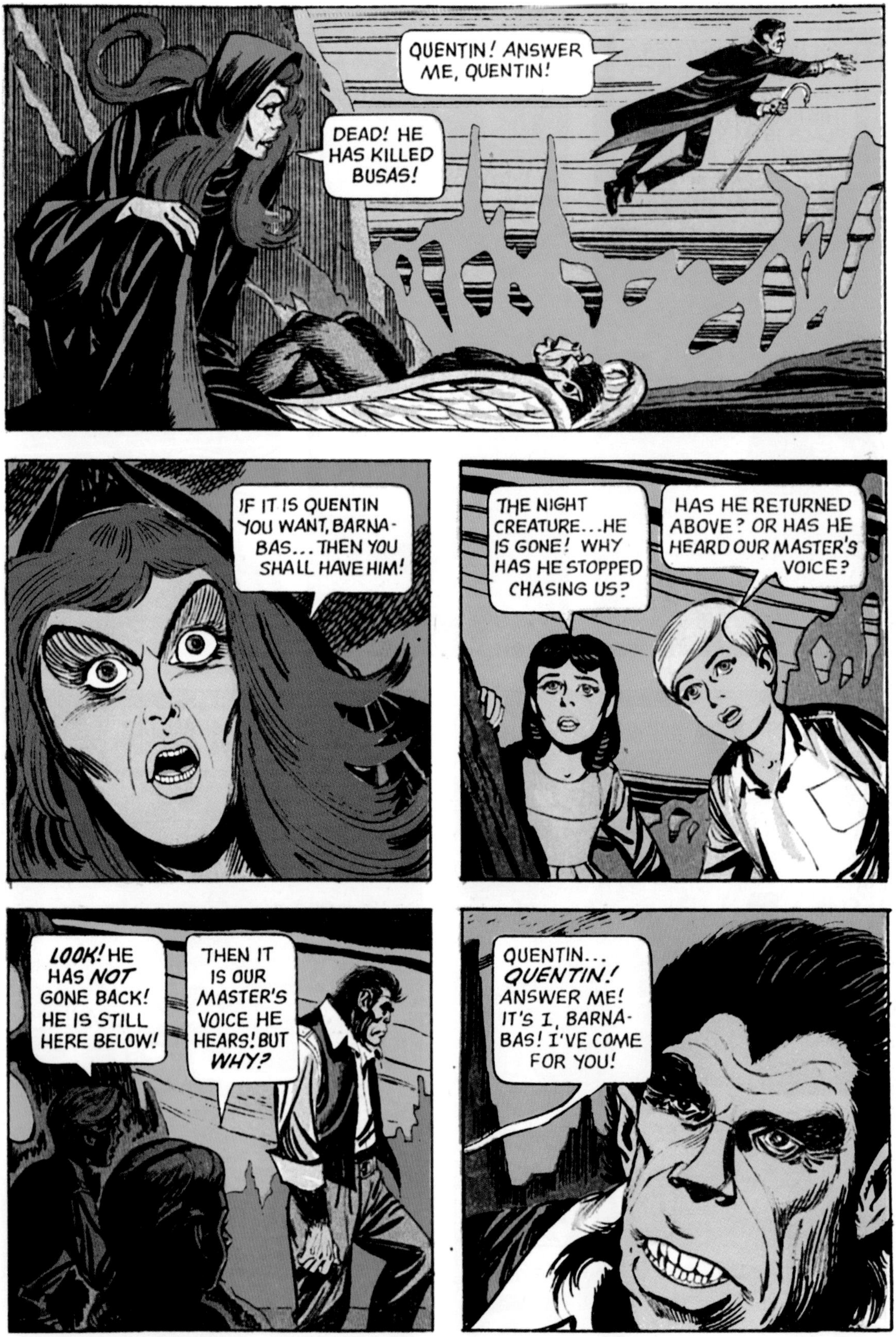
QUENTIN! ANSWER ME, QUENTIN!
DEAD! HE HAS KILLED BUSAS!
IF IT IS QUENTIN YOU WANT, BARNA-BAS... THEN YOU SHALL HAVE HIM!
THE NIGHT CREATURE...HE IS GONE! WHY HAS HE STOPPED CHASING US?
HAS HE RETURNED ABOVE? OR HAS HE HEARD OUR MASTER'S VOICE?
LOOK! HE HAS NOT GONE BACK! HE IS STILL HERE BELOW!
THEN IT IS OUR MASTER'S VOICE HE HEARS! BUT WHY?
QUENTIN... QUENTIN! ANSWER ME! IT'S I, BARNA-BAS! I'VE COME FOR YOU!

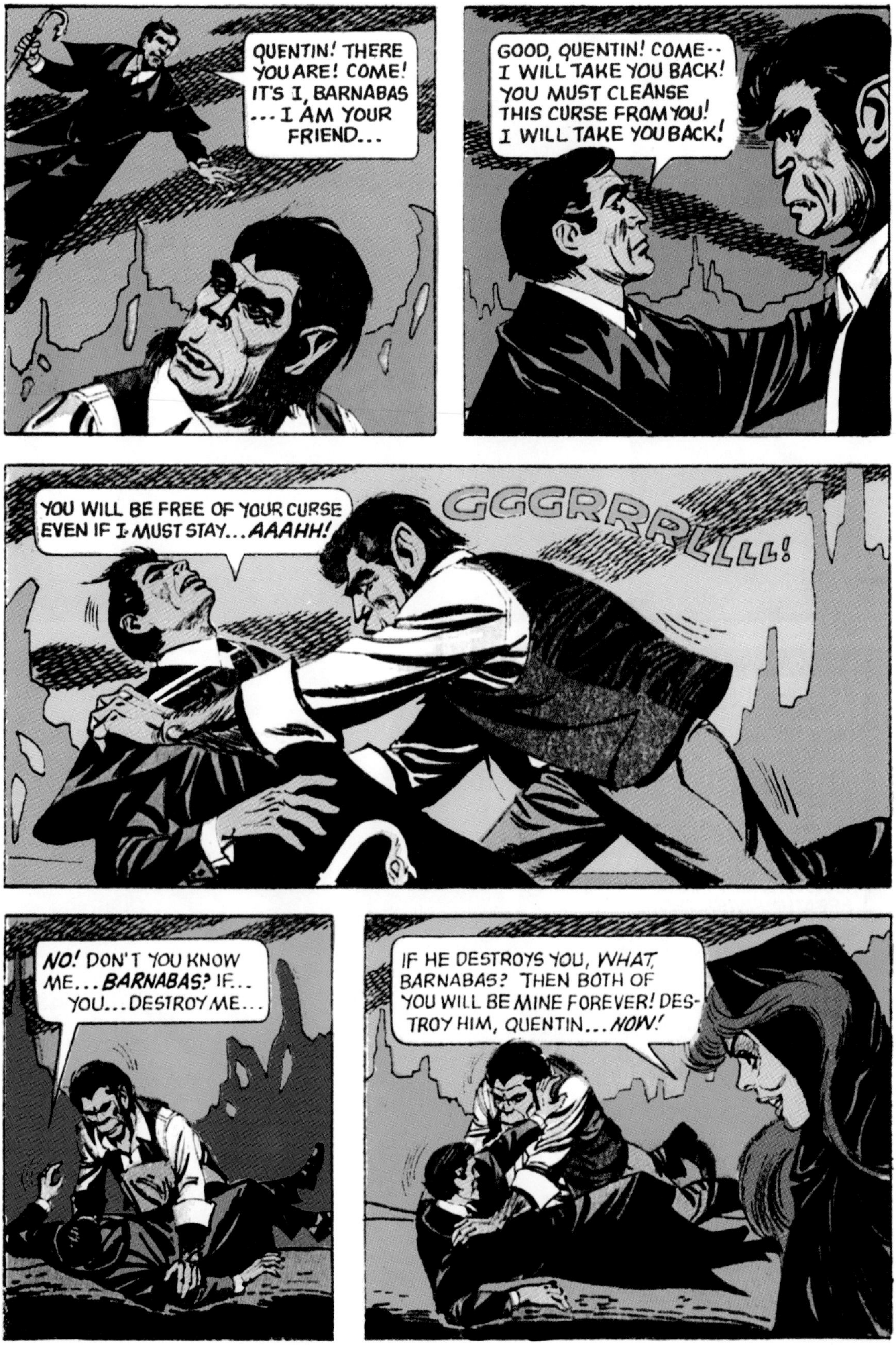
QUENTIN! THERE YOU ARE! COME! IT'S I, BARNABAS ... I AM YOUR FRIEND...
GOOD, QUENTIN! COME-- I WILL TAKE YOU BACK! YOU MUST CLEANSE THIS CURSE FROM YOU! I WILL TAKE YOU BACK!
YOU WILL BE FREE OF YOUR CURSE EVEN IF I MUST STAY... AAAHH!
GGGRRRRLLLLL!
NO! DON'T YOU KNOW ME... BARNABAS? IF... YOU... DESTROY ME...
IF HE DESTROYS YOU, WHAT, BARNABAS? THEN BOTH OF YOU WILL BE MINE FOREVER! DESTROY HIM, QUENTIN... NOW!

BUT AT THAT MOMENT IN THE OVERWORLD, THE WORLD OF MORTALS, THE FULL MOON FOLLOWS ITS ETERNAL PATH...

AND AS THE MOON SETS, ITS DEADLY GRIP ON QUENTIN FADES IN THE WORLD BELOW...

AHHHH...

QUENTIN!

BUT BARNABAS'S SALVATION FROM ONE FATE ONLY THROWS *BOTH* OF THEM INTO ANOTHER, MORE HORRIBLE FATE ...THE *HARPPES*...

GO! THIS IS THEIR FINAL HOUR...THEIR FINAL BREATH! *FINISH THEM!*

HHHHHHHHHHHHH...

YOU HAD YOUR CHANCE TO STAY WITH ME, BARNABAS! YOU DENIED ME! NOW I HAVE MY REVENGE AT LAST! *HA HA HA HA!*

AAAHH!

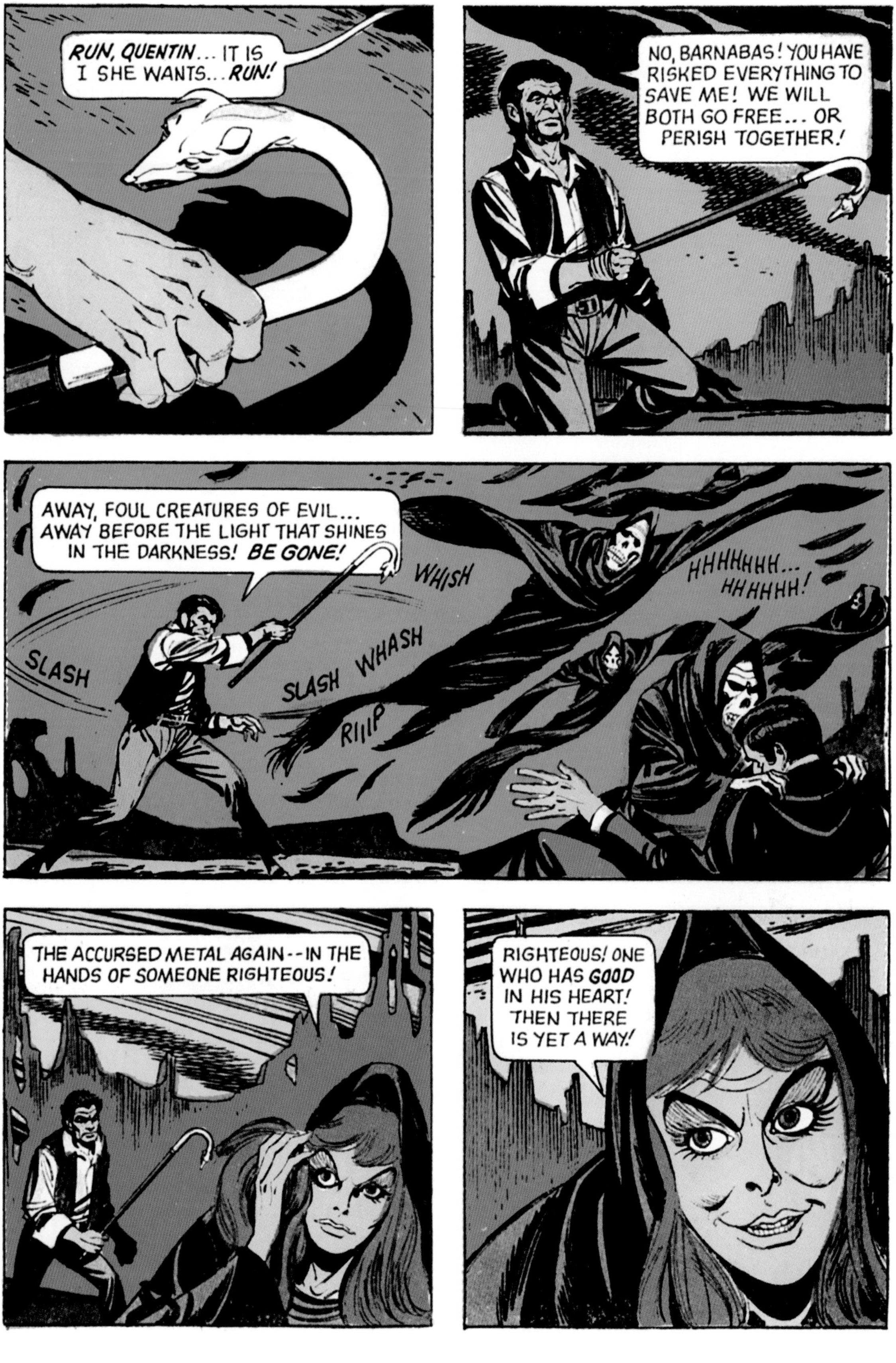
RUN, QUENTIN... IT IS I SHE WANTS... RUN!
NO, BARNABAS! YOU HAVE RISKED EVERYTHING TO SAVE ME! WE WILL BOTH GO FREE... OR PERISH TOGETHER!
AWAY, FOUL CREATURES OF EVIL... AWAY BEFORE THE LIGHT THAT SHINES IN THE DARKNESS! BE GONE!
WHISH
HHHHHHH... HHHHHH!
SLASH
SLASH
WHASH
RIIIP
THE ACCURSED METAL AGAIN--IN THE HANDS OF SOMEONE RIGHTEOUS!
RIGHTEOUS! ONE WHO HAS GOOD IN HIS HEART! THEN THERE IS YET A WAY!

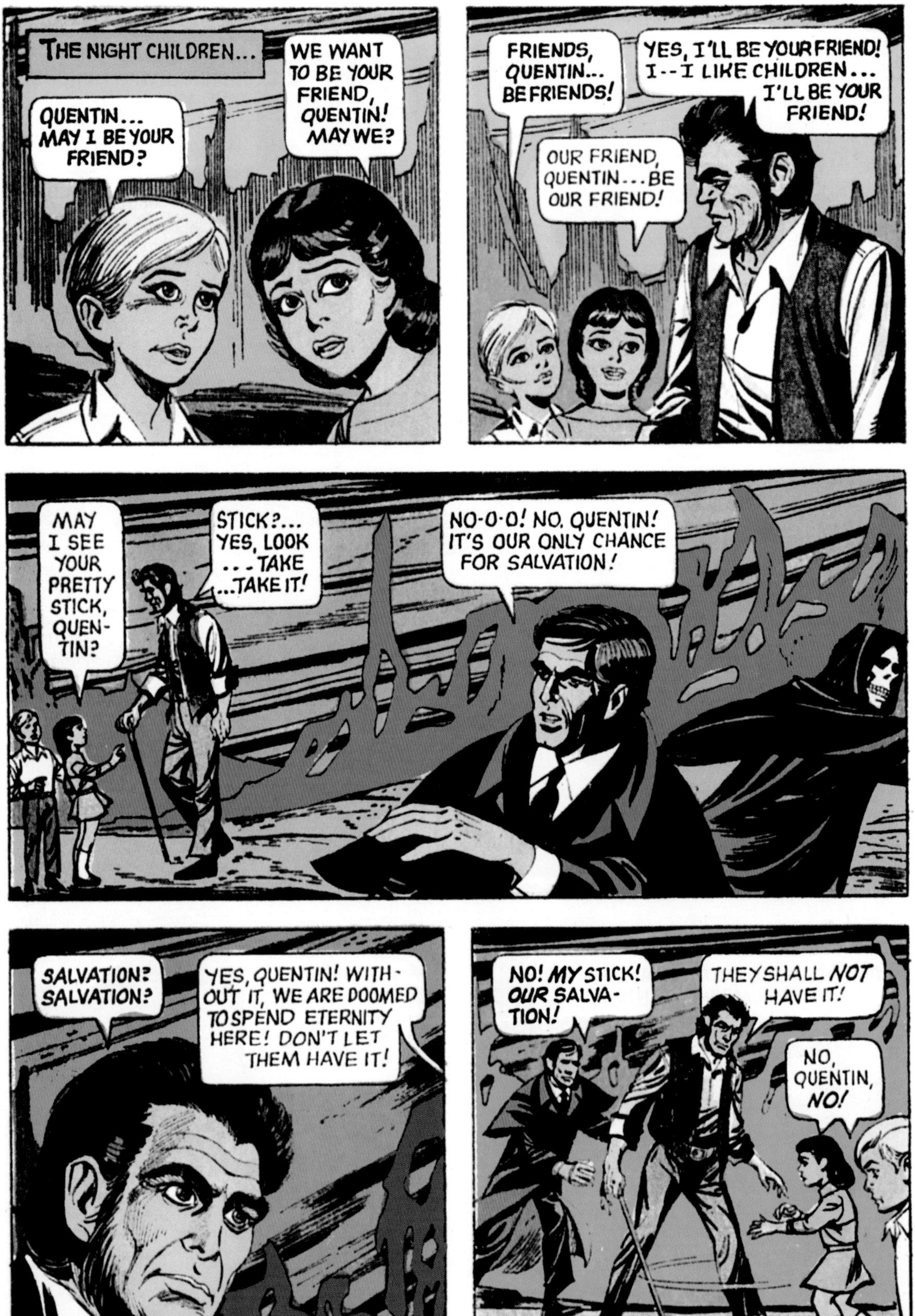
THE NIGHT CHILDREN...
QUENTIN... MAY I BE YOUR FRIEND?
WE WANT TO BE YOUR FRIEND, QUENTIN! MAY WE?
FRIENDS, QUENTIN... BE FRIENDS!
YES, I'LL BE YOUR FRIEND! I--I LIKE CHILDREN... I'LL BE YOUR FRIEND!
OUR FRIEND, QUENTIN... BE OUR FRIEND!
MAY I SEE YOUR PRETTY STICK, QUEN-TIN?
STICK?... YES, LOOK ...TAKE ...TAKE IT!
NO-O-O! NO, QUENTIN! IT'S OUR ONLY CHANCE FOR SALVATION!
SALVATION? SALVATION?
YES, QUENTIN! WITH-OUT IT, WE ARE DOOMED TO SPEND ETERNITY HERE! DON'T LET THEM HAVE IT!
NO! MY STICK! OUR SALVA-TION!
THEY SHALL NOT HAVE IT!
NO, QUENTIN, NO!

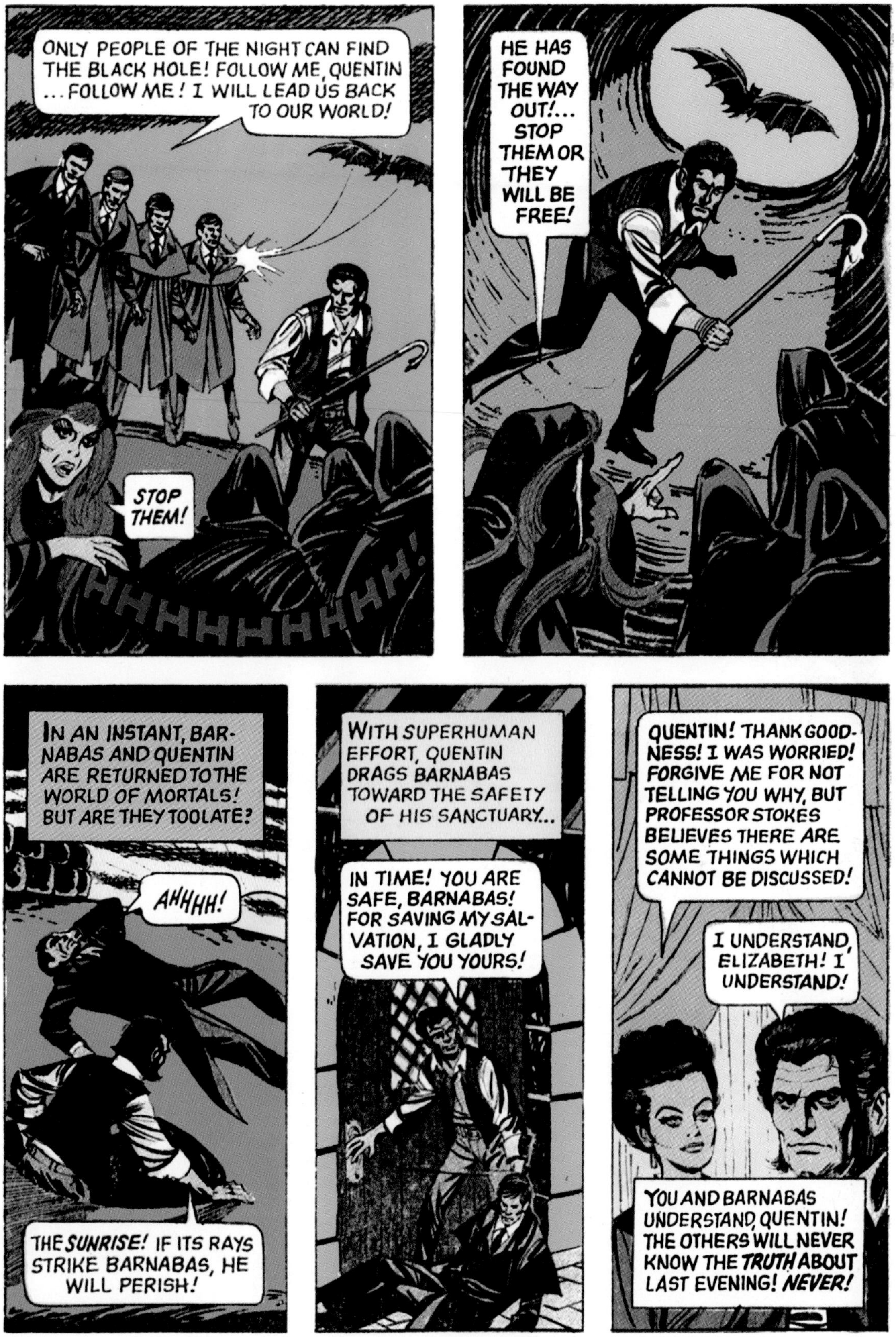
ONLY PEOPLE OF THE NIGHT CAN FIND THE BLACK HOLE! FOLLOW ME, QUENTIN ... FOLLOW ME! I WILL LEAD US BACK TO OUR WORLD!
STOP THEM!
HE HAS FOUND THE WAY OUT!... STOP THEM OR THEY WILL BE FREE!
IN AN INSTANT, BARNABAS AND QUENTIN ARE RETURNED TO THE WORLD OF MORTALS! BUT ARE THEY TOO LATE?
AHHHH!
THE SUNRISE! IF ITS RAYS STRIKE BARNABAS, HE WILL PERISH!
WITH SUPERHUMAN EFFORT, QUENTIN DRAGS BARNABAS TOWARD THE SAFETY OF HIS SANCTUARY...
IN TIME! YOU ARE SAFE, BARNABAS! FOR SAVING MY SALVATION, I GLADLY SAVE YOU YOURS!
QUENTIN! THANK GOODNESS! I WAS WORRIED! FORGIVE ME FOR NOT TELLING YOU WHY, BUT PROFESSOR STOKES BELIEVES THERE ARE SOME THINGS WHICH CANNOT BE DISCUSSED!
I UNDERSTAND, ELIZABETH! I UNDERSTAND!
YOU AND BARNABAS UNDERSTAND, QUENTIN! THE OTHERS WILL NEVER KNOW THE TRUTH ABOUT LAST EVENING! NEVER!

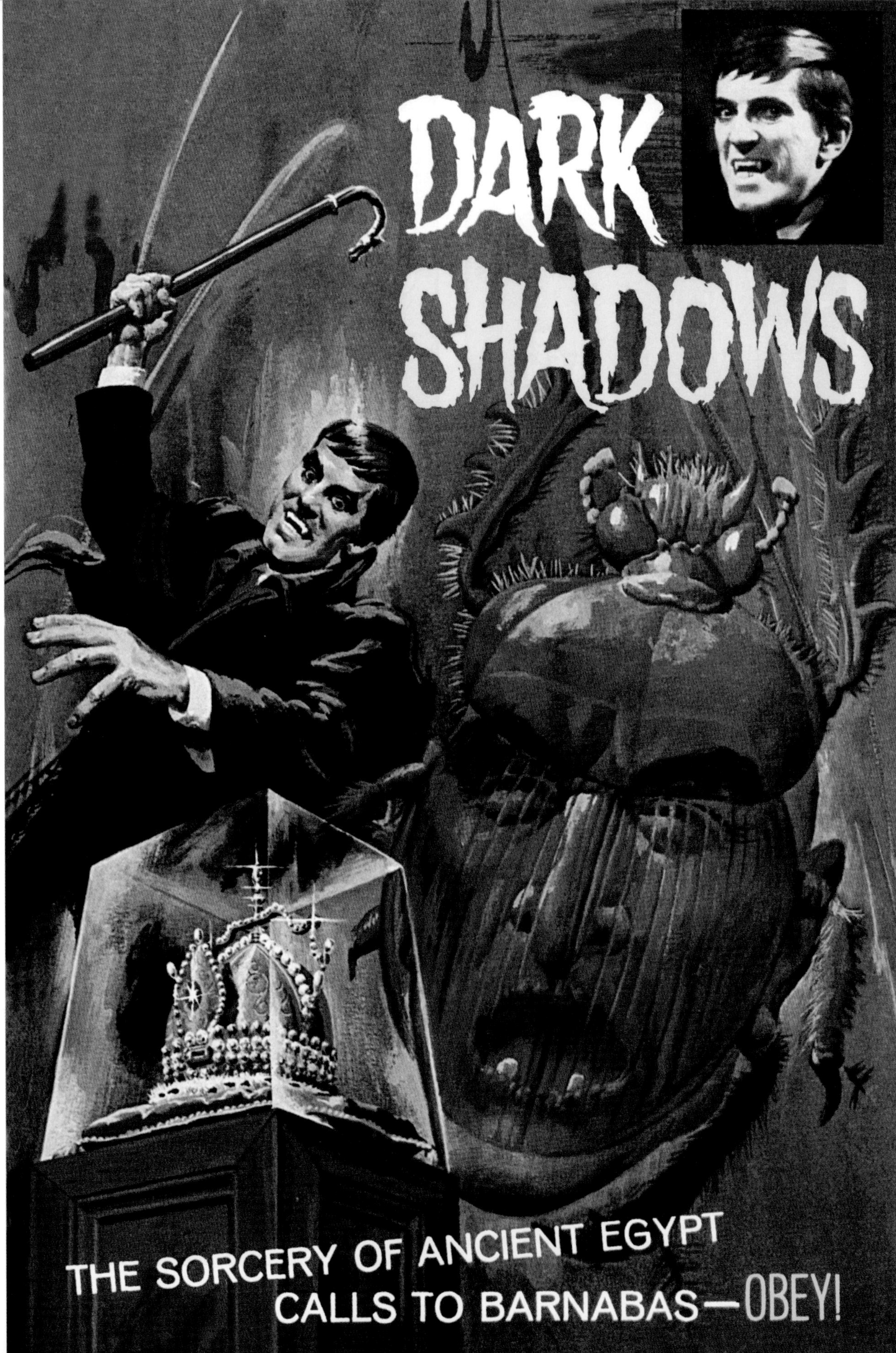
DARK SHADOWS
THE SORCERY OF ANCIENT EGYPT
CALLS TO BARNABAS—OBEY!

DARK SHADOWS

The Scarab

PART 1: The SPELL OF POTIPHAR

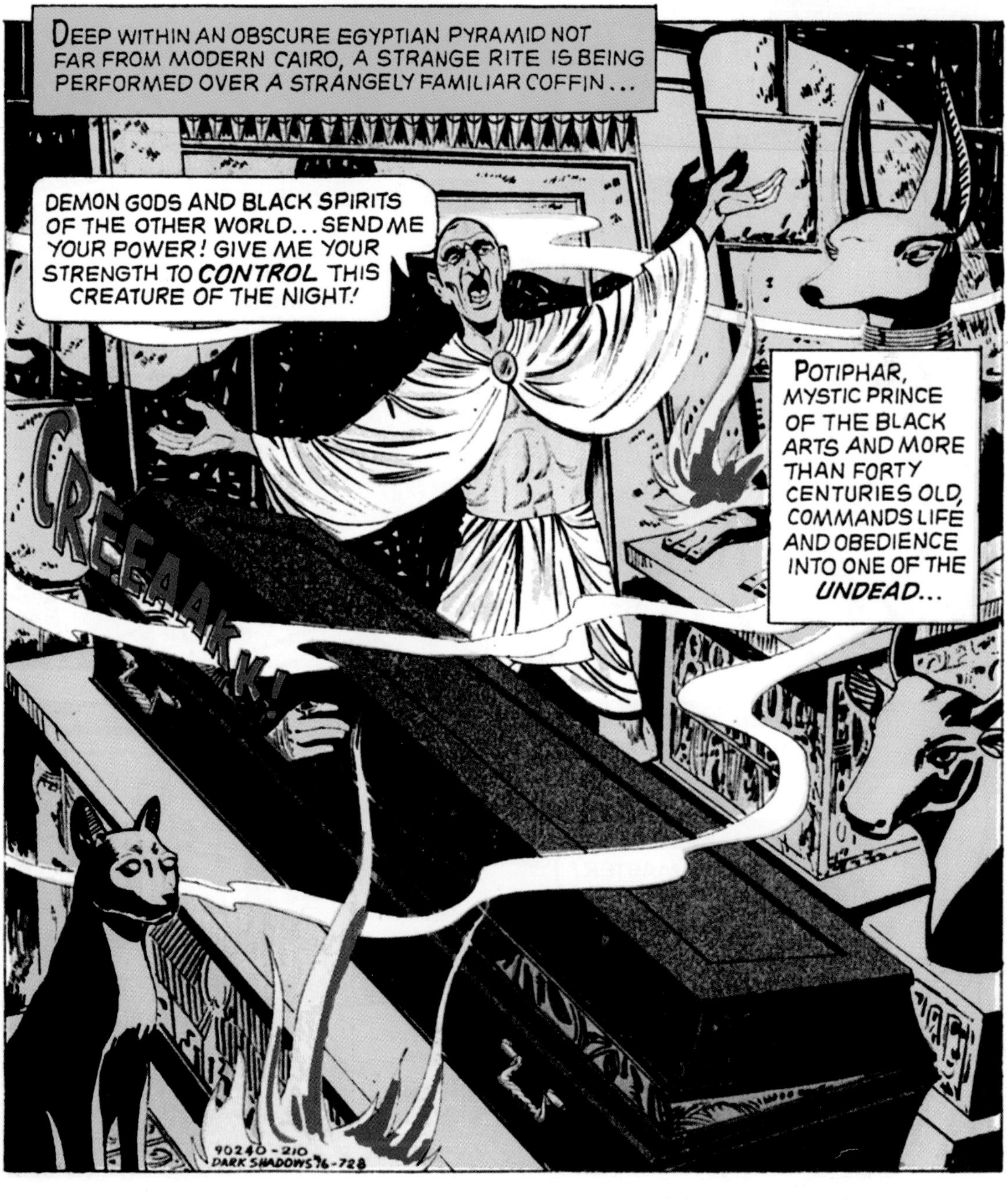

DEEP WITHIN AN OBSCURE EGYPTIAN PYRAMID NOT FAR FROM MODERN CAIRO, A STRANGE RITE IS BEING PERFORMED OVER A STRANGELY FAMILIAR COFFIN...
DEMON GODS AND BLACK SPIRITS OF THE OTHER WORLD... SEND ME YOUR POWER! GIVE ME YOUR STRENGTH TO *CONTROL* THIS CREATURE OF THE NIGHT!
POTIPHAR, MYSTIC PRINCE OF THE BLACK ARTS AND MORE THAN FORTY CENTURIES OLD, COMMANDS LIFE AND OBEDIENCE INTO ONE OF THE *UNDEAD*...
CREEAAAKK!
90240-210
DARK SHADOWS 76-728

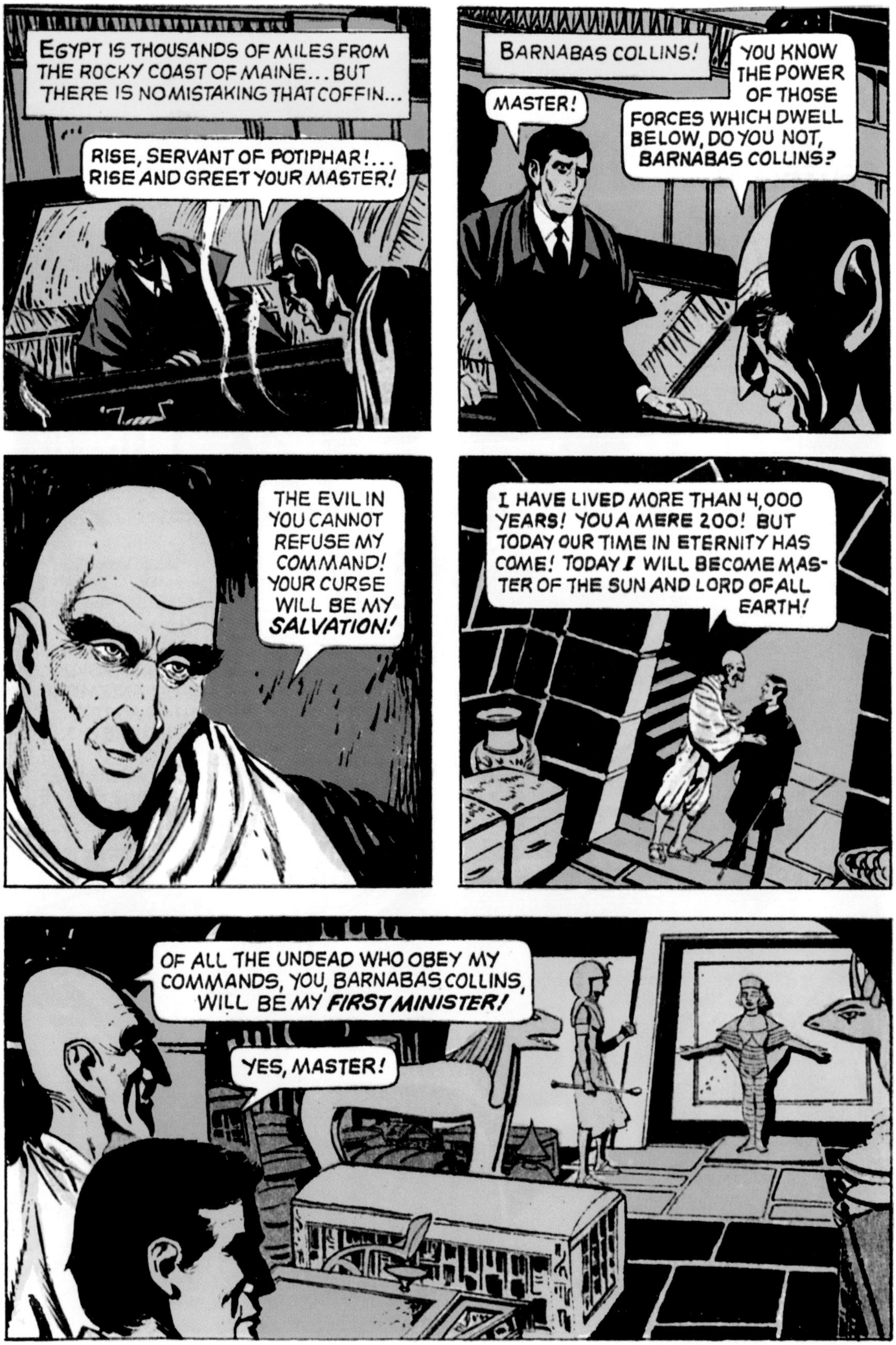
EGYPT IS THOUSANDS OF MILES FROM THE ROCKY COAST OF MAINE... BUT THERE IS NO MISTAKING THAT COFFIN...
RISE, SERVANT OF POTIPHAR!... RISE AND GREET YOUR MASTER!
BARNABAS COLLINS!
MASTER!
YOU KNOW THE POWER OF THOSE FORCES WHICH DWELL BELOW, DO YOU NOT, BARNABAS COLLINS?
THE EVIL IN YOU CANNOT REFUSE MY COMMAND! YOUR CURSE WILL BE MY SALVATION!
I HAVE LIVED MORE THAN 4,000 YEARS! YOU A MERE 200! BUT TODAY OUR TIME IN ETERNITY HAS COME! TODAY I WILL BECOME MASTER OF THE SUN AND LORD OF ALL EARTH!
OF ALL THE UNDEAD WHO OBEY MY COMMANDS, YOU, BARNABAS COLLINS, WILL BE MY FIRST MINISTER!
YES, MASTER!

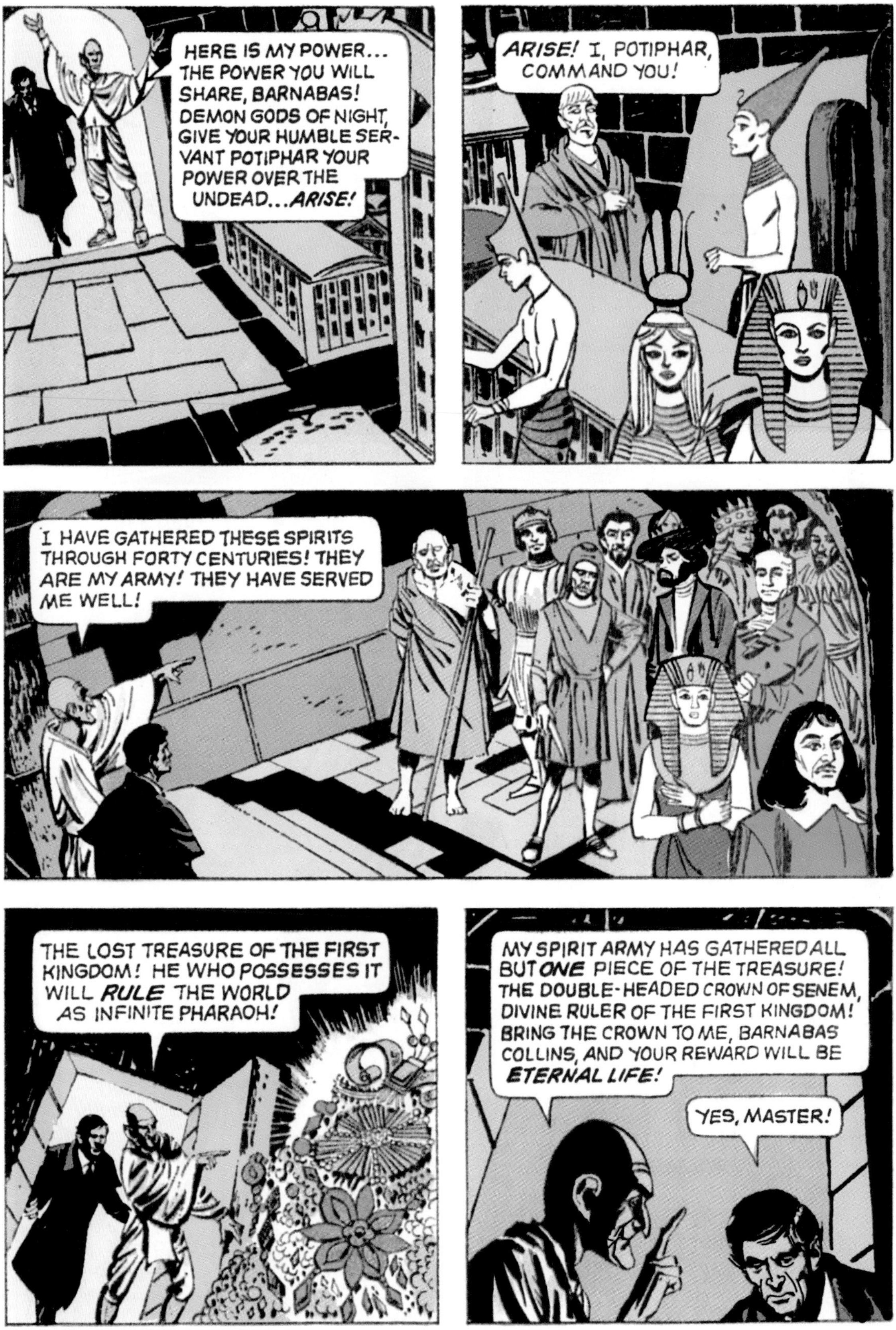
HERE IS MY POWER... THE POWER YOU WILL SHARE, BARNABAS! DEMON GODS OF NIGHT, GIVE YOUR HUMBLE SERVANT POTIPHAR YOUR POWER OVER THE UNDEAD... ARISE!
ARISE! I, POTIPHAR, COMMAND YOU!
I HAVE GATHERED THESE SPIRITS THROUGH FORTY CENTURIES! THEY ARE MY ARMY! THEY HAVE SERVED ME WELL!
THE LOST TREASURE OF THE FIRST KINGDOM! HE WHO POSSESSES IT WILL RULE THE WORLD AS INFINITE PHARAOH!
MY SPIRIT ARMY HAS GATHERED ALL BUT ONE PIECE OF THE TREASURE! THE DOUBLE-HEADED CROWN OF SENEM, DIVINE RULER OF THE FIRST KINGDOM! BRING THE CROWN TO ME, BARNABAS COLLINS, AND YOUR REWARD WILL BE ETERNAL LIFE!
YES, MASTER!

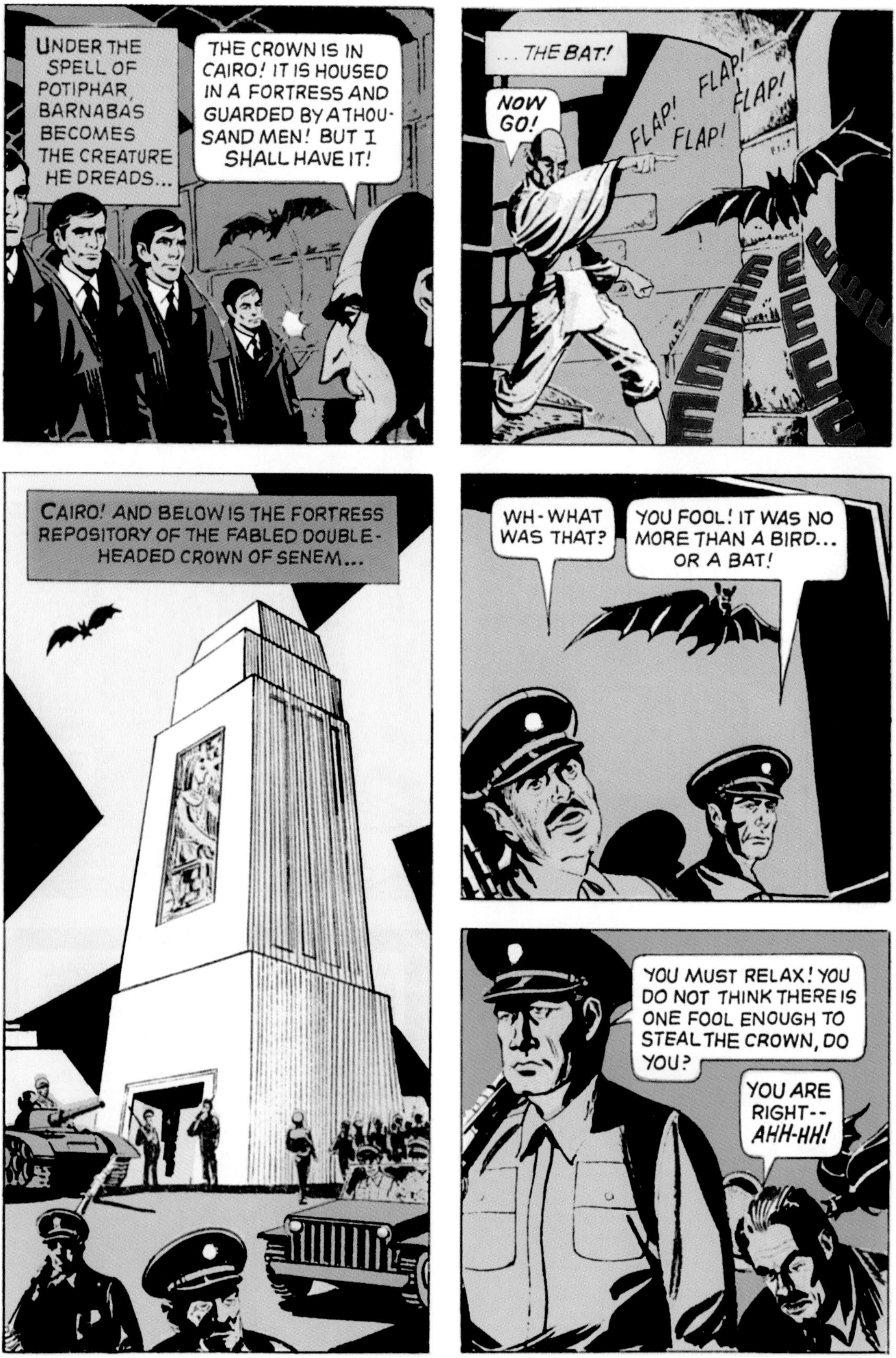
UNDER THE SPELL OF POTIPHAR, BARNABAS BECOMES THE CREATURE HE DREADS...
THE CROWN IS IN CAIRO! IT IS HOUSED IN A FORTRESS AND GUARDED BY A THOUSAND MEN! BUT I SHALL HAVE IT!
...THE BAT!
NOW GO!
FLAP! FLAP! FLAP! FLAP!
EEEEEEE
EEEEEEEE
CAIRO! AND BELOW IS THE FORTRESS REPOSITORY OF THE FABLED DOUBLE-HEADED CROWN OF SENEM...
WH-WHAT WAS THAT?
YOU FOOL! IT WAS NO MORE THAN A BIRD... OR A BAT!
YOU MUST RELAX! YOU DO NOT THINK THERE IS ONE FOOL ENOUGH TO STEAL THE CROWN, DO YOU?
YOU ARE RIGHT-- AHH-HH!

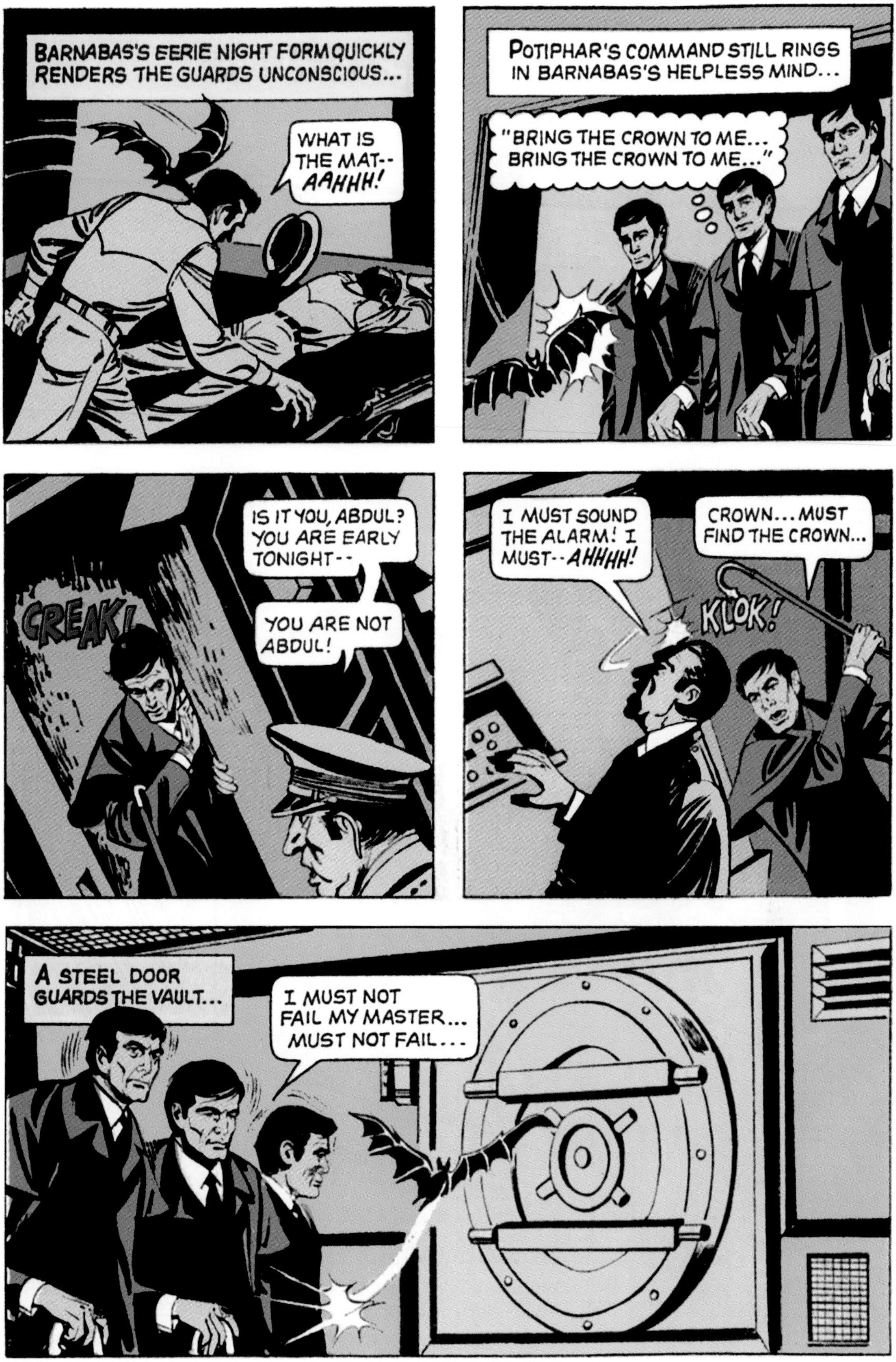
BARNABAS'S EERIE NIGHT FORM QUICKLY RENDERS THE GUARDS UNCONSCIOUS...
WHAT IS THE MAT--AAHHH!
POTIPHAR'S COMMAND STILL RINGS IN BARNABAS'S HELPLESS MIND...
"BRING THE CROWN TO ME... BRING THE CROWN TO ME..."
CREAK!
IS IT YOU, ABDUL? YOU ARE EARLY TONIGHT--
YOU ARE NOT ABDUL!
I MUST SOUND THE ALARM! I MUST--AHHHH!
CROWN... MUST FIND THE CROWN...
KLOK!
A STEEL DOOR GUARDS THE VAULT...
I MUST NOT FAIL MY MASTER... MUST NOT FAIL...

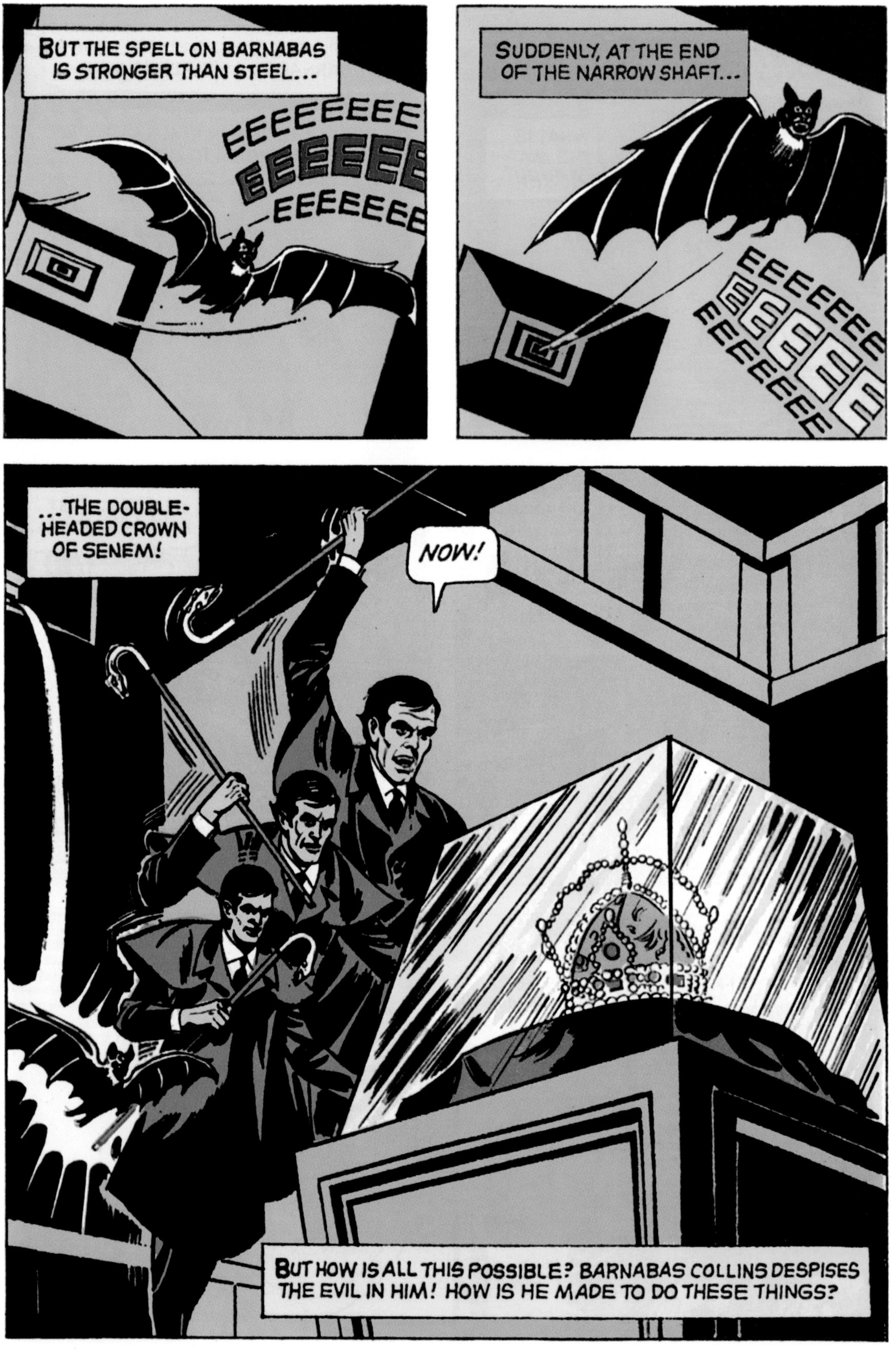
BUT THE SPELL ON BARNABAS IS STRONGER THAN STEEL...
EEEEEEEE
EEEEEE
EEEEEEE
SUDDENLY, AT THE END OF THE NARROW SHAFT...
...THE DOUBLE-HEADED CROWN OF SENEM!
NOW!
BUT HOW IS ALL THIS POSSIBLE? BARNABAS COLLINS DESPISES THE EVIL IN HIM! HOW IS HE MADE TO DO THESE THINGS?

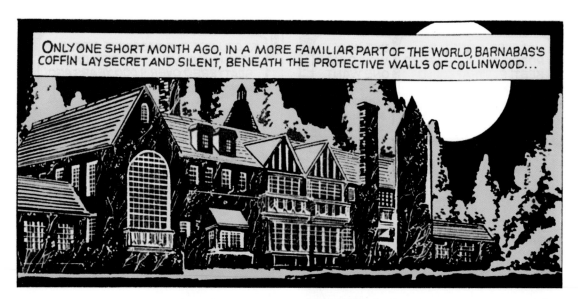

ONLY ONE SHORT MONTH AGO, IN A MORE FAMILIAR PART OF THE WORLD, BARNABAS'S COFFIN LAY SECRET AND SILENT, BENEATH THE PROTECTIVE WALLS OF COLLINWOOD...

WHILE UPSTAIRS, IN THE STATELY MANSION...

IF BARNABAS DOESN'T ARRIVE SOON, I SHALL HAVE TO BEGIN DINNER WITHOUT HIM!

LET'S WAIT! I WANT TO HEAR THE REST OF PROFESSOR STOKES'S STORY!

YOU WERE GOING TO TELL US YOUR *THEORY* ABOUT THE RASH OF MUSEUM ROBBERIES, PROFESSOR!

HUMPH! YES...

AS YOU KNOW, I WAS CALLED INTO THE INVESTIGATION BECAUSE OF MY-- HARRUMPH, EXPERTISE IN THE OCCULT!

BUT WHAT'S THE CONNECTION?

THERE IS AN ANCIENT EGYPTIAN LEGEND THAT SAYS AN EVIL PRIEST OF THE BLACK ARTS, POTIPHAR, BY NAME, COULD TURN HIM- SELF INTO A *SCARAB!*

YOU MEAN, A *BEETLE?*

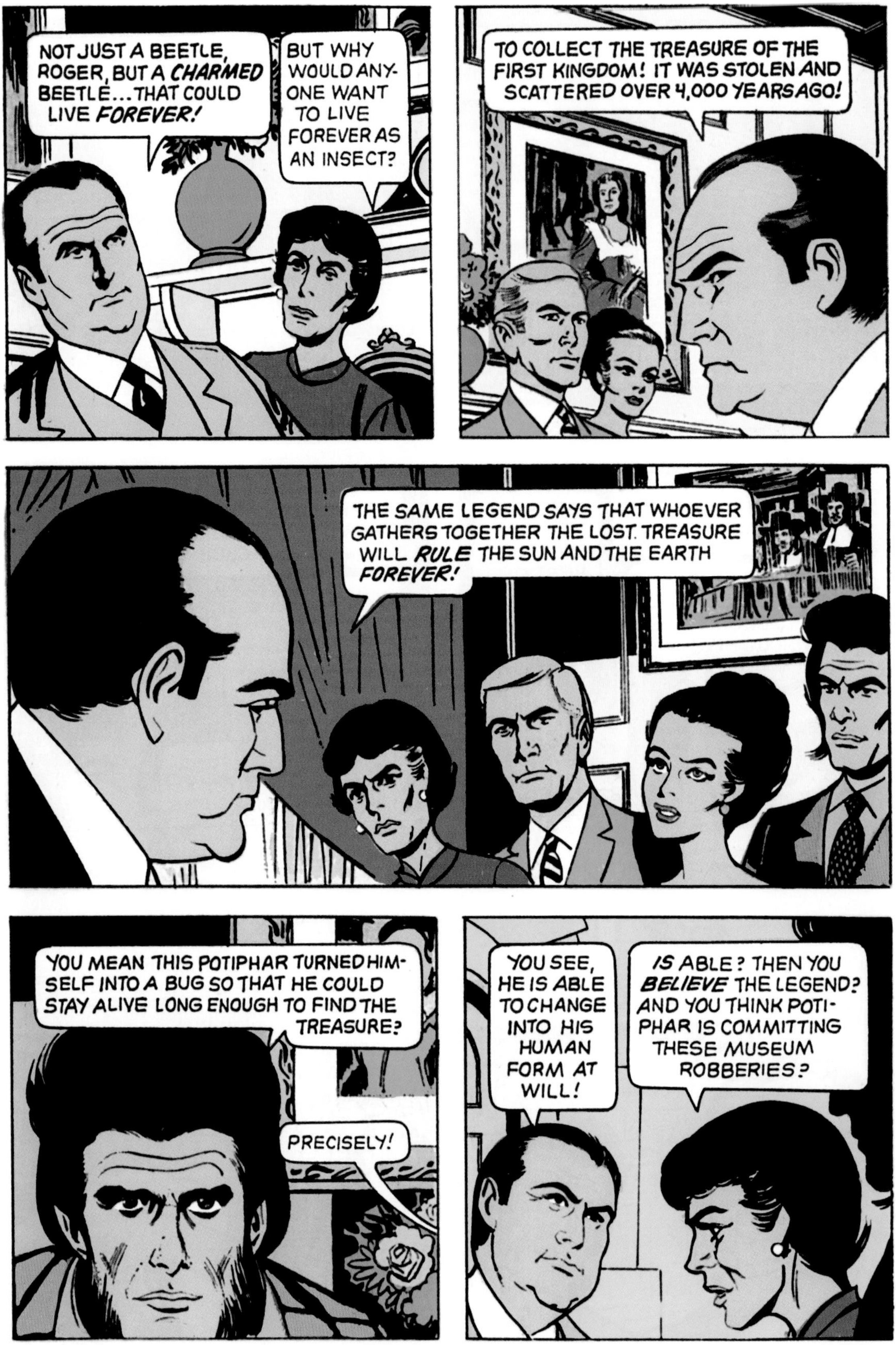
NOT JUST A BEETLE, ROGER, BUT A CHARMED BEETLE... THAT COULD LIVE FOREVER!
BUT WHY WOULD ANYONE WANT TO LIVE FOREVER AS AN INSECT?
TO COLLECT THE TREASURE OF THE FIRST KINGDOM! IT WAS STOLEN AND SCATTERED OVER 4,000 YEARS AGO!
THE SAME LEGEND SAYS THAT WHOEVER GATHERS TOGETHER THE LOST TREASURE WILL RULE THE SUN AND THE EARTH FOREVER!
YOU MEAN THIS POTIPHAR TURNED HIMSELF INTO A BUG SO THAT HE COULD STAY ALIVE LONG ENOUGH TO FIND THE TREASURE?
PRECISELY!
YOU SEE, HE IS ABLE TO CHANGE INTO HIS HUMAN FORM AT WILL!
IS ABLE? THEN YOU BELIEVE THE LEGEND? AND YOU THINK POTIPHAR IS COMMITTING THESE MUSEUM ROBBERIES?

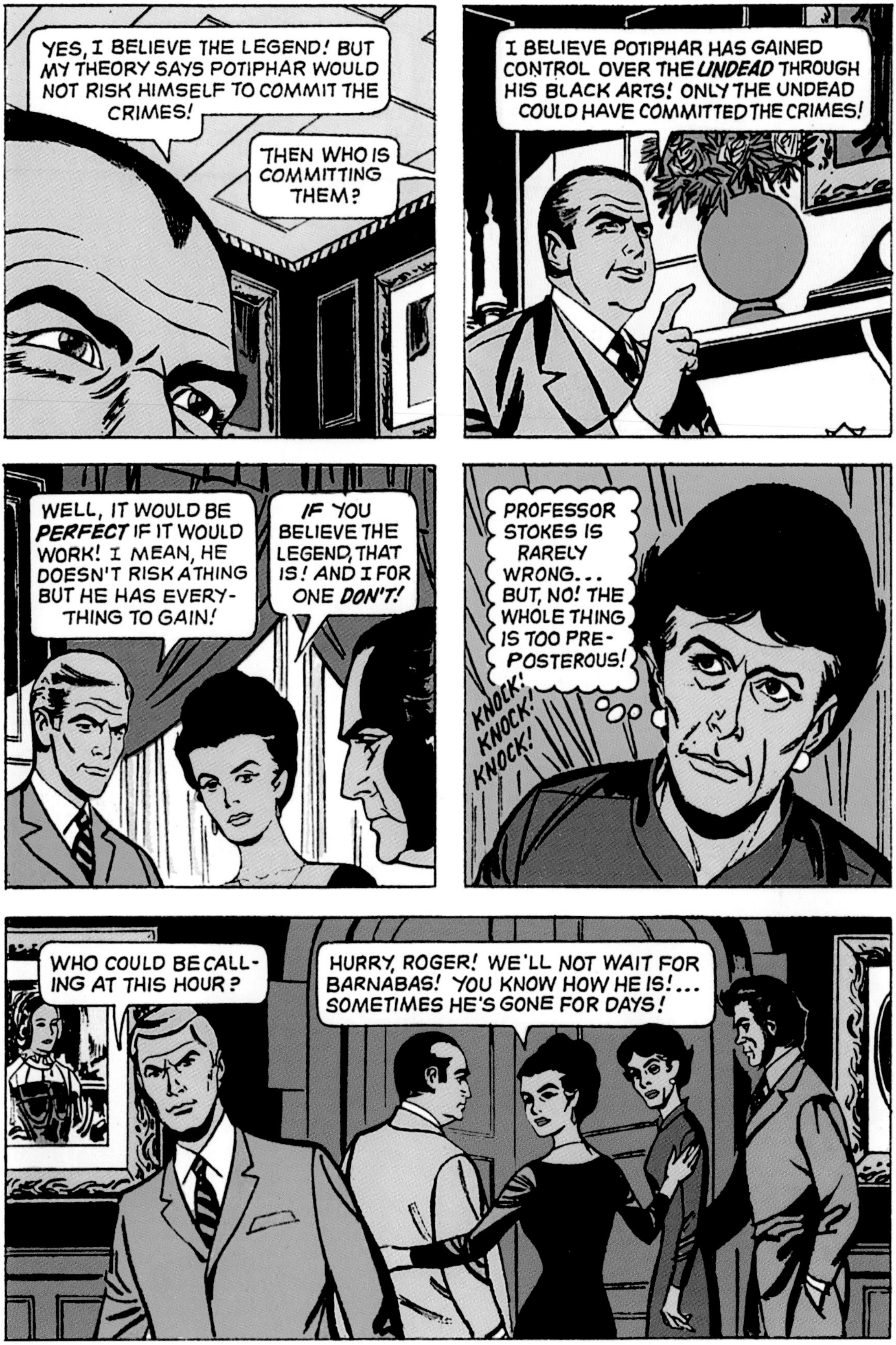
YES, I BELIEVE THE LEGEND! BUT MY THEORY SAYS POTIPHAR WOULD NOT RISK HIMSELF TO COMMIT THE CRIMES!
THEN WHO IS COMMITTING THEM?
I BELIEVE POTIPHAR HAS GAINED CONTROL OVER THE UNDEAD THROUGH HIS BLACK ARTS! ONLY THE UNDEAD COULD HAVE COMMITTED THE CRIMES!
WELL, IT WOULD BE PERFECT IF IT WOULD WORK! I MEAN, HE DOESN'T RISK A THING BUT HE HAS EVERYTHING TO GAIN!
IF YOU BELIEVE THE LEGEND, THAT IS! AND I FOR ONE DON'T!
PROFESSOR STOKES IS RARELY WRONG... BUT, NO! THE WHOLE THING IS TOO PREPOSTEROUS!
KNOCK! KNOCK! KNOCK!
WHO COULD BE CALLING AT THIS HOUR?
HURRY, ROGER! WE'LL NOT WAIT FOR BARNABAS! YOU KNOW HOW HE IS!... SOMETIMES HE'S GONE FOR DAYS!

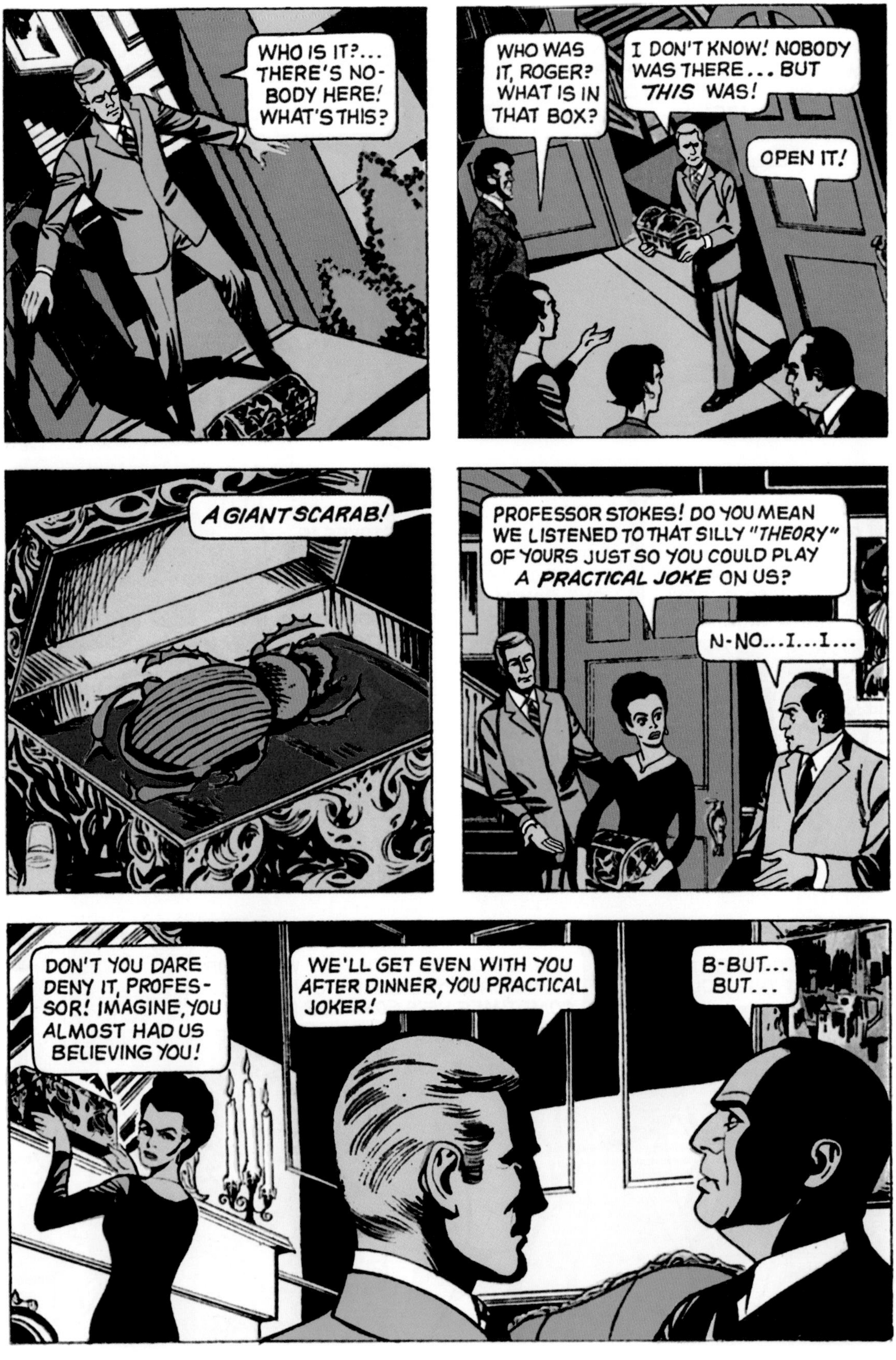
WHO IS IT?... THERE'S NO-BODY HERE! WHAT'S THIS?
WHO WAS IT, ROGER? WHAT IS IN THAT BOX?
I DON'T KNOW! NOBODY WAS THERE... BUT THIS WAS!
OPEN IT!
A GIANT SCARAB!
PROFESSOR STOKES! DO YOU MEAN WE LISTENED TO THAT SILLY "THEORY" OF YOURS JUST SO YOU COULD PLAY A PRACTICAL JOKE ON US?
N-NO...I...I...
DON'T YOU DARE DENY IT, PROFES-SOR! IMAGINE, YOU ALMOST HAD US BELIEVING YOU!
WE'LL GET EVEN WITH YOU AFTER DINNER, YOU PRACTICAL JOKER!
B-BUT... BUT...

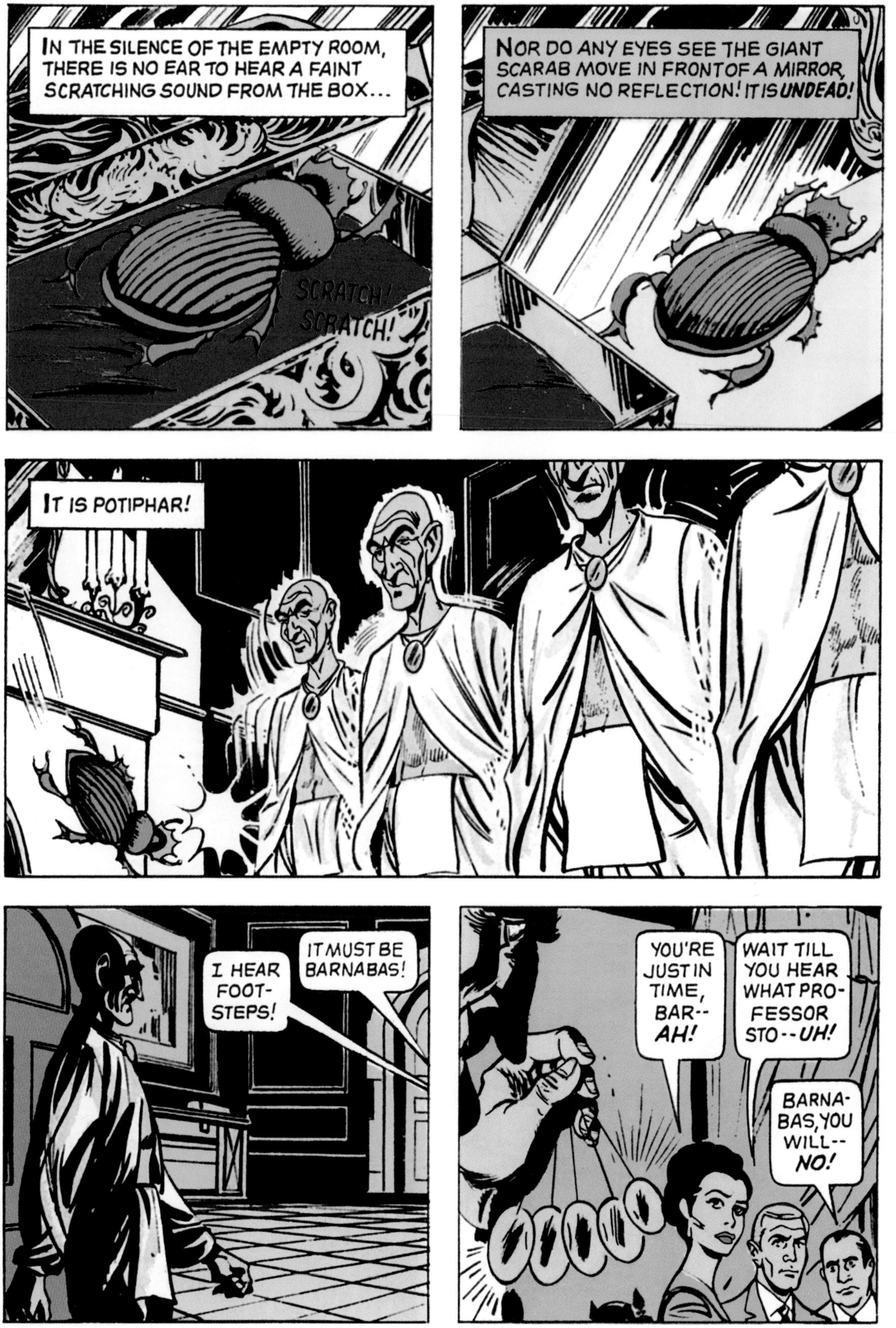
IN THE SILENCE OF THE EMPTY ROOM, THERE IS NO EAR TO HEAR A FAINT SCRATCHING SOUND FROM THE BOX...
SCRATCH! SCRATCH!
NOR DO ANY EYES SEE THE GIANT SCARAB MOVE IN FRONT OF A MIRROR, CASTING NO REFLECTION! IT IS UNDEAD!
IT IS POTIPHAR!
I HEAR FOOT-STEPS!
IT MUST BE BARNABAS!
YOU'RE JUST IN TIME, BAR-- AH!
WAIT TILL YOU HEAR WHAT PRO-FESSOR STO--UH!
BARNA-BAS, YOU WILL-- NO!

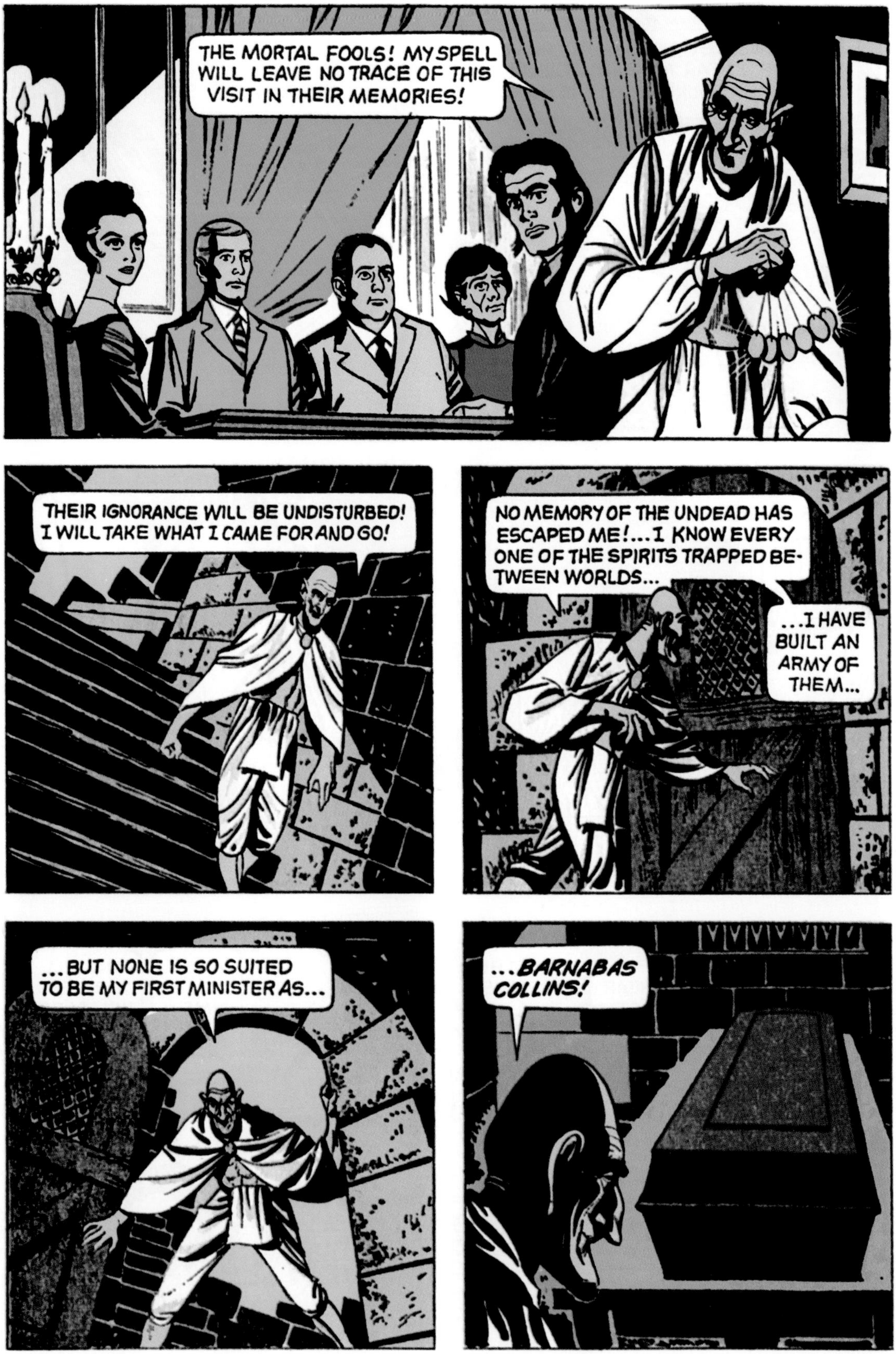
THE MORTAL FOOLS! MY SPELL WILL LEAVE NO TRACE OF THIS VISIT IN THEIR MEMORIES!
THEIR IGNORANCE WILL BE UNDISTURBED! I WILL TAKE WHAT I CAME FOR AND GO!
NO MEMORY OF THE UNDEAD HAS ESCAPED ME!... I KNOW EVERY ONE OF THE SPIRITS TRAPPED BETWEEN WORLDS...
...I HAVE BUILT AN ARMY OF THEM...
... BUT NONE IS SO SUITED TO BE MY FIRST MINISTER AS...
... BARNABAS COLLINS!

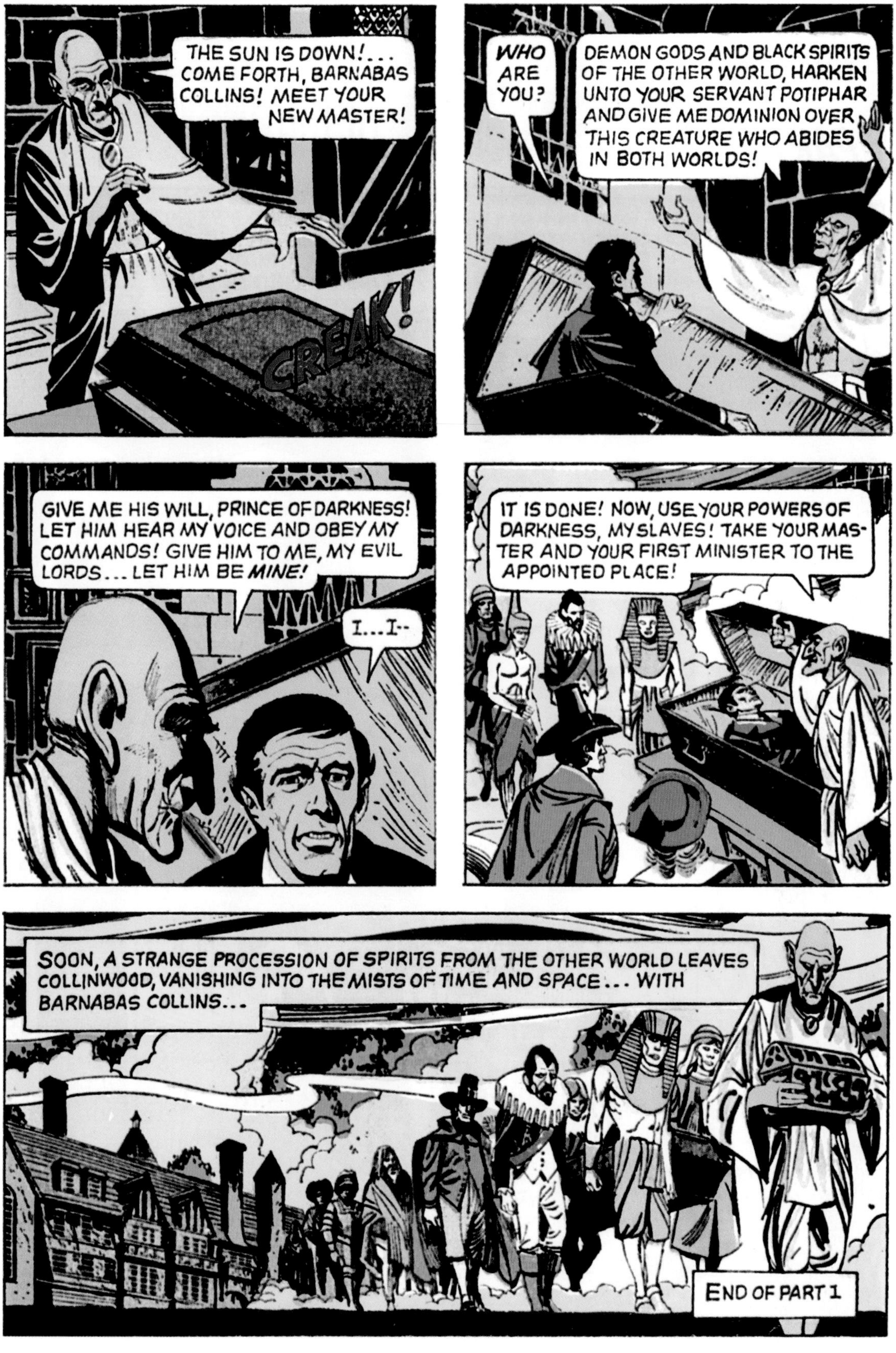
THE SUN IS DOWN!... COME FORTH, BARNABAS COLLINS! MEET YOUR NEW MASTER!
CREAK!
WHO ARE YOU?
DEMON GODS AND BLACK SPIRITS OF THE OTHER WORLD, HARKEN UNTO YOUR SERVANT POTIPHAR AND GIVE ME DOMINION OVER THIS CREATURE WHO ABIDES IN BOTH WORLDS!
GIVE ME HIS WILL, PRINCE OF DARKNESS! LET HIM HEAR MY VOICE AND OBEY MY COMMANDS! GIVE HIM TO ME, MY EVIL LORDS... LET HIM BE MINE!
I...I-
IT IS DONE! NOW, USE YOUR POWERS OF DARKNESS, MY SLAVES! TAKE YOUR MASTER AND YOUR FIRST MINISTER TO THE APPOINTED PLACE!
SOON, A STRANGE PROCESSION OF SPIRITS FROM THE OTHER WORLD LEAVES COLLINWOOD, VANISHING INTO THE MISTS OF TIME AND SPACE... WITH BARNABAS COLLINS...
END OF PART 1

DARK SHADOWS

The Scarab
PART 2: TREASURE of the UNDEAD

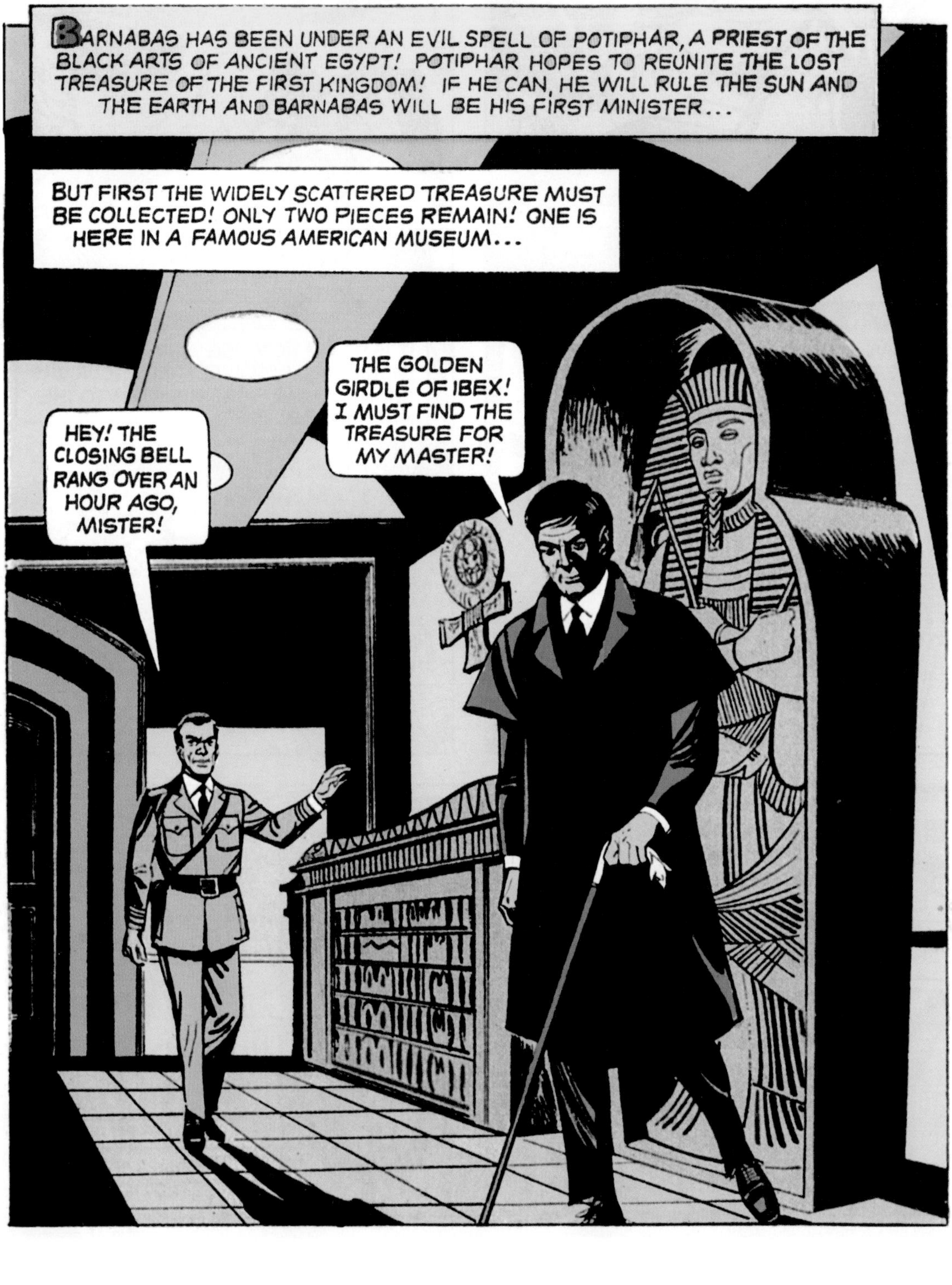

BARNABAS HAS BEEN UNDER AN EVIL SPELL OF POTIPHAR, A PRIEST OF THE BLACK ARTS OF ANCIENT EGYPT! POTIPHAR HOPES TO REUNITE THE LOST TREASURE OF THE FIRST KINGDOM! IF HE CAN, HE WILL RULE THE SUN AND THE EARTH AND BARNABAS WILL BE HIS FIRST MINISTER...
BUT FIRST THE WIDELY SCATTERED TREASURE MUST BE COLLECTED! ONLY TWO PIECES REMAIN! ONE IS HERE IN A FAMOUS AMERICAN MUSEUM...
HEY! THE CLOSING BELL RANG OVER AN HOUR AGO, MISTER!
THE GOLDEN GIRDLE OF IBEX! I MUST FIND THE TREASURE FOR MY MASTER!

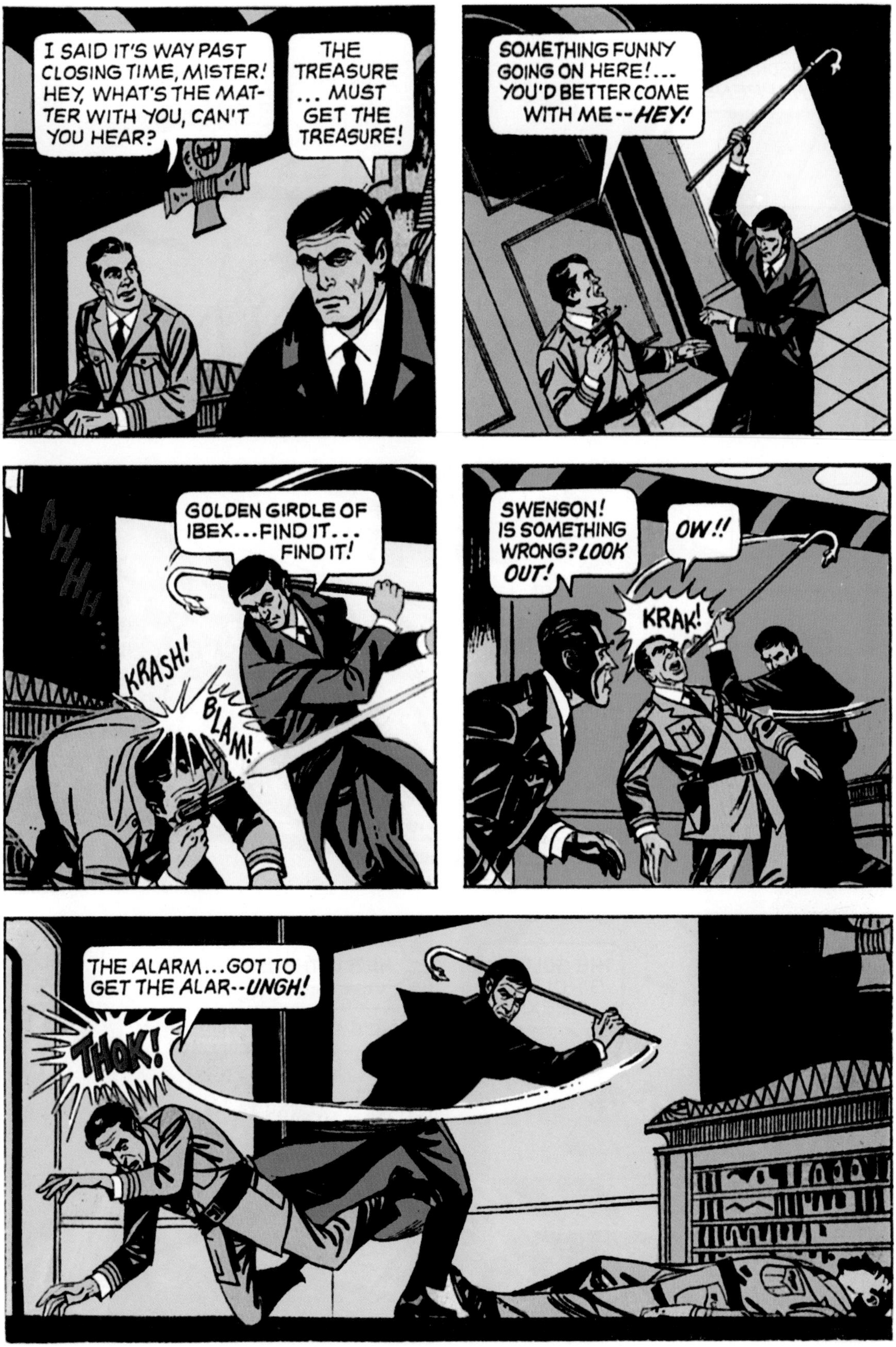
I SAID IT'S WAY PAST CLOSING TIME, MISTER! HEY, WHAT'S THE MATTER WITH YOU, CAN'T YOU HEAR?
THE TREASURE ... MUST GET THE TREASURE!
SOMETHING FUNNY GOING ON HERE!... YOU'D BETTER COME WITH ME--HEY!
AHHH...
GOLDEN GIRDLE OF IBEX...FIND IT... FIND IT!
KRASH!
BLAM!
SWENSON! IS SOMETHING WRONG? LOOK OUT!
OW!!
KRAK!
THE ALARM...GOT TO GET THE ALAR--UNGH!
THOK!

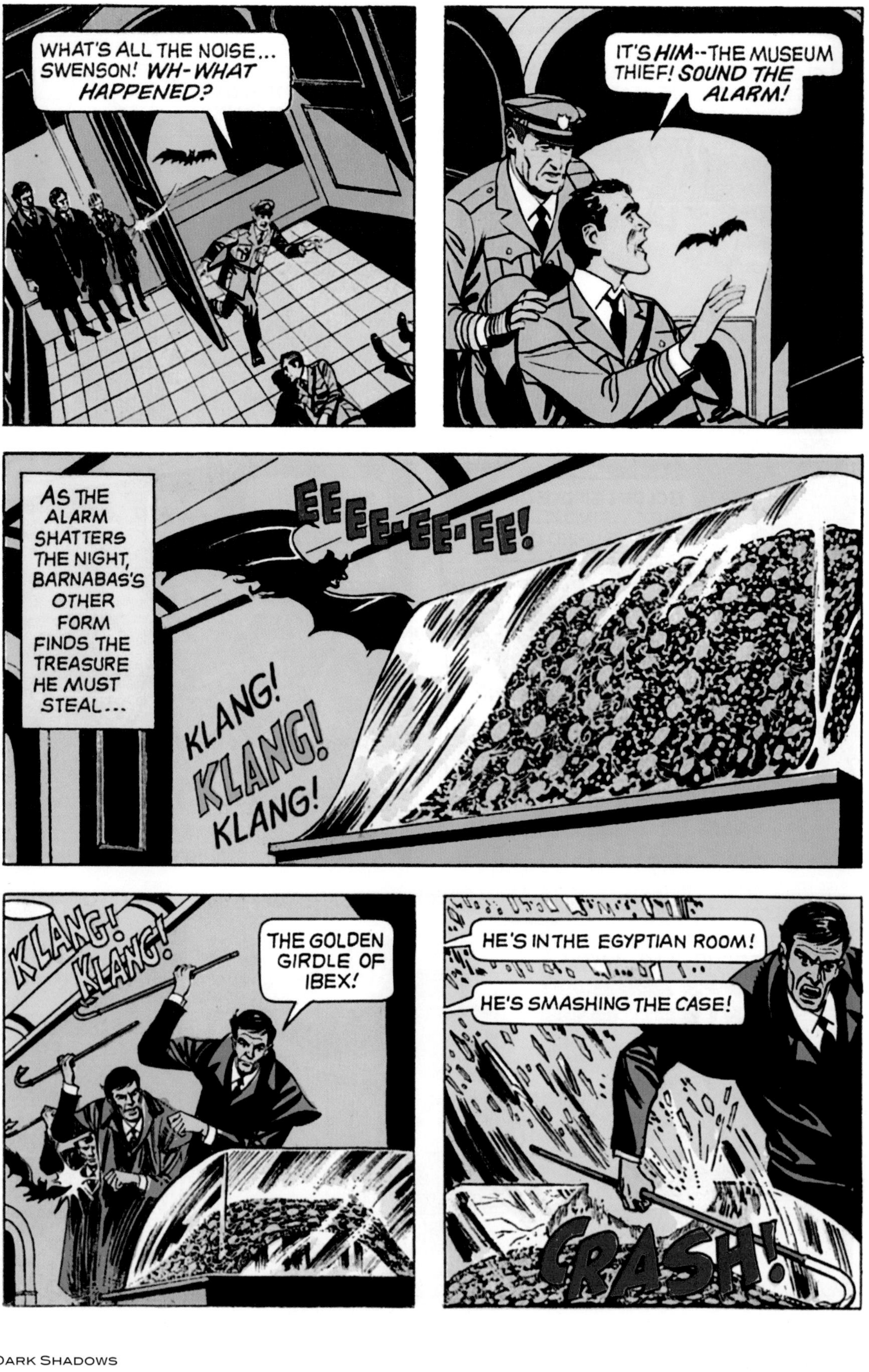
WHAT'S ALL THE NOISE... SWENSON! WH-WHAT HAPPENED?
IT'S HIM--THE MUSEUM THIEF! SOUND THE ALARM!
AS THE ALARM SHATTERS THE NIGHT, BARNABAS'S OTHER FORM FINDS THE TREASURE HE MUST STEAL...
EEEE-EE-EE!
KLANG! KLANG! KLANG!
KLANG! KLANG!
THE GOLDEN GIRDLE OF IBEX!
HE'S IN THE EGYPTIAN ROOM!
HE'S SMASHING THE CASE!
CRASH!

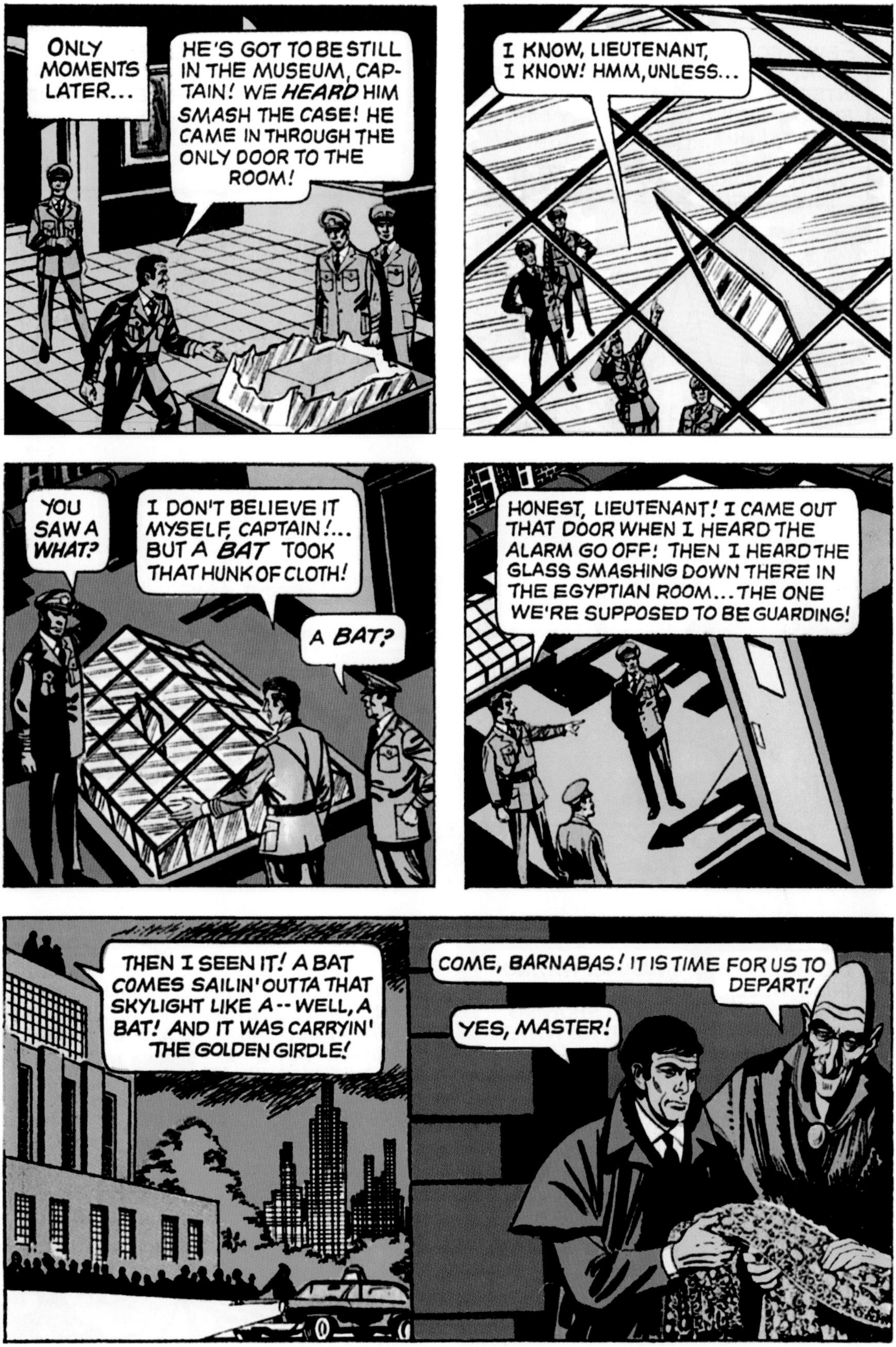
ONLY MOMENTS LATER...
HE'S GOT TO BE STILL IN THE MUSEUM, CAPTAIN! WE HEARD HIM SMASH THE CASE! HE CAME IN THROUGH THE ONLY DOOR TO THE ROOM!
I KNOW, LIEUTENANT, I KNOW! HMM, UNLESS...
YOU SAW A WHAT?
I DON'T BELIEVE IT MYSELF, CAPTAIN!... BUT A BAT TOOK THAT HUNK OF CLOTH!
A BAT?
HONEST, LIEUTENANT! I CAME OUT THAT DOOR WHEN I HEARD THE ALARM GO OFF! THEN I HEARD THE GLASS SMASHING DOWN THERE IN THE EGYPTIAN ROOM... THE ONE WE'RE SUPPOSED TO BE GUARDING!
THEN I SEEN IT! A BAT COMES SAILIN' OUTTA THAT SKYLIGHT LIKE A -- WELL, A BAT! AND IT WAS CARRYIN' THE GOLDEN GIRDLE!
COME, BARNABAS! IT IS TIME FOR US TO DEPART!
YES, MASTER!

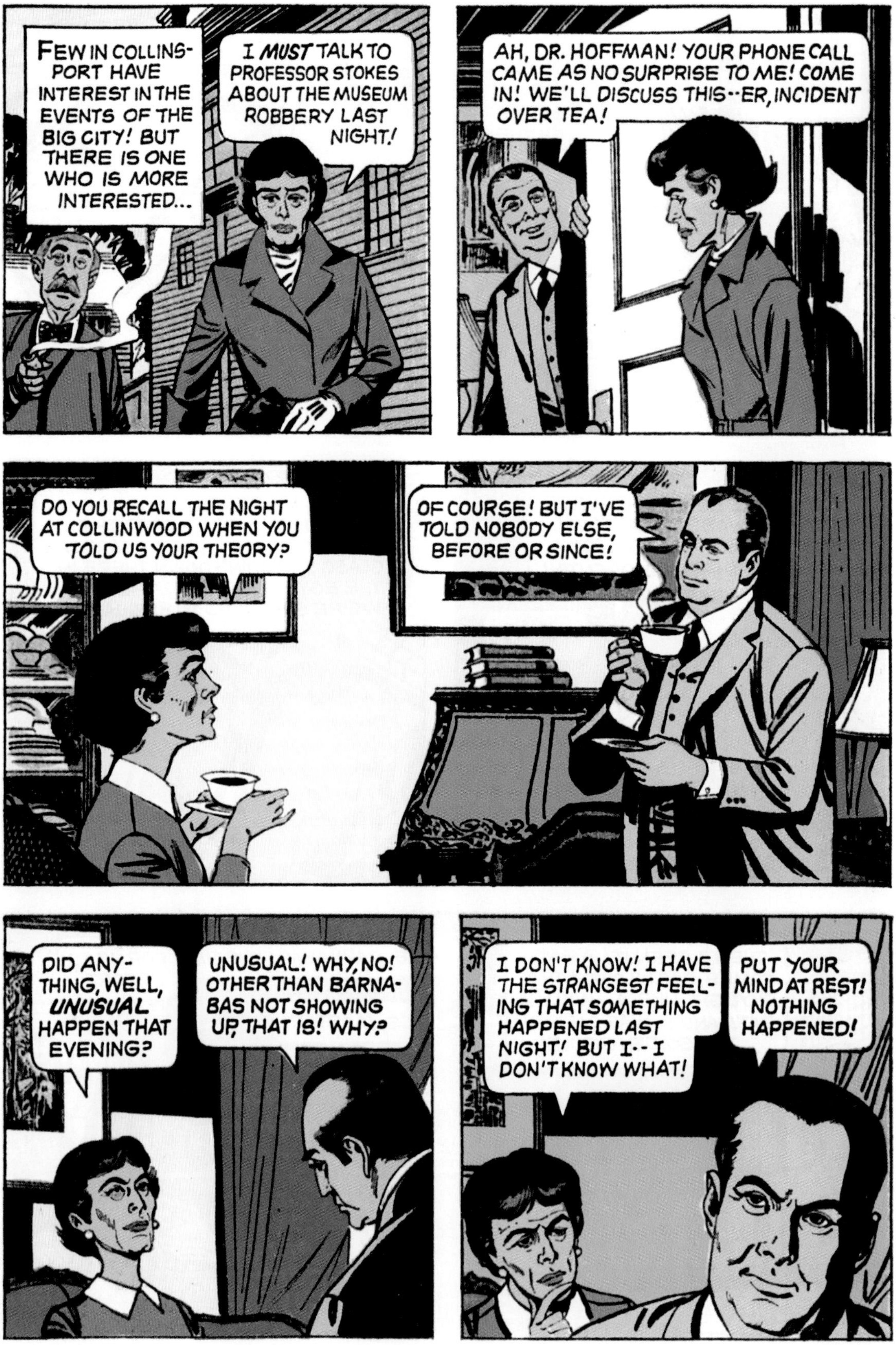
FEW IN COLLINSPORT HAVE INTEREST IN THE EVENTS OF THE BIG CITY! BUT THERE IS ONE WHO IS MORE INTERESTED...
I MUST TALK TO PROFESSOR STOKES ABOUT THE MUSEUM ROBBERY LAST NIGHT!
AH, DR. HOFFMAN! YOUR PHONE CALL CAME AS NO SURPRISE TO ME! COME IN! WE'LL DISCUSS THIS--ER, INCIDENT OVER TEA!
DO YOU RECALL THE NIGHT AT COLLINWOOD WHEN YOU TOLD US YOUR THEORY?
OF COURSE! BUT I'VE TOLD NOBODY ELSE, BEFORE OR SINCE!
DID ANYTHING, WELL, UNUSUAL HAPPEN THAT EVENING?
UNUSUAL! WHY, NO! OTHER THAN BARNABAS NOT SHOWING UP, THAT IS! WHY?
I DON'T KNOW! I HAVE THE STRANGEST FEELING THAT SOMETHING HAPPENED LAST NIGHT! BUT I-- I DON'T KNOW WHAT!
PUT YOUR MIND AT REST! NOTHING HAPPENED!

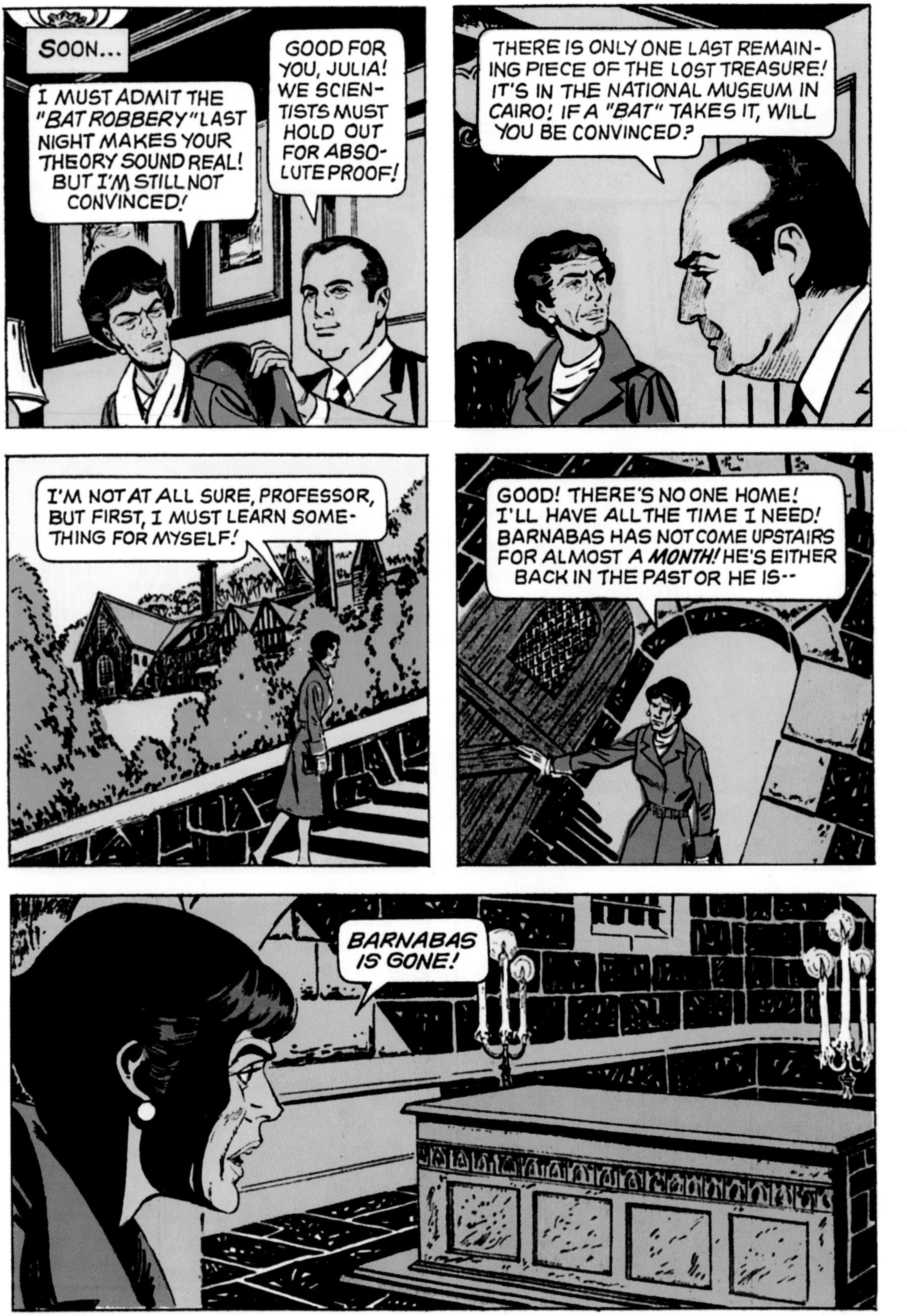
SOON...
I MUST ADMIT THE "BAT ROBBERY" LAST NIGHT MAKES YOUR THEORY SOUND REAL! BUT I'M STILL NOT CONVINCED!
GOOD FOR YOU, JULIA! WE SCIENTISTS MUST HOLD OUT FOR ABSOLUTE PROOF!
THERE IS ONLY ONE LAST REMAINING PIECE OF THE LOST TREASURE! IT'S IN THE NATIONAL MUSEUM IN CAIRO! IF A "BAT" TAKES IT, WILL YOU BE CONVINCED?
I'M NOT AT ALL SURE, PROFESSOR, BUT FIRST, I MUST LEARN SOMETHING FOR MYSELF!
GOOD! THERE'S NO ONE HOME! I'LL HAVE ALL THE TIME I NEED! BARNABAS HAS NOT COME UPSTAIRS FOR ALMOST A *MONTH!* HE'S EITHER BACK IN THE PAST OR HE IS--
BARNABAS IS GONE!

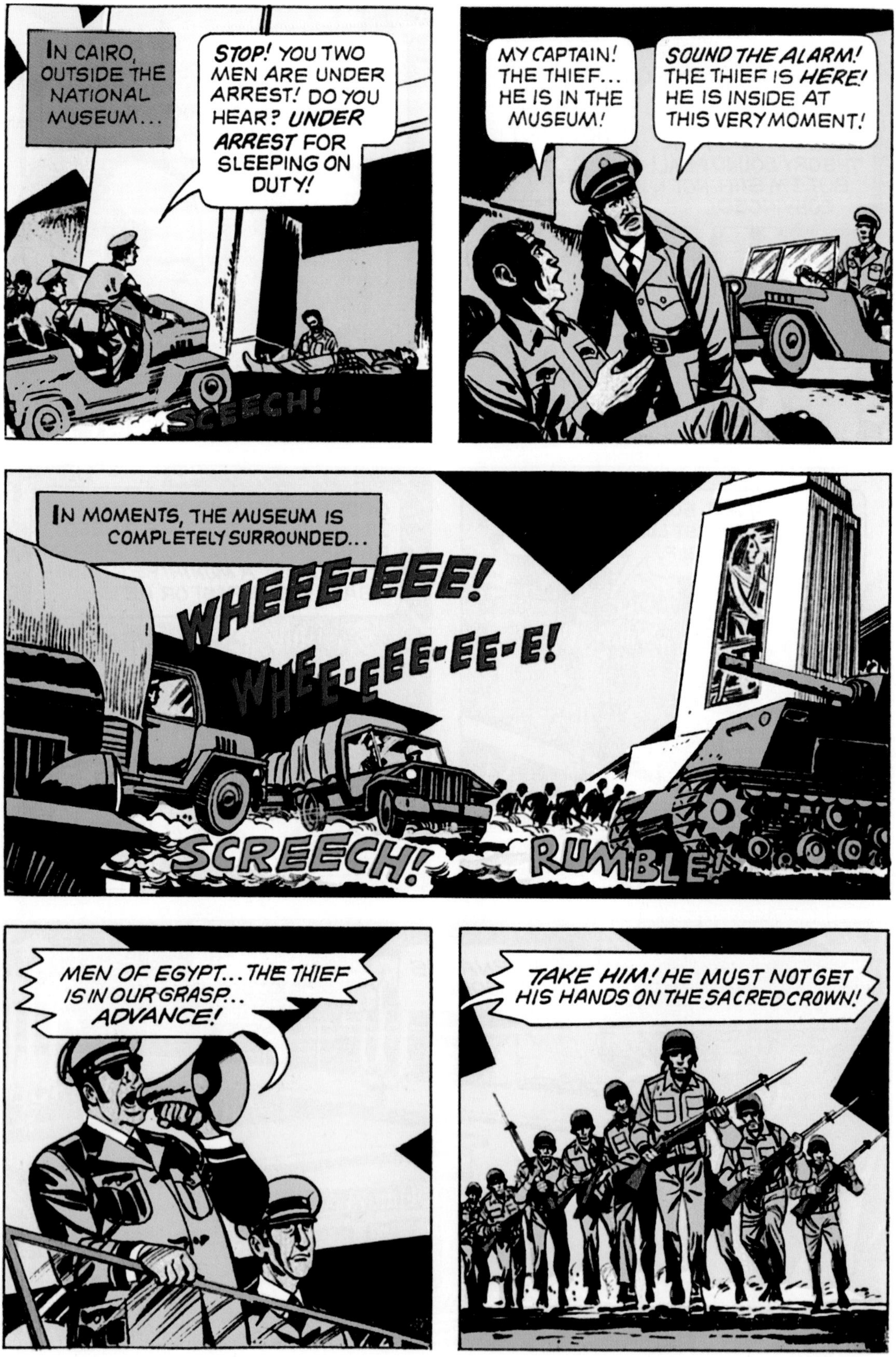

IN CAIRO, OUTSIDE THE NATIONAL MUSEUM...
STOP! YOU TWO MEN ARE UNDER ARREST! DO YOU HEAR? UNDER ARREST FOR SLEEPING ON DUTY!
SCEECH!
MY CAPTAIN! THE THIEF... HE IS IN THE MUSEUM!
SOUND THE ALARM! THE THIEF IS HERE! HE IS INSIDE AT THIS VERY MOMENT!
IN MOMENTS, THE MUSEUM IS COMPLETELY SURROUNDED...
WHEEE-EEE!
WHEE-EEE-EE-E!
SCREECH!
RUMBLE!
MEN OF EGYPT... THE THIEF IS IN OUR GRASP.. ADVANCE!
TAKE HIM! HE MUST NOT GET HIS HANDS ON THE SACRED CROWN!

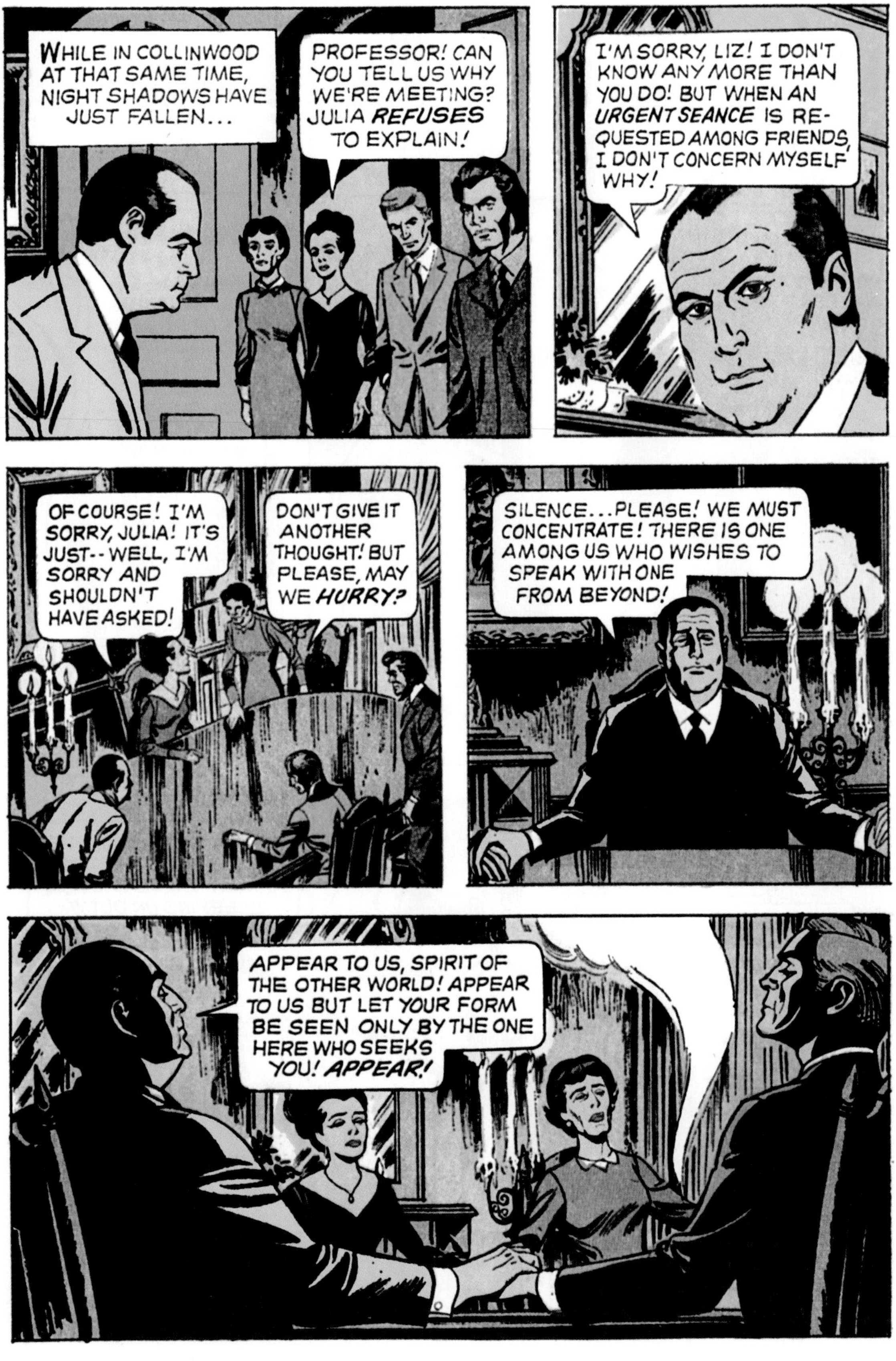
WHILE IN COLLINWOOD AT THAT SAME TIME, NIGHT SHADOWS HAVE JUST FALLEN...
PROFESSOR! CAN YOU TELL US WHY WE'RE MEETING? JULIA REFUSES TO EXPLAIN!
I'M SORRY, LIZ! I DON'T KNOW ANY MORE THAN YOU DO! BUT WHEN AN URGENT SEANCE IS REQUESTED AMONG FRIENDS, I DON'T CONCERN MYSELF WHY!
OF COURSE! I'M SORRY, JULIA! IT'S JUST--WELL, I'M SORRY AND SHOULDN'T HAVE ASKED!
DON'T GIVE IT ANOTHER THOUGHT! BUT PLEASE, MAY WE HURRY?
SILENCE...PLEASE! WE MUST CONCENTRATE! THERE IS ONE AMONG US WHO WISHES TO SPEAK WITH ONE FROM BEYOND!
APPEAR TO US, SPIRIT OF THE OTHER WORLD! APPEAR TO US BUT LET YOUR FORM BE SEEN ONLY BY THE ONE HERE WHO SEEKS YOU! APPEAR!

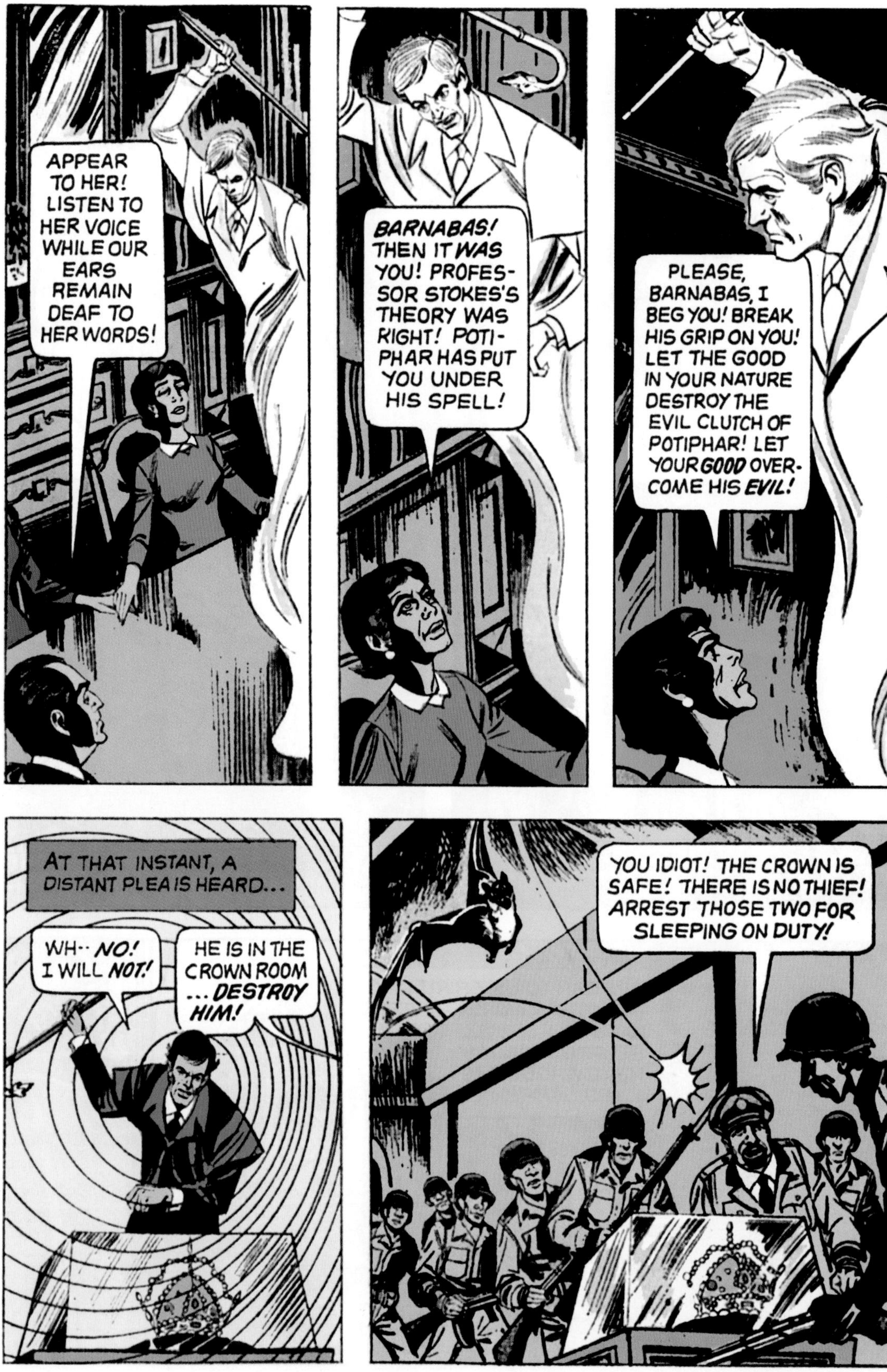
APPEAR TO HER! LISTEN TO HER VOICE WHILE OUR EARS REMAIN DEAF TO HER WORDS!
BARNABAS! THEN IT WAS YOU! PROFESSOR STOKES'S THEORY WAS RIGHT! POTIPHAR HAS PUT YOU UNDER HIS SPELL!
PLEASE, BARNABAS, I BEG YOU! BREAK HIS GRIP ON YOU! LET THE GOOD IN YOUR NATURE DESTROY THE EVIL CLUTCH OF POTIPHAR! LET YOUR GOOD OVERCOME HIS EVIL!
AT THAT INSTANT, A DISTANT PLEA IS HEARD...
WH-- NO! I WILL NOT!
HE IS IN THE CROWN ROOM ... DESTROY HIM!
YOU IDIOT! THE CROWN IS SAFE! THERE IS NO THIEF! ARREST THOSE TWO FOR SLEEPING ON DUTY!

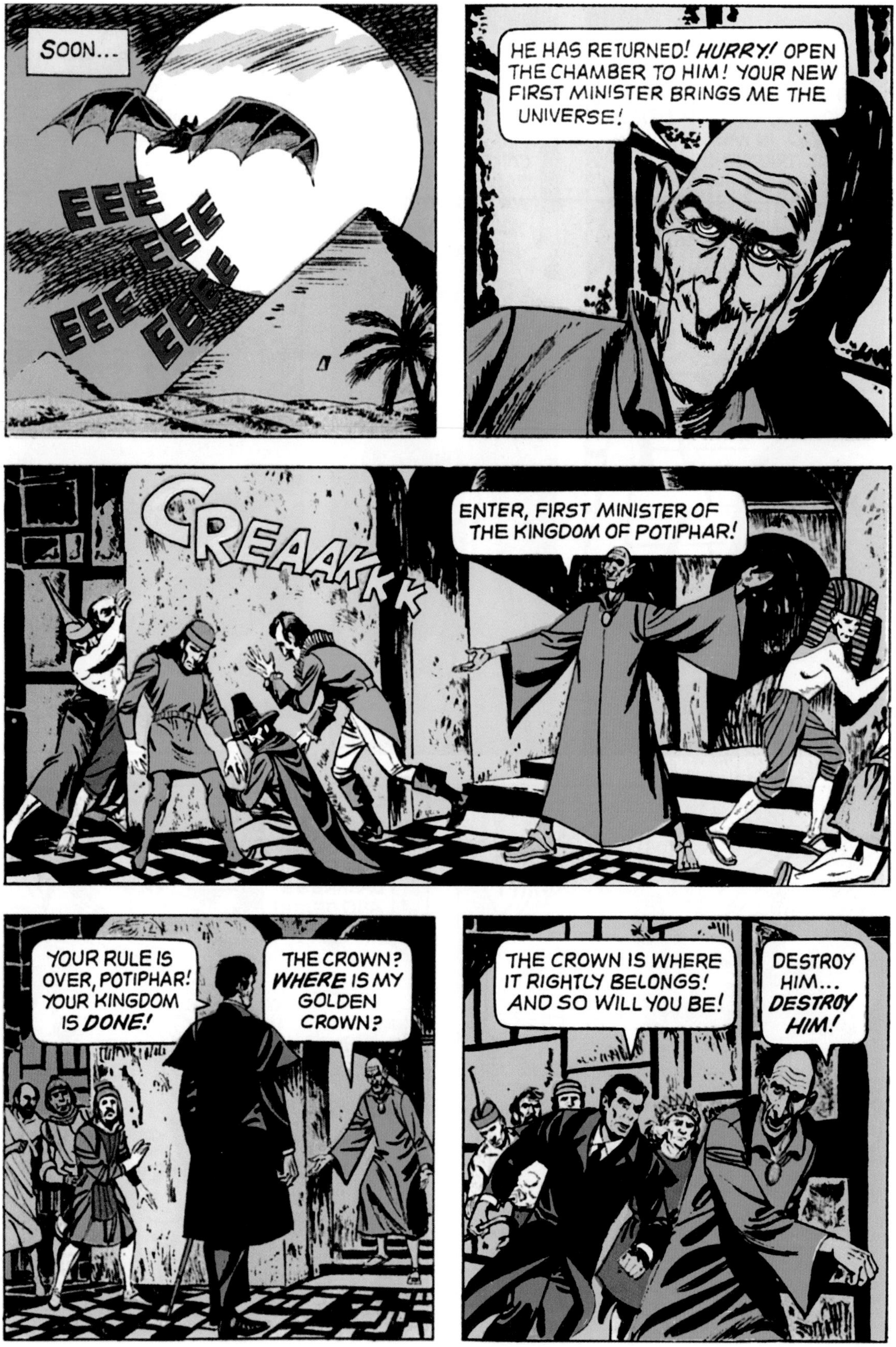
SOON...
EEE EEE EEE EEE
HE HAS RETURNED! HURRY! OPEN THE CHAMBER TO HIM! YOUR NEW FIRST MINISTER BRINGS ME THE UNIVERSE!
CREAAKKK
ENTER, FIRST MINISTER OF THE KINGDOM OF POTIPHAR!
YOUR RULE IS OVER, POTIPHAR! YOUR KINGDOM IS DONE!
THE CROWN? WHERE IS MY GOLDEN CROWN?
THE CROWN IS WHERE IT RIGHTLY BELONGS! AND SO WILL YOU BE!
DESTROY HIM... DESTROY HIM!

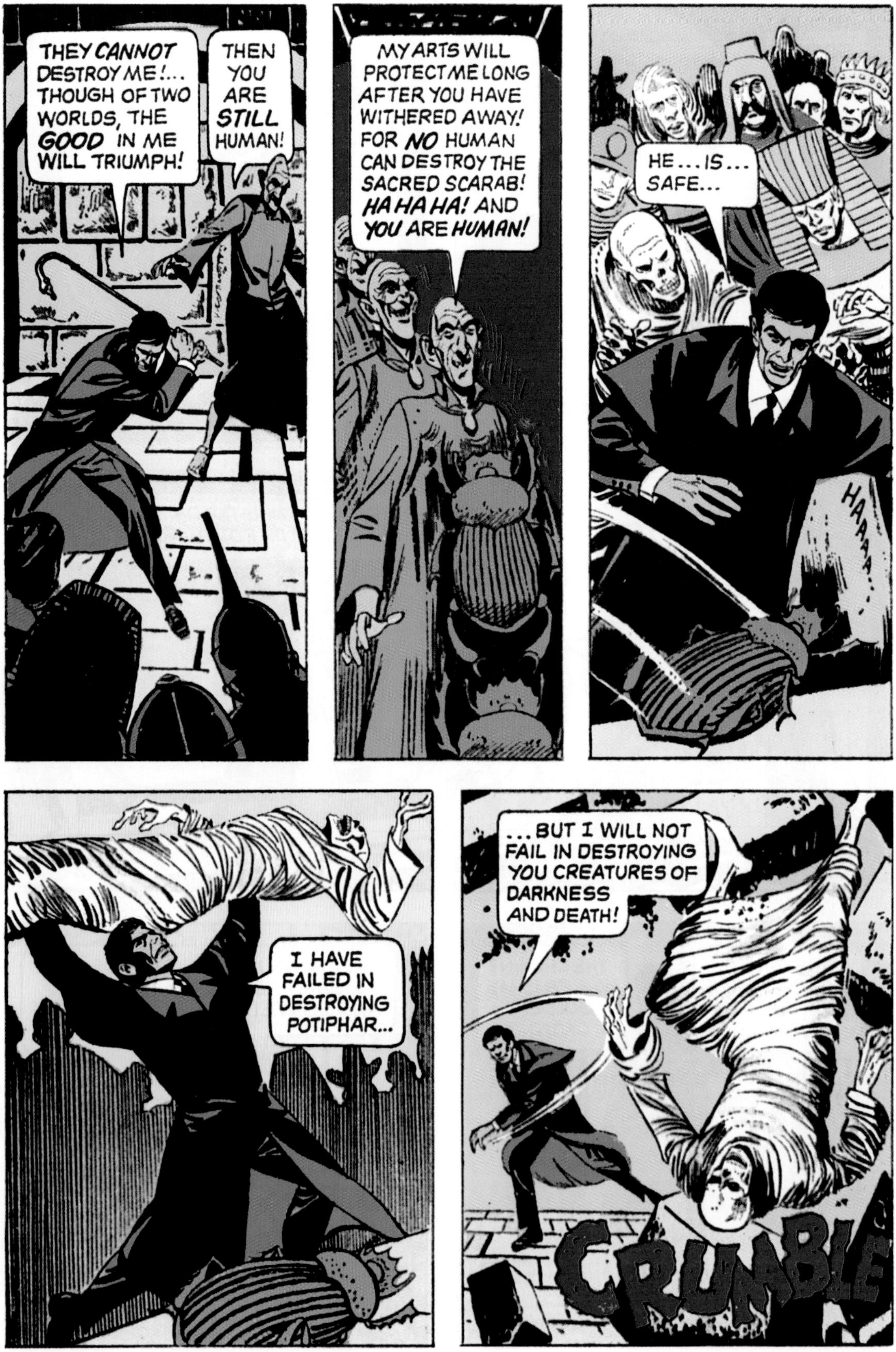
THEY CANNOT DESTROY ME!... THOUGH OF TWO WORLDS, THE GOOD IN ME WILL TRIUMPH!
THEN YOU ARE STILL HUMAN!
MY ARTS WILL PROTECT ME LONG AFTER YOU HAVE WITHERED AWAY! FOR NO HUMAN CAN DESTROY THE SACRED SCARAB! HA HA HA! AND YOU ARE HUMAN!
HE... IS... SAFE...
HAAAA...
I HAVE FAILED IN DESTROYING POTIPHAR...
...BUT I WILL NOT FAIL IN DESTROYING YOU CREATURES OF DARKNESS AND DEATH!
CRUMBLE

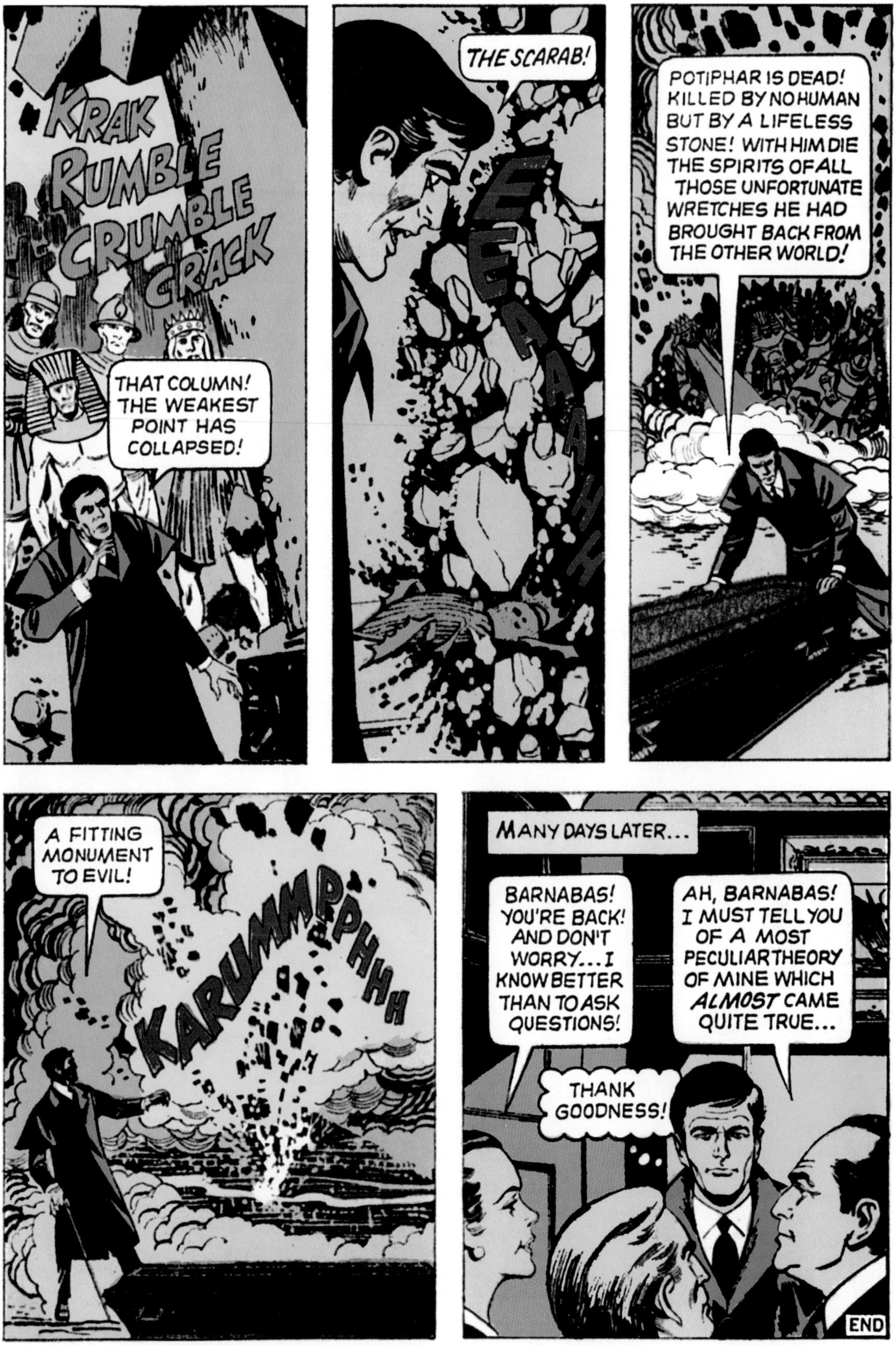
KRAK
RUMBLE
CRUMBLE
CRACK
THAT COLUMN! THE WEAKEST POINT HAS COLLAPSED!
THE SCARAB!
EEEAAAAHHH
POTIPHAR IS DEAD! KILLED BY NO HUMAN BUT BY A LIFELESS STONE! WITH HIM DIE THE SPIRITS OF ALL THOSE UNFORTUNATE WRETCHES HE HAD BROUGHT BACK FROM THE OTHER WORLD!
A FITTING MONUMENT TO EVIL!
KARUMMPPHHH
MANY DAYS LATER...
BARNABAS! YOU'RE BACK! AND DON'T WORRY...I KNOW BETTER THAN TO ASK QUESTIONS!
AH, BARNABAS! I MUST TELL YOU OF A MOST PECULIAR THEORY OF MINE WHICH ALMOST CAME QUITE TRUE...
THANK GOODNESS!
END

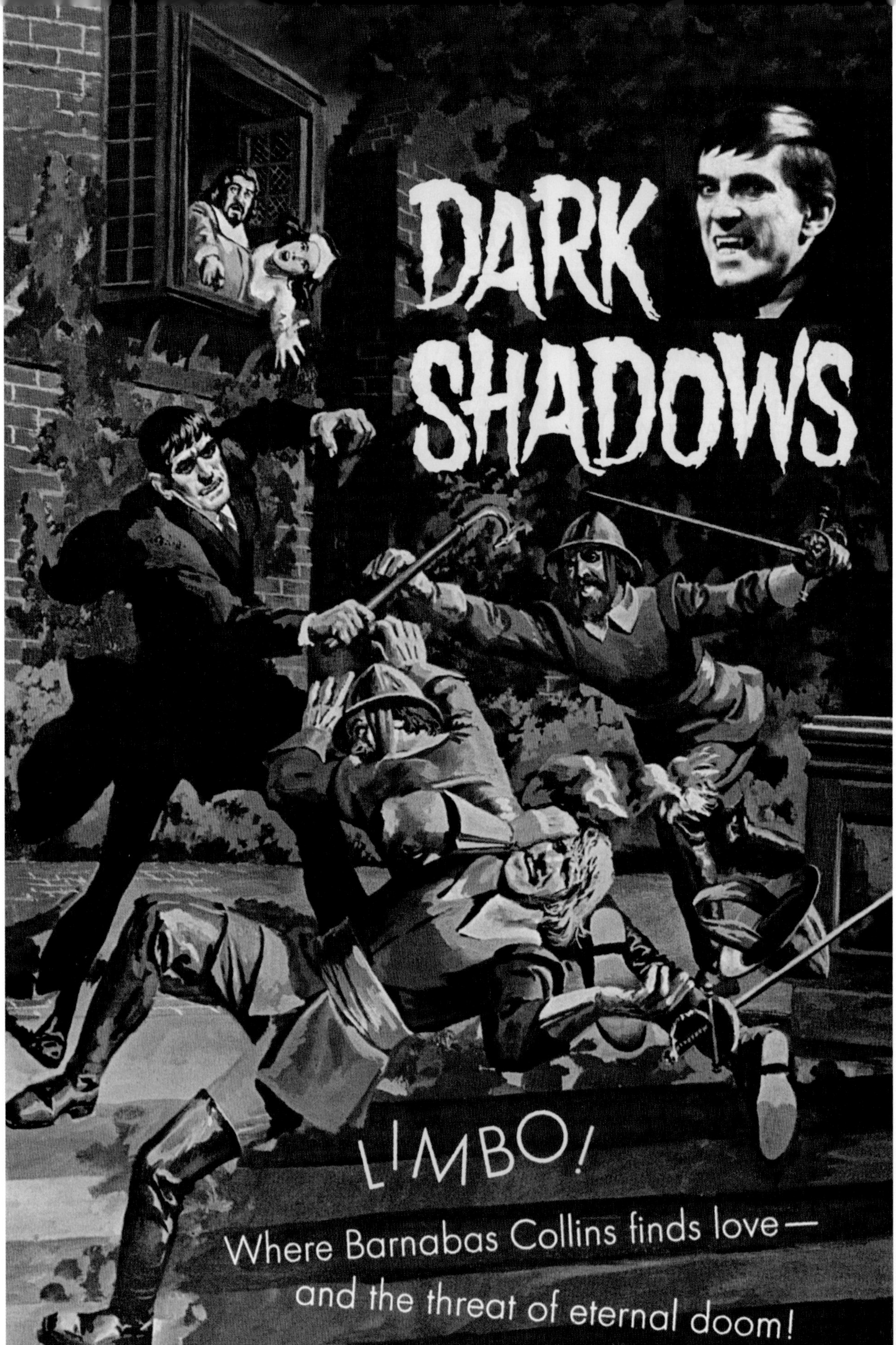
DARK SHADOWS
LIMBO!
Where Barnabas Collins finds love—
and the threat of eternal doom!

DARK SHADOWS

The Bride of Barnabas Collins

PART 1: MISTS OF TIME

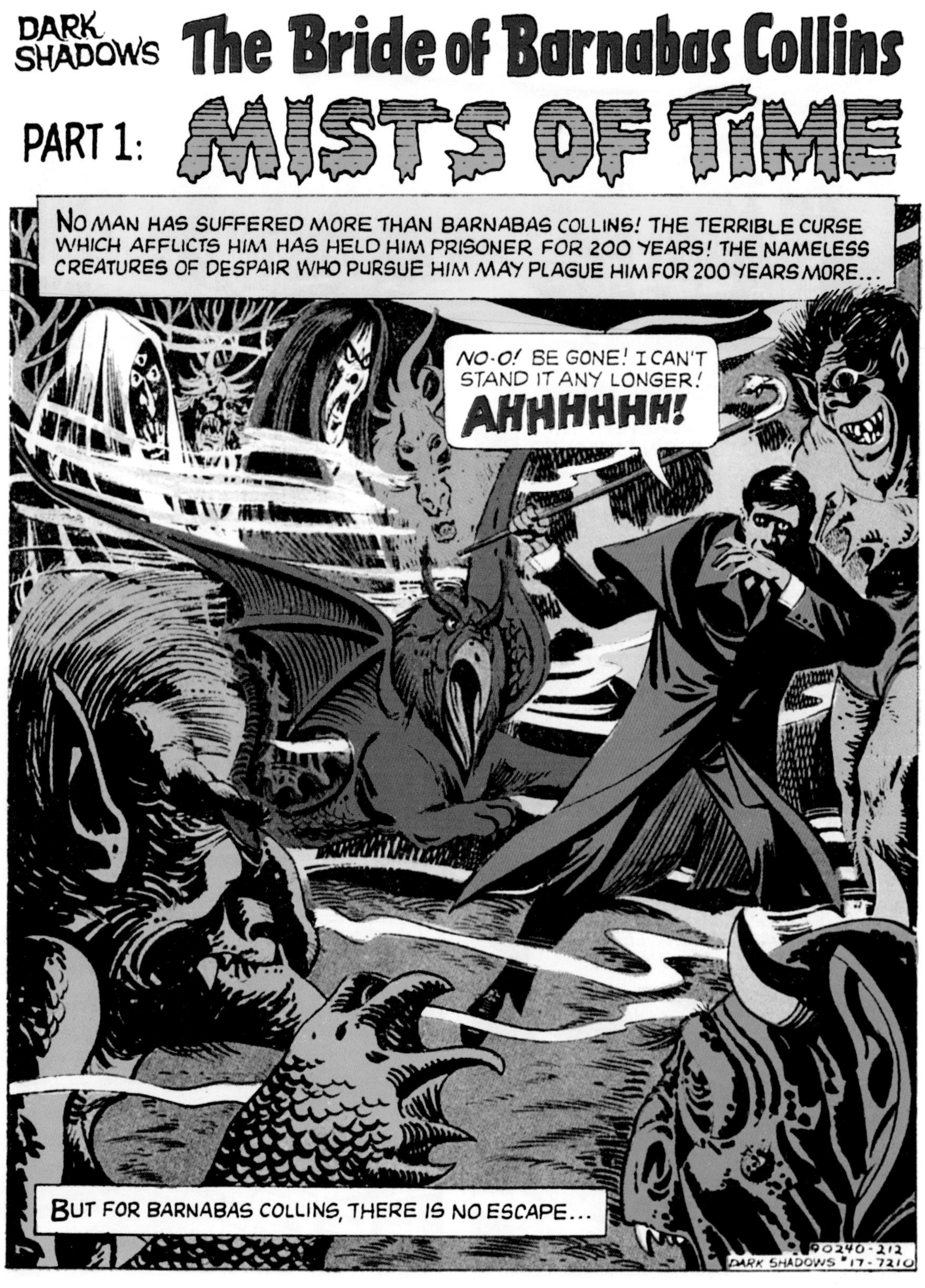
NO MAN HAS SUFFERED MORE THAN BARNABAS COLLINS! THE TERRIBLE CURSE WHICH AFFLICTS HIM HAS HELD HIM PRISONER FOR 200 YEARS! THE NAMELESS CREATURES OF DESPAIR WHO PURSUE HIM MAY PLAGUE HIM FOR 200 YEARS MORE...
NO-O! BE GONE! I CAN'T STAND IT ANY LONGER! AHHHHHH!
BUT FOR BARNABAS COLLINS, THERE IS NO ESCAPE...
90240-212
DARK SHADOWS #17-7210

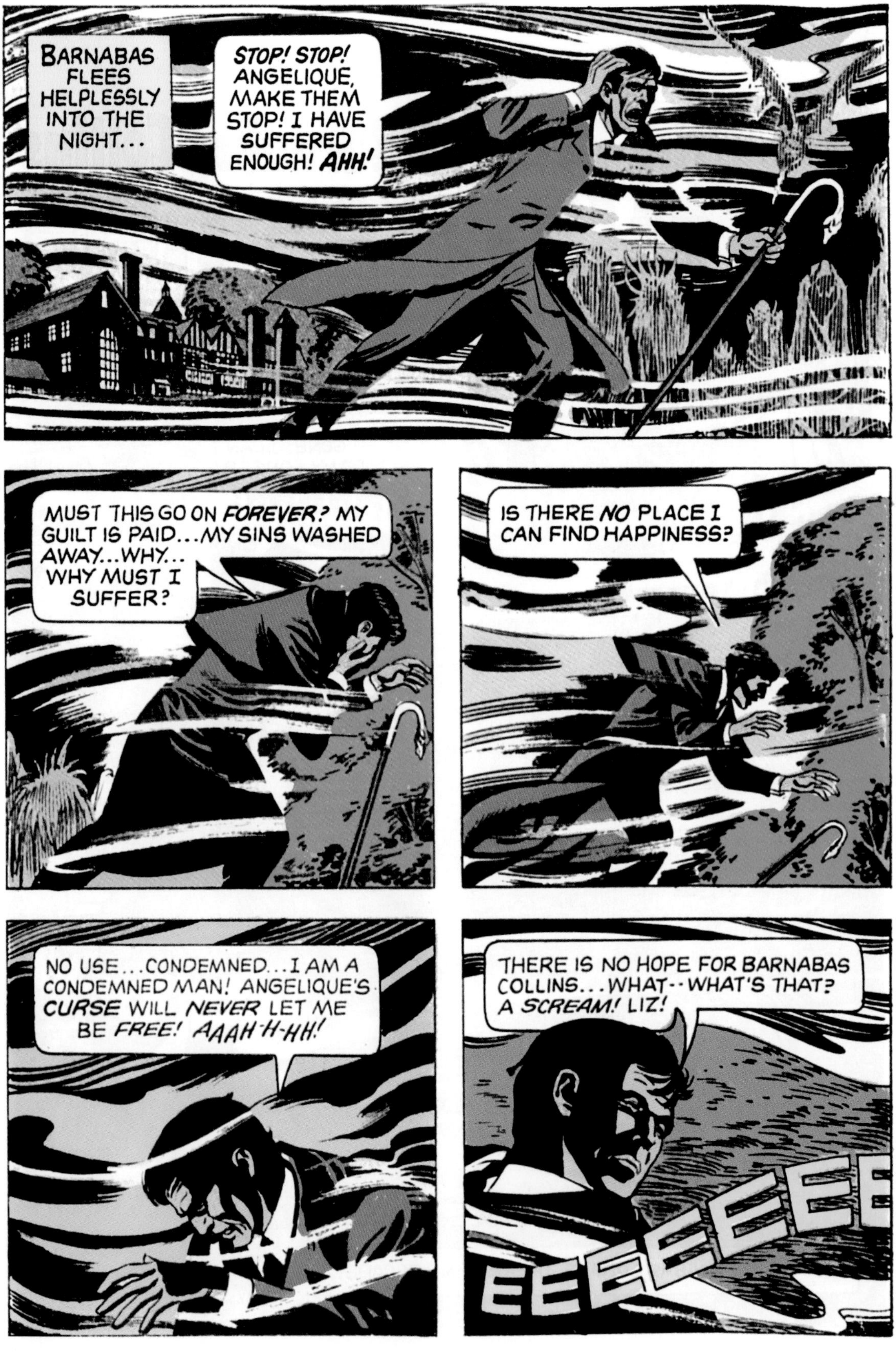
BARNABAS FLEES HELPLESSLY INTO THE NIGHT...
STOP! STOP! ANGELIQUE, MAKE THEM STOP! I HAVE SUFFERED ENOUGH! AHH!
MUST THIS GO ON FOREVER? MY GUILT IS PAID...MY SINS WASHED AWAY...WHY... WHY MUST I SUFFER?
IS THERE NO PLACE I CAN FIND HAPPINESS?
NO USE...CONDEMNED...I AM A CONDEMNED MAN! ANGELIQUE'S CURSE WILL NEVER LET ME BE FREE! AAAH-H-HH!
THERE IS NO HOPE FOR BARNABAS COLLINS...WHAT--WHAT'S THAT? A SCREAM! LIZ!
EEEEEEEE

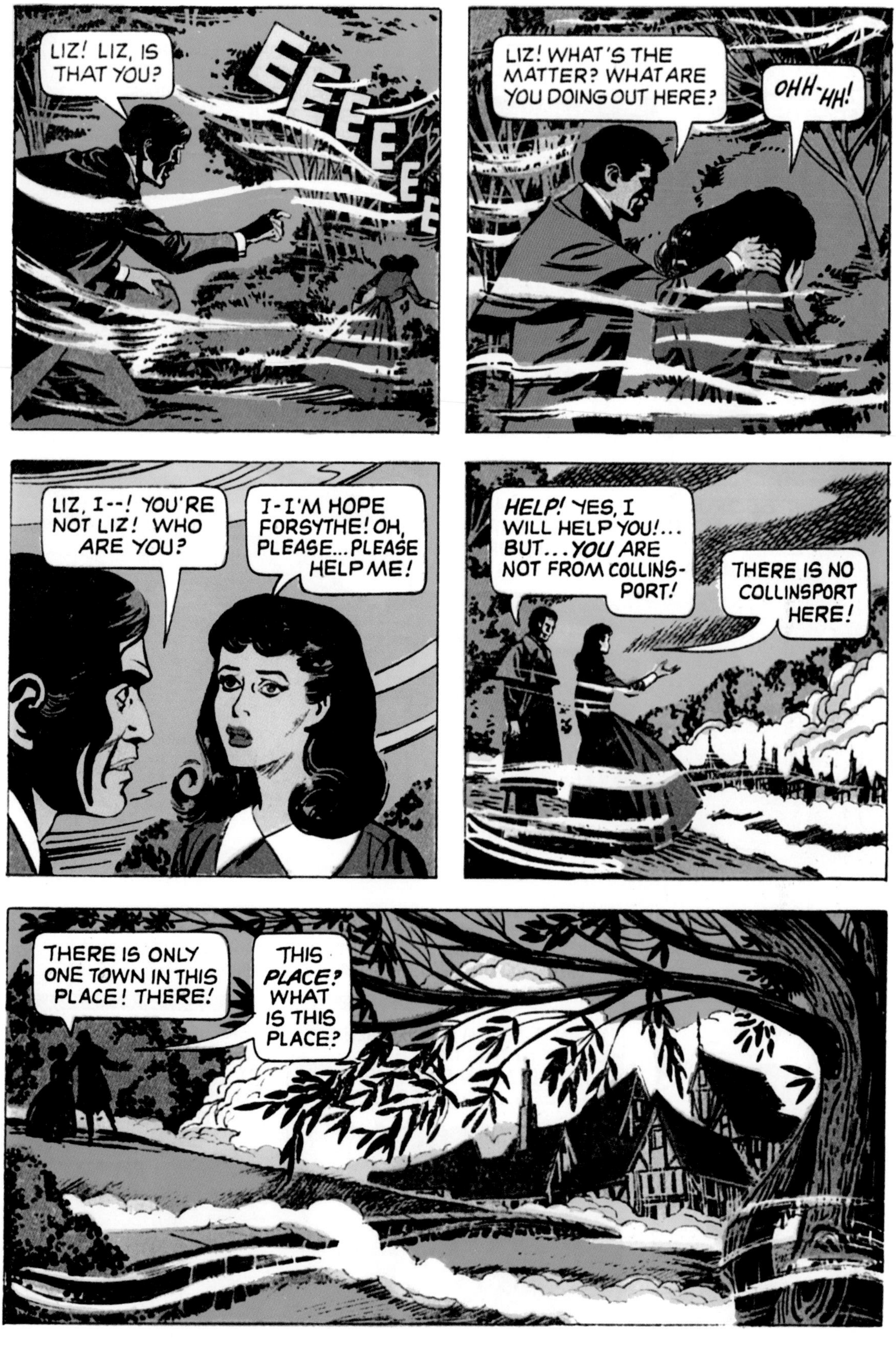

LIZ! LIZ, IS THAT YOU?
EEEEEEE
LIZ! WHAT'S THE MATTER? WHAT ARE YOU DOING OUT HERE?
OHH-HH!
LIZ, I--! YOU'RE NOT LIZ! WHO ARE YOU?
I-I'M HOPE FORSYTHE! OH, PLEASE...PLEASE HELP ME!
HELP! YES, I WILL HELP YOU!... BUT...YOU ARE NOT FROM COLLINS-PORT!
THERE IS NO COLLINSPORT HERE!
THERE IS ONLY ONE TOWN IN THIS PLACE! THERE!
THIS PLACE? WHAT IS THIS PLACE?

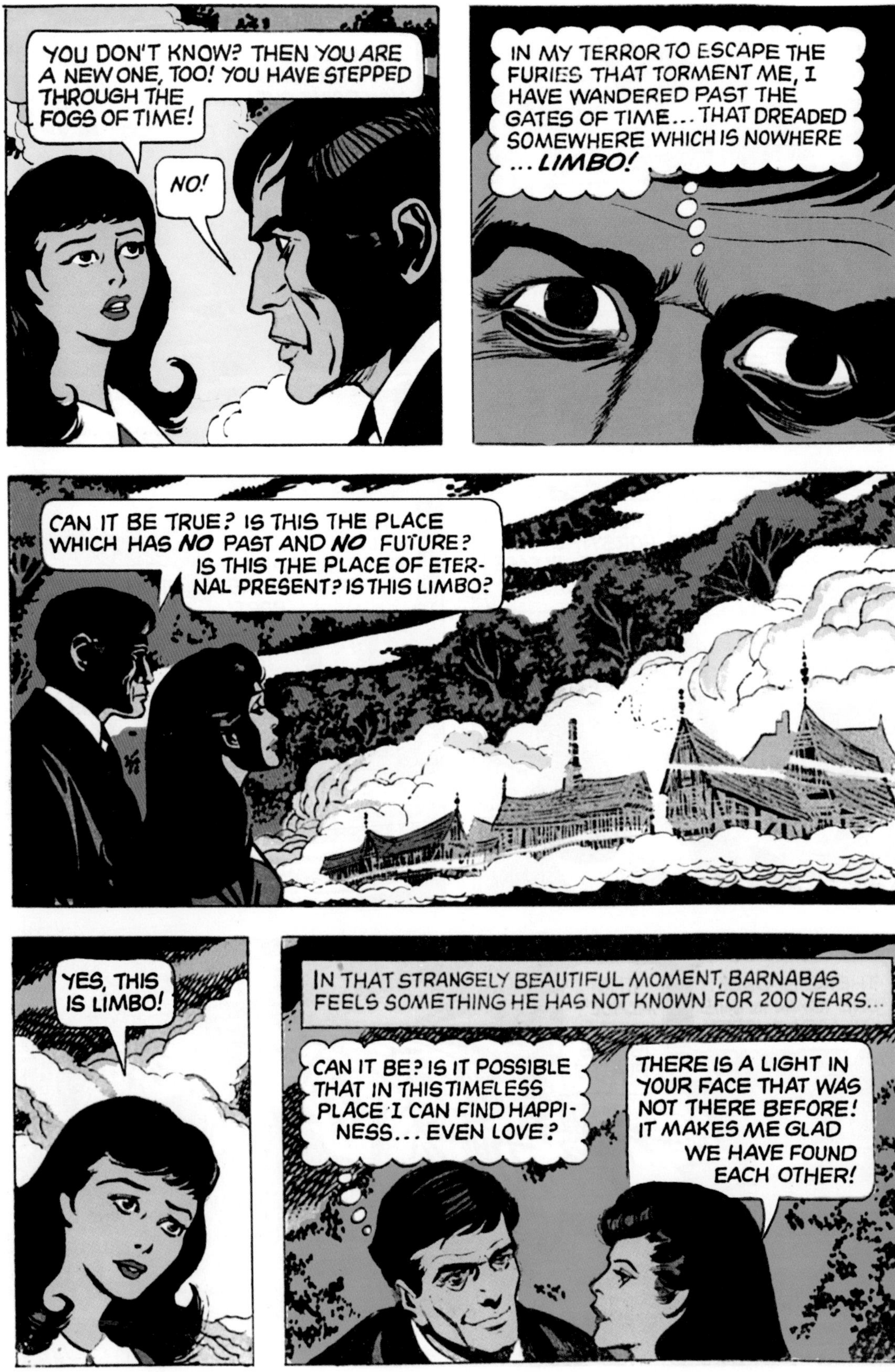

YOU DON'T KNOW? THEN YOU ARE A NEW ONE, TOO! YOU HAVE STEPPED THROUGH THE FOGS OF TIME!
NO!
IN MY TERROR TO ESCAPE THE FURIES THAT TORMENT ME, I HAVE WANDERED PAST THE GATES OF TIME... THAT DREADED SOMEWHERE WHICH IS NOWHERE ...LIMBO!
CAN IT BE TRUE? IS THIS THE PLACE WHICH HAS NO PAST AND NO FUTURE? IS THIS THE PLACE OF ETERNAL PRESENT? IS THIS LIMBO?
YES, THIS IS LIMBO!
IN THAT STRANGELY BEAUTIFUL MOMENT, BARNABAS FEELS SOMETHING HE HAS NOT KNOWN FOR 200 YEARS...
CAN IT BE? IS IT POSSIBLE THAT IN THIS TIMELESS PLACE I CAN FIND HAPPINESS... EVEN LOVE?
THERE IS A LIGHT IN YOUR FACE THAT WAS NOT THERE BEFORE! IT MAKES ME GLAD WE HAVE FOUND EACH OTHER!

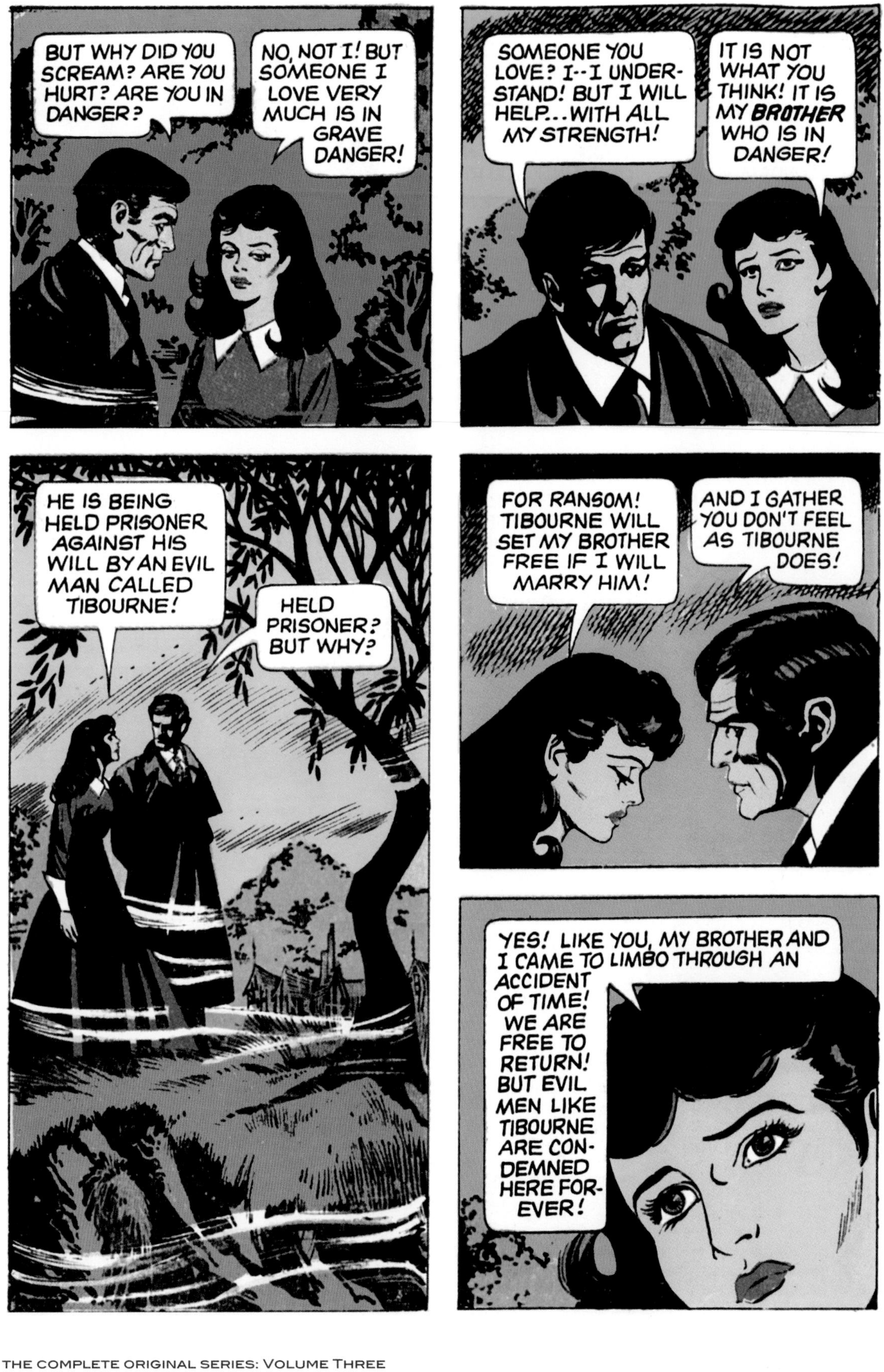
BUT WHY DID YOU SCREAM? ARE YOU HURT? ARE YOU IN DANGER?
NO, NOT I! BUT SOMEONE I LOVE VERY MUCH IS IN GRAVE DANGER!
SOMEONE YOU LOVE? I--I UNDERSTAND! BUT I WILL HELP...WITH ALL MY STRENGTH!
IT IS NOT WHAT YOU THINK! IT IS MY BROTHER WHO IS IN DANGER!
HE IS BEING HELD PRISONER AGAINST HIS WILL BY AN EVIL MAN CALLED TIBOURNE!
HELD PRISONER? BUT WHY?
FOR RANSOM! TIBOURNE WILL SET MY BROTHER FREE IF I WILL MARRY HIM!
AND I GATHER YOU DON'T FEEL AS TIBOURNE DOES!
YES! LIKE YOU, MY BROTHER AND I CAME TO LIMBO THROUGH AN ACCIDENT OF TIME! WE ARE FREE TO RETURN! BUT EVIL MEN LIKE TIBOURNE ARE CONDEMNED HERE FOREVER!

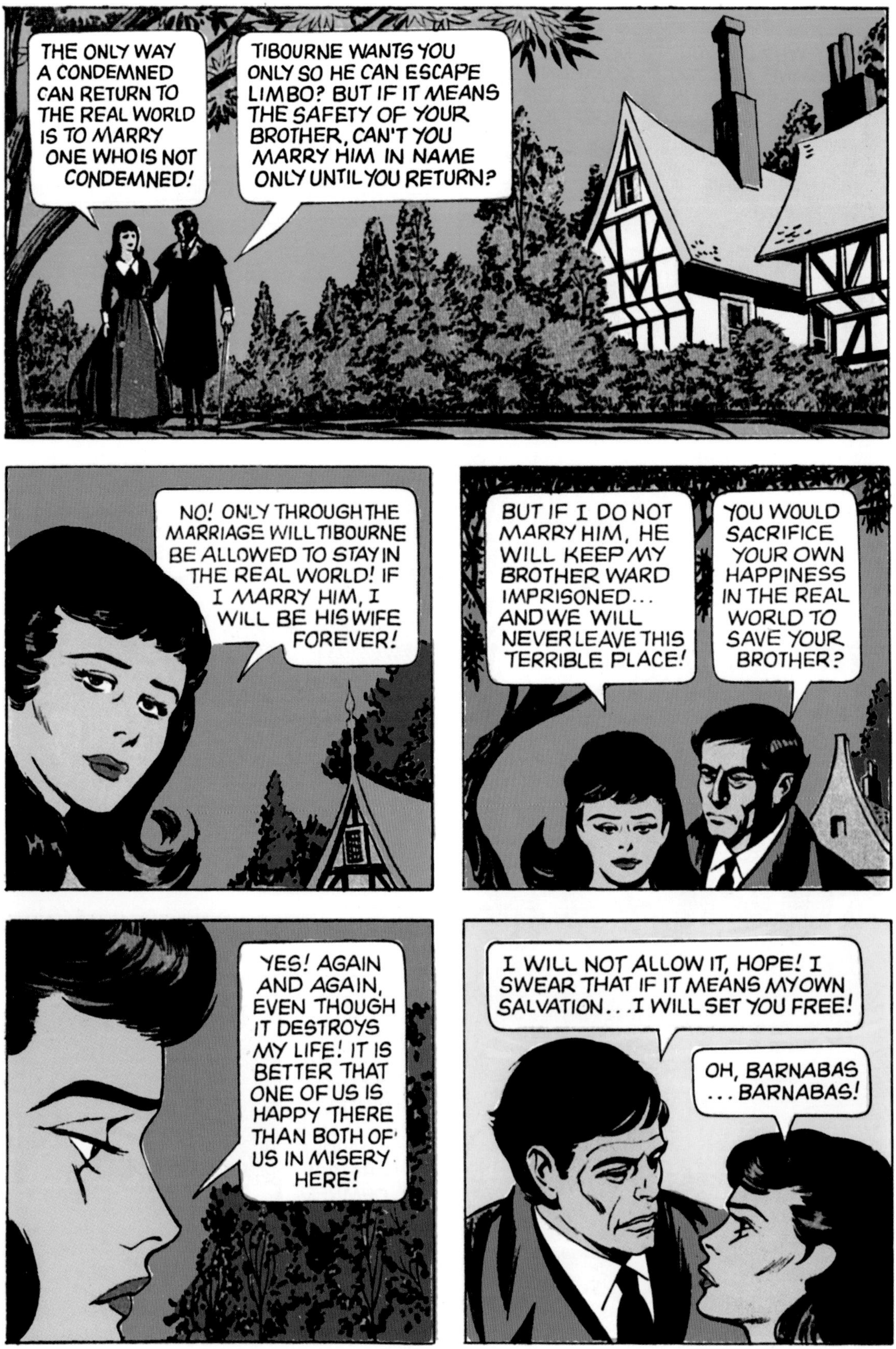
THE ONLY WAY A CONDEMNED CAN RETURN TO THE REAL WORLD IS TO MARRY ONE WHO IS NOT CONDEMNED!
TIBOURNE WANTS YOU ONLY SO HE CAN ESCAPE LIMBO? BUT IF IT MEANS THE SAFETY OF YOUR BROTHER, CAN'T YOU MARRY HIM IN NAME ONLY UNTIL YOU RETURN?
NO! ONLY THROUGH THE MARRIAGE WILL TIBOURNE BE ALLOWED TO STAY IN THE REAL WORLD! IF I MARRY HIM, I WILL BE HIS WIFE FOREVER!
BUT IF I DO NOT MARRY HIM, HE WILL KEEP MY BROTHER WARD IMPRISONED... AND WE WILL NEVER LEAVE THIS TERRIBLE PLACE!
YOU WOULD SACRIFICE YOUR OWN HAPPINESS IN THE REAL WORLD TO SAVE YOUR BROTHER?
YES! AGAIN AND AGAIN, EVEN THOUGH IT DESTROYS MY LIFE! IT IS BETTER THAT ONE OF US IS HAPPY THERE THAN BOTH OF US IN MISERY HERE!
I WILL NOT ALLOW IT, HOPE! I SWEAR THAT IF IT MEANS MY OWN SALVATION...I WILL SET YOU FREE!
OH, BARNABAS ...BARNABAS!

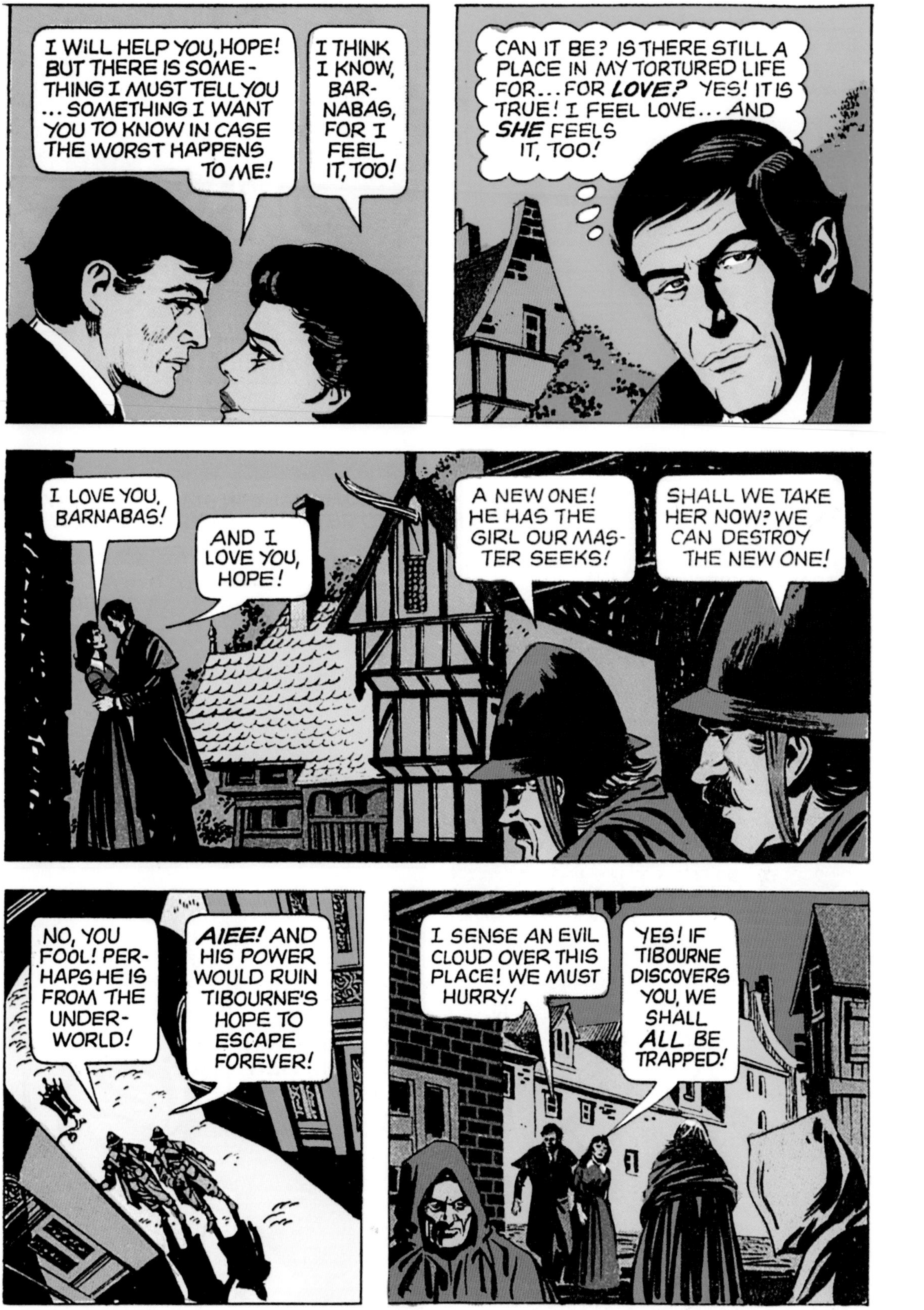
I WILL HELP YOU, HOPE! BUT THERE IS SOME-THING I MUST TELL YOU ... SOMETHING I WANT YOU TO KNOW IN CASE THE WORST HAPPENS TO ME!
I THINK I KNOW, BAR-NABAS, FOR I FEEL IT, TOO!
CAN IT BE? IS THERE STILL A PLACE IN MY TORTURED LIFE FOR... FOR LOVE? YES! IT IS TRUE! I FEEL LOVE... AND SHE FEELS IT, TOO!
I LOVE YOU, BARNABAS!
AND I LOVE YOU, HOPE!
A NEW ONE! HE HAS THE GIRL OUR MAS-TER SEEKS!
SHALL WE TAKE HER NOW? WE CAN DESTROY THE NEW ONE!
NO, YOU FOOL! PER-HAPS HE IS FROM THE UNDER-WORLD!
AIEE! AND HIS POWER WOULD RUIN TIBOURNE'S HOPE TO ESCAPE FOREVER!
I SENSE AN EVIL CLOUD OVER THIS PLACE! WE MUST HURRY!
YES! IF TIBOURNE DISCOVERS YOU, WE SHALL ALL BE TRAPPED!

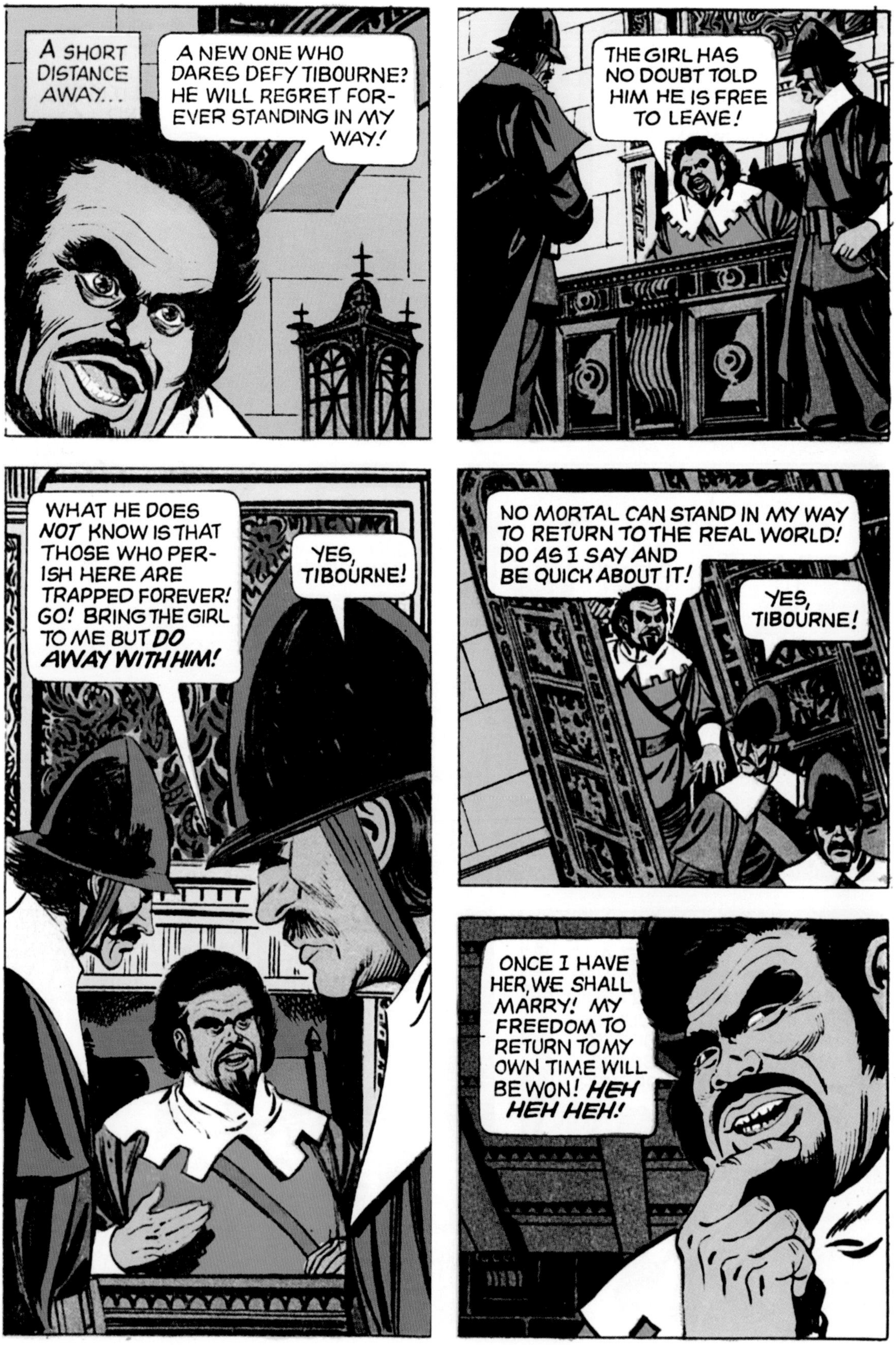
A SHORT DISTANCE AWAY...
A NEW ONE WHO DARES DEFY TIBOURNE? HE WILL REGRET FOR-EVER STANDING IN MY WAY!
THE GIRL HAS NO DOUBT TOLD HIM HE IS FREE TO LEAVE!
WHAT HE DOES *NOT* KNOW IS THAT THOSE WHO PER-ISH HERE ARE TRAPPED FOREVER! GO! BRING THE GIRL TO ME BUT ***DO AWAY WITH HIM!***
YES, TIBOURNE!
NO MORTAL CAN STAND IN MY WAY TO RETURN TO THE REAL WORLD! DO AS I SAY AND BE QUICK ABOUT IT!
YES, TIBOURNE!
ONCE I HAVE HER, WE SHALL MARRY! MY FREEDOM TO RETURN TO MY OWN TIME WILL BE WON! ***HEH HEH HEH!***

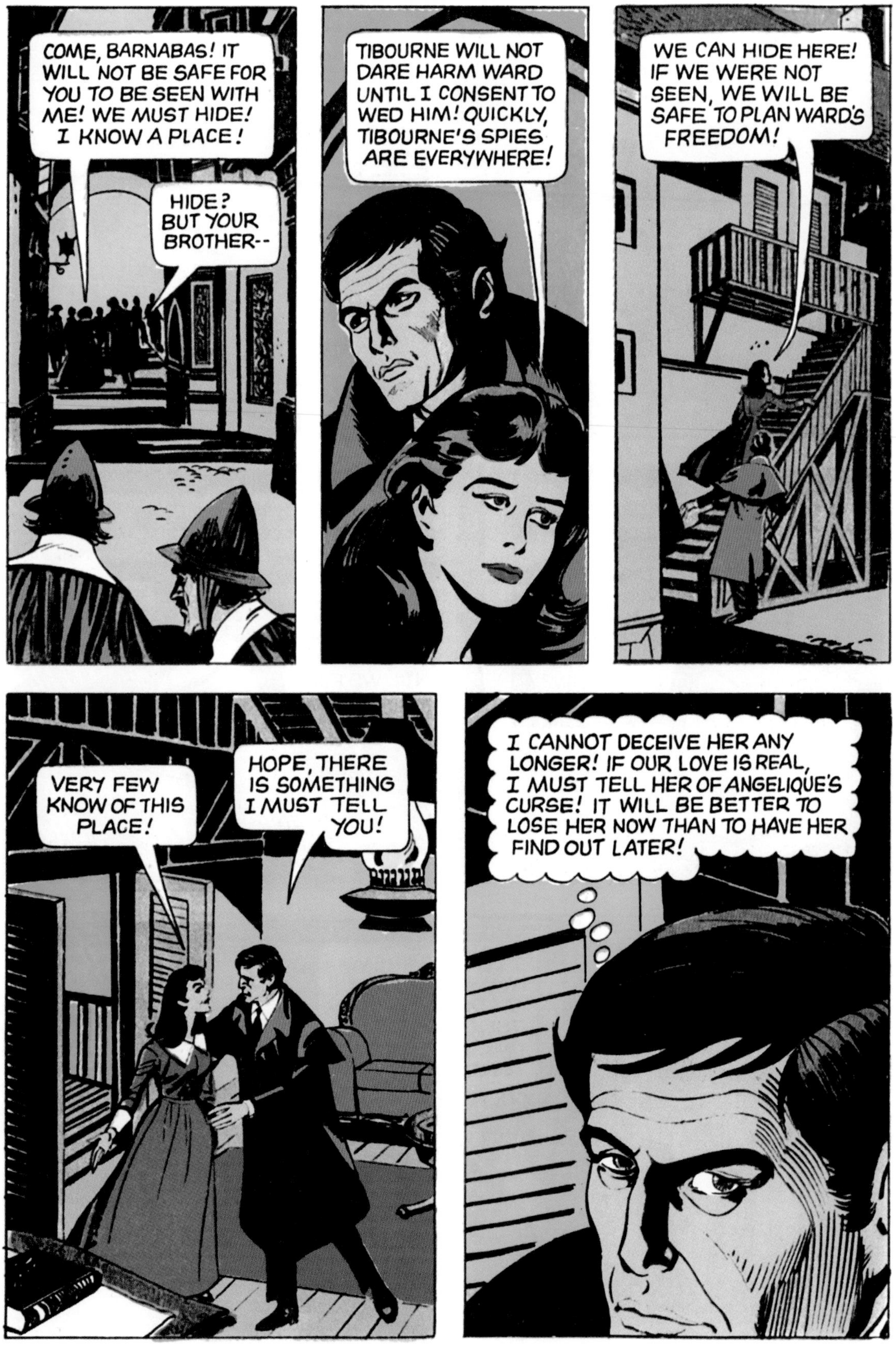
COME, BARNABAS! IT WILL NOT BE SAFE FOR YOU TO BE SEEN WITH ME! WE MUST HIDE! I KNOW A PLACE!
HIDE? BUT YOUR BROTHER--
TIBOURNE WILL NOT DARE HARM WARD UNTIL I CONSENT TO WED HIM! QUICKLY, TIBOURNE'S SPIES ARE EVERYWHERE!
WE CAN HIDE HERE! IF WE WERE NOT SEEN, WE WILL BE SAFE TO PLAN WARD'S FREEDOM!
VERY FEW KNOW OF THIS PLACE!
HOPE, THERE IS SOMETHING I MUST TELL YOU!
I CANNOT DECEIVE HER ANY LONGER! IF OUR LOVE IS REAL, I MUST TELL HER OF ANGELIQUE'S CURSE! IT WILL BE BETTER TO LOSE HER NOW THAN TO HAVE HER FIND OUT LATER!

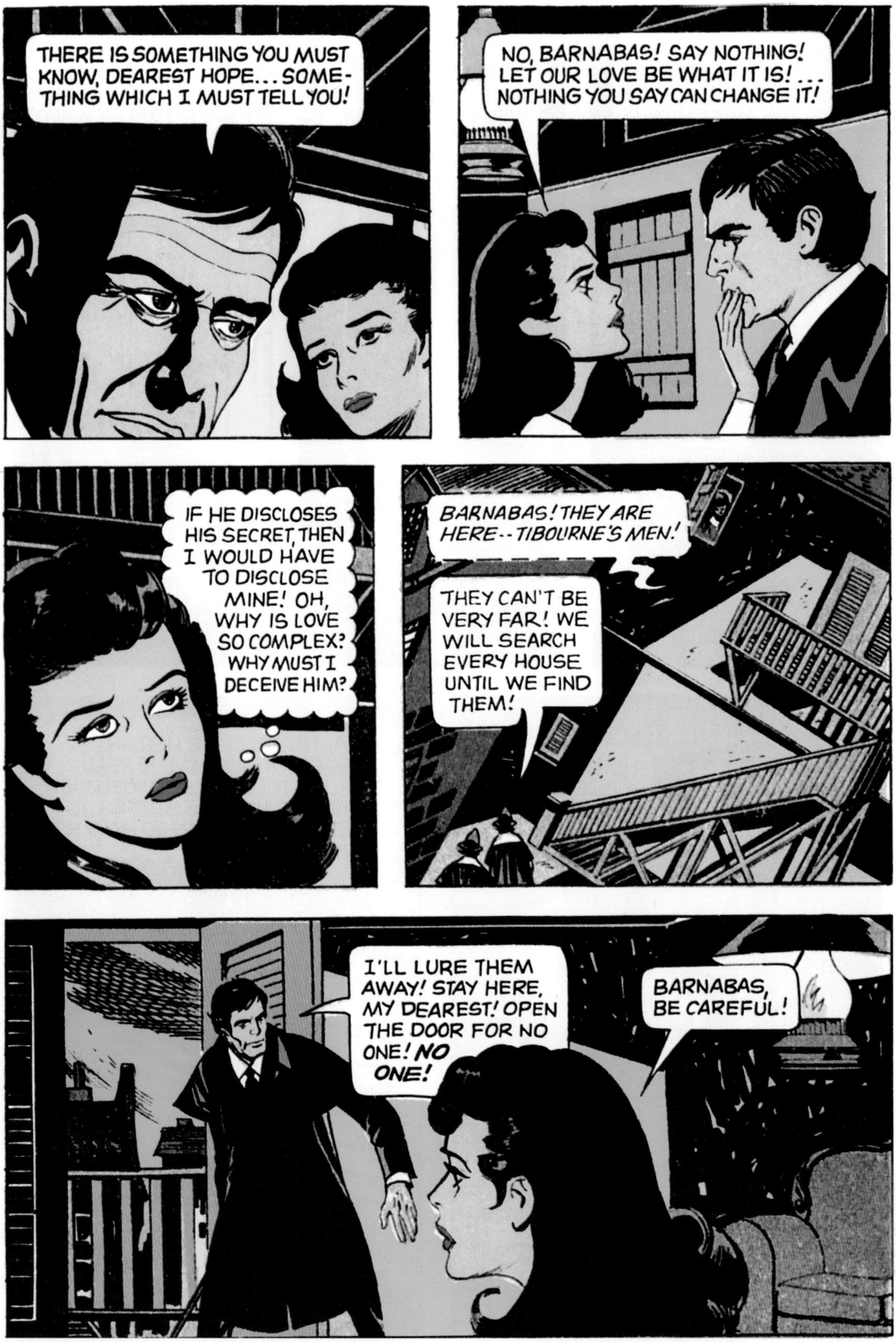
THERE IS SOMETHING YOU MUST KNOW, DEAREST HOPE... SOMETHING WHICH I MUST TELL YOU!
NO, BARNABAS! SAY NOTHING! LET OUR LOVE BE WHAT IT IS!... NOTHING YOU SAY CAN CHANGE IT!
IF HE DISCLOSES HIS SECRET, THEN I WOULD HAVE TO DISCLOSE MINE! OH, WHY IS LOVE SO COMPLEX? WHY MUST I DECEIVE HIM?
BARNABAS! THEY ARE HERE--TIBOURNE'S MEN!
THEY CAN'T BE VERY FAR! WE WILL SEARCH EVERY HOUSE UNTIL WE FIND THEM!
I'LL LURE THEM AWAY! STAY HERE, MY DEAREST! OPEN THE DOOR FOR NO ONE! NO ONE!
BARNABAS, BE CAREFUL!

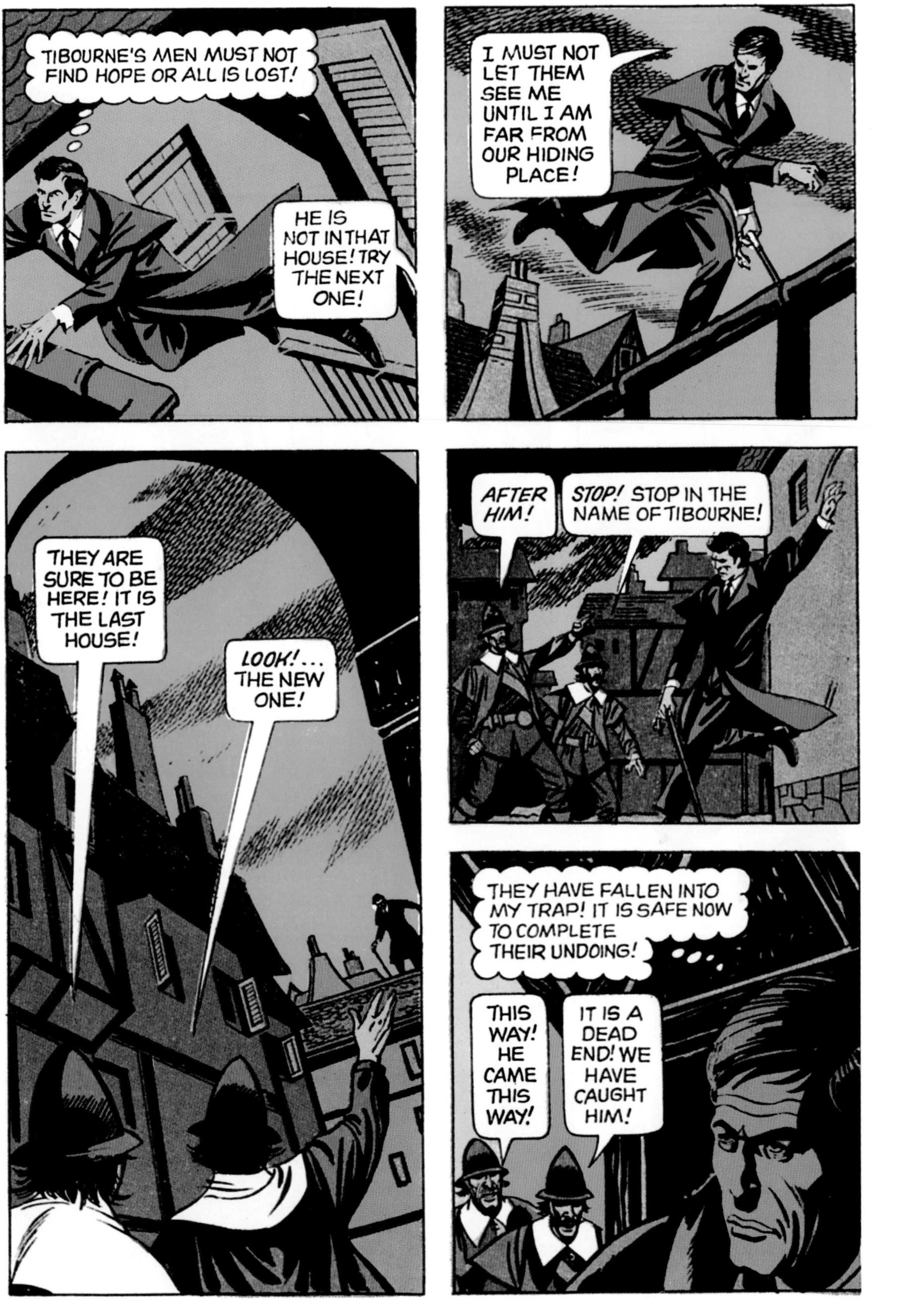
TIBOURNE'S MEN MUST NOT FIND HOPE OR ALL IS LOST!
HE IS NOT IN THAT HOUSE! TRY THE NEXT ONE!
I MUST NOT LET THEM SEE ME UNTIL I AM FAR FROM OUR HIDING PLACE!
THEY ARE SURE TO BE HERE! IT IS THE LAST HOUSE!
LOOK!... THE NEW ONE!
AFTER HIM!
STOP! STOP IN THE NAME OF TIBOURNE!
THEY HAVE FALLEN INTO MY TRAP! IT IS SAFE NOW TO COMPLETE THEIR UNDOING!
THIS WAY! HE CAME THIS WAY!
IT IS A DEAD END! WE HAVE CAUGHT HIM!

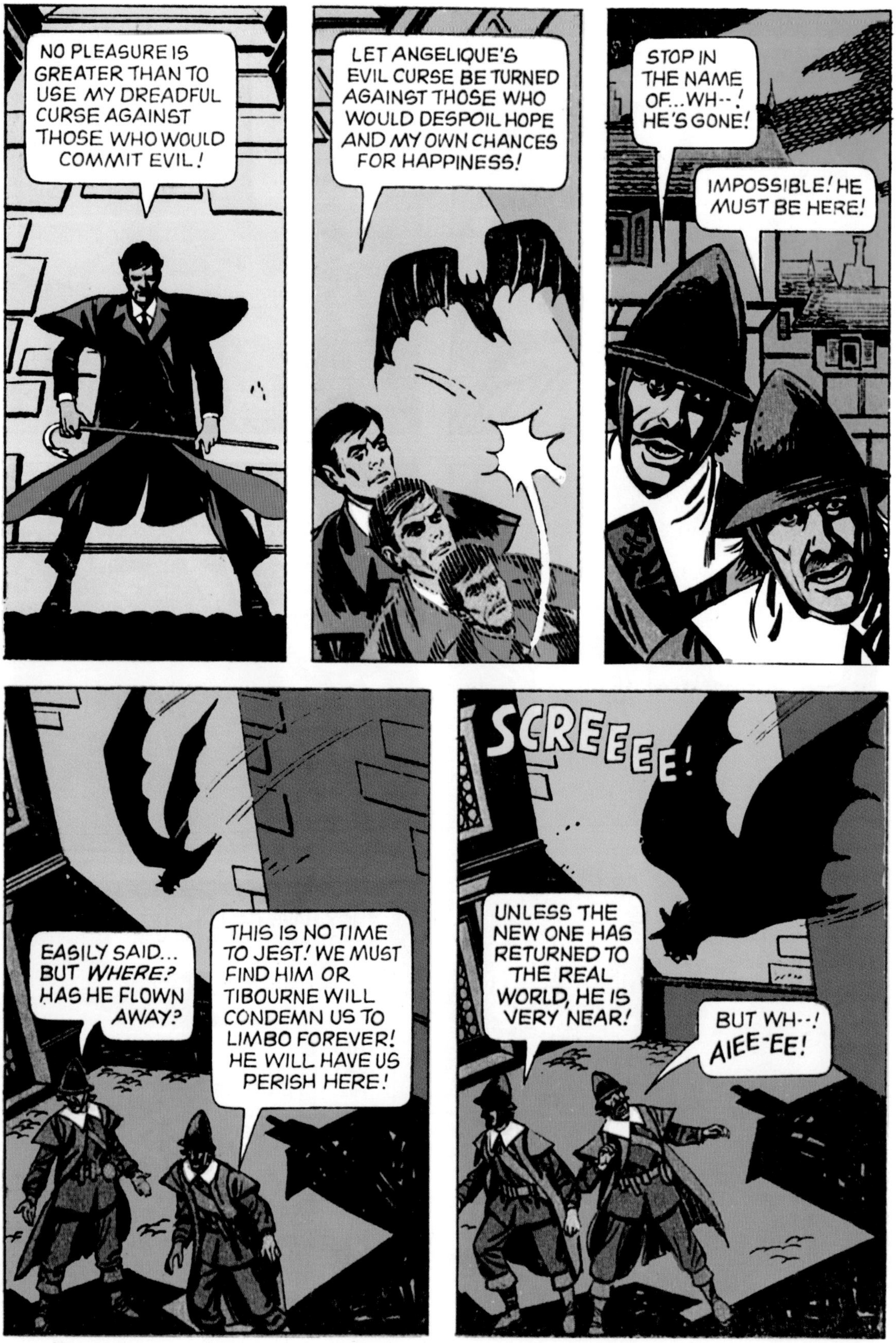
NO PLEASURE IS GREATER THAN TO USE MY DREADFUL CURSE AGAINST THOSE WHO WOULD COMMIT EVIL!
LET ANGELIQUE'S EVIL CURSE BE TURNED AGAINST THOSE WHO WOULD DESPOIL HOPE AND MY OWN CHANCES FOR HAPPINESS!
STOP IN THE NAME OF...WH--! HE'S GONE!
IMPOSSIBLE! HE MUST BE HERE!
EASILY SAID... BUT *WHERE?* HAS HE FLOWN AWAY?
THIS IS NO TIME TO JEST! WE MUST FIND HIM OR TIBOURNE WILL CONDEMN US TO LIMBO FOREVER! HE WILL HAVE US PERISH HERE!
SCREEEEE!
UNLESS THE NEW ONE HAS RETURNED TO THE REAL WORLD, HE IS VERY NEAR!
BUT WH--! AIEE-EE!

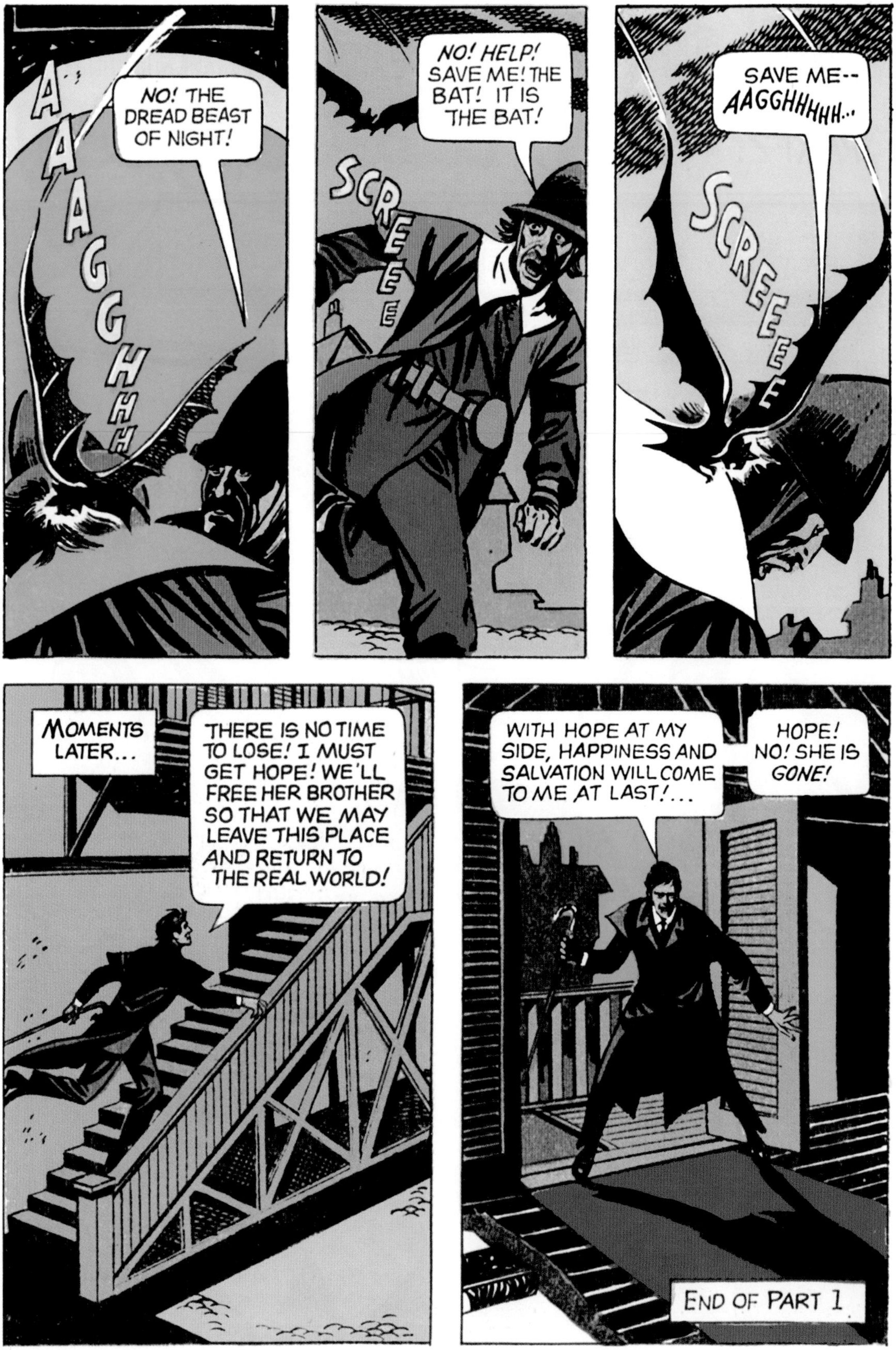

AAAAGGHHH
NO! THE DREAD BEAST OF NIGHT!
NO! HELP! SAVE ME! THE BAT! IT IS THE BAT!
SCREEEE
SAVE ME-- AAGGHHHHH...
SCREEEEE
MOMENTS LATER...
THERE IS NO TIME TO LOSE! I MUST GET HOPE! WE'LL FREE HER BROTHER SO THAT WE MAY LEAVE THIS PLACE AND RETURN TO THE REAL WORLD!
WITH HOPE AT MY SIDE, HAPPINESS AND SALVATION WILL COME TO ME AT LAST!...
HOPE! NO! SHE IS GONE!
END OF PART 1

DARK SHADOWS

The Bride of Barnabas Collins

PART 2: The Wedding Day

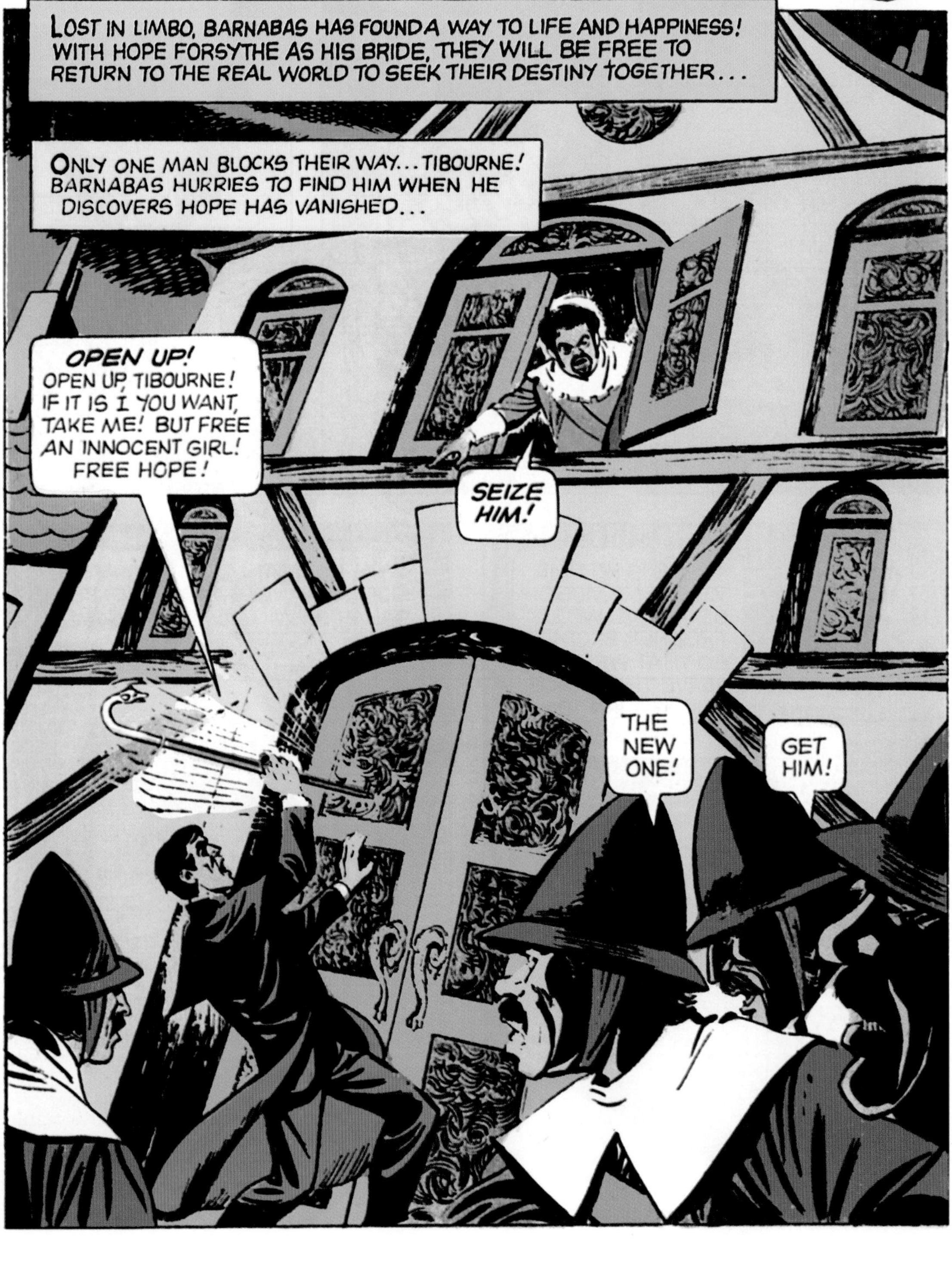
LOST IN LIMBO, BARNABAS HAS FOUND A WAY TO LIFE AND HAPPINESS! WITH HOPE FORSYTHE AS HIS BRIDE, THEY WILL BE FREE TO RETURN TO THE REAL WORLD TO SEEK THEIR DESTINY TOGETHER...
ONLY ONE MAN BLOCKS THEIR WAY... TIBOURNE! BARNABAS HURRIES TO FIND HIM WHEN HE DISCOVERS HOPE HAS VANISHED...
OPEN UP! OPEN UP, TIBOURNE! IF IT IS I YOU WANT, TAKE ME! BUT FREE AN INNOCENT GIRL! FREE HOPE!
SEIZE HIM!
THE NEW ONE!
GET HIM!

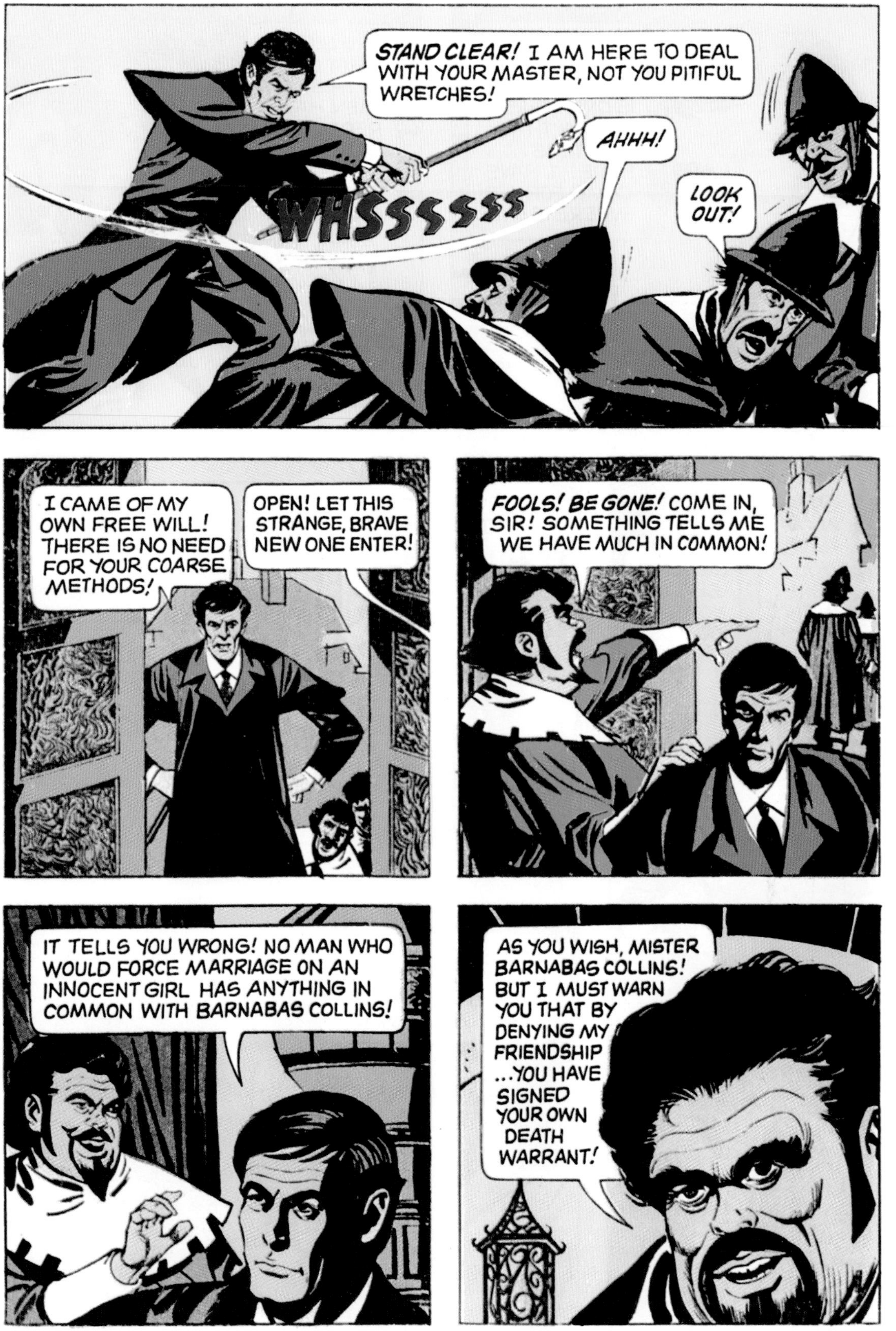
STAND CLEAR! I AM HERE TO DEAL WITH YOUR MASTER, NOT YOU PITIFUL WRETCHES!
AHHH!
LOOK OUT!
WHSSSSSS
I CAME OF MY OWN FREE WILL! THERE IS NO NEED FOR YOUR COARSE METHODS!
OPEN! LET THIS STRANGE, BRAVE NEW ONE ENTER!
FOOLS! BE GONE! COME IN, SIR! SOMETHING TELLS ME WE HAVE MUCH IN COMMON!
IT TELLS YOU WRONG! NO MAN WHO WOULD FORCE MARRIAGE ON AN INNOCENT GIRL HAS ANYTHING IN COMMON WITH BARNABAS COLLINS!
AS YOU WISH, MISTER BARNABAS COLLINS! BUT I MUST WARN YOU THAT BY DENYING MY FRIENDSHIP ...YOU HAVE SIGNED YOUR OWN DEATH WARRANT!

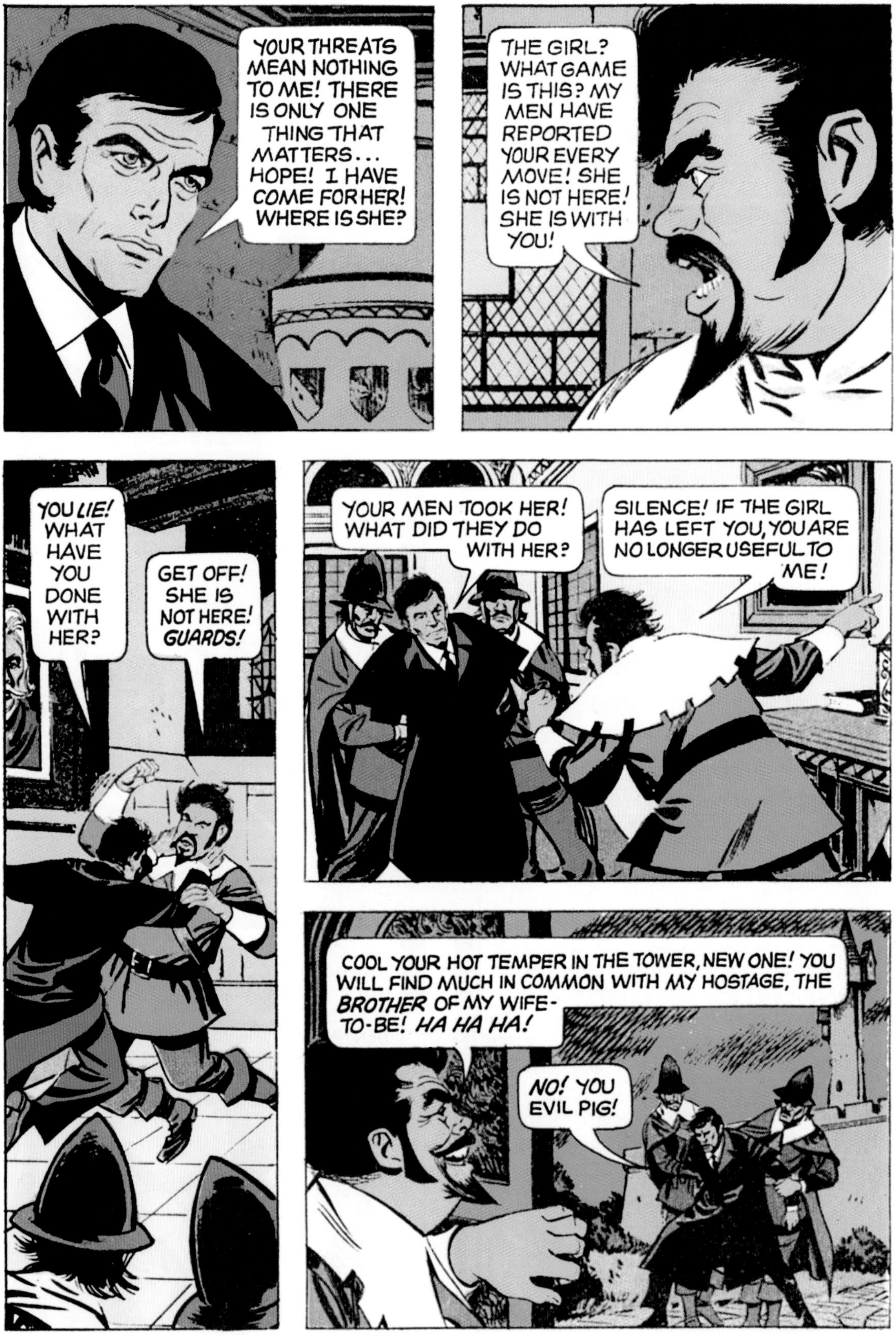
YOUR THREATS MEAN NOTHING TO ME! THERE IS ONLY ONE THING THAT MATTERS... HOPE! I HAVE COME FOR HER! WHERE IS SHE?
THE GIRL? WHAT GAME IS THIS? MY MEN HAVE REPORTED YOUR EVERY MOVE! SHE IS NOT HERE! SHE IS WITH YOU!
YOU LIE! WHAT HAVE YOU DONE WITH HER?
GET OFF! SHE IS NOT HERE! GUARDS!
YOUR MEN TOOK HER! WHAT DID THEY DO WITH HER?
SILENCE! IF THE GIRL HAS LEFT YOU, YOU ARE NO LONGER USEFUL TO ME!
COOL YOUR HOT TEMPER IN THE TOWER, NEW ONE! YOU WILL FIND MUCH IN COMMON WITH MY HOSTAGE, THE BROTHER OF MY WIFE-TO-BE! HA HA HA!
NO! YOU EVIL PIG!

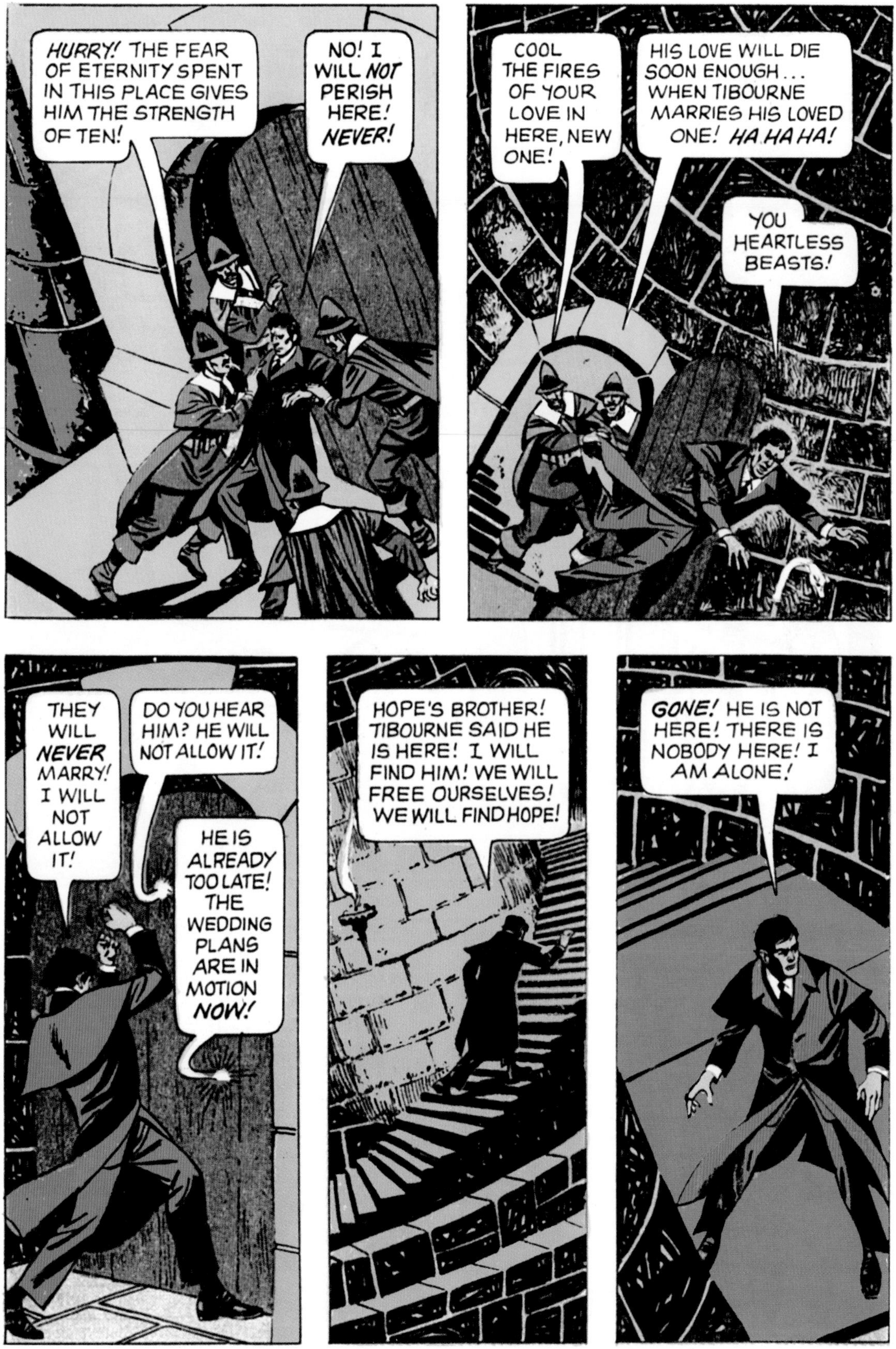
HURRY! THE FEAR OF ETERNITY SPENT IN THIS PLACE GIVES HIM THE STRENGTH OF TEN!
NO! I WILL NOT PERISH HERE! NEVER!
COOL THE FIRES OF YOUR LOVE IN HERE, NEW ONE!
HIS LOVE WILL DIE SOON ENOUGH . . . WHEN TIBOURNE MARRIES HIS LOVED ONE! HA HA HA!
YOU HEARTLESS BEASTS!
THEY WILL NEVER MARRY! I WILL NOT ALLOW IT!
DO YOU HEAR HIM? HE WILL NOT ALLOW IT!
HE IS ALREADY TOO LATE! THE WEDDING PLANS ARE IN MOTION NOW!
HOPE'S BROTHER! TIBOURNE SAID HE IS HERE! I WILL FIND HIM! WE WILL FREE OURSELVES! WE WILL FIND HOPE!
GONE! HE IS NOT HERE! THERE IS NOBODY HERE! I AM ALONE!

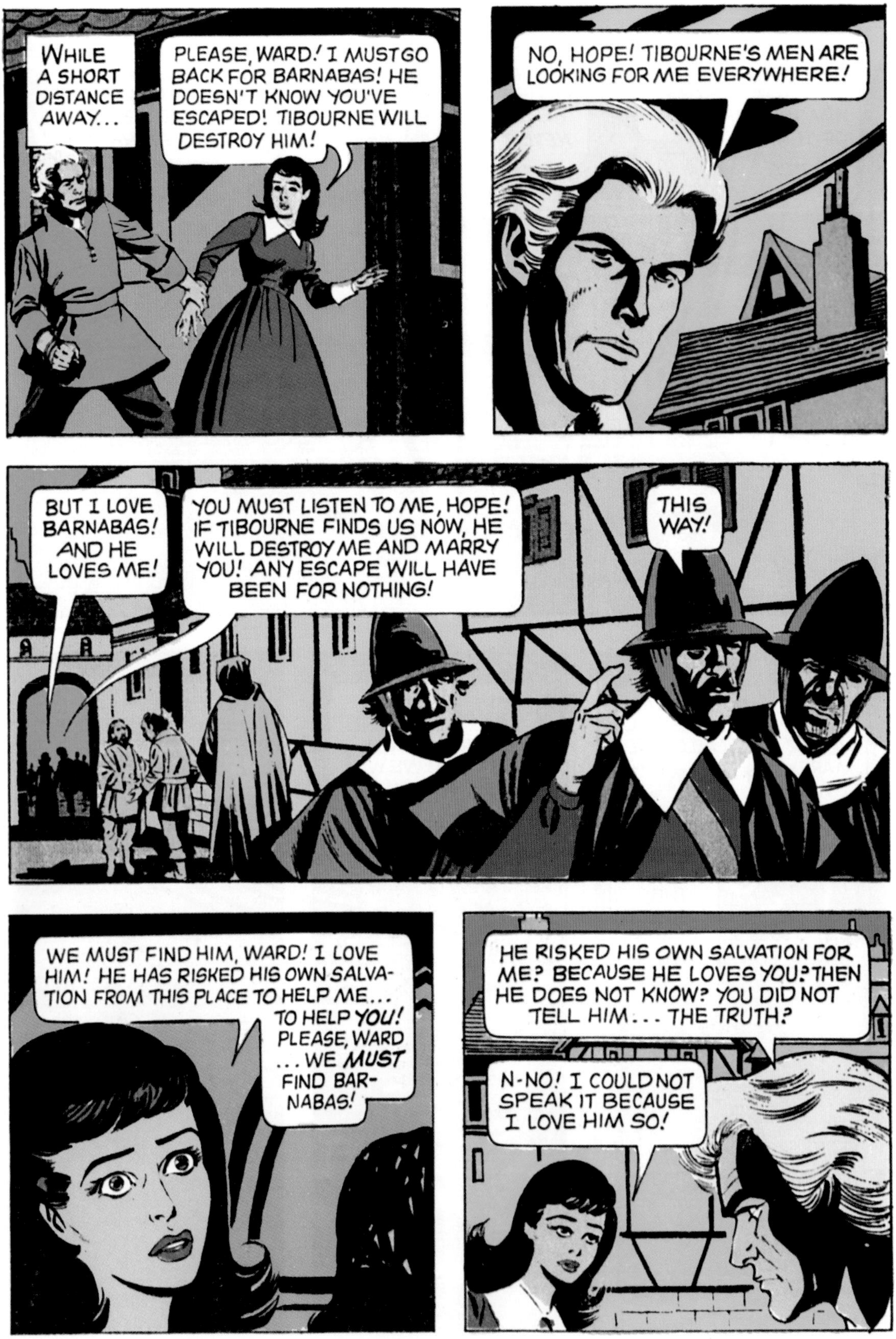

WHILE A SHORT DISTANCE AWAY...
PLEASE, WARD! I MUST GO BACK FOR BARNABAS! HE DOESN'T KNOW YOU'VE ESCAPED! TIBOURNE WILL DESTROY HIM!
NO, HOPE! TIBOURNE'S MEN ARE LOOKING FOR ME EVERYWHERE!
BUT I LOVE BARNABAS! AND HE LOVES ME!
YOU MUST LISTEN TO ME, HOPE! IF TIBOURNE FINDS US NOW, HE WILL DESTROY ME AND MARRY YOU! ANY ESCAPE WILL HAVE BEEN FOR NOTHING!
THIS WAY!
WE MUST FIND HIM, WARD! I LOVE HIM! HE HAS RISKED HIS OWN SALVATION FROM THIS PLACE TO HELP ME... TO HELP YOU! PLEASE, WARD ... WE MUST FIND BARNABAS!
HE RISKED HIS OWN SALVATION FOR ME? BECAUSE HE LOVES YOU? THEN HE DOES NOT KNOW? YOU DID NOT TELL HIM... THE TRUTH?
N-NO! I COULD NOT SPEAK IT BECAUSE I LOVE HIM SO!

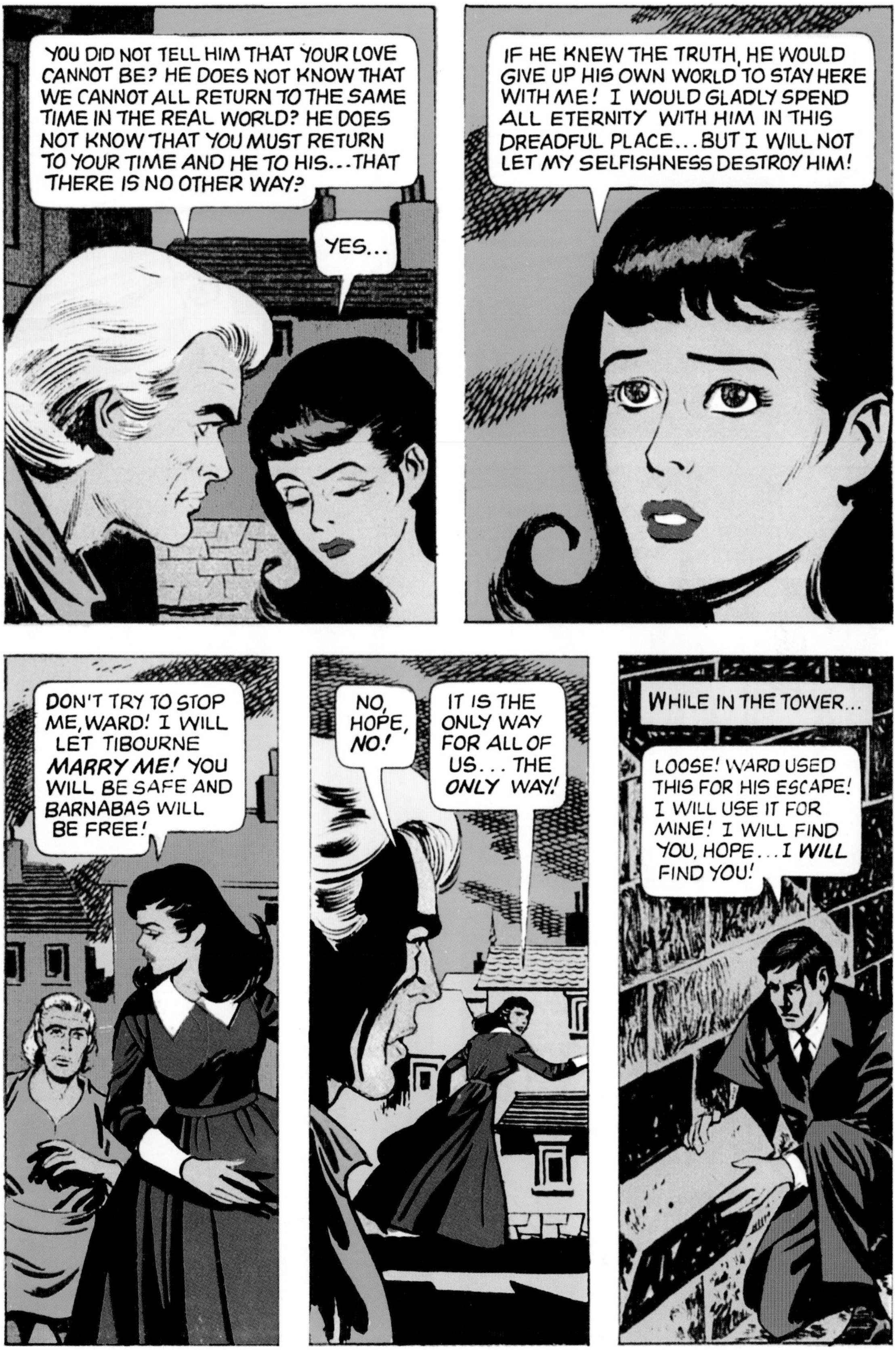
YOU DID NOT TELL HIM THAT YOUR LOVE CANNOT BE? HE DOES NOT KNOW THAT WE CANNOT ALL RETURN TO THE SAME TIME IN THE REAL WORLD? HE DOES NOT KNOW THAT YOU MUST RETURN TO YOUR TIME AND HE TO HIS...THAT THERE IS NO OTHER WAY?
YES...
IF HE KNEW THE TRUTH, HE WOULD GIVE UP HIS OWN WORLD TO STAY HERE WITH ME! I WOULD GLADLY SPEND ALL ETERNITY WITH HIM IN THIS DREADFUL PLACE...BUT I WILL NOT LET MY SELFISHNESS DESTROY HIM!
DON'T TRY TO STOP ME, WARD! I WILL LET TIBOURNE MARRY ME! YOU WILL BE SAFE AND BARNABAS WILL BE FREE!
NO, HOPE, NO!
IT IS THE ONLY WAY FOR ALL OF US... THE ONLY WAY!
WHILE IN THE TOWER...
LOOSE! WARD USED THIS FOR HIS ESCAPE! I WILL USE IT FOR MINE! I WILL FIND YOU, HOPE...I WILL FIND YOU!

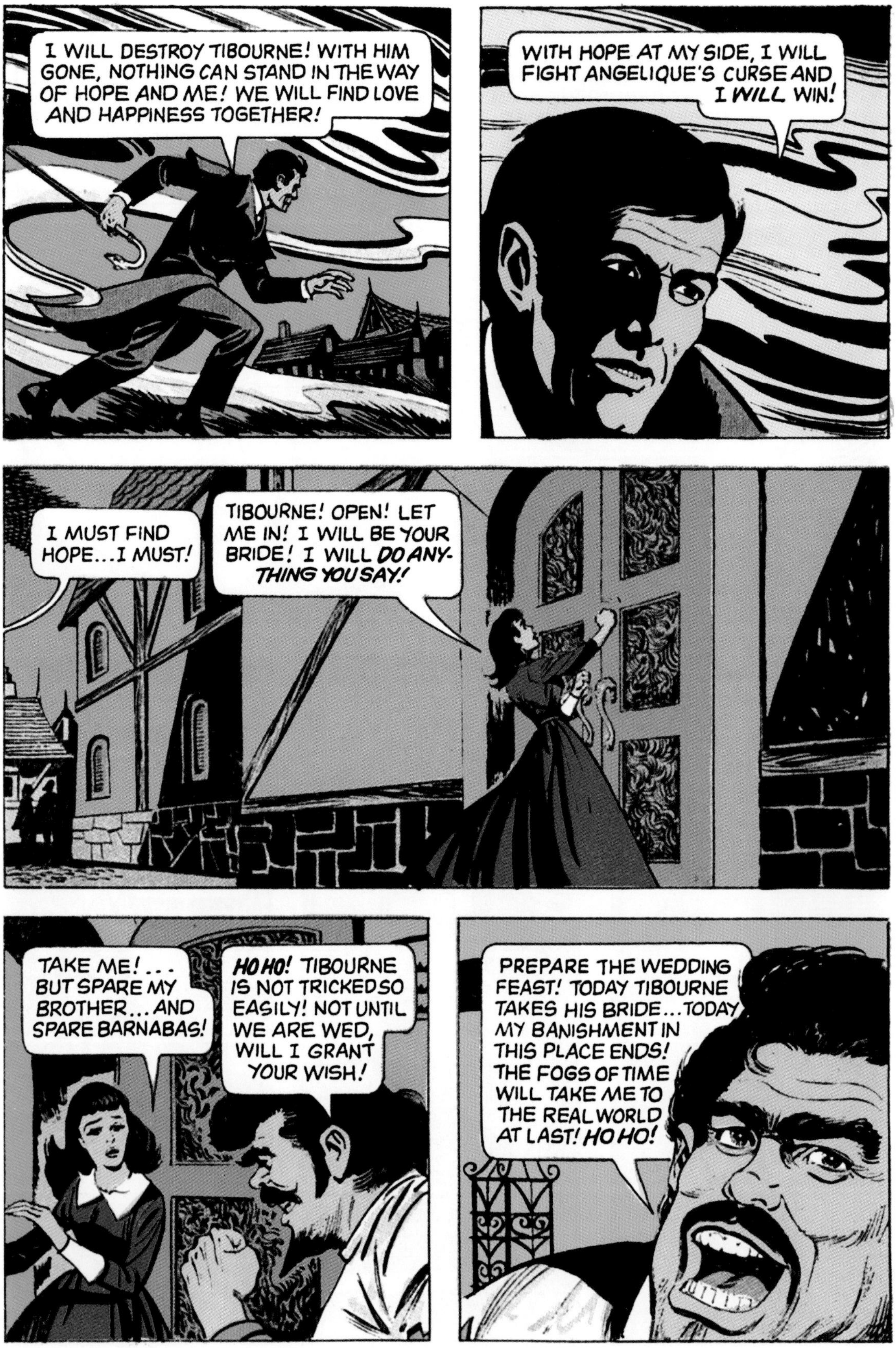
I WILL DESTROY TIBOURNE! WITH HIM GONE, NOTHING CAN STAND IN THE WAY OF HOPE AND ME! WE WILL FIND LOVE AND HAPPINESS TOGETHER!
WITH HOPE AT MY SIDE, I WILL FIGHT ANGELIQUE'S CURSE AND I *WILL* WIN!
I MUST FIND HOPE... I MUST!
TIBOURNE! OPEN! LET ME IN! I WILL BE YOUR BRIDE! I WILL *DO ANYTHING YOU SAY!*
TAKE ME! ... BUT SPARE MY BROTHER... AND SPARE BARNABAS!
HO HO! TIBOURNE IS NOT TRICKED SO EASILY! NOT UNTIL WE ARE WED, WILL I GRANT YOUR WISH!
PREPARE THE WEDDING FEAST! TODAY TIBOURNE TAKES HIS BRIDE... TODAY MY BANISHMENT IN THIS PLACE ENDS! THE FOGS OF TIME WILL TAKE ME TO THE REAL WORLD AT LAST! *HO HO!*

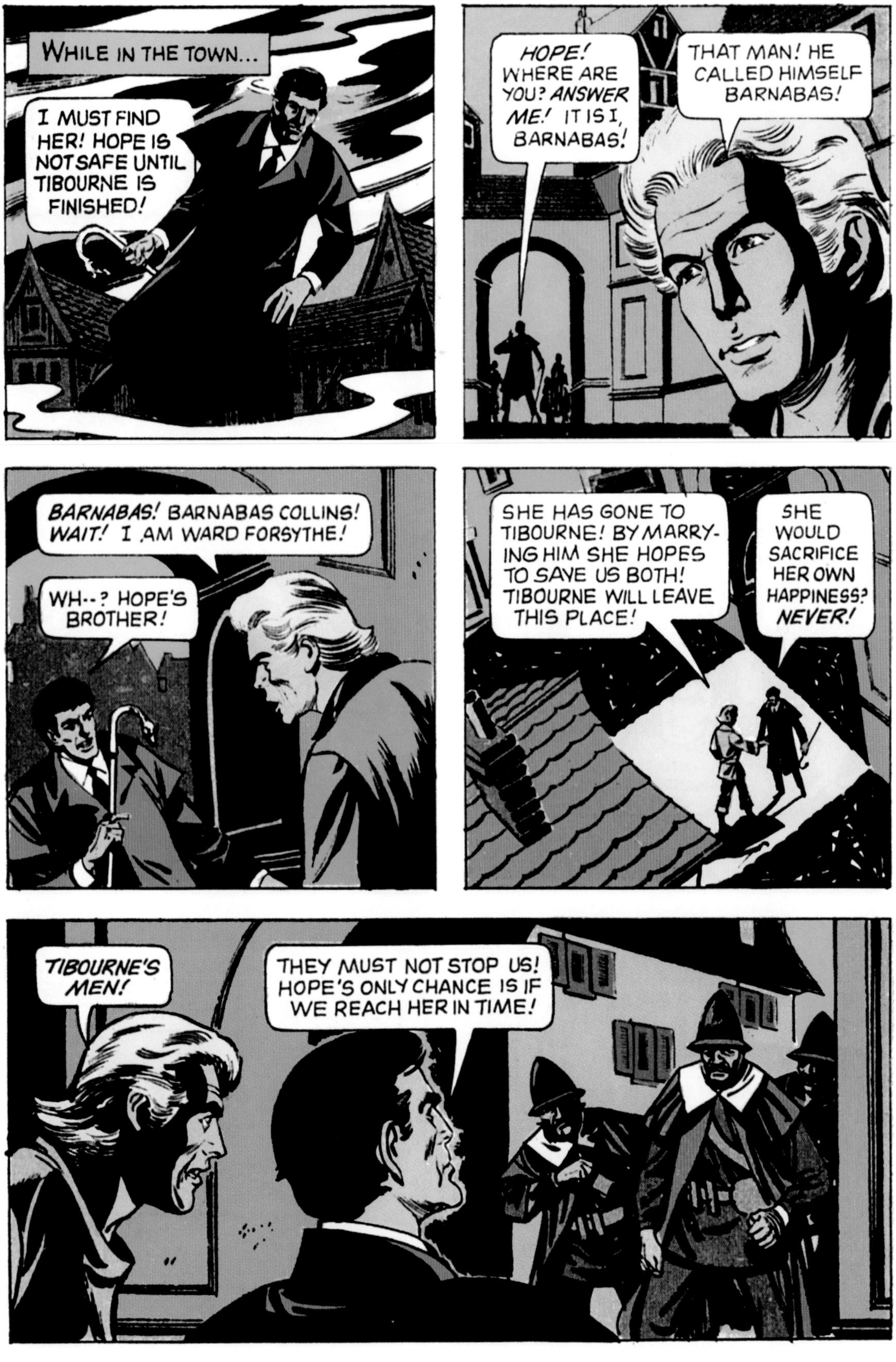
WHILE IN THE TOWN...
I MUST FIND HER! HOPE IS NOT SAFE UNTIL TIBOURNE IS FINISHED!
HOPE! WHERE ARE YOU? ANSWER ME! IT IS I, BARNABAS!
THAT MAN! HE CALLED HIMSELF BARNABAS!
BARNABAS! BARNABAS COLLINS! WAIT! I AM WARD FORSYTHE!
WH--? HOPE'S BROTHER!
SHE HAS GONE TO TIBOURNE! BY MARRYING HIM SHE HOPES TO SAVE US BOTH! TIBOURNE WILL LEAVE THIS PLACE!
SHE WOULD SACRIFICE HER OWN HAPPINESS? NEVER!
TIBOURNE'S MEN!
THEY MUST NOT STOP US! HOPE'S ONLY CHANCE IS IF WE REACH HER IN TIME!

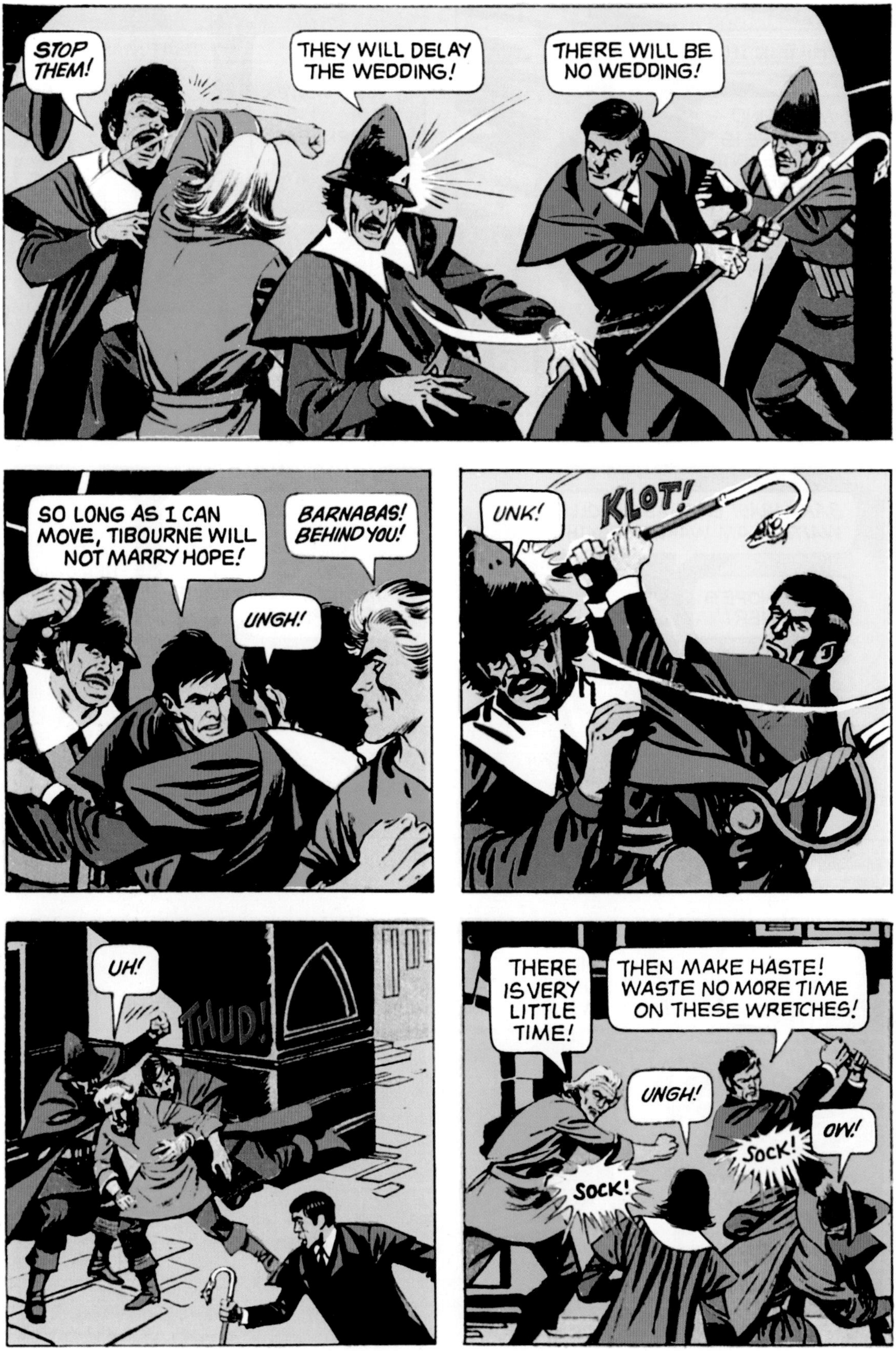
STOP THEM!
THEY WILL DELAY THE WEDDING!
THERE WILL BE NO WEDDING!
SO LONG AS I CAN MOVE, TIBOURNE WILL NOT MARRY HOPE!
BARNABAS! BEHIND YOU!
UNGH!
UNK!
KLOT!
UH!
THUD!
THERE IS VERY LITTLE TIME!
THEN MAKE HASTE! WASTE NO MORE TIME ON THESE WRETCHES!
UNGH!
OW!
SOCK!
SOCK!

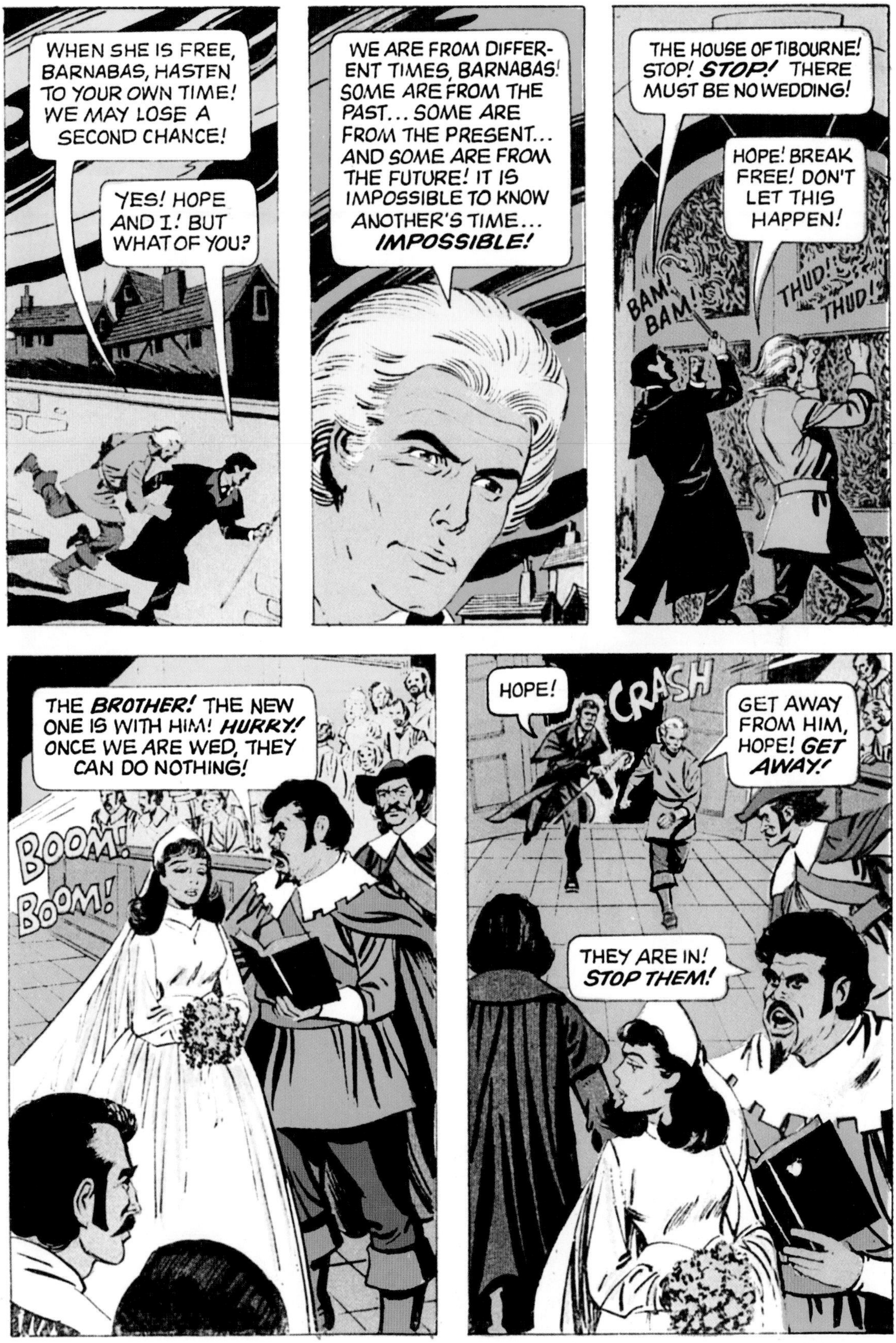
WHEN SHE IS FREE, BARNABAS, HASTEN TO YOUR OWN TIME! WE MAY LOSE A SECOND CHANCE!
YES! HOPE AND I! BUT WHAT OF YOU?
WE ARE FROM DIFFERENT TIMES, BARNABAS! SOME ARE FROM THE PAST... SOME ARE FROM THE PRESENT... AND SOME ARE FROM THE FUTURE! IT IS IMPOSSIBLE TO KNOW ANOTHER'S TIME... IMPOSSIBLE!
THE HOUSE OF TIBOURNE! STOP! STOP! THERE MUST BE NO WEDDING!
HOPE! BREAK FREE! DON'T LET THIS HAPPEN!
BAM! BAM!
THUD! THUD!
THE BROTHER! THE NEW ONE IS WITH HIM! HURRY! ONCE WE ARE WED, THEY CAN DO NOTHING!
BOOM! BOOM!
HOPE!
CRASH
GET AWAY FROM HIM, HOPE! GET AWAY!
THEY ARE IN! STOP THEM!

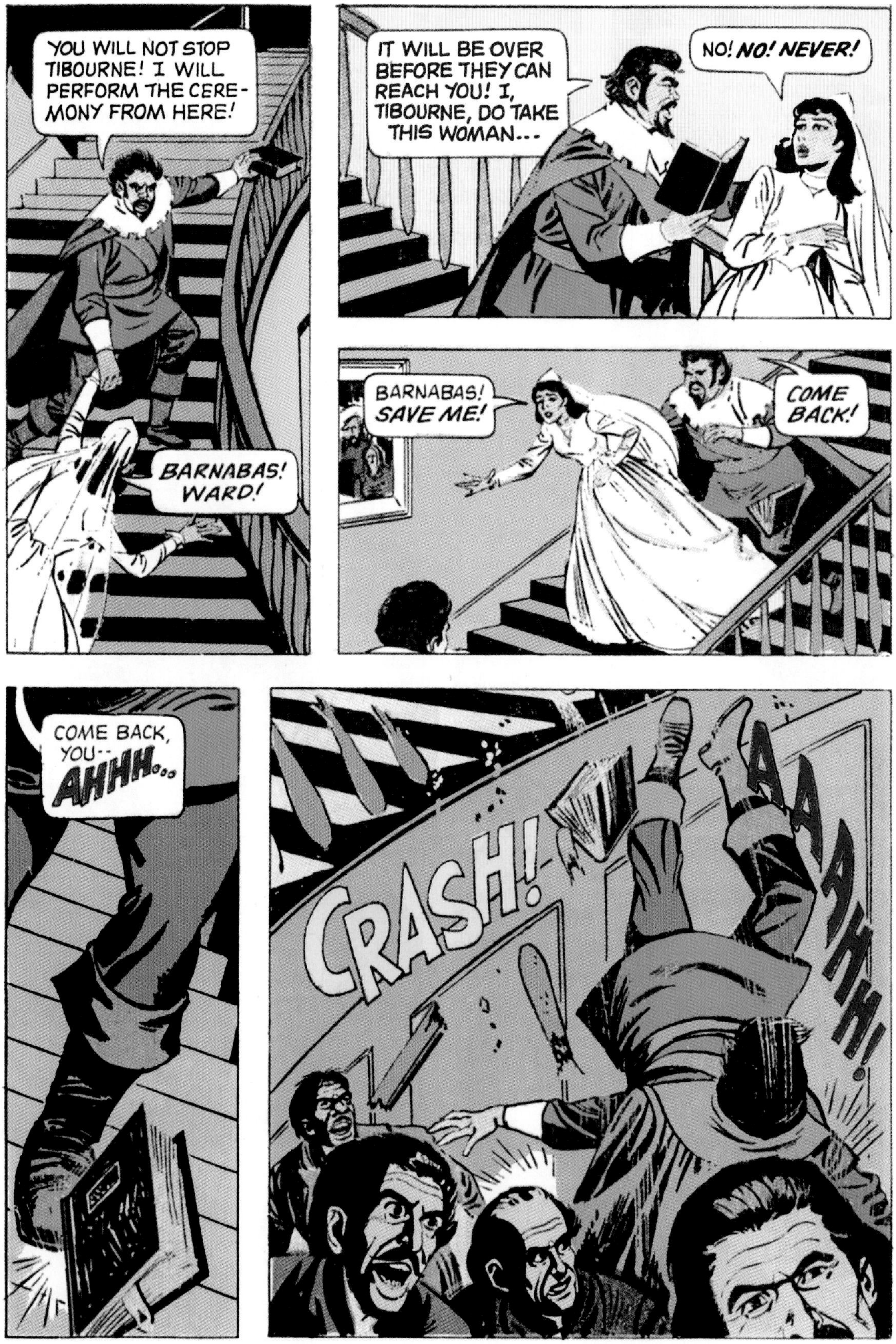
YOU WILL NOT STOP TIBOURNE! I WILL PERFORM THE CERE-MONY FROM HERE!
BARNABAS! WARD!
IT WILL BE OVER BEFORE THEY CAN REACH YOU! I, TIBOURNE, DO TAKE THIS WOMAN...
NO! NO! NEVER!
BARNABAS! SAVE ME!
COME BACK!
COME BACK, YOU-- AHHH...
CRASH!
AAAHH!

A SHORT WHILE LATER...

TIBOURNE IS GONE! THOSE WHO PERISH HERE VANISH FOREVER! THERE IS NO HOPE FOR THEIR SALVATION!

BUT WE CAN RETURN SAFELY TO THE REAL WORLD TOGETHER!

TELL HIM, HOPE!... TELL HIM THE TRUTH!

THE TRUTH? WHAT IS IT, DEAREST HOPE? IS IT THAT YOU NO LONGER WISH TO BECOME MY BRIDE? IF YOU HAVE CHANGED YOUR MIND, I WILL UNDERSTAND!

NO, DEAR BARNABAS, IT IS NOT THAT! WALK ON AHEAD SO I MAY SAY GOODBYE TO WARD!

WHY WON'T YOU TELL HIM YOUR TIME AND HIS TIME ARE DIFFERENT? WON'T YOU TELL HIM THAT ONCE HE PASSES THROUGH THE FOGS OF TIME, YOU WILL BE SEPARATED FOREVER?

NO! IF I DID, HE WOULD STAY! HE WOULD GIVE UP HIS OWN DESTINY TO BE WITH ME! IT IS BETTER THIS WAY!

HOPE! COME! THIS FOG...IT IS SO THICK! I -- HOPE!... HOPE!

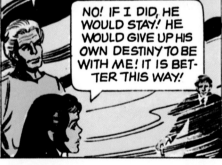

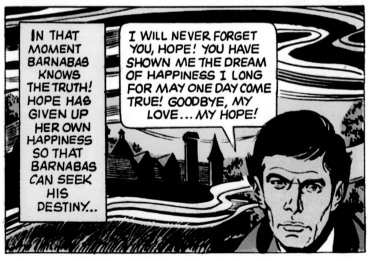

IN THAT MOMENT BARNABAS KNOWS THE TRUTH! HOPE HAS GIVEN UP HER OWN HAPPINESS SO THAT BARNABAS CAN SEEK HIS DESTINY...

I WILL NEVER FORGET YOU, HOPE! YOU HAVE SHOWN ME THE DREAM OF HAPPINESS I LONG FOR MAY ONE DAY COME TRUE! GOODBYE, MY LOVE... MY HOPE!

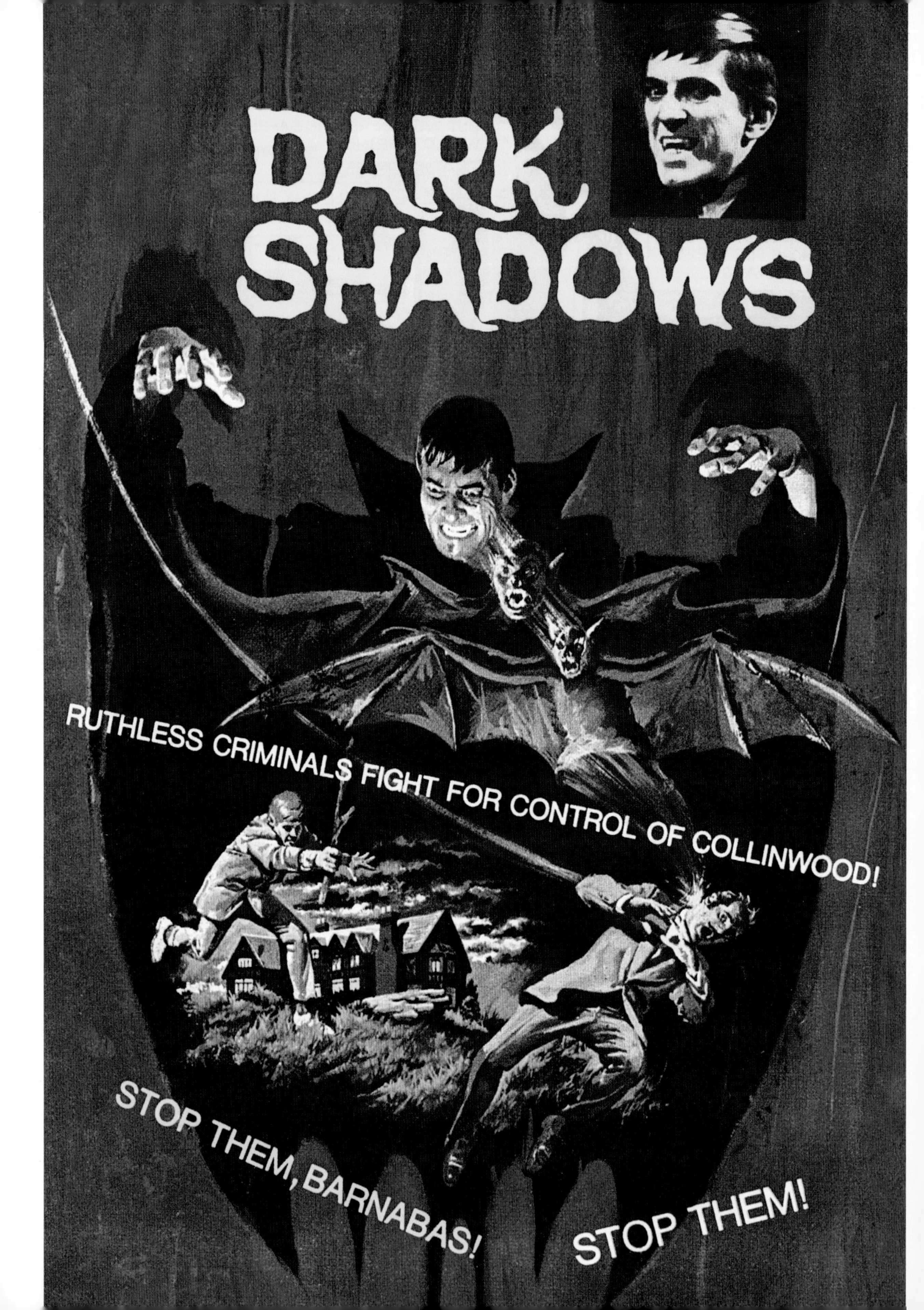
DARK SHADOWS
RUTHLESS CRIMINALS FIGHT FOR CONTROL OF COLLINWOOD!
STOP THEM, BARNABAS!
STOP THEM!

DARK SHADOWS

GUEST in the HOUSE

PART 1

THE MAN FROM NEW YORK

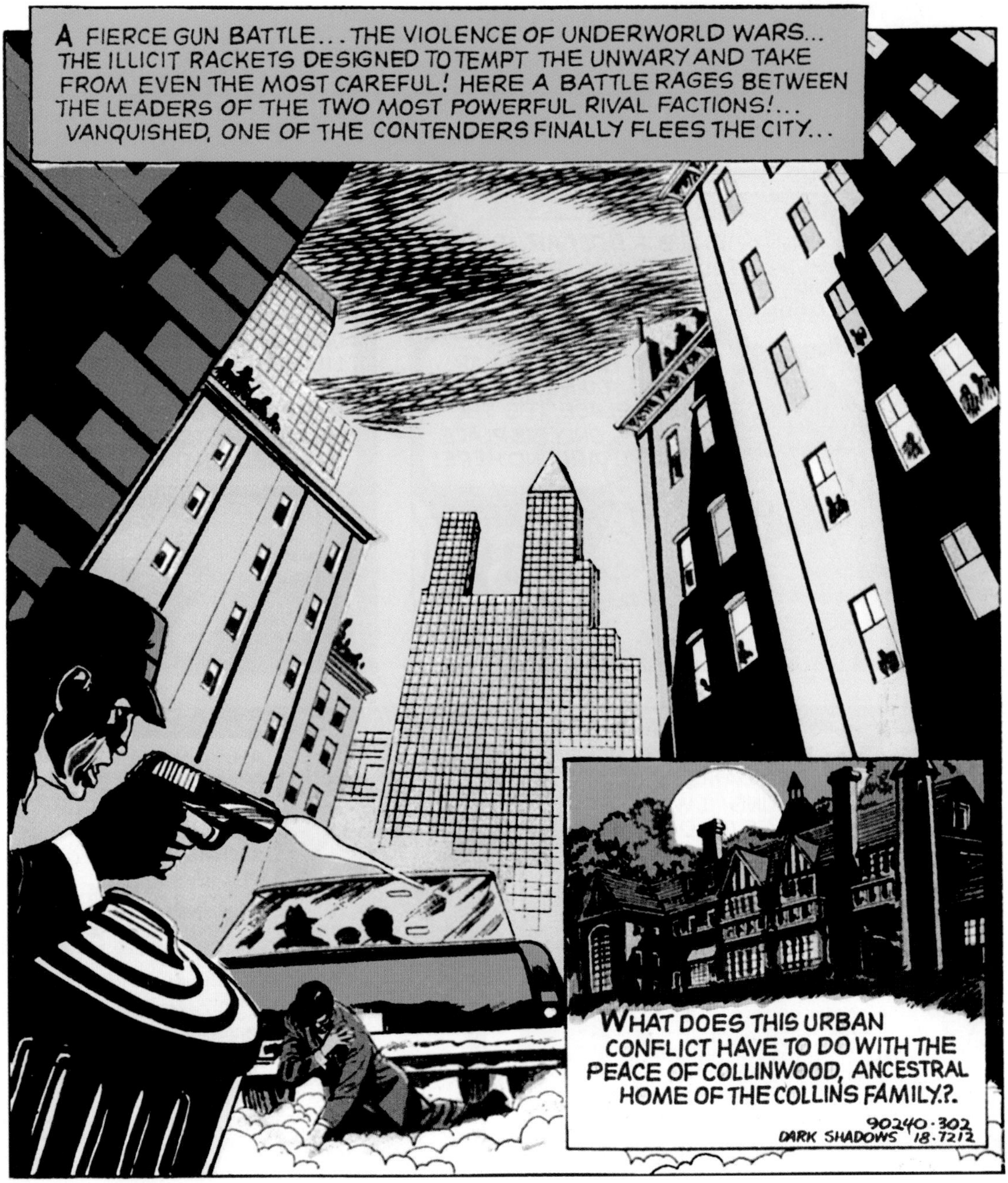
A FIERCE GUN BATTLE... THE VIOLENCE OF UNDERWORLD WARS... THE ILLICIT RACKETS DESIGNED TO TEMPT THE UNWARY AND TAKE FROM EVEN THE MOST CAREFUL! HERE A BATTLE RAGES BETWEEN THE LEADERS OF THE TWO MOST POWERFUL RIVAL FACTIONS!... VANQUISHED, ONE OF THE CONTENDERS FINALLY FLEES THE CITY...
WHAT DOES THIS URBAN CONFLICT HAVE TO DO WITH THE PEACE OF COLLINWOOD, ANCESTRAL HOME OF THE COLLINS FAMILY?.
90240-302
DARK SHADOWS 18-7212

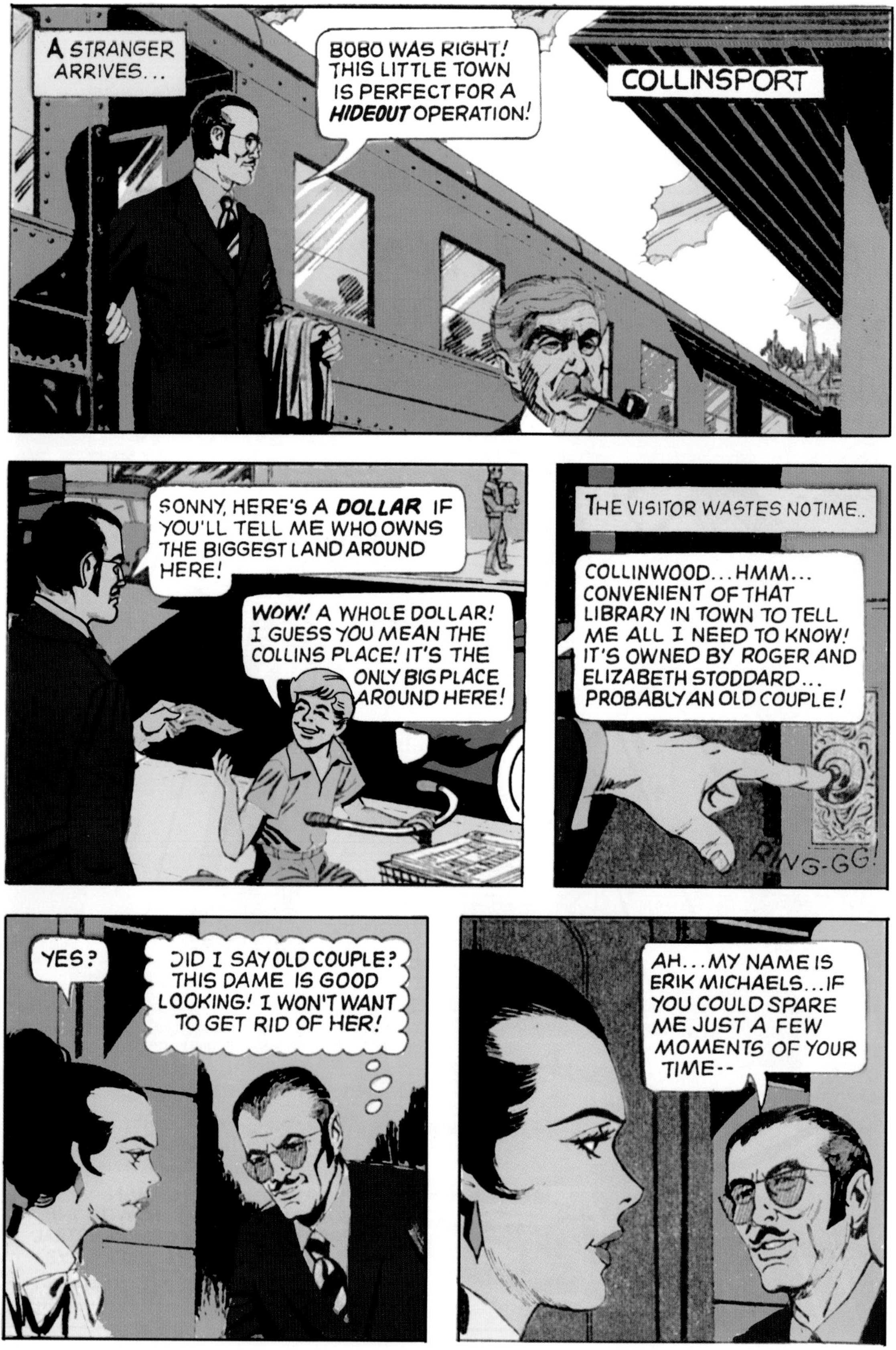

A STRANGER ARRIVES...
BOBO WAS RIGHT! THIS LITTLE TOWN IS PERFECT FOR A HIDEOUT OPERATION!
COLLINSPORT
SONNY, HERE'S A DOLLAR IF YOU'LL TELL ME WHO OWNS THE BIGGEST LAND AROUND HERE!
WOW! A WHOLE DOLLAR! I GUESS YOU MEAN THE COLLINS PLACE! IT'S THE ONLY BIG PLACE AROUND HERE!
THE VISITOR WASTES NO TIME..
COLLINWOOD...HMM... CONVENIENT OF THAT LIBRARY IN TOWN TO TELL ME ALL I NEED TO KNOW! IT'S OWNED BY ROGER AND ELIZABETH STODDARD... PROBABLY AN OLD COUPLE!
RING-GG!
YES?
DID I SAY OLD COUPLE? THIS DAME IS GOOD LOOKING! I WON'T WANT TO GET RID OF HER!
AH...MY NAME IS ERIK MICHAELS...IF YOU COULD SPARE ME JUST A FEW MOMENTS OF YOUR TIME--

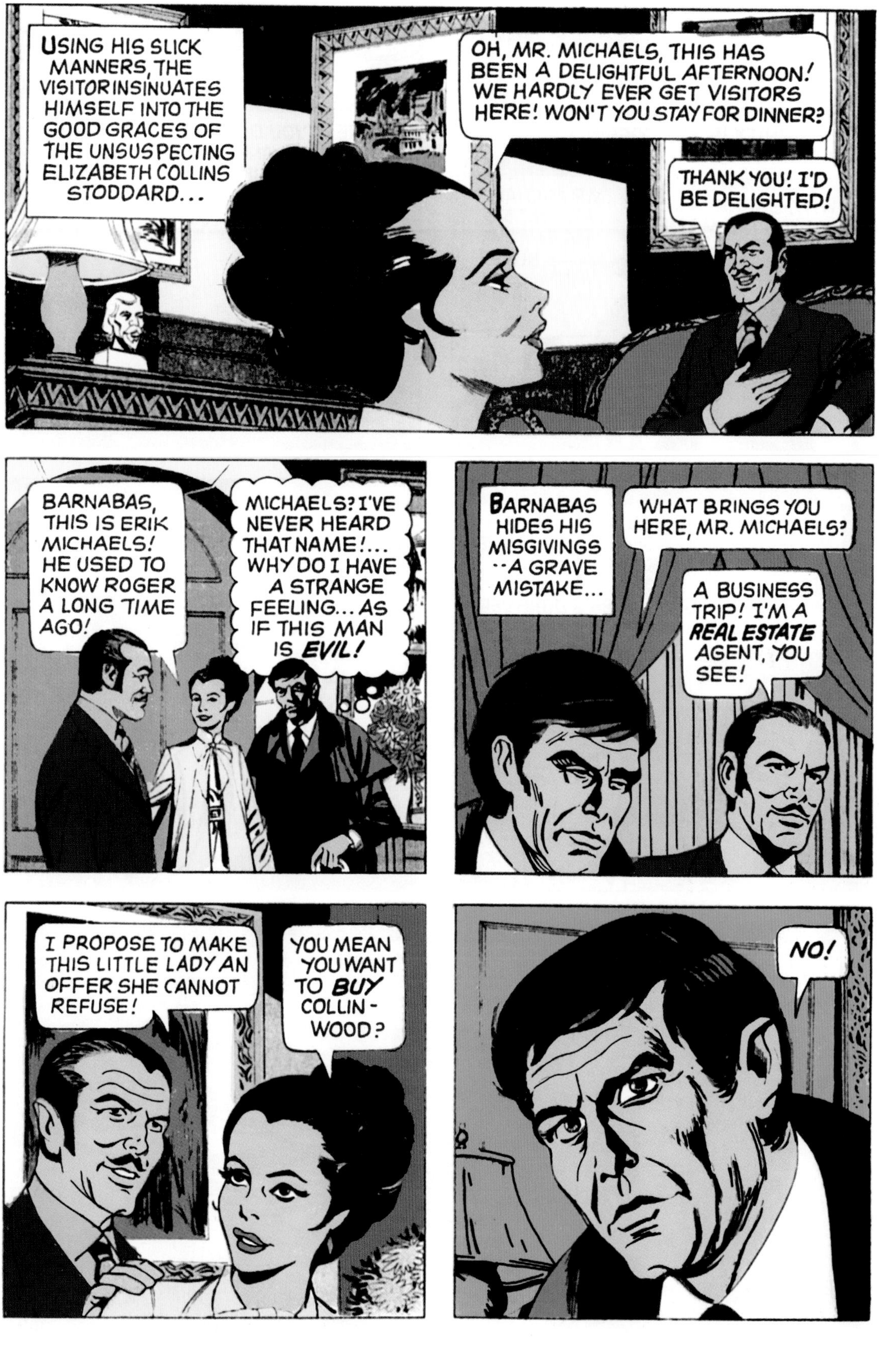
USING HIS SLICK MANNERS, THE VISITOR INSINUATES HIMSELF INTO THE GOOD GRACES OF THE UNSUSPECTING ELIZABETH COLLINS STODDARD...
OH, MR. MICHAELS, THIS HAS BEEN A DELIGHTFUL AFTERNOON! WE HARDLY EVER GET VISITORS HERE! WON'T YOU STAY FOR DINNER?
THANK YOU! I'D BE DELIGHTED!
BARNABAS, THIS IS ERIK MICHAELS! HE USED TO KNOW ROGER A LONG TIME AGO!
MICHAELS? I'VE NEVER HEARD THAT NAME!... WHY DO I HAVE A STRANGE FEELING... AS IF THIS MAN IS EVIL!
BARNABAS HIDES HIS MISGIVINGS --A GRAVE MISTAKE...
WHAT BRINGS YOU HERE, MR. MICHAELS?
A BUSINESS TRIP! I'M A REAL ESTATE AGENT, YOU SEE!
I PROPOSE TO MAKE THIS LITTLE LADY AN OFFER SHE CANNOT REFUSE!
YOU MEAN YOU WANT TO BUY COLLIN-WOOD?
NO!

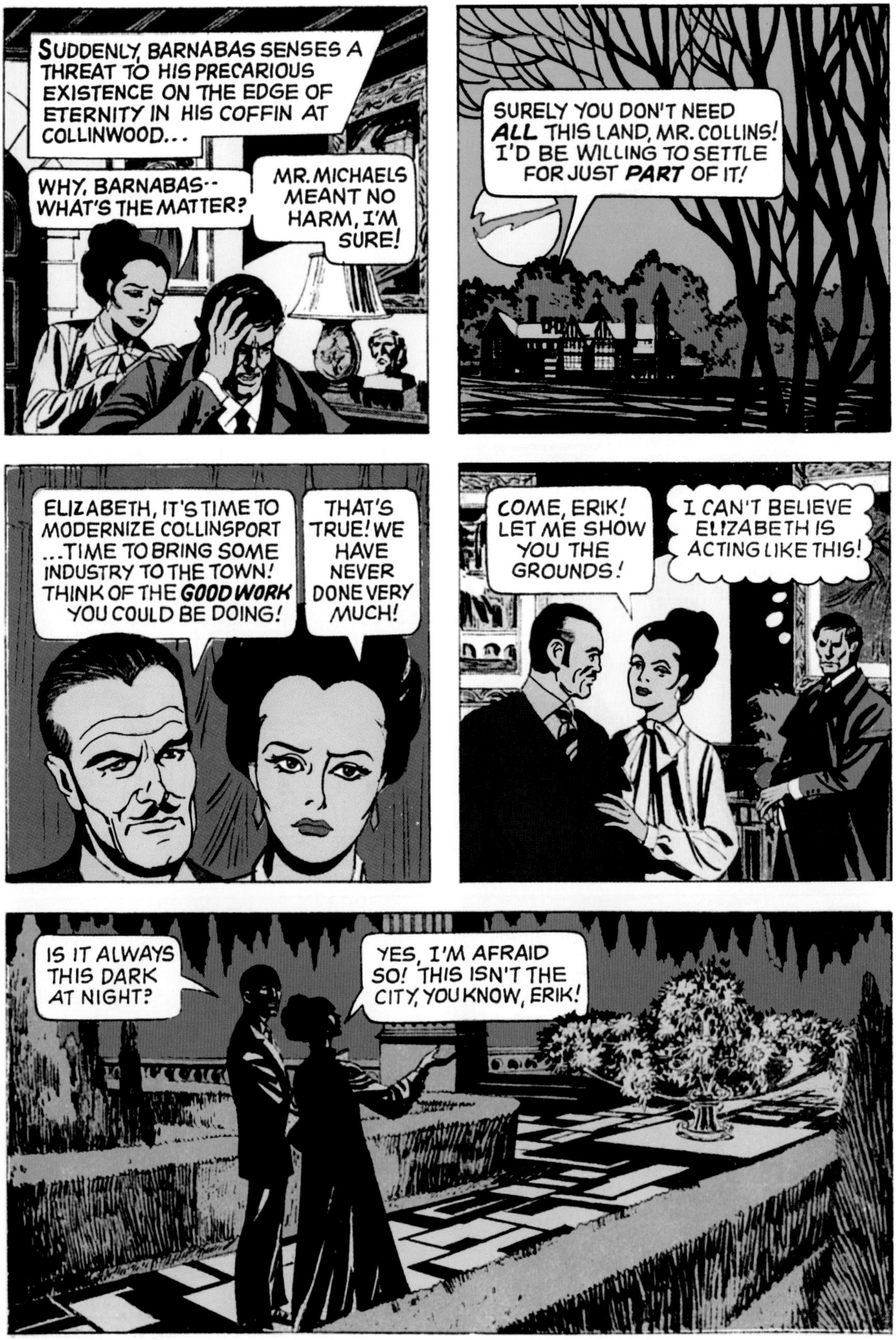
SUDDENLY, BARNABAS SENSES A THREAT TO HIS PRECARIOUS EXISTENCE ON THE EDGE OF ETERNITY IN HIS COFFIN AT COLLINWOOD...
WHY, BARNABAS-- WHAT'S THE MATTER?
MR. MICHAELS MEANT NO HARM, I'M SURE!
SURELY YOU DON'T NEED ALL THIS LAND, MR. COLLINS! I'D BE WILLING TO SETTLE FOR JUST PART OF IT!
ELIZABETH, IT'S TIME TO MODERNIZE COLLINSPORT ...TIME TO BRING SOME INDUSTRY TO THE TOWN! THINK OF THE GOOD WORK YOU COULD BE DOING!
THAT'S TRUE! WE HAVE NEVER DONE VERY MUCH!
COME, ERIK! LET ME SHOW YOU THE GROUNDS!
I CAN'T BELIEVE ELIZABETH IS ACTING LIKE THIS!
IS IT ALWAYS THIS DARK AT NIGHT?
YES, I'M AFRAID SO! THIS ISN'T THE CITY, YOU KNOW, ERIK!

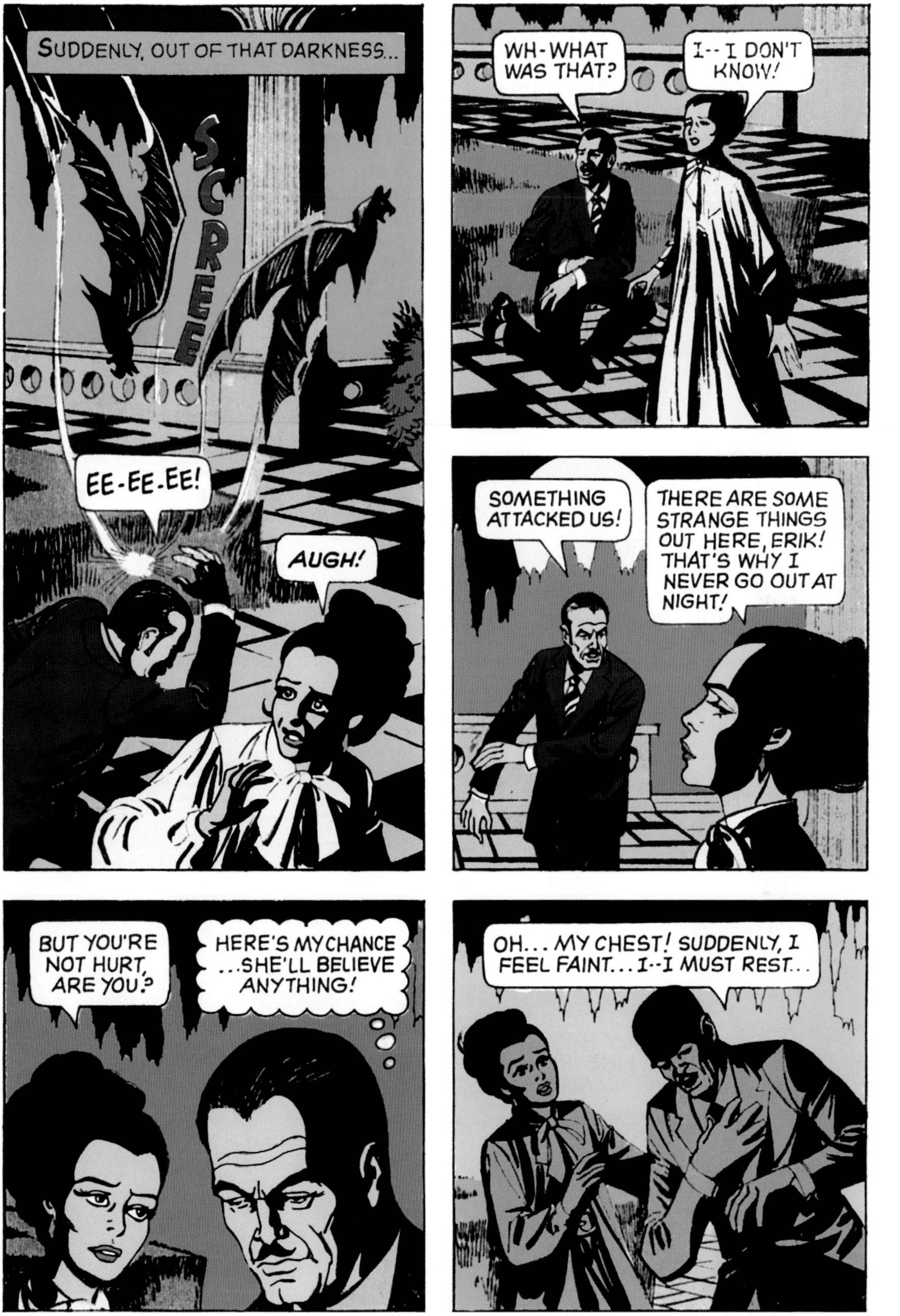
SUDDENLY, OUT OF THAT DARKNESS...
SCREE
EE-EE-EE!
AUGH!
WH-WHAT WAS THAT?
I-- I DON'T KNOW!
SOMETHING ATTACKED US!
THERE ARE SOME STRANGE THINGS OUT HERE, ERIK! THAT'S WHY I NEVER GO OUT AT NIGHT!
BUT YOU'RE NOT HURT, ARE YOU?
HERE'S MY CHANCE ...SHE'LL BELIEVE ANYTHING!
OH... MY CHEST! SUDDENLY, I FEEL FAINT... I--I MUST REST...

LATER, TAKING ADVANTAGE OF HIS PRETENDED SHOCK TO ACCEPT ELIZABETH'S OFFER TO REMAIN A FEW DAYS AT COLLINWOOD...

WHAT A SETUP! MY BOYS CAN MOVE IN AND NO ONE WILL EVER SUSPECT THIS IS A FRONT OPERATION!

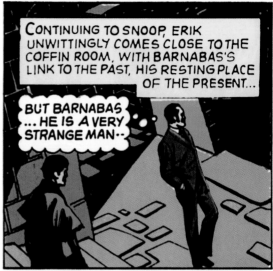

CONTINUING TO SNOOP, ERIK UNWITTINGLY COMES CLOSE TO THE COFFIN ROOM, WITH BARNABAS'S LINK TO THE PAST, HIS RESTING PLACE OF THE PRESENT...

BUT BARNABAS ...HE IS A VERY STRANGE MAN--

OH, MR. MICHAELS! DID I STARTLE YOU?

WOULDN'T YOU LIKE TO SEE THE *LIBRARY?* IT'S *THIS* WAY!

WHAT WAS HE DOING THERE? DID HE SEE THE COFFIN?

THIS GUY HAS A GRIP LIKE IRON! IT'S HARDLY *HUMAN!*

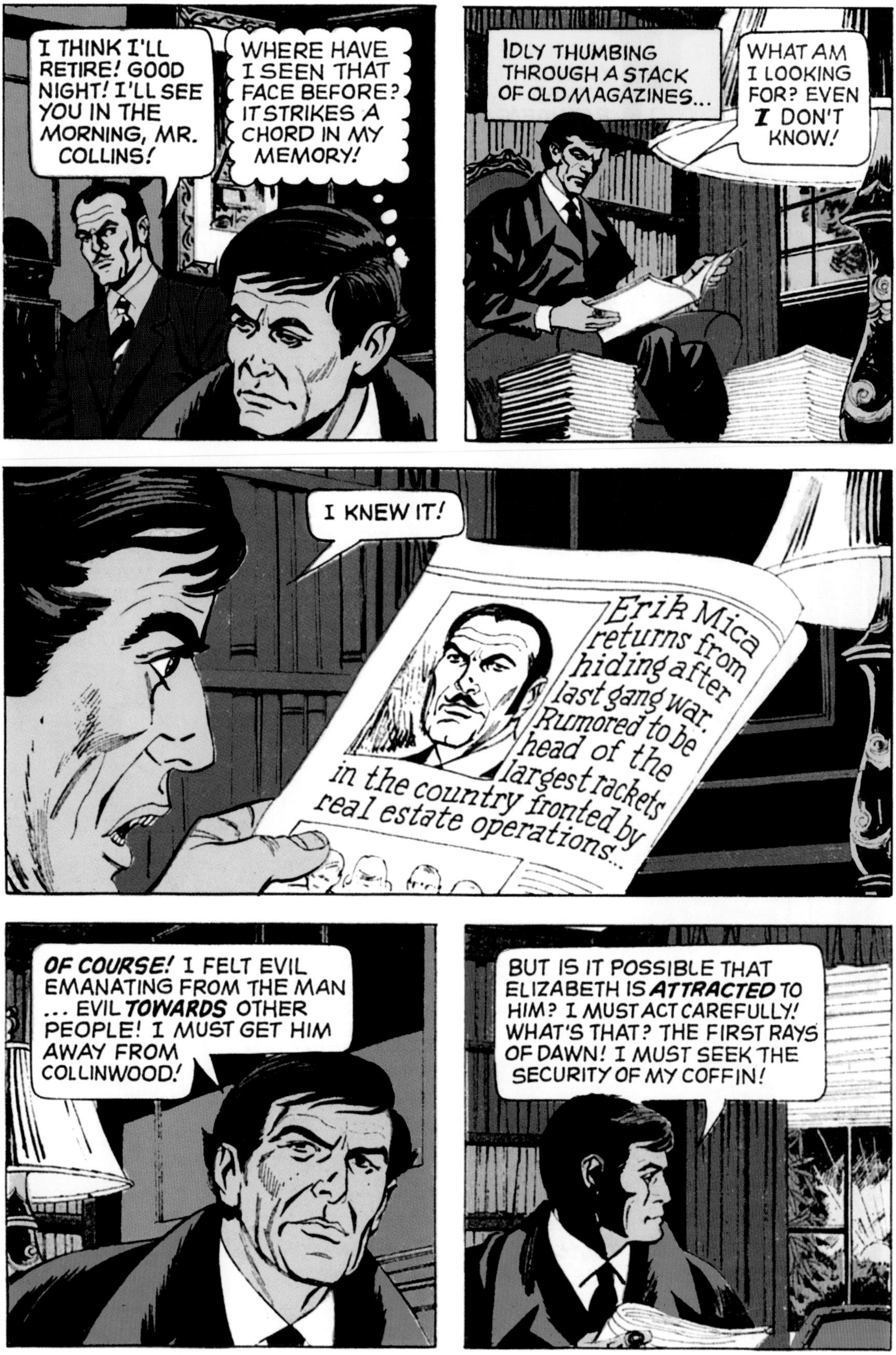
I THINK I'LL RETIRE! GOOD NIGHT! I'LL SEE YOU IN THE MORNING, MR. COLLINS!
WHERE HAVE I SEEN THAT FACE BEFORE? IT STRIKES A CHORD IN MY MEMORY!
IDLY THUMBING THROUGH A STACK OF OLD MAGAZINES...
WHAT AM I LOOKING FOR? EVEN I DON'T KNOW!
I KNEW IT!
Erik Mica returns from hiding after last gang war. Rumored to be head of the largest rackets in the country fronted by real estate operations...
OF COURSE! I FELT EVIL EMANATING FROM THE MAN ... EVIL TOWARDS OTHER PEOPLE! I MUST GET HIM AWAY FROM COLLINWOOD!
BUT IS IT POSSIBLE THAT ELIZABETH IS ATTRACTED TO HIM? I MUST ACT CAREFULLY! WHAT'S THAT? THE FIRST RAYS OF DAWN! I MUST SEEK THE SECURITY OF MY COFFIN!

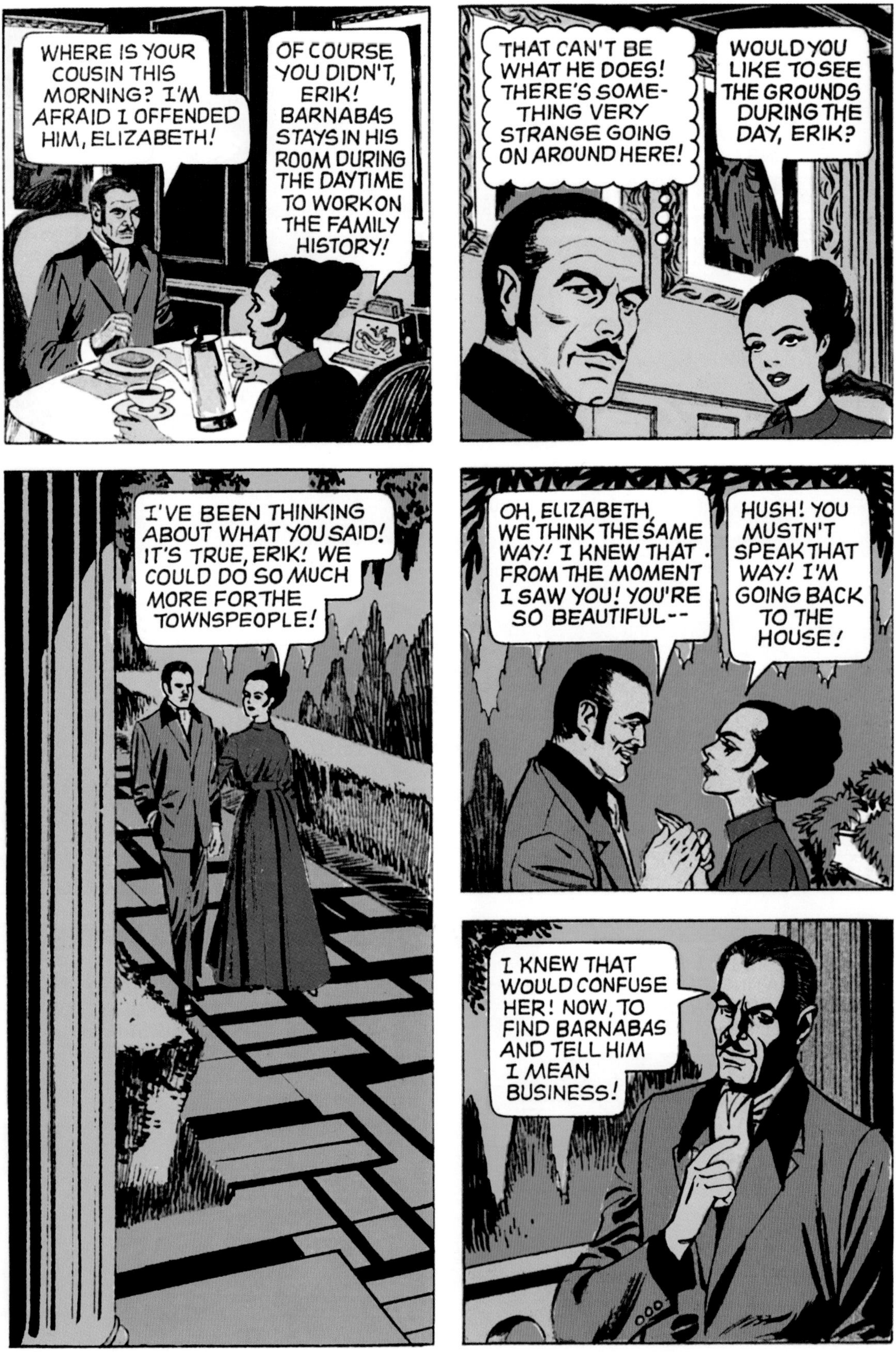
WHERE IS YOUR COUSIN THIS MORNING? I'M AFRAID I OFFENDED HIM, ELIZABETH!
OF COURSE YOU DIDN'T, ERIK! BARNABAS STAYS IN HIS ROOM DURING THE DAYTIME TO WORK ON THE FAMILY HISTORY!
THAT CAN'T BE WHAT HE DOES! THERE'S SOMETHING VERY STRANGE GOING ON AROUND HERE!
WOULD YOU LIKE TO SEE THE GROUNDS DURING THE DAY, ERIK?
I'VE BEEN THINKING ABOUT WHAT YOU SAID! IT'S TRUE, ERIK! WE COULD DO SO MUCH MORE FOR THE TOWNSPEOPLE!
OH, ELIZABETH, WE THINK THE SAME WAY! I KNEW THAT FROM THE MOMENT I SAW YOU! YOU'RE SO BEAUTIFUL--
HUSH! YOU MUSTN'T SPEAK THAT WAY! I'M GOING BACK TO THE HOUSE!
I KNEW THAT WOULD CONFUSE HER! NOW, TO FIND BARNABAS AND TELL HIM I MEAN BUSINESS!

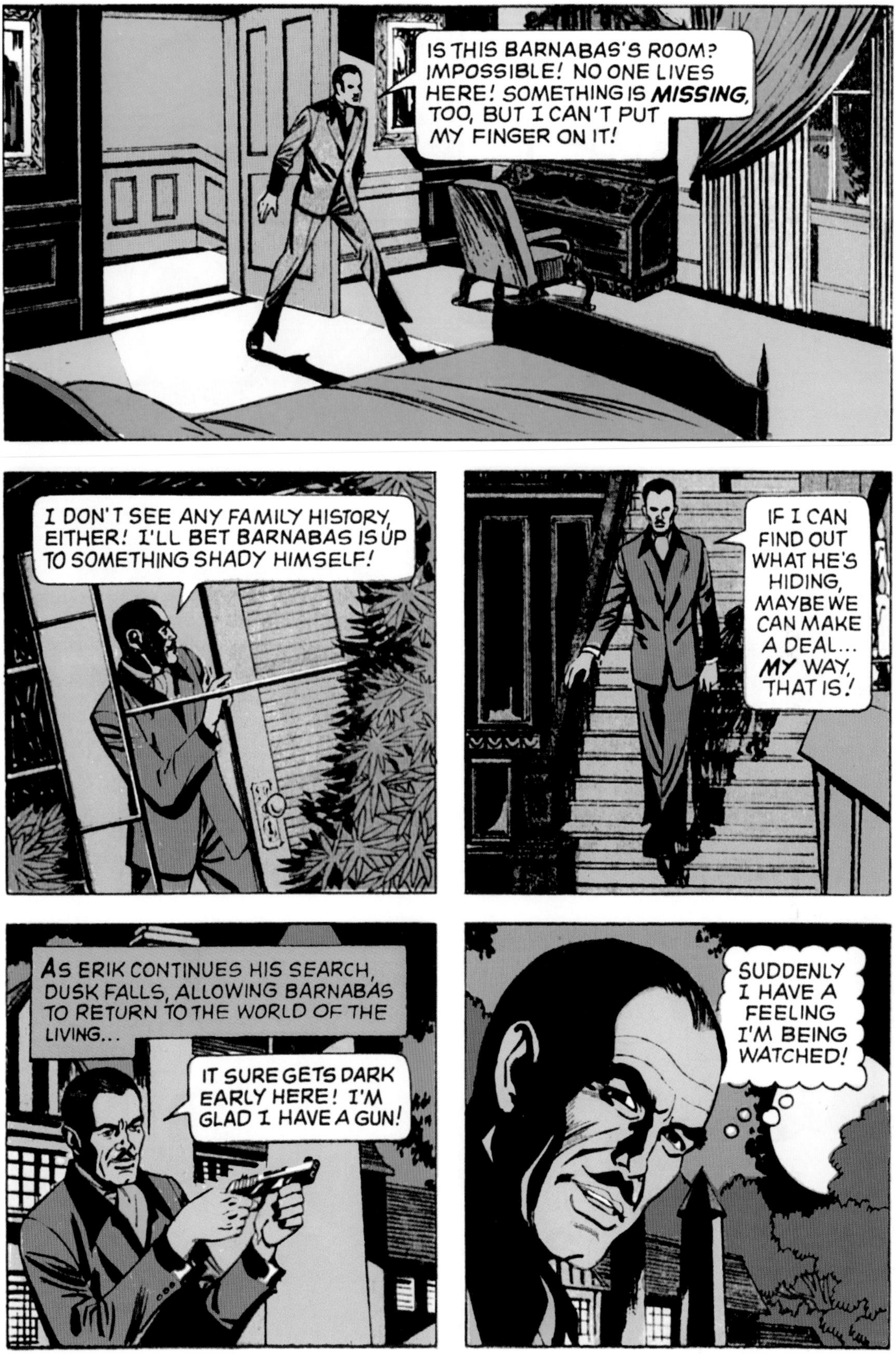
IS THIS BARNABAS'S ROOM? IMPOSSIBLE! NO ONE LIVES HERE! SOMETHING IS MISSING, TOO, BUT I CAN'T PUT MY FINGER ON IT!
I DON'T SEE ANY FAMILY HISTORY, EITHER! I'LL BET BARNABAS IS UP TO SOMETHING SHADY HIMSELF!
IF I CAN FIND OUT WHAT HE'S HIDING, MAYBE WE CAN MAKE A DEAL... MY WAY, THAT IS!
AS ERIK CONTINUES HIS SEARCH, DUSK FALLS, ALLOWING BARNABAS TO RETURN TO THE WORLD OF THE LIVING...
IT SURE GETS DARK EARLY HERE! I'M GLAD I HAVE A GUN!
SUDDENLY I HAVE A FEELING I'M BEING WATCHED!

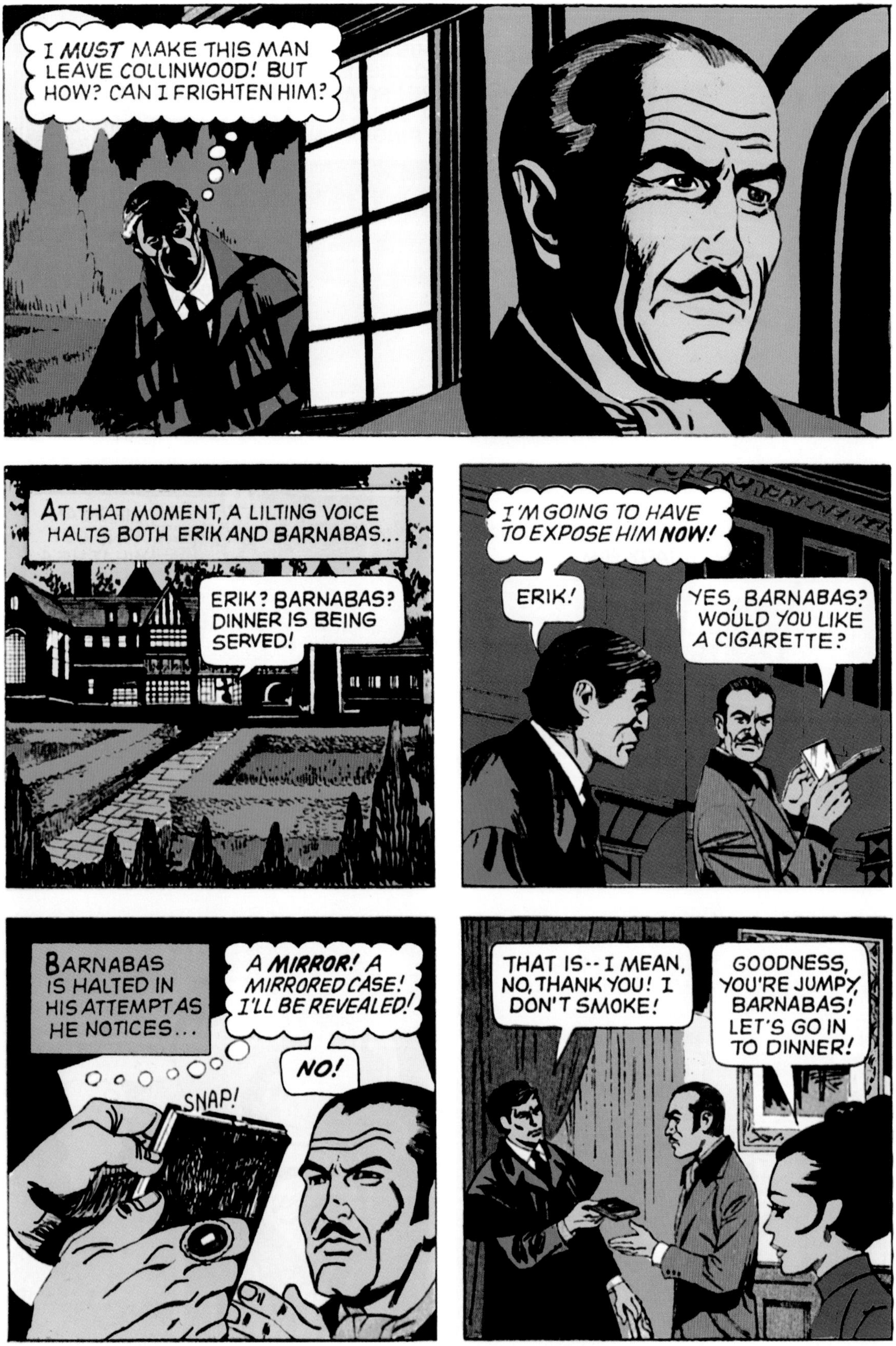
I MUST MAKE THIS MAN LEAVE COLLINWOOD! BUT HOW? CAN I FRIGHTEN HIM?
AT THAT MOMENT, A LILTING VOICE HALTS BOTH ERIK AND BARNABAS...
ERIK? BARNABAS? DINNER IS BEING SERVED!
I'M GOING TO HAVE TO EXPOSE HIM NOW!
ERIK!
YES, BARNABAS? WOULD YOU LIKE A CIGARETTE?
BARNABAS IS HALTED IN HIS ATTEMPT AS HE NOTICES...
A MIRROR! A MIRRORED CASE! I'LL BE REVEALED!
NO!
SNAP!
THAT IS-- I MEAN, NO, THANK YOU! I DON'T SMOKE!
GOODNESS, YOU'RE JUMPY, BARNABAS! LET'S GO IN TO DINNER!

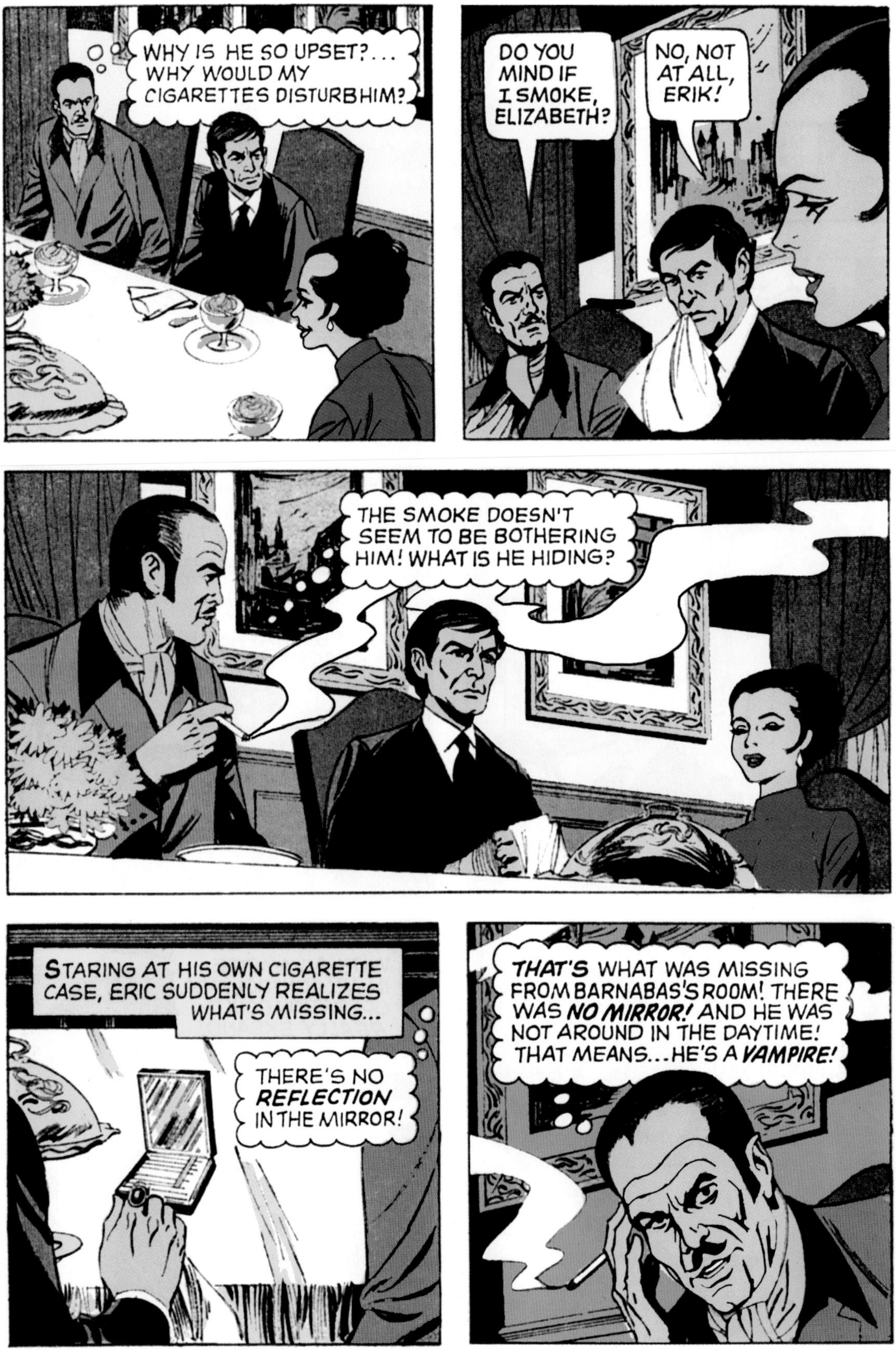
WHY IS HE SO UPSET?... WHY WOULD MY CIGARETTES DISTURB HIM?
DO YOU MIND IF I SMOKE, ELIZABETH?
NO, NOT AT ALL, ERIK!
THE SMOKE DOESN'T SEEM TO BE BOTHERING HIM! WHAT IS HE HIDING?
STARING AT HIS OWN CIGARETTE CASE, ERIC SUDDENLY REALIZES WHAT'S MISSING...
THERE'S NO REFLECTION IN THE MIRROR!
THAT'S WHAT WAS MISSING FROM BARNABAS'S ROOM! THERE WAS NO MIRROR! AND HE WAS NOT AROUND IN THE DAYTIME! THAT MEANS...HE'S A VAMPIRE!

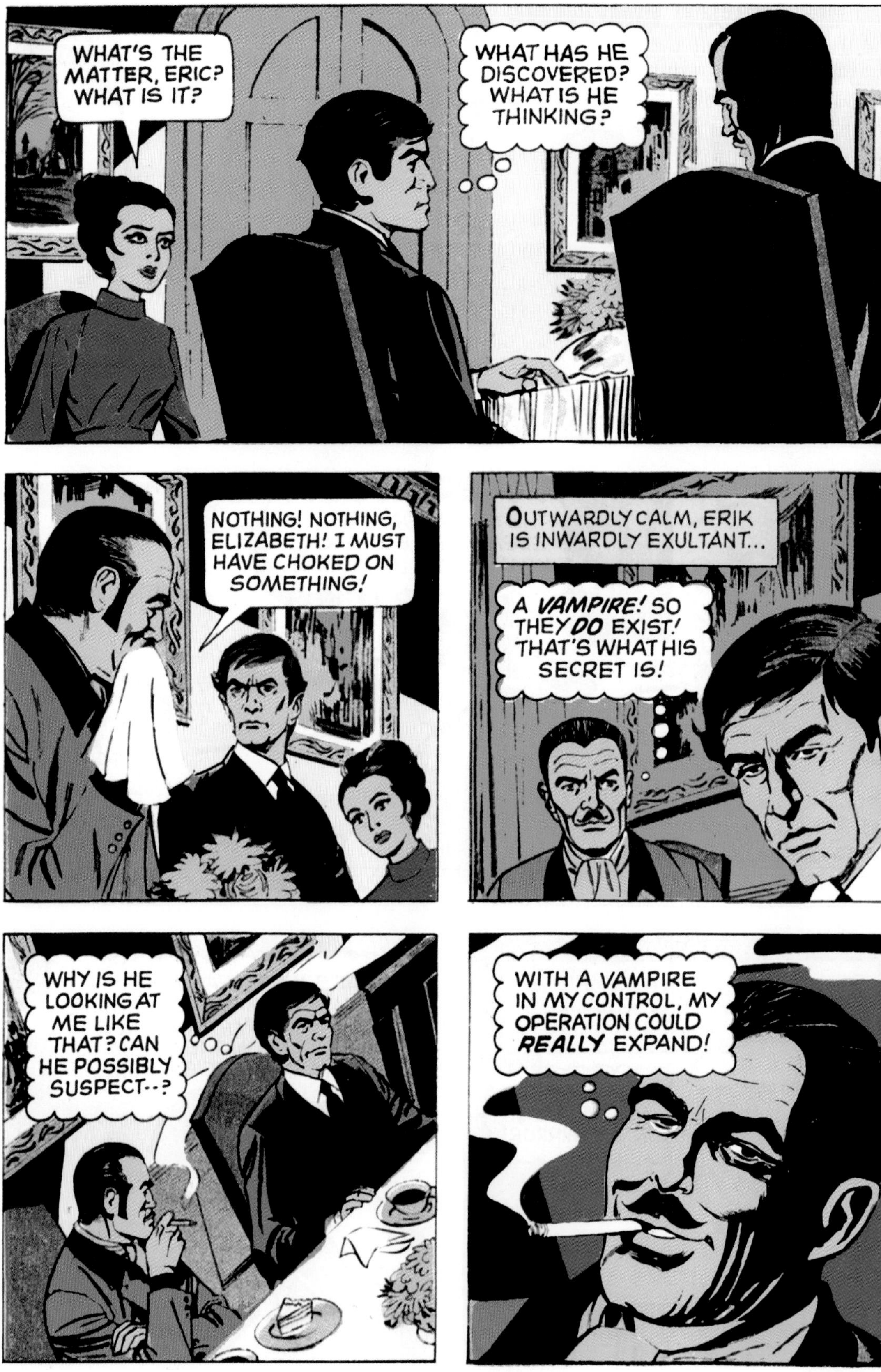
WHAT'S THE MATTER, ERIC? WHAT IS IT?
WHAT HAS HE DISCOVERED? WHAT IS HE THINKING?
NOTHING! NOTHING, ELIZABETH! I MUST HAVE CHOKED ON SOMETHING!
OUTWARDLY CALM, ERIK IS INWARDLY EXULTANT...
A VAMPIRE! SO THEY DO EXIST! THAT'S WHAT HIS SECRET IS!
WHY IS HE LOOKING AT ME LIKE THAT? CAN HE POSSIBLY SUSPECT--?
WITH A VAMPIRE IN MY CONTROL, MY OPERATION COULD REALLY EXPAND!

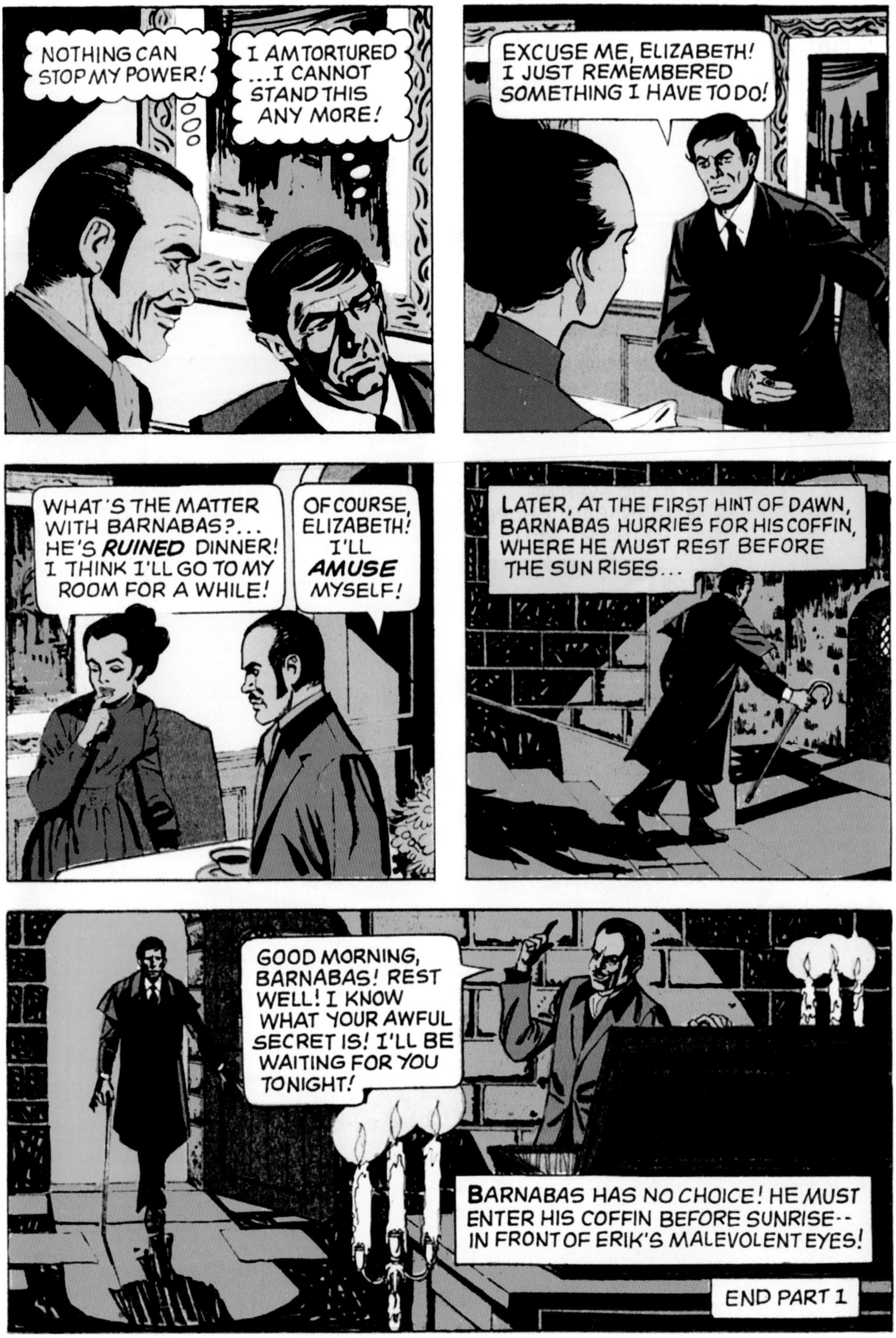
NOTHING CAN STOP MY POWER!
I AM TORTURED ...I CANNOT STAND THIS ANY MORE!
EXCUSE ME, ELIZABETH! I JUST REMEMBERED SOMETHING I HAVE TO DO!
WHAT'S THE MATTER WITH BARNABAS?... HE'S **RUINED** DINNER! I THINK I'LL GO TO MY ROOM FOR A WHILE!
OF COURSE, ELIZABETH! I'LL **AMUSE** MYSELF!
LATER, AT THE FIRST HINT OF DAWN, BARNABAS HURRIES FOR HIS COFFIN, WHERE HE MUST REST BEFORE THE SUN RISES...
GOOD MORNING, BARNABAS! REST WELL! I KNOW WHAT YOUR AWFUL SECRET IS! I'LL BE WAITING FOR YOU TONIGHT!
BARNABAS HAS NO CHOICE! HE MUST ENTER HIS COFFIN BEFORE SUNRISE-- IN FRONT OF ERIK'S MALEVOLENT EYES!
END PART 1

DARK SHADOWS' GUEST in the HOUSE

PART 2: A Second Visitor

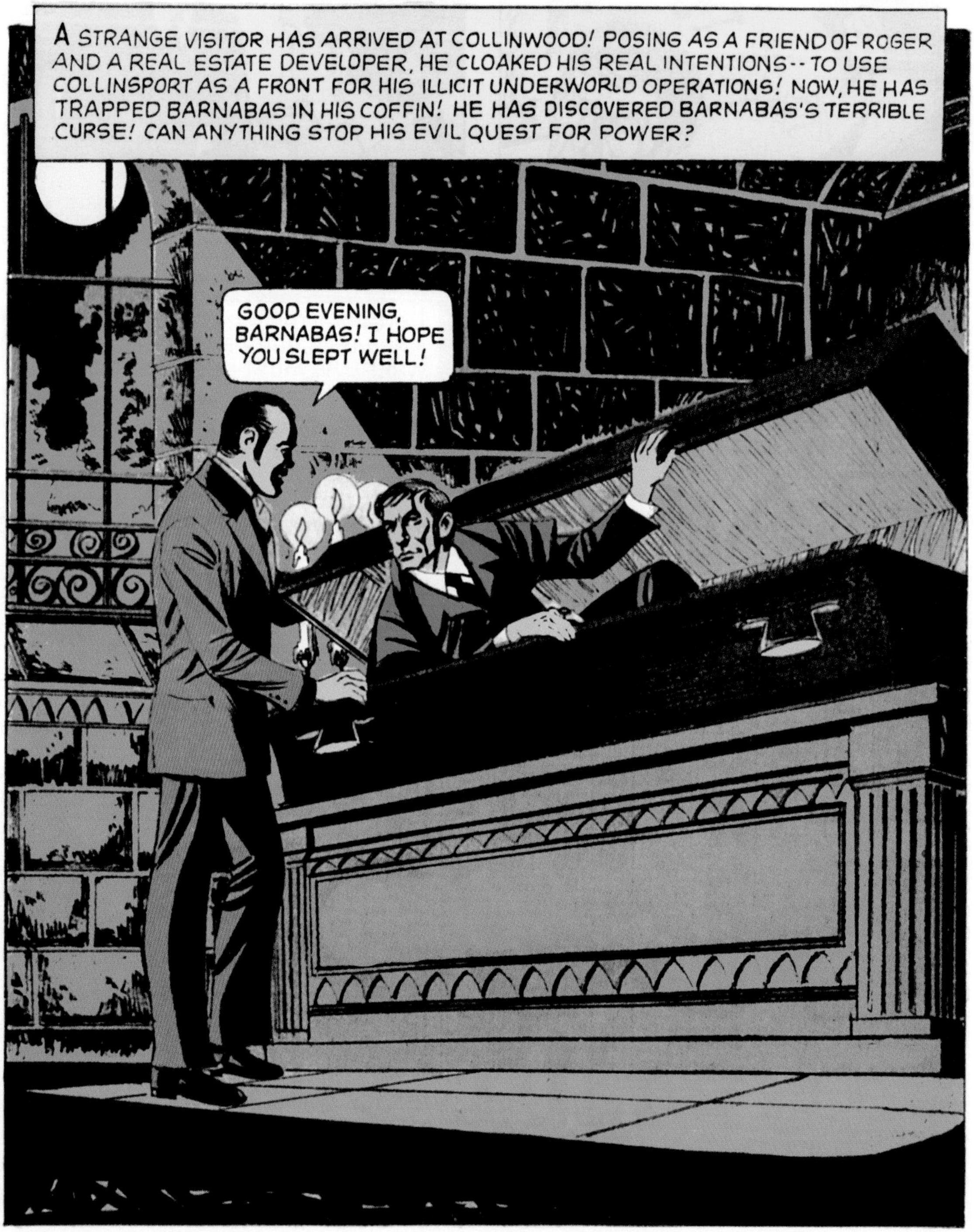
A STRANGE VISITOR HAS ARRIVED AT COLLINWOOD! POSING AS A FRIEND OF ROGER AND A REAL ESTATE DEVELOPER, HE CLOAKED HIS REAL INTENTIONS -- TO USE COLLINSPORT AS A FRONT FOR HIS ILLICIT UNDERWORLD OPERATIONS! NOW, HE HAS TRAPPED BARNABAS IN HIS COFFIN! HE HAS DISCOVERED BARNABAS'S TERRIBLE CURSE! CAN ANYTHING STOP HIS EVIL QUEST FOR POWER?
GOOD EVENING, BARNABAS! I HOPE YOU SLEPT WELL!

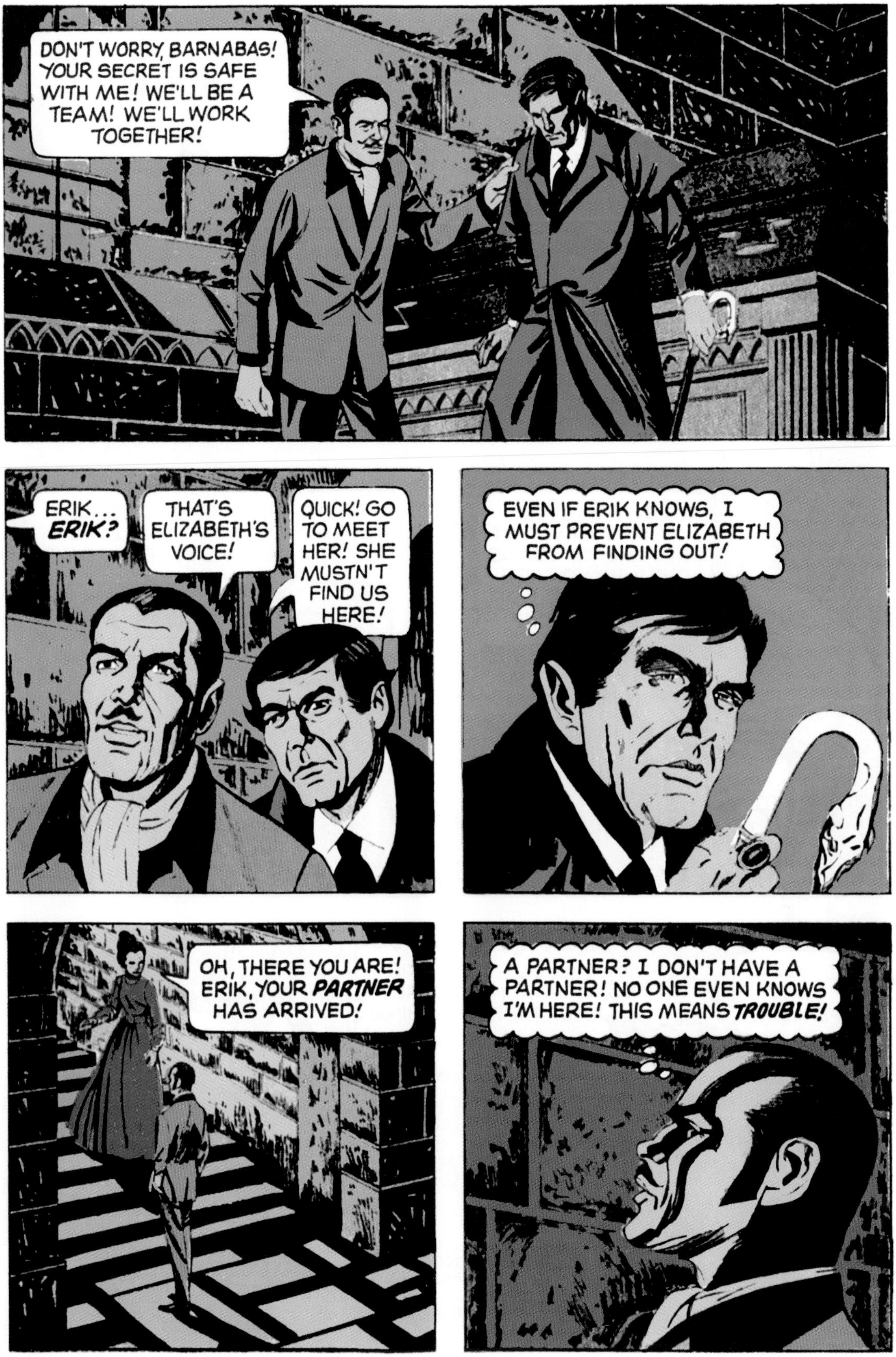
DON'T WORRY, BARNABAS! YOUR SECRET IS SAFE WITH ME! WE'LL BE A TEAM! WE'LL WORK TOGETHER!
ERIK... ERIK?
THAT'S ELIZABETH'S VOICE!
QUICK! GO TO MEET HER! SHE MUSTN'T FIND US HERE!
EVEN IF ERIK KNOWS, I MUST PREVENT ELIZABETH FROM FINDING OUT!
OH, THERE YOU ARE! ERIK, YOUR PARTNER HAS ARRIVED!
A PARTNER? I DON'T HAVE A PARTNER! NO ONE EVEN KNOWS I'M HERE! THIS MEANS TROUBLE!

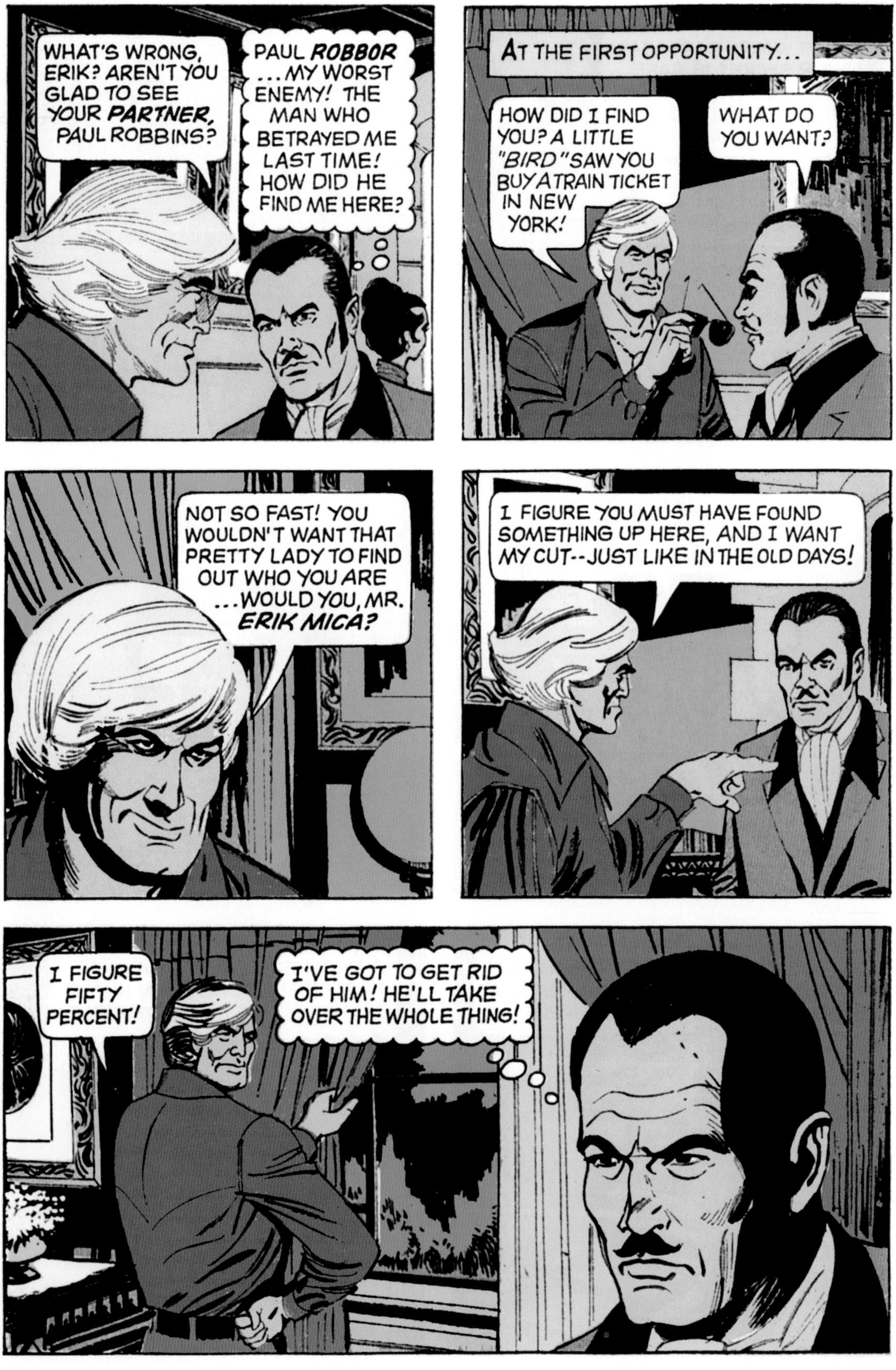
WHAT'S WRONG, ERIK? AREN'T YOU GLAD TO SEE YOUR PARTNER, PAUL ROBBINS?
PAUL ROBBOR ...MY WORST ENEMY! THE MAN WHO BETRAYED ME LAST TIME! HOW DID HE FIND ME HERE?
AT THE FIRST OPPORTUNITY...
HOW DID I FIND YOU? A LITTLE "BIRD" SAW YOU BUY A TRAIN TICKET IN NEW YORK!
WHAT DO YOU WANT?
NOT SO FAST! YOU WOULDN'T WANT THAT PRETTY LADY TO FIND OUT WHO YOU ARE ...WOULD YOU, MR. ERIK MICA?
I FIGURE YOU MUST HAVE FOUND SOMETHING UP HERE, AND I WANT MY CUT--JUST LIKE IN THE OLD DAYS!
I FIGURE FIFTY PERCENT!
I'VE GOT TO GET RID OF HIM! HE'LL TAKE OVER THE WHOLE THING!

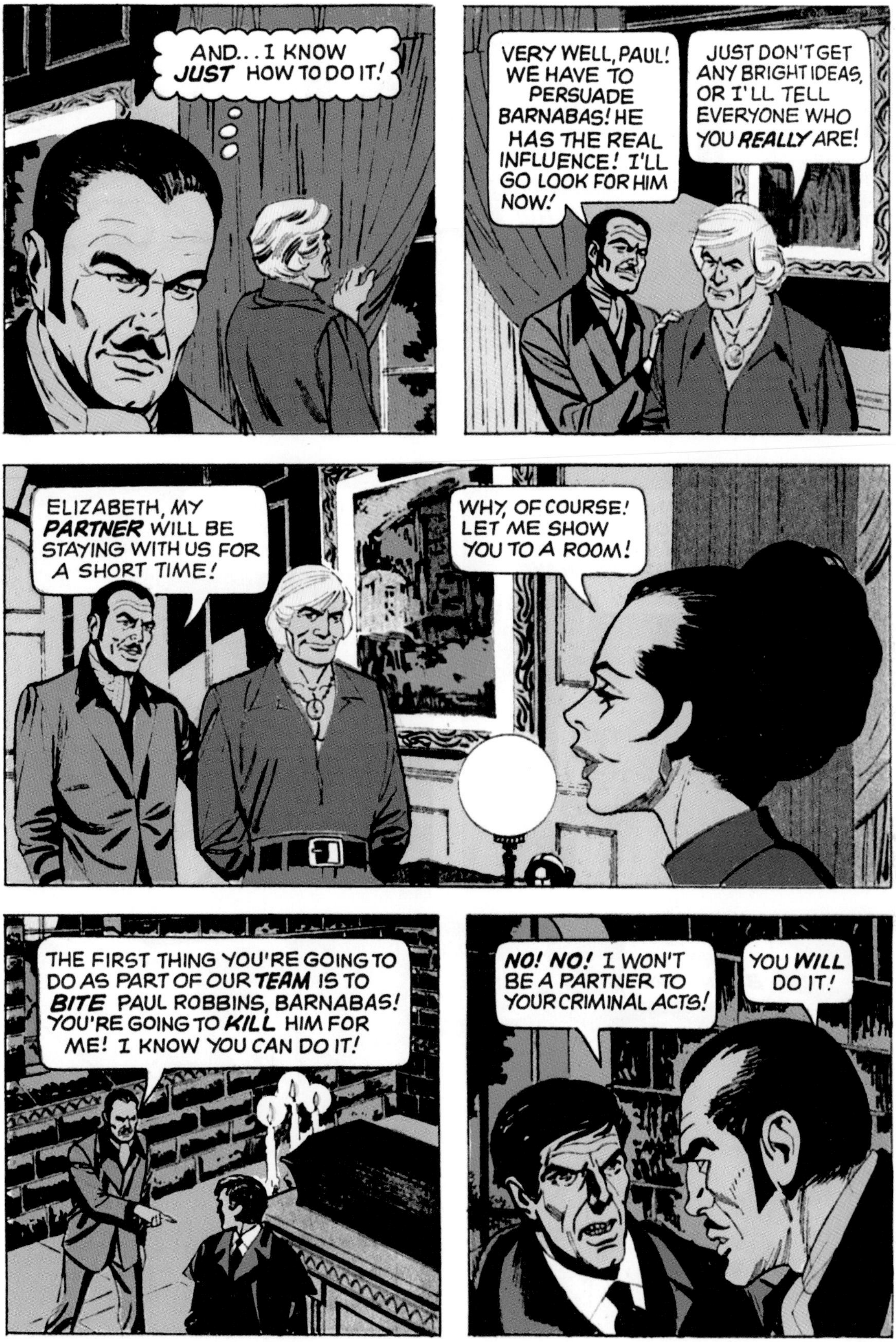
AND...I KNOW JUST HOW TO DO IT!
VERY WELL, PAUL! WE HAVE TO PERSUADE BARNABAS! HE HAS THE REAL INFLUENCE! I'LL GO LOOK FOR HIM NOW!
JUST DON'T GET ANY BRIGHT IDEAS, OR I'LL TELL EVERYONE WHO YOU REALLY ARE!
ELIZABETH, MY PARTNER WILL BE STAYING WITH US FOR A SHORT TIME!
WHY, OF COURSE! LET ME SHOW YOU TO A ROOM!
THE FIRST THING YOU'RE GOING TO DO AS PART OF OUR TEAM IS TO BITE PAUL ROBBINS, BARNABAS! YOU'RE GOING TO KILL HIM FOR ME! I KNOW YOU CAN DO IT!
NO! NO! I WON'T BE A PARTNER TO YOUR CRIMINAL ACTS!
YOU WILL DO IT!

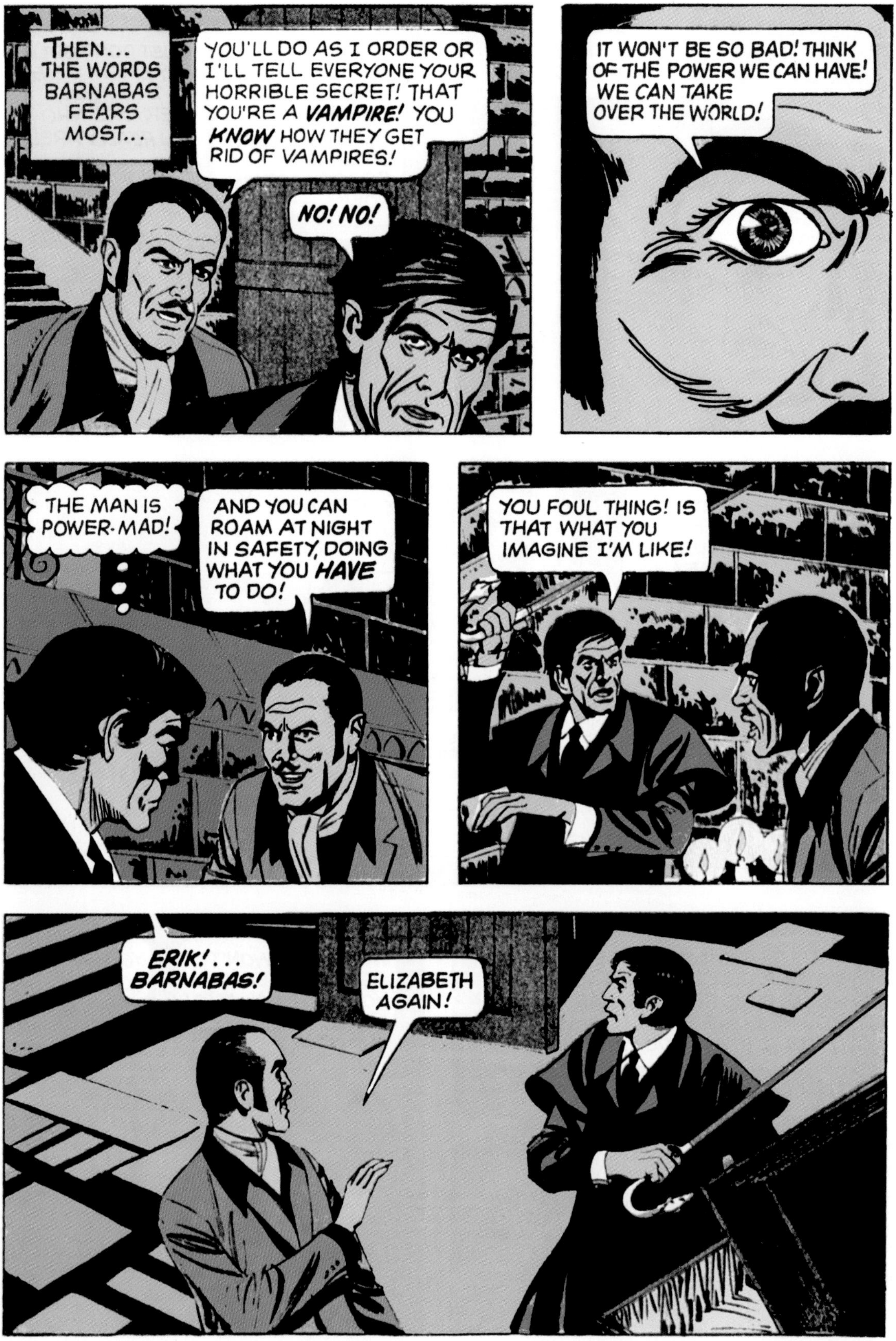
THEN... THE WORDS BARNABAS FEARS MOST...
YOU'LL DO AS I ORDER OR I'LL TELL EVERYONE YOUR HORRIBLE SECRET! THAT YOU'RE A VAMPIRE! YOU KNOW HOW THEY GET RID OF VAMPIRES!
NO! NO!
IT WON'T BE SO BAD! THINK OF THE POWER WE CAN HAVE! WE CAN TAKE OVER THE WORLD!
THE MAN IS POWER-MAD!
AND YOU CAN ROAM AT NIGHT IN SAFETY, DOING WHAT YOU HAVE TO DO!
YOU FOUL THING! IS THAT WHAT YOU IMAGINE I'M LIKE!
ERIK!... BARNABAS!
ELIZABETH AGAIN!

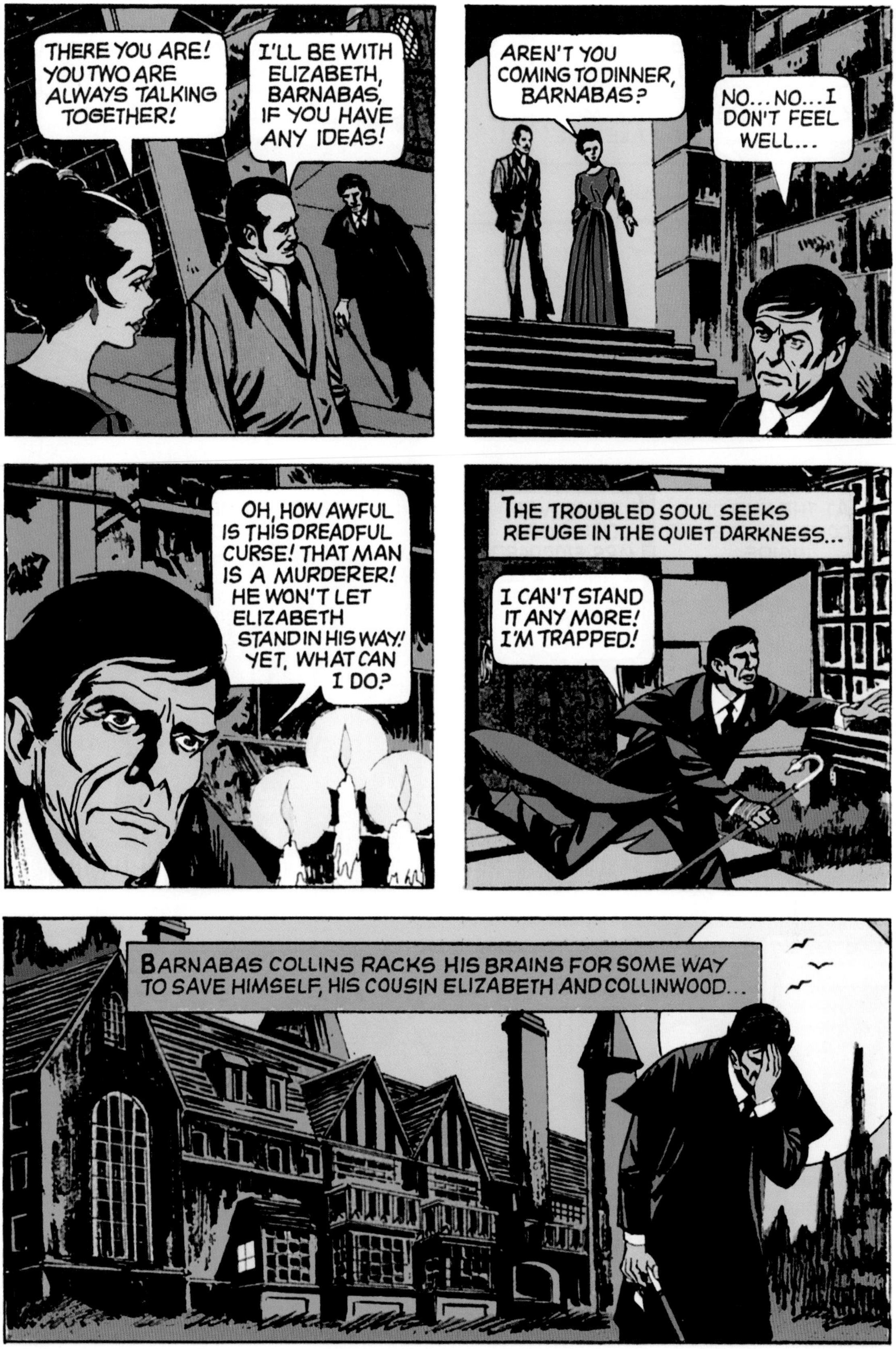
THERE YOU ARE! YOU TWO ARE ALWAYS TALKING TOGETHER!
I'LL BE WITH ELIZABETH, BARNABAS, IF YOU HAVE ANY IDEAS!
AREN'T YOU COMING TO DINNER, BARNABAS?
NO... NO... I DON'T FEEL WELL...
OH, HOW AWFUL IS THIS DREADFUL CURSE! THAT MAN IS A MURDERER! HE WON'T LET ELIZABETH STAND IN HIS WAY! YET, WHAT CAN I DO?
THE TROUBLED SOUL SEEKS REFUGE IN THE QUIET DARKNESS...
I CAN'T STAND IT ANY MORE! I'M TRAPPED!
BARNABAS COLLINS RACKS HIS BRAINS FOR SOME WAY TO SAVE HIMSELF, HIS COUSIN ELIZABETH AND COLLINWOOD...

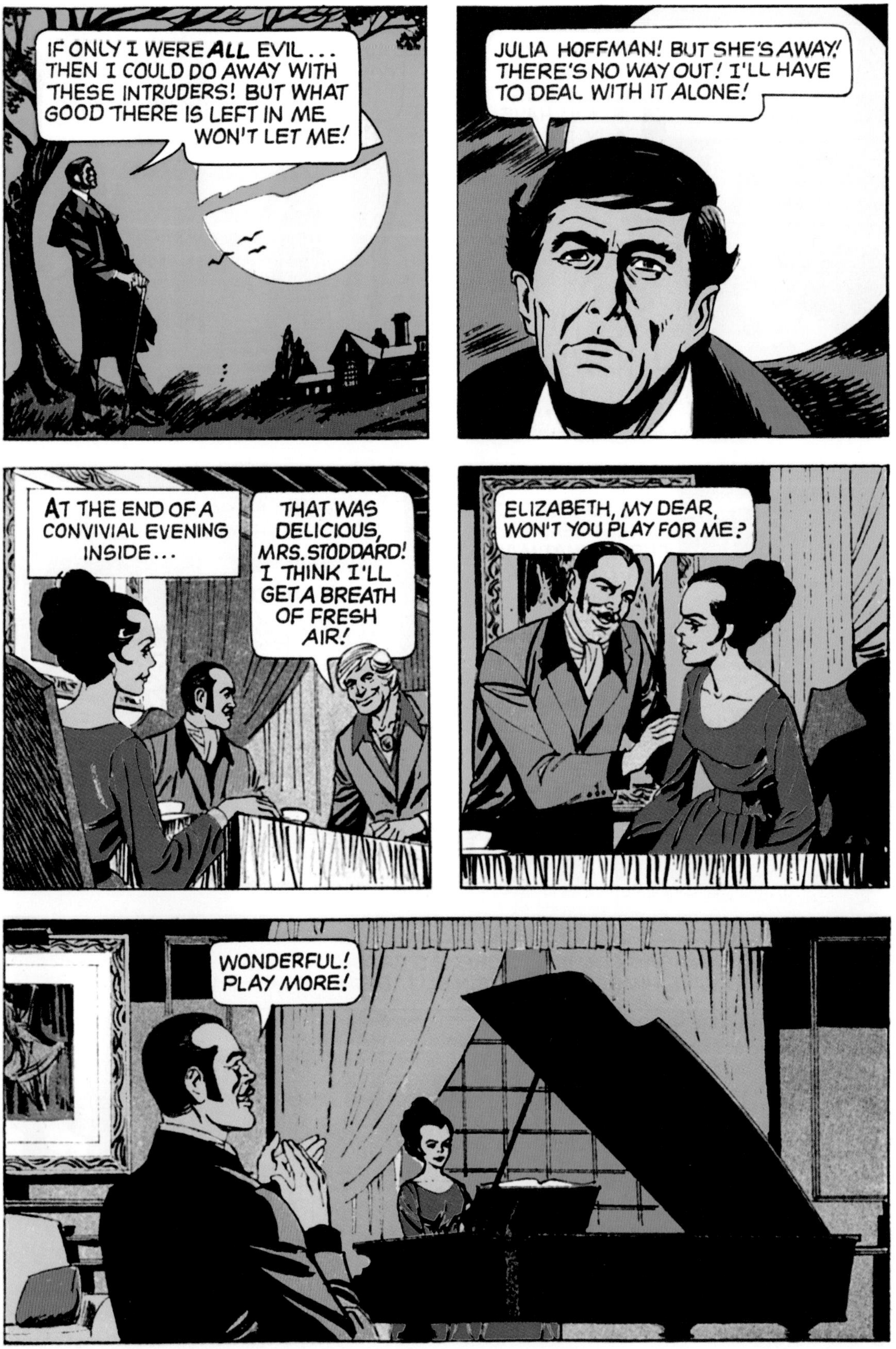
IF ONLY I WERE ALL EVIL... THEN I COULD DO AWAY WITH THESE INTRUDERS! BUT WHAT GOOD THERE IS LEFT IN ME WON'T LET ME!
JULIA HOFFMAN! BUT SHE'S AWAY! THERE'S NO WAY OUT! I'LL HAVE TO DEAL WITH IT ALONE!
AT THE END OF A CONVIVIAL EVENING INSIDE...
THAT WAS DELICIOUS, MRS. STODDARD! I THINK I'LL GET A BREATH OF FRESH AIR!
ELIZABETH, MY DEAR, WON'T YOU PLAY FOR ME?
WONDERFUL! PLAY MORE!

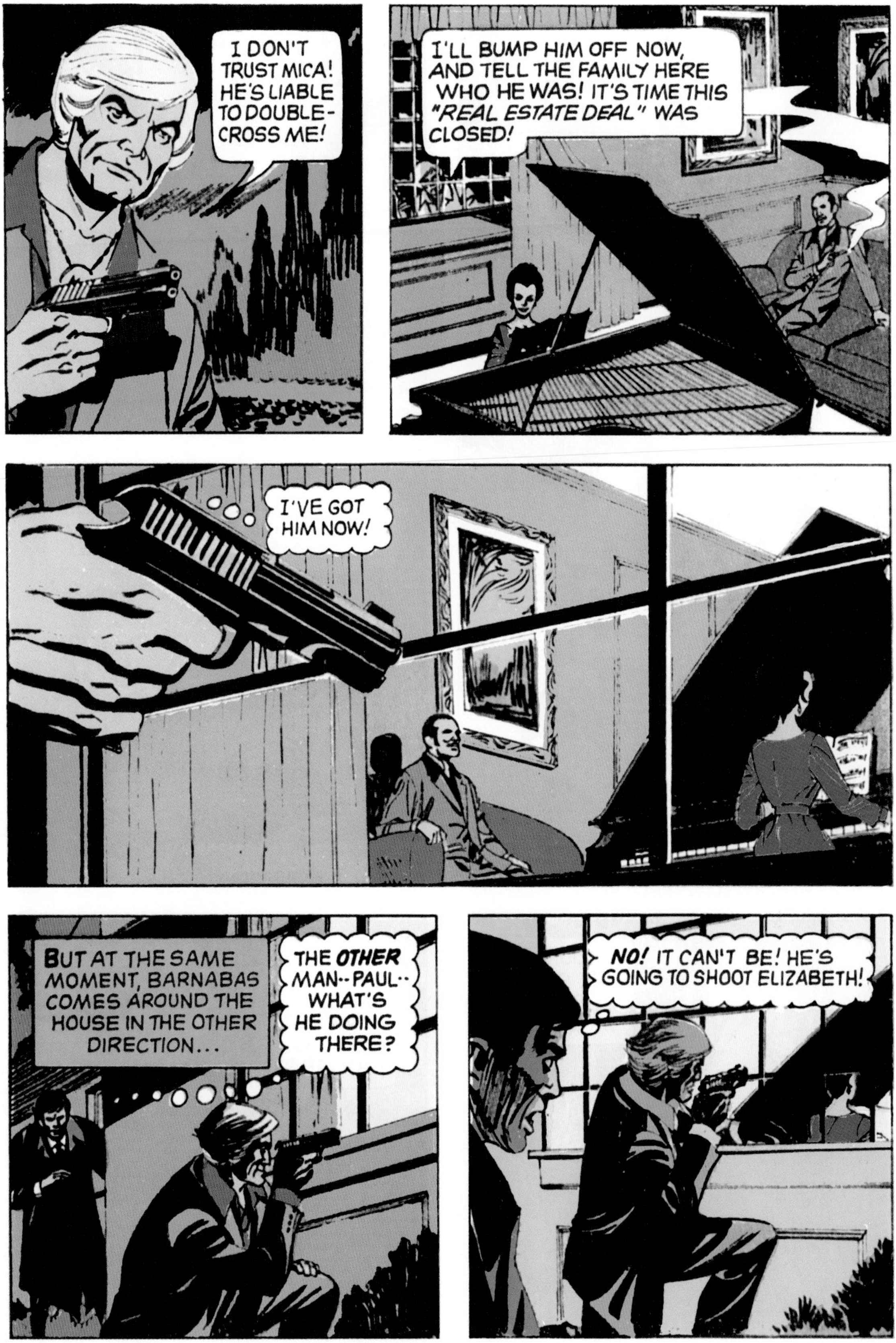
I DON'T TRUST MICA! HE'S LIABLE TO DOUBLE-CROSS ME!
I'LL BUMP HIM OFF NOW, AND TELL THE FAMILY HERE WHO HE WAS! IT'S TIME THIS "REAL ESTATE DEAL" WAS CLOSED!
I'VE GOT HIM NOW!
BUT AT THE SAME MOMENT, BARNABAS COMES AROUND THE HOUSE IN THE OTHER DIRECTION...
THE OTHER MAN--PAUL-- WHAT'S HE DOING THERE?
NO! IT CAN'T BE! HE'S GOING TO SHOOT ELIZABETH!

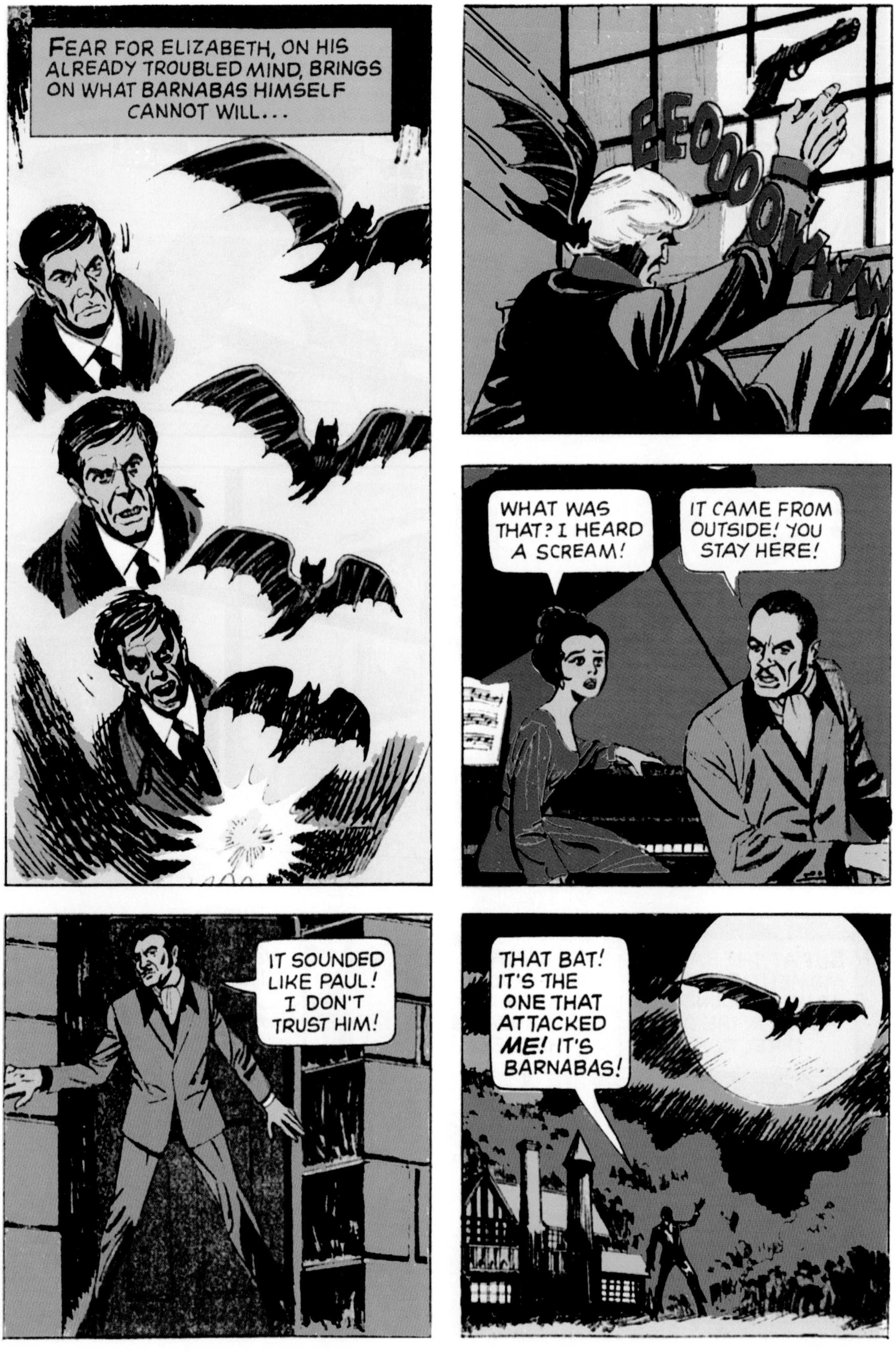
FEAR FOR ELIZABETH, ON HIS ALREADY TROUBLED MIND, BRINGS ON WHAT BARNABAS HIMSELF CANNOT WILL...
EEOOOOOWWW
WHAT WAS THAT? I HEARD A SCREAM!
IT CAME FROM OUTSIDE! YOU STAY HERE!
IT SOUNDED LIKE PAUL! I DON'T TRUST HIM!
THAT BAT! IT'S THE ONE THAT ATTACKED ME! IT'S BARNABAS!

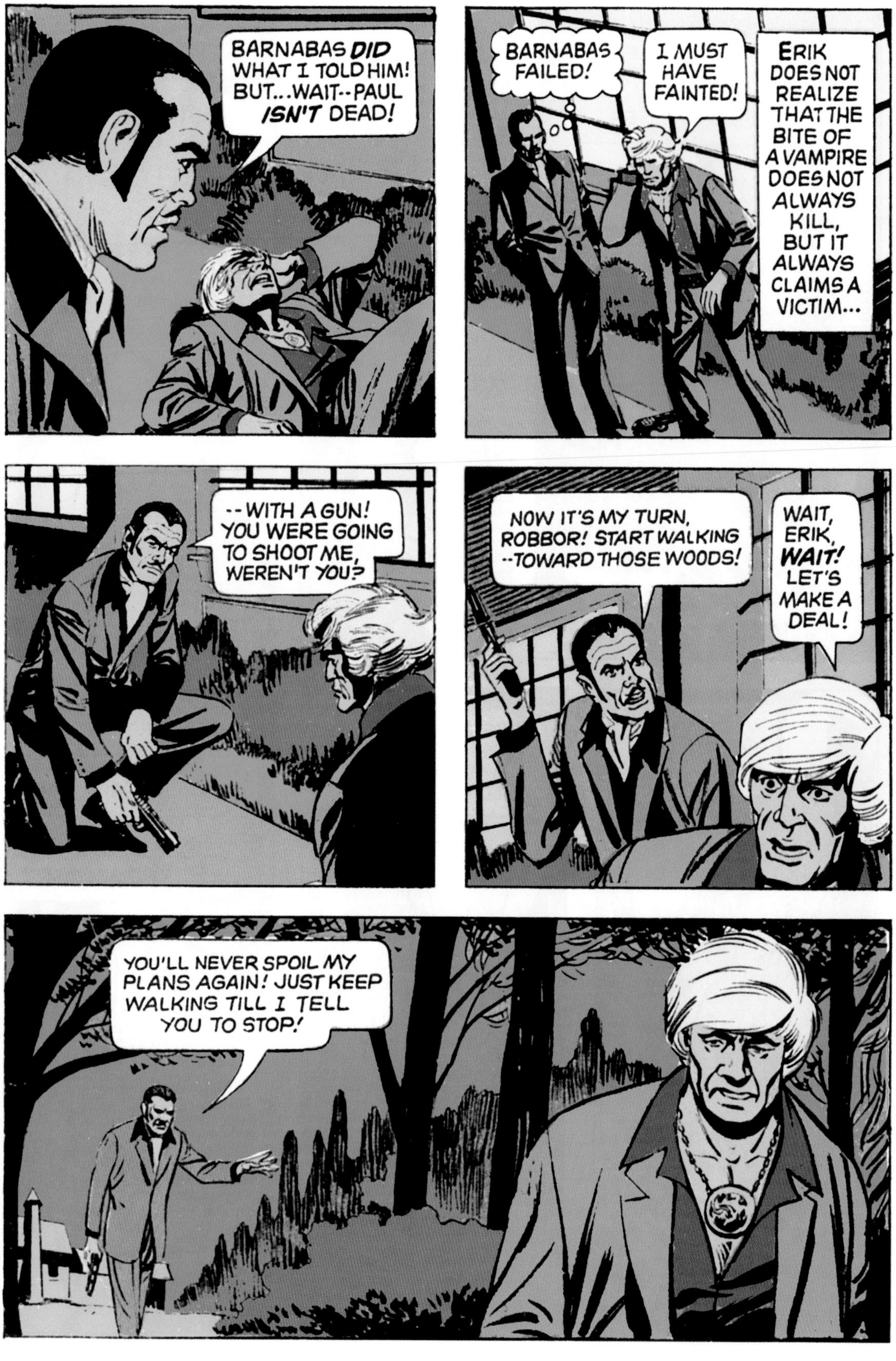

BARNABAS *DID* WHAT I TOLD HIM! BUT...WAIT--PAUL *ISN'T* DEAD!
BARNABAS FAILED!
I MUST HAVE FAINTED!
ERIK DOES NOT REALIZE THAT THE BITE OF A VAMPIRE DOES NOT ALWAYS KILL, BUT IT ALWAYS CLAIMS A VICTIM...
--WITH A GUN! YOU WERE GOING TO SHOOT ME, WEREN'T YOU?
NOW IT'S MY TURN, ROBBOR! START WALKING --TOWARD THOSE WOODS!
WAIT, ERIK, *WAIT!* LET'S MAKE A DEAL!
YOU'LL NEVER SPOIL MY PLANS AGAIN! JUST KEEP WALKING TILL I TELL YOU TO STOP!

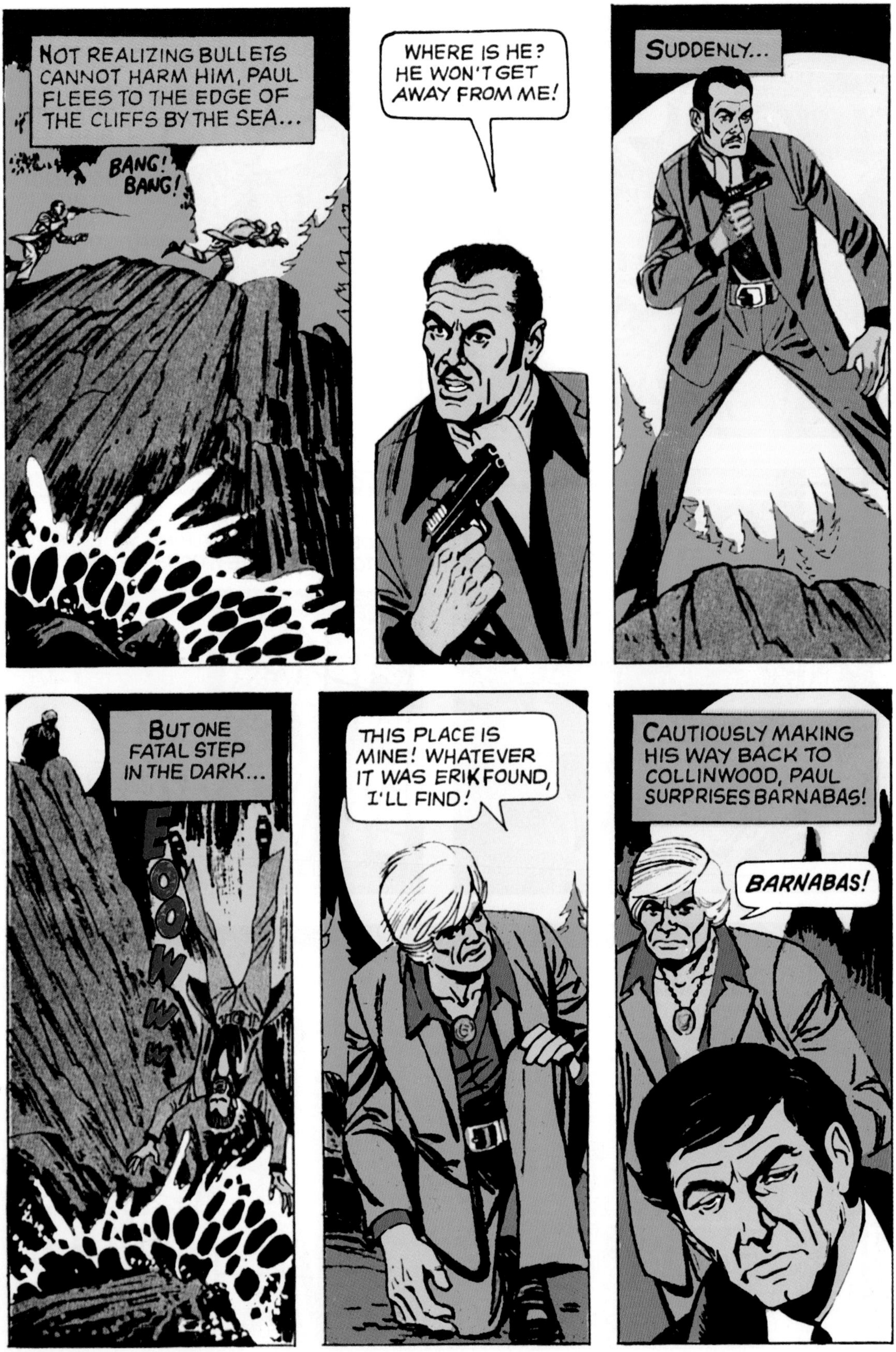
NOT REALIZING BULLETS CANNOT HARM HIM, PAUL FLEES TO THE EDGE OF THE CLIFFS BY THE SEA...
BANG! BANG!
WHERE IS HE? HE WON'T GET AWAY FROM ME!
SUDDENLY...
BUT ONE FATAL STEP IN THE DARK...
EEOOOWWW
THIS PLACE IS MINE! WHATEVER IT WAS ERIK FOUND, I'LL FIND!
CAUTIOUSLY MAKING HIS WAY BACK TO COLLINWOOD, PAUL SURPRISES BARNABAS!
BARNABAS!

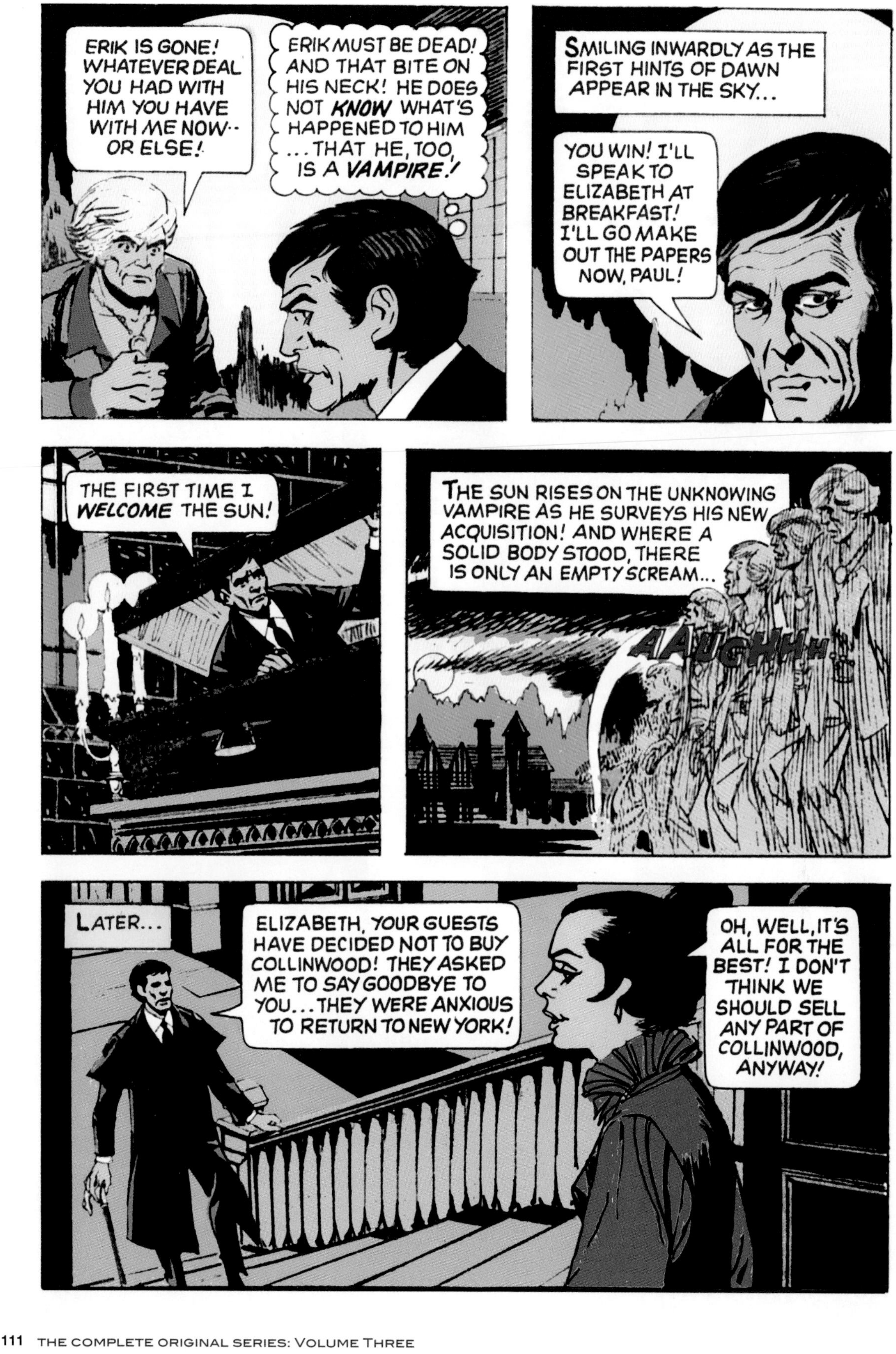
ERIK IS GONE! WHATEVER DEAL YOU HAD WITH HIM YOU HAVE WITH ME NOW-- OR ELSE!
ERIK MUST BE DEAD! AND THAT BITE ON HIS NECK! HE DOES NOT KNOW WHAT'S HAPPENED TO HIM ...THAT HE, TOO, IS A VAMPIRE!
SMILING INWARDLY AS THE FIRST HINTS OF DAWN APPEAR IN THE SKY...
YOU WIN! I'LL SPEAK TO ELIZABETH AT BREAKFAST! I'LL GO MAKE OUT THE PAPERS NOW, PAUL!
THE FIRST TIME I WELCOME THE SUN!
THE SUN RISES ON THE UNKNOWING VAMPIRE AS HE SURVEYS HIS NEW ACQUISITION! AND WHERE A SOLID BODY STOOD, THERE IS ONLY AN EMPTY SCREAM...
AAUCHHH
LATER...
ELIZABETH, YOUR GUESTS HAVE DECIDED NOT TO BUY COLLINWOOD! THEY ASKED ME TO SAY GOODBYE TO YOU... THEY WERE ANXIOUS TO RETURN TO NEW YORK!
OH, WELL, IT'S ALL FOR THE BEST! I DON'T THINK WE SHOULD SELL ANY PART OF COLLINWOOD, ANYWAY!

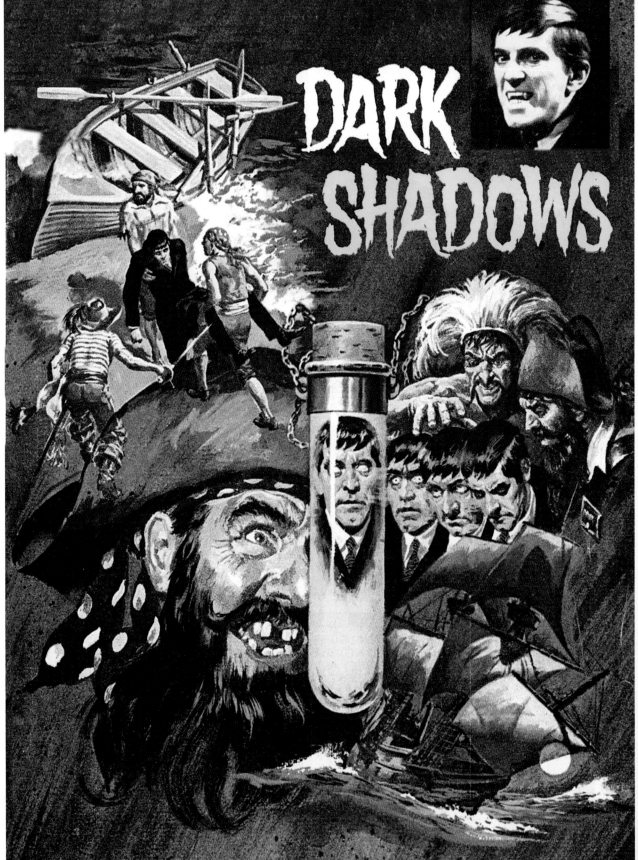

DARK SHADOWS

Pirates who have the secret of eternal life
condemn Barnabas to ETERNAL DOOM!

DARK SHADOWS ISLAND OF ETERNAL LIFE

PART 1: THE PHANTOM GALLEON

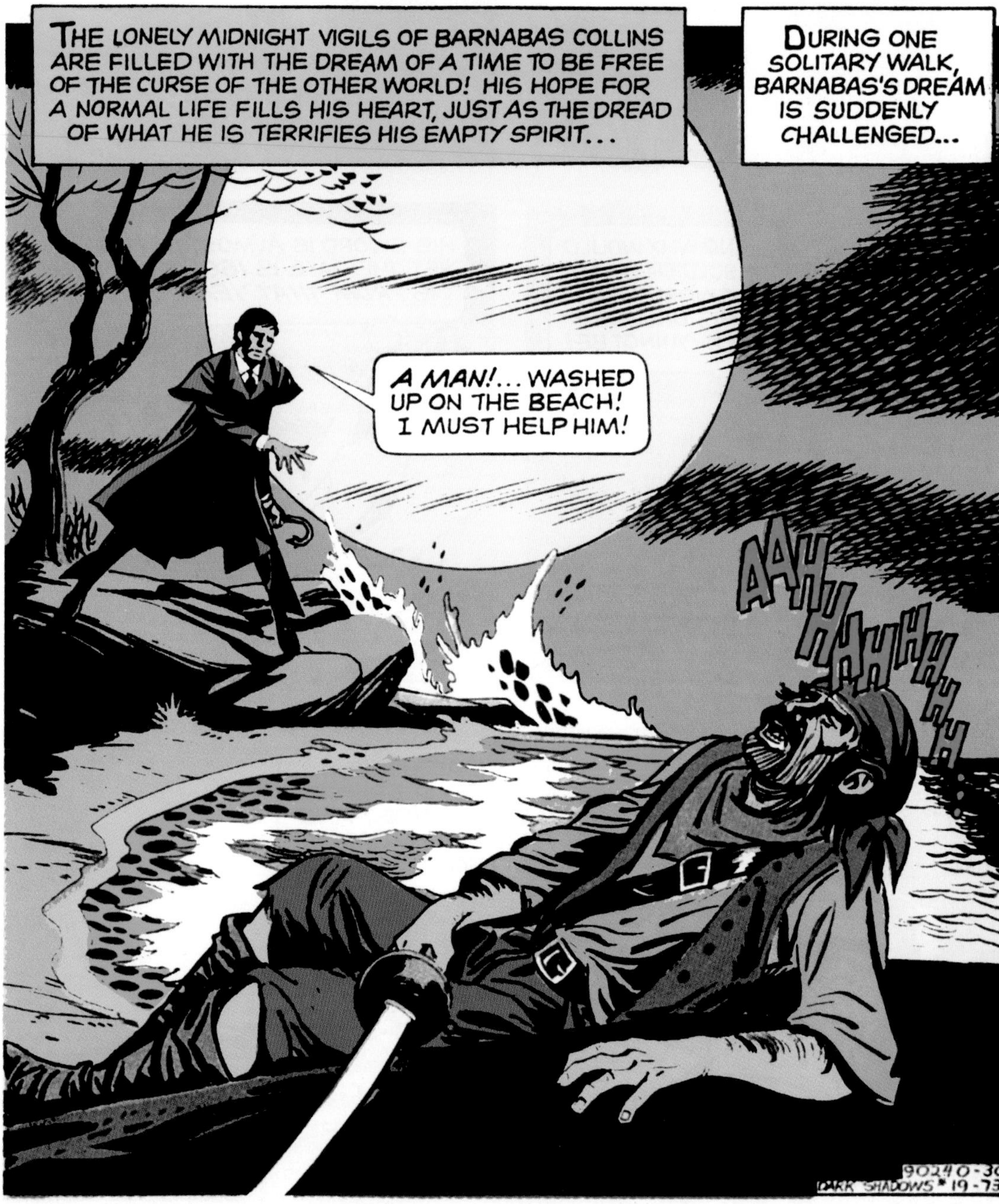

THE LONELY MIDNIGHT VIGILS OF BARNABAS COLLINS ARE FILLED WITH THE DREAM OF A TIME TO BE FREE OF THE CURSE OF THE OTHER WORLD! HIS HOPE FOR A NORMAL LIFE FILLS HIS HEART, JUST AS THE DREAD OF WHAT HE IS TERRIFIES HIS EMPTY SPIRIT...
DURING ONE SOLITARY WALK, BARNABAS'S DREAM IS SUDDENLY CHALLENGED...
A MAN!... WASHED UP ON THE BEACH! I MUST HELP HIM!
AAHHHHHHHHH

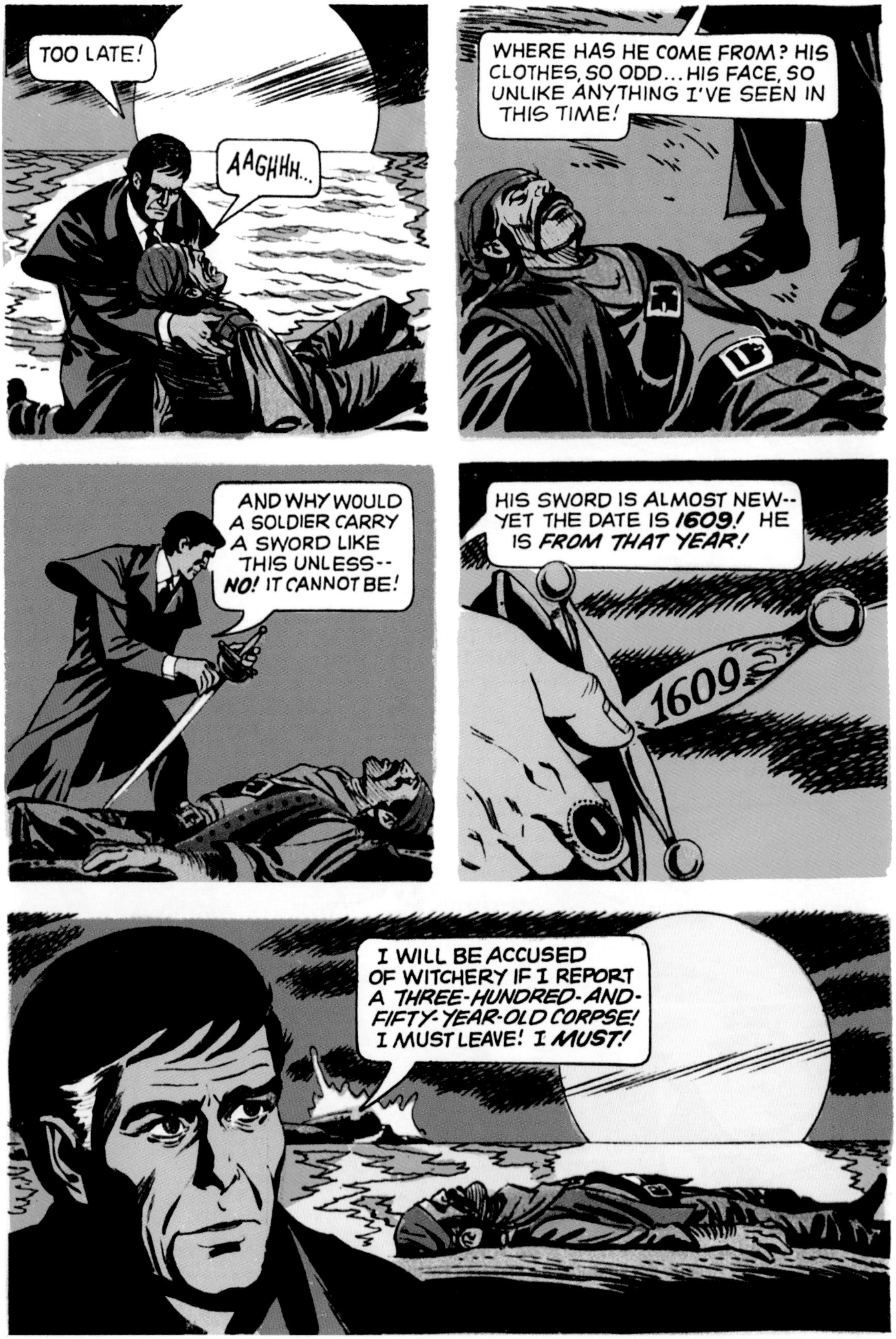
TOO LATE!
AAGHHH...
WHERE HAS HE COME FROM? HIS CLOTHES, SO ODD... HIS FACE, SO UNLIKE ANYTHING I'VE SEEN IN THIS TIME!
AND WHY WOULD A SOLDIER CARRY A SWORD LIKE THIS UNLESS-- NO! IT CANNOT BE!
HIS SWORD IS ALMOST NEW-- YET THE DATE IS 1609! HE IS FROM THAT YEAR!
1609
I WILL BE ACCUSED OF WITCHERY IF I REPORT A THREE-HUNDRED-AND-FIFTY-YEAR-OLD CORPSE! I MUST LEAVE! I MUST!

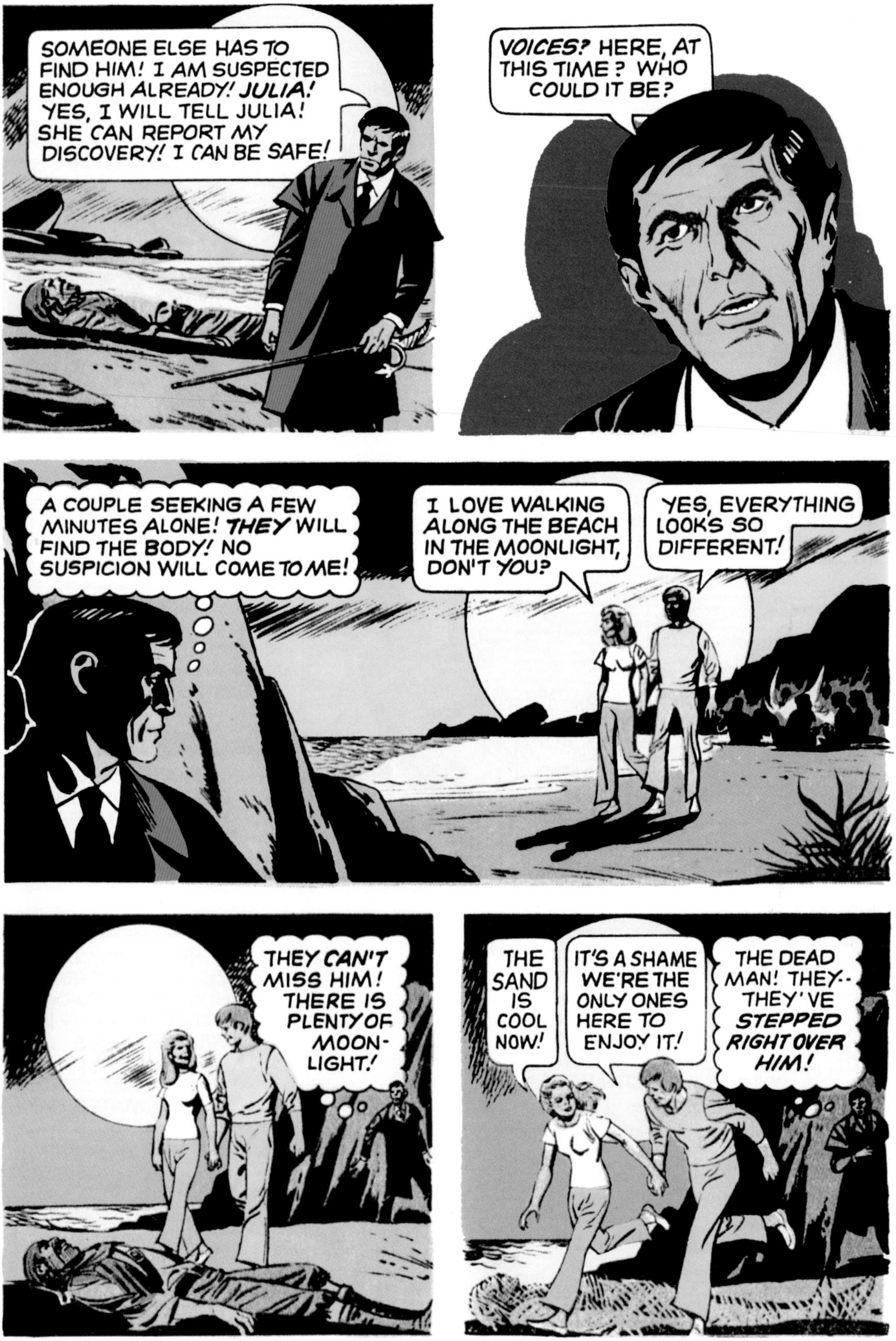
SOMEONE ELSE HAS TO FIND HIM! I AM SUSPECTED ENOUGH ALREADY! JULIA! YES, I WILL TELL JULIA! SHE CAN REPORT MY DISCOVERY! I CAN BE SAFE!
VOICES? HERE, AT THIS TIME? WHO COULD IT BE?
A COUPLE SEEKING A FEW MINUTES ALONE! THEY WILL FIND THE BODY! NO SUSPICION WILL COME TO ME!
I LOVE WALKING ALONG THE BEACH IN THE MOONLIGHT, DON'T YOU?
YES, EVERYTHING LOOKS SO DIFFERENT!
THEY CAN'T MISS HIM! THERE IS PLENTY OF MOON-LIGHT!
THE SAND IS COOL NOW!
IT'S A SHAME WE'RE THE ONLY ONES HERE TO ENJOY IT!
THE DEAD MAN! THEY-- THEY'VE STEPPED RIGHT OVER HIM!

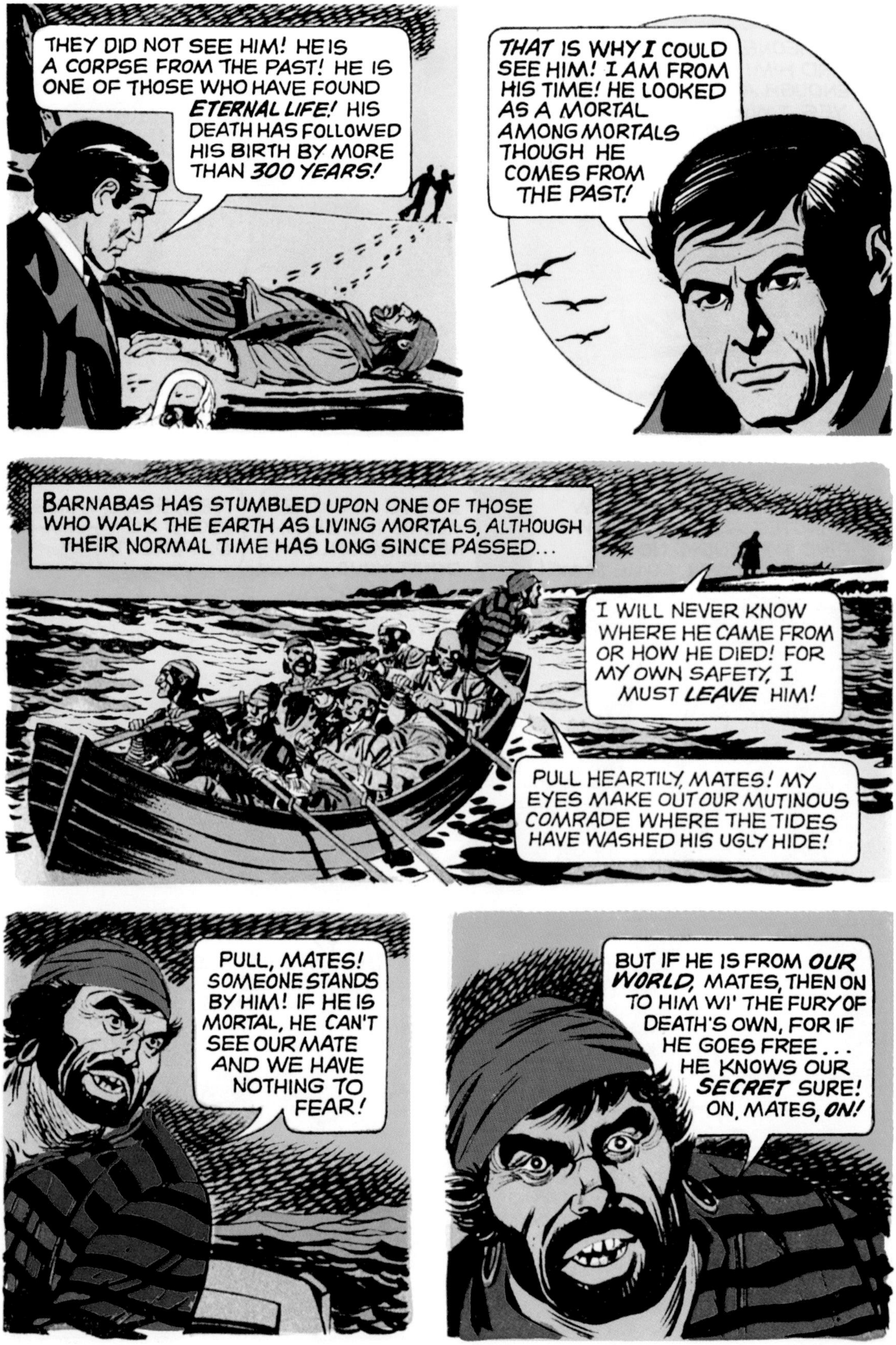
THEY DID NOT SEE HIM! HE IS A CORPSE FROM THE PAST! HE IS ONE OF THOSE WHO HAVE FOUND ETERNAL LIFE! HIS DEATH HAS FOLLOWED HIS BIRTH BY MORE THAN 300 YEARS!
THAT IS WHY I COULD SEE HIM! I AM FROM HIS TIME! HE LOOKED AS A MORTAL AMONG MORTALS THOUGH HE COMES FROM THE PAST!
BARNABAS HAS STUMBLED UPON ONE OF THOSE WHO WALK THE EARTH AS LIVING MORTALS, ALTHOUGH THEIR NORMAL TIME HAS LONG SINCE PASSED...
I WILL NEVER KNOW WHERE HE CAME FROM OR HOW HE DIED! FOR MY OWN SAFETY, I MUST LEAVE HIM!
PULL HEARTILY, MATES! MY EYES MAKE OUT OUR MUTINOUS COMRADE WHERE THE TIDES HAVE WASHED HIS UGLY HIDE!
PULL, MATES! SOMEONE STANDS BY HIM! IF HE IS MORTAL, HE CAN'T SEE OUR MATE AND WE HAVE NOTHING TO FEAR!
BUT IF HE IS FROM OUR WORLD, MATES, THEN ON TO HIM WI' THE FURY OF DEATH'S OWN, FOR IF HE GOES FREE... HE KNOWS OUR SECRET SURE! ON, MATES, ON!

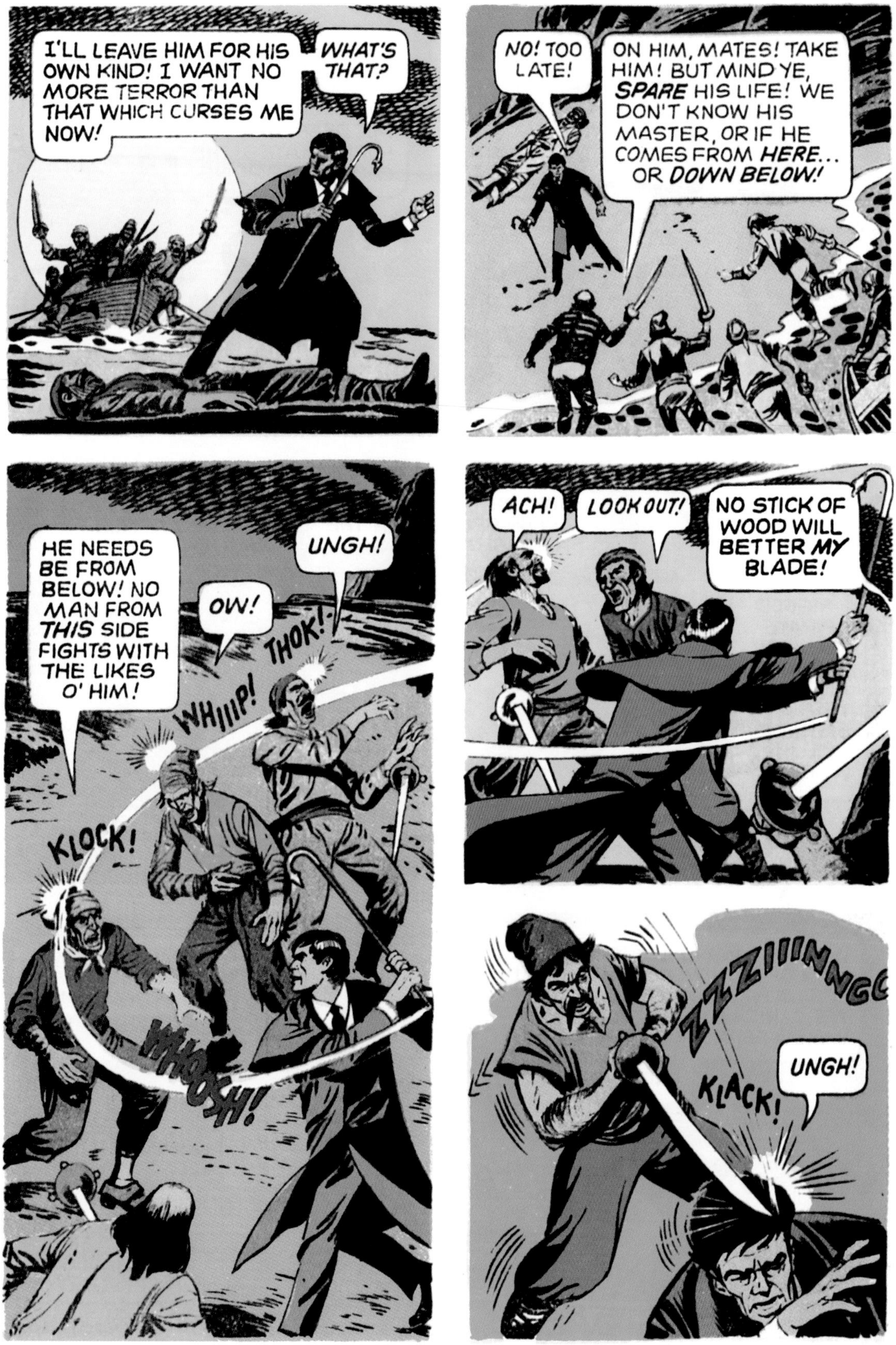
I'LL LEAVE HIM FOR HIS OWN KIND! I WANT NO MORE TERROR THAN THAT WHICH CURSES ME NOW!
WHAT'S THAT?
NO! TOO LATE!
ON HIM, MATES! TAKE HIM! BUT MIND YE, SPARE HIS LIFE! WE DON'T KNOW HIS MASTER, OR IF HE COMES FROM HERE... OR DOWN BELOW!
HE NEEDS BE FROM BELOW! NO MAN FROM THIS SIDE FIGHTS WITH THE LIKES O' HIM!
OW!
UNGH!
THOK!
WHIIIP!
KLOCK!
WHOOSH!
ACH!
LOOK OUT!
NO STICK OF WOOD WILL BETTER MY BLADE!
ZZZIIIINNGG
KLACK!
UNGH!

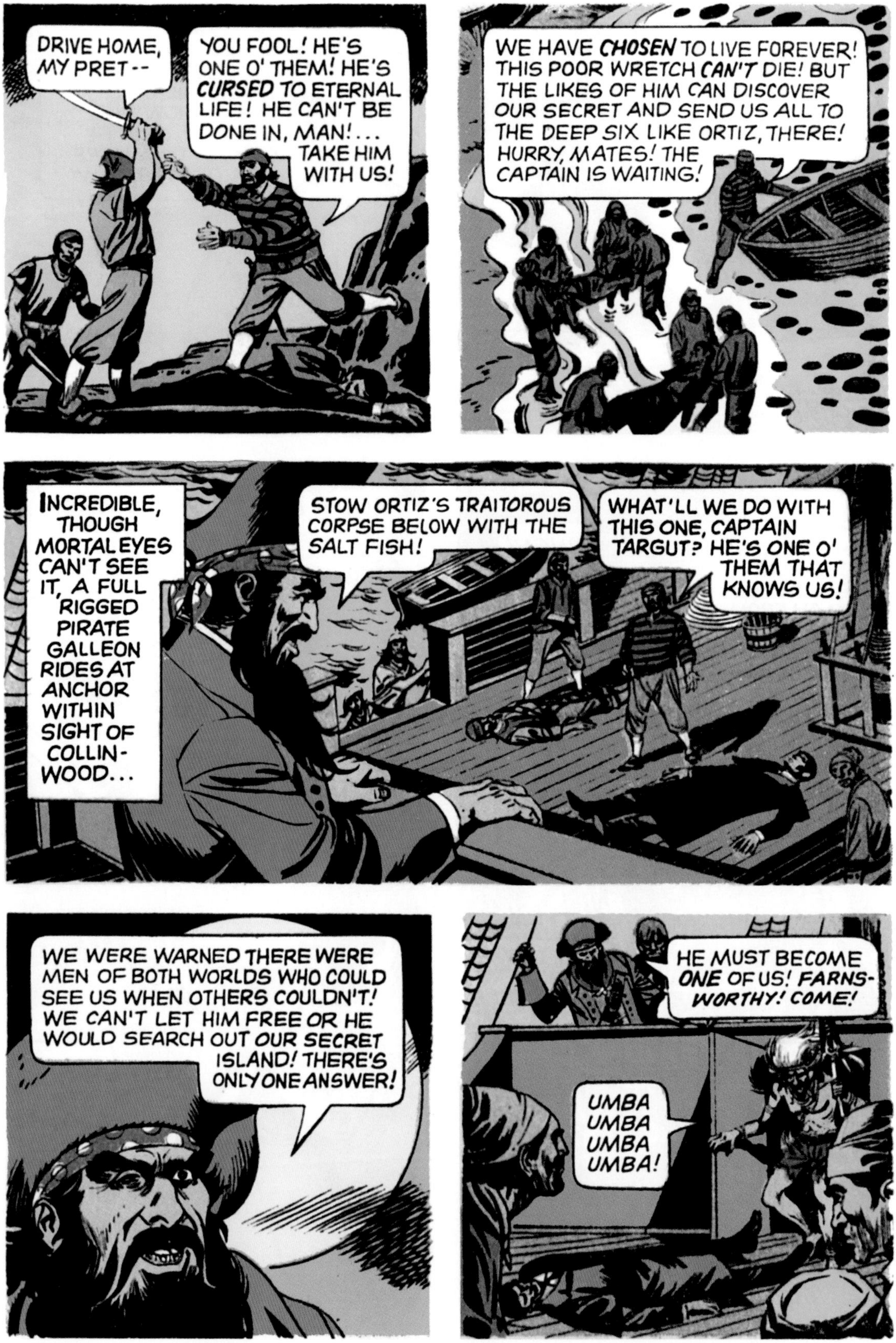
DRIVE HOME, MY PRET--
YOU FOOL! HE'S ONE O' THEM! HE'S CURSED TO ETERNAL LIFE! HE CAN'T BE DONE IN, MAN!... TAKE HIM WITH US!
WE HAVE CHOSEN TO LIVE FOREVER! THIS POOR WRETCH CAN'T DIE! BUT THE LIKES OF HIM CAN DISCOVER OUR SECRET AND SEND US ALL TO THE DEEP SIX LIKE ORTIZ, THERE! HURRY, MATES! THE CAPTAIN IS WAITING!
INCREDIBLE, THOUGH MORTAL EYES CAN'T SEE IT, A FULL RIGGED PIRATE GALLEON RIDES AT ANCHOR WITHIN SIGHT OF COLLIN-WOOD...
STOW ORTIZ'S TRAITOROUS CORPSE BELOW WITH THE SALT FISH!
WHAT'LL WE DO WITH THIS ONE, CAPTAIN TARGUT? HE'S ONE O' THEM THAT KNOWS US!
WE WERE WARNED THERE WERE MEN OF BOTH WORLDS WHO COULD SEE US WHEN OTHERS COULDN'T! WE CAN'T LET HIM FREE OR HE WOULD SEARCH OUT OUR SECRET ISLAND! THERE'S ONLY ONE ANSWER!
HE MUST BECOME ONE OF US! FARNS-WORTHY! COME!
UMBA UMBA UMBA UMBA!

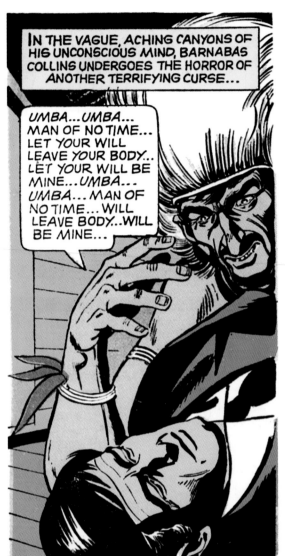

IN THE VAGUE, ACHING CANYONS OF HIS UNCONSCIOUS MIND, BARNABAS COLLINS UNDERGOES THE HORROR OF ANOTHER TERRIFYING CURSE...

UMBA...UMBA... MAN OF NO TIME... LET YOUR WILL LEAVE YOUR BODY... LET YOUR WILL BE MINE...UMBA... UMBA... MAN OF NO TIME... WILL LEAVE BODY...WILL BE MINE...

HIS PAST IS GONE, CAPTAIN! HIS FORMER LIFE MEANS NOTHING! WHOEVER HE WAS, WHATEVER HE WAS, HIS WILL IS NOW IN THIS VIAL...IT IS YOURS, CAPTAIN!

GOOD WORK, FARNS- WORTHY! YOU'VE LEARNED OUR ISLAND'S SECRETS WELL!

GET UP! YOUR WILL IS NO LONGER YOURS! GET UP AND MEET YOUR NEW CAPTAIN!

WH-WHERE IS THIS PLACE? WHO ARE YOU?

YOU KNOW THIS PLACE BETTER THAN I, STRANGE ONE! IS THAT NOT YOUR HOME?

YES, I COME FROM THERE! BUT...WHERE DO YOU COME FROM?

HO HO HO! THAT, MY NEW FRIEND, IS ANOTHER QUESTION! MAKE SAIL! THE TIDE IS WITH US! YOU SHALL SEE! YOU SHALL SEE, STRANGE ONE! HO HO HO!

UNSEEN, YET IN FULL VIEW OF COLLINWOOD, A GALLEON OF ANOTHER AGE UNFURLS ITS SAIL AND CATCHES THE MORNING WINDS FOR PARTS... UNKNOWN...

NO! THE SUN! YOU MUST FREE ME! I MUST NOT BE LEFT TO PERISH IN THE RAYS OF THE MORNING SUN!

THE SUN? WHAT OF THE SUN?

HO HO! SO YOU ARE ONE OF THEM! FEAR NOT, CREATURE OF NIGHT! AS LONG AS YOUR WILL REMAINS IN THIS MAGICAL VIAL, YOU WILL LIVE AS ONE OF US... FOREVER!

I-- I DO NOT UNDERSTAND! WHO ARE YOU? WHERE DO YOU COME FROM?

ENOUGH! I'VE A SHIP TO SAIL! YOUR QUESTIONS WILL BE ANSWERED IN DUE TIME!

WITHOUT A WILL OF HIS OWN, BARNABAS COLLINS WONDERS WHAT HIS FATE WILL BE WHILE AT THE MERCY OF A CREW AND A SHIP FROM ANOTHER TIME...

IS THERE NO ESCAPE? WILL I BECOME ONE OF THEM... WHOEVER AND WHATEVER THEY ARE?

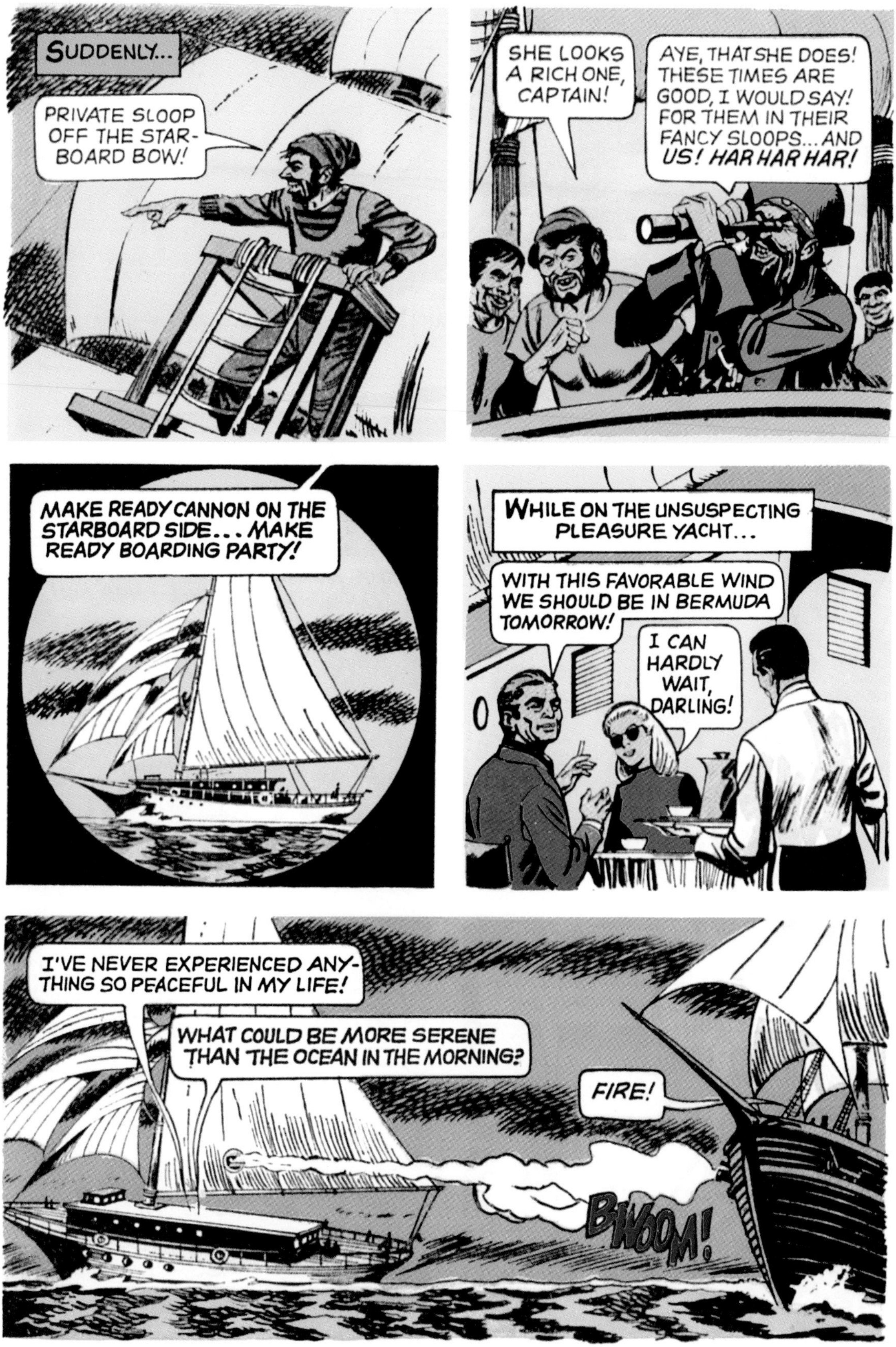
SUDDENLY...
PRIVATE SLOOP OFF THE STAR-BOARD BOW!
SHE LOOKS A RICH ONE, CAPTAIN!
AYE, THAT SHE DOES! THESE TIMES ARE GOOD, I WOULD SAY! FOR THEM IN THEIR FANCY SLOOPS... AND US! HAR HAR HAR!
MAKE READY CANNON ON THE STARBOARD SIDE... MAKE READY BOARDING PARTY!
WHILE ON THE UNSUSPECTING PLEASURE YACHT...
WITH THIS FAVORABLE WIND WE SHOULD BE IN BERMUDA TOMORROW!
I CAN HARDLY WAIT, DARLING!
I'VE NEVER EXPERIENCED ANY-THING SO PEACEFUL IN MY LIFE!
WHAT COULD BE MORE SERENE THAN THE OCEAN IN THE MORNING?
FIRE!
BWOOM!

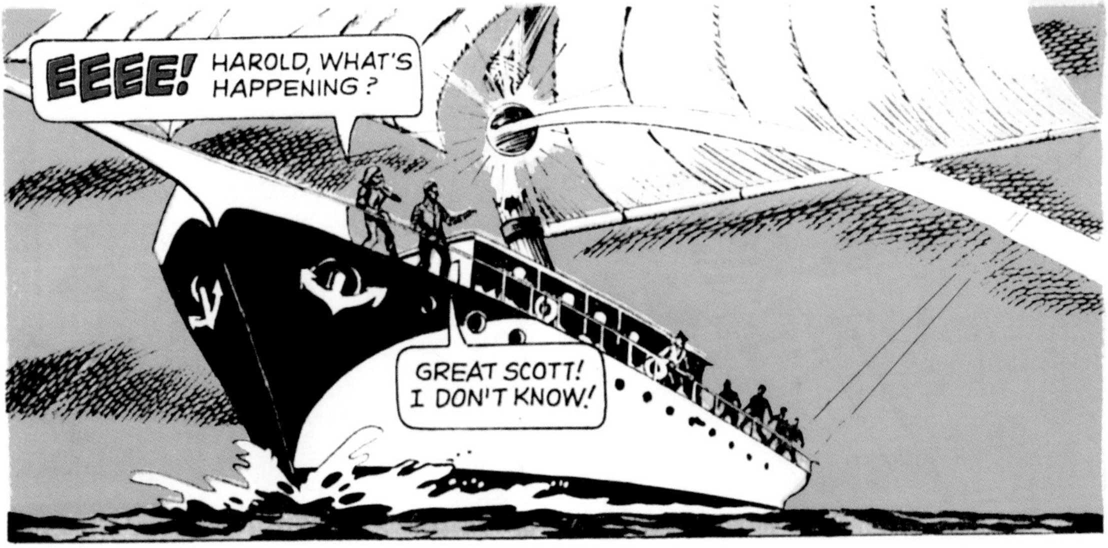
EEEE! HAROLD, WHAT'S HAPPENING?
GREAT SCOTT! I DON'T KNOW!

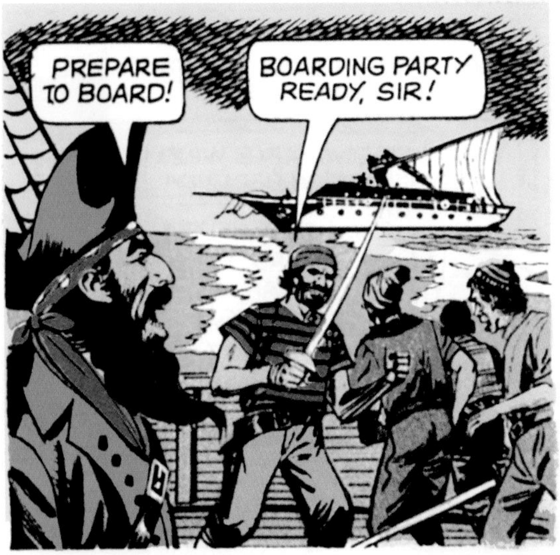
PREPARE TO BOARD!
BOARDING PARTY READY, SIR!

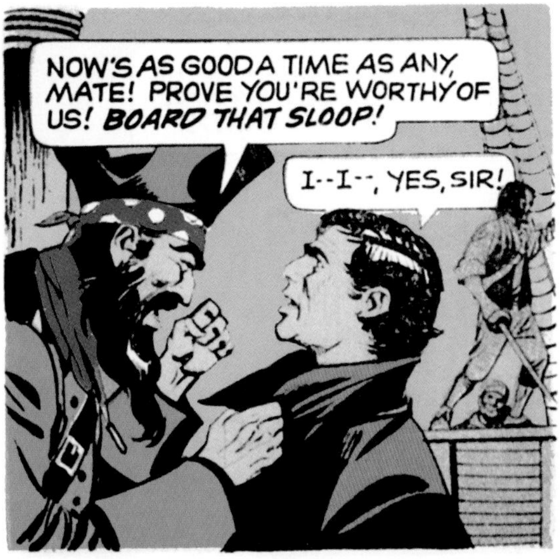
NOW'S AS GOOD A TIME AS ANY, MATE! PROVE YOU'RE WORTHY OF US! BOARD THAT SLOOP!
I--I--, YES, SIR!

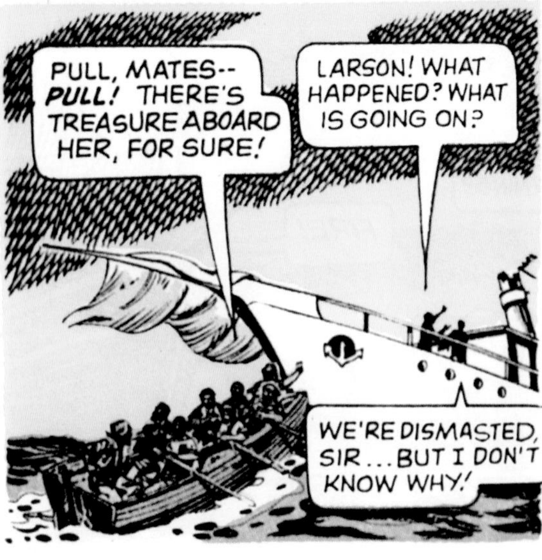
PULL, MATES-- PULL! THERE'S TREASURE ABOARD HER, FOR SURE!
LARSON! WHAT HAPPENED? WHAT IS GOING ON?
WE'RE DISMASTED, SIR... BUT I DON'T KNOW WHY!

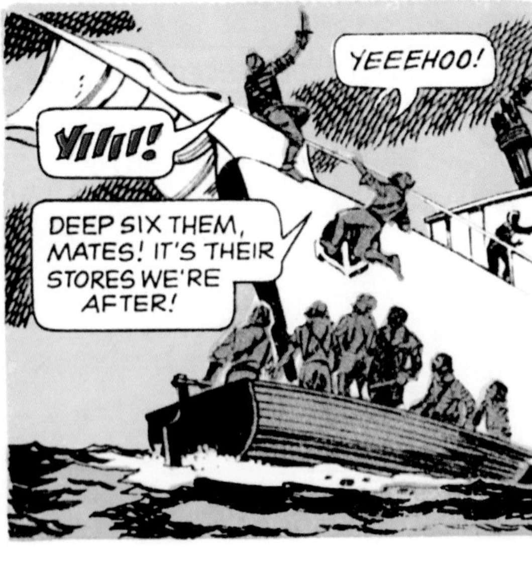
YEEEHOO!
YIIII!
DEEP SIX THEM, MATES! IT'S THEIR STORES WE'RE AFTER!

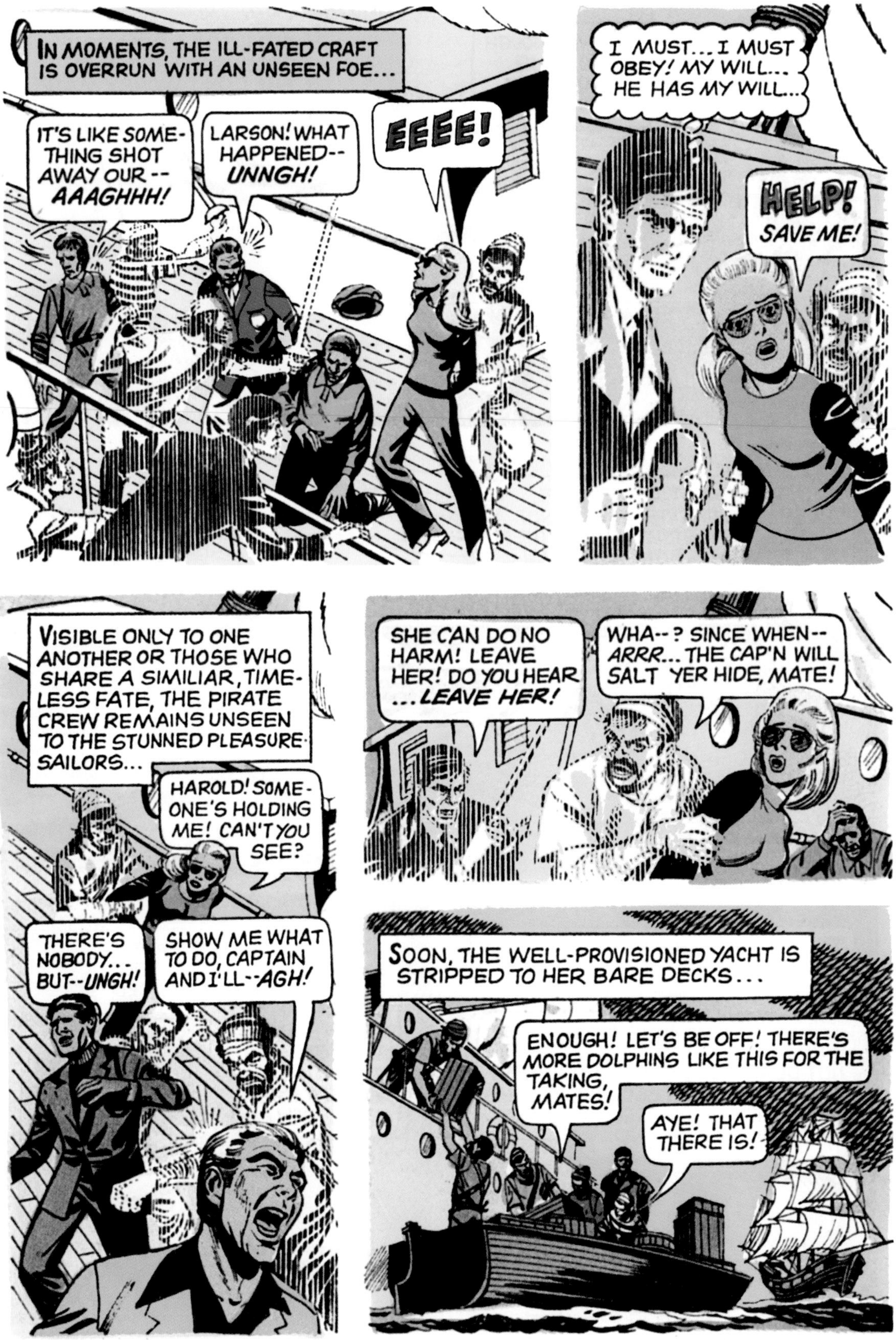
IN MOMENTS, THE ILL-FATED CRAFT IS OVERRUN WITH AN UNSEEN FOE...
IT'S LIKE SOMETHING SHOT AWAY OUR -- AAAGHHH!
LARSON! WHAT HAPPENED-- UNNGH!
EEEE!
I MUST... I MUST OBEY! MY WILL... HE HAS MY WILL...
HELP! SAVE ME!
VISIBLE ONLY TO ONE ANOTHER OR THOSE WHO SHARE A SIMILIAR, TIMELESS FATE, THE PIRATE CREW REMAINS UNSEEN TO THE STUNNED PLEASURE-SAILORS...
HAROLD! SOMEONE'S HOLDING ME! CAN'T YOU SEE?
THERE'S NOBODY... BUT--UNGH!
SHOW ME WHAT TO DO, CAPTAIN AND I'LL--AGH!
SHE CAN DO NO HARM! LEAVE HER! DO YOU HEAR ...LEAVE HER!
WHA--? SINCE WHEN-- ARRR... THE CAP'N WILL SALT YER HIDE, MATE!
SOON, THE WELL-PROVISIONED YACHT IS STRIPPED TO HER BARE DECKS...
ENOUGH! LET'S BE OFF! THERE'S MORE DOLPHINS LIKE THIS FOR THE TAKING, MATES!
AYE! THAT THERE IS!

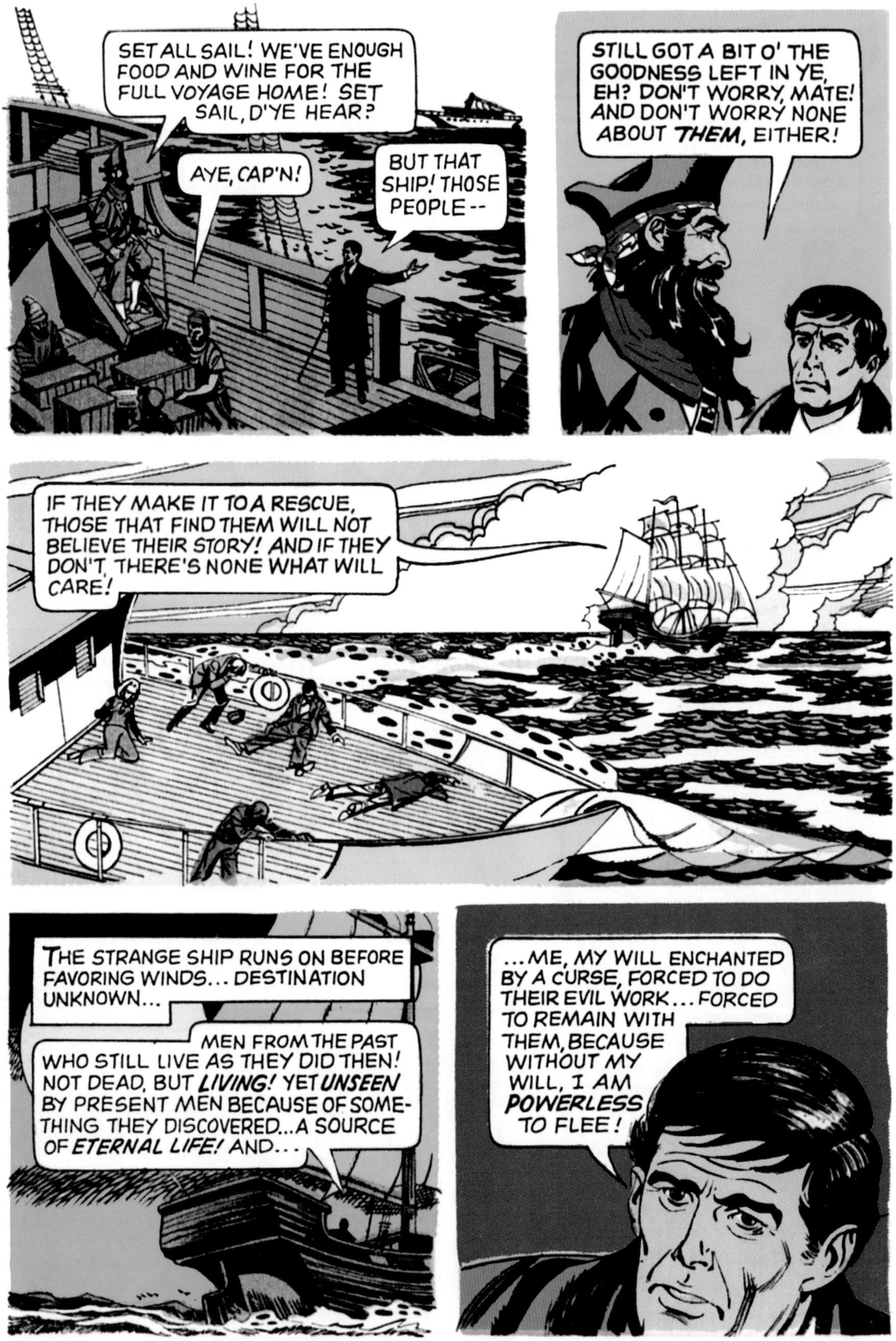
SET ALL SAIL! WE'VE ENOUGH FOOD AND WINE FOR THE FULL VOYAGE HOME! SET SAIL, D'YE HEAR?
AYE, CAP'N!
BUT THAT SHIP! THOSE PEOPLE--
STILL GOT A BIT O' THE GOODNESS LEFT IN YE, EH? DON'T WORRY, MATE! AND DON'T WORRY NONE ABOUT THEM, EITHER!
IF THEY MAKE IT TO A RESCUE, THOSE THAT FIND THEM WILL NOT BELIEVE THEIR STORY! AND IF THEY DON'T, THERE'S NONE WHAT WILL CARE!
THE STRANGE SHIP RUNS ON BEFORE FAVORING WINDS... DESTINATION UNKNOWN...
MEN FROM THE PAST WHO STILL LIVE AS THEY DID THEN! NOT DEAD, BUT LIVING! YET UNSEEN BY PRESENT MEN BECAUSE OF SOMETHING THEY DISCOVERED...A SOURCE OF ETERNAL LIFE! AND...
...ME, MY WILL ENCHANTED BY A CURSE, FORCED TO DO THEIR EVIL WORK... FORCED TO REMAIN WITH THEM, BECAUSE WITHOUT MY WILL, I AM POWERLESS TO FLEE!

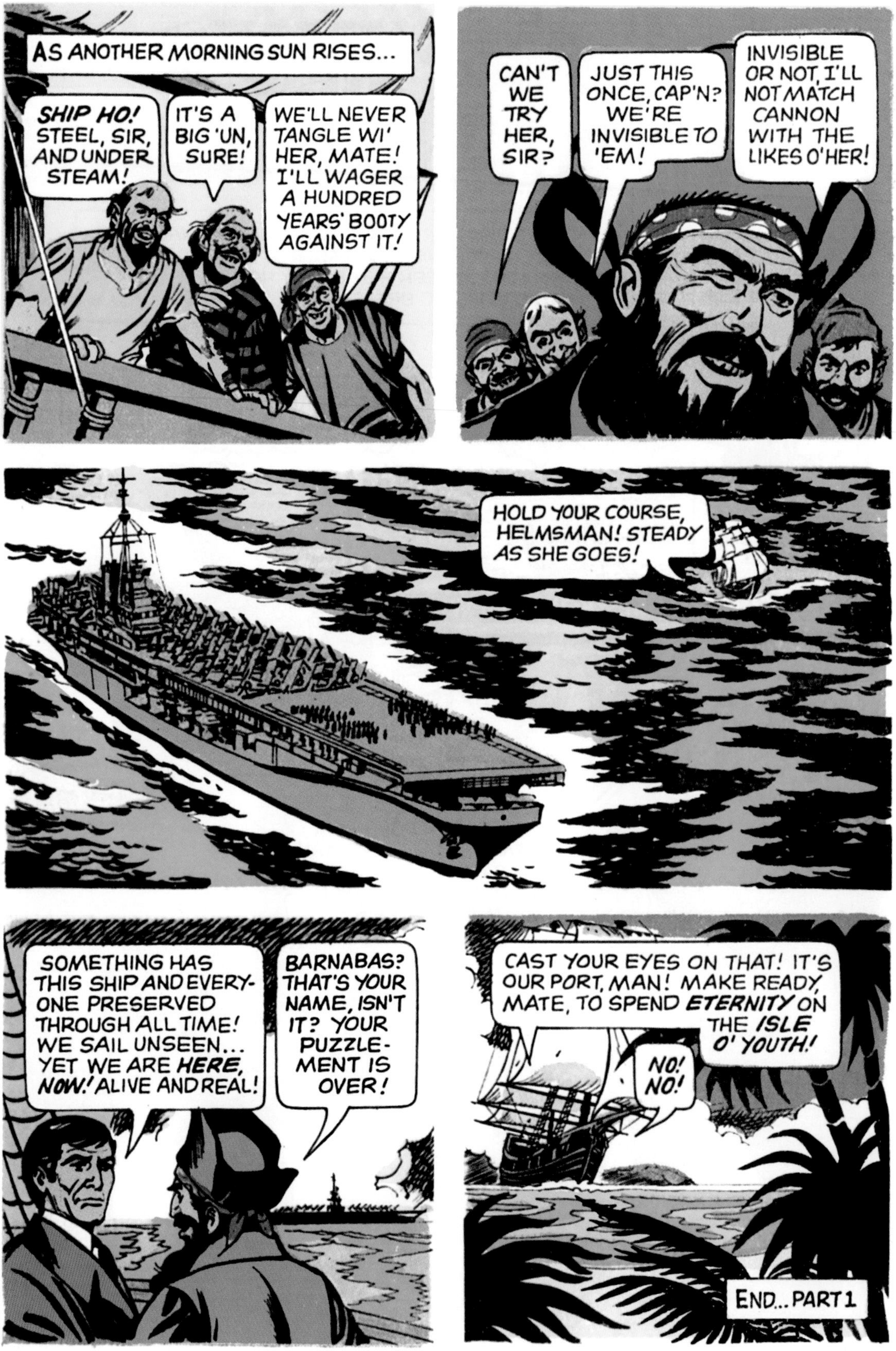
AS ANOTHER MORNING SUN RISES...
SHIP HO! STEEL, SIR, AND UNDER STEAM!
IT'S A BIG 'UN, SURE!
WE'LL NEVER TANGLE WI' HER, MATE! I'LL WAGER A HUNDRED YEARS' BOOTY AGAINST IT!
CAN'T WE TRY HER, SIR?
JUST THIS ONCE, CAP'N? WE'RE INVISIBLE TO 'EM!
INVISIBLE OR NOT, I'LL NOT MATCH CANNON WITH THE LIKES O'HER!
HOLD YOUR COURSE, HELMSMAN! STEADY AS SHE GOES!
SOMETHING HAS THIS SHIP AND EVERYONE PRESERVED THROUGH ALL TIME! WE SAIL UNSEEN... YET WE ARE HERE, NOW! ALIVE AND REAL!
BARNABAS? THAT'S YOUR NAME, ISN'T IT? YOUR PUZZLEMENT IS OVER!
CAST YOUR EYES ON THAT! IT'S OUR PORT, MAN! MAKE READY, MATE, TO SPEND ETERNITY ON THE ISLE O' YOUTH!
NO! NO!
END... PART 1

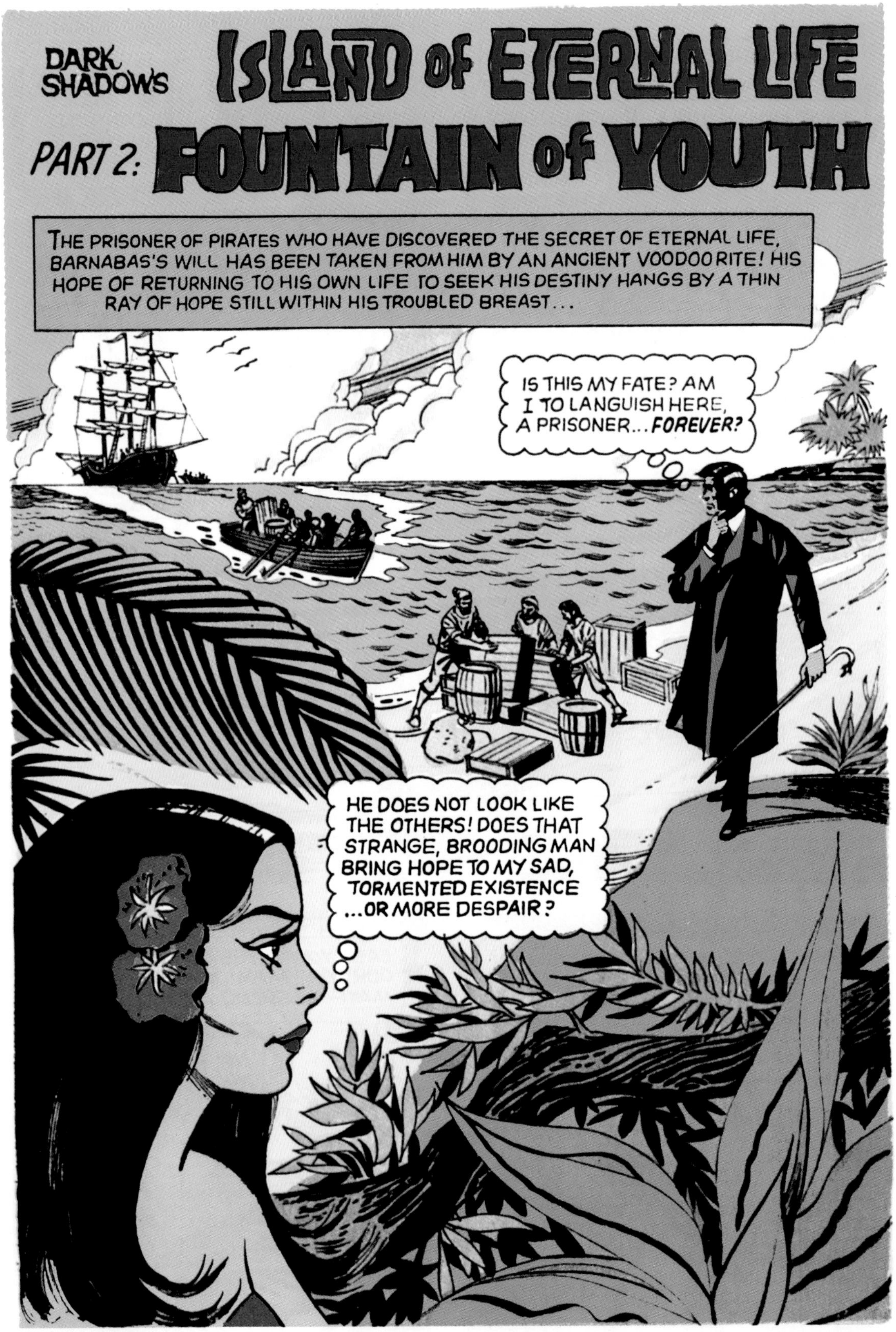

DARK SHADOWS
ISLAND OF ETERNAL LIFE
PART 2: FOUNTAIN OF YOUTH
THE PRISONER OF PIRATES WHO HAVE DISCOVERED THE SECRET OF ETERNAL LIFE, BARNABAS'S WILL HAS BEEN TAKEN FROM HIM BY AN ANCIENT VOODOO RITE! HIS HOPE OF RETURNING TO HIS OWN LIFE TO SEEK HIS DESTINY HANGS BY A THIN RAY OF HOPE STILL WITHIN HIS TROUBLED BREAST...
IS THIS MY FATE? AM I TO LANGUISH HERE, A PRISONER... FOREVER?
HE DOES NOT LOOK LIKE THE OTHERS! DOES THAT STRANGE, BROODING MAN BRING HOPE TO MY SAD, TORMENTED EXISTENCE ...OR MORE DESPAIR?

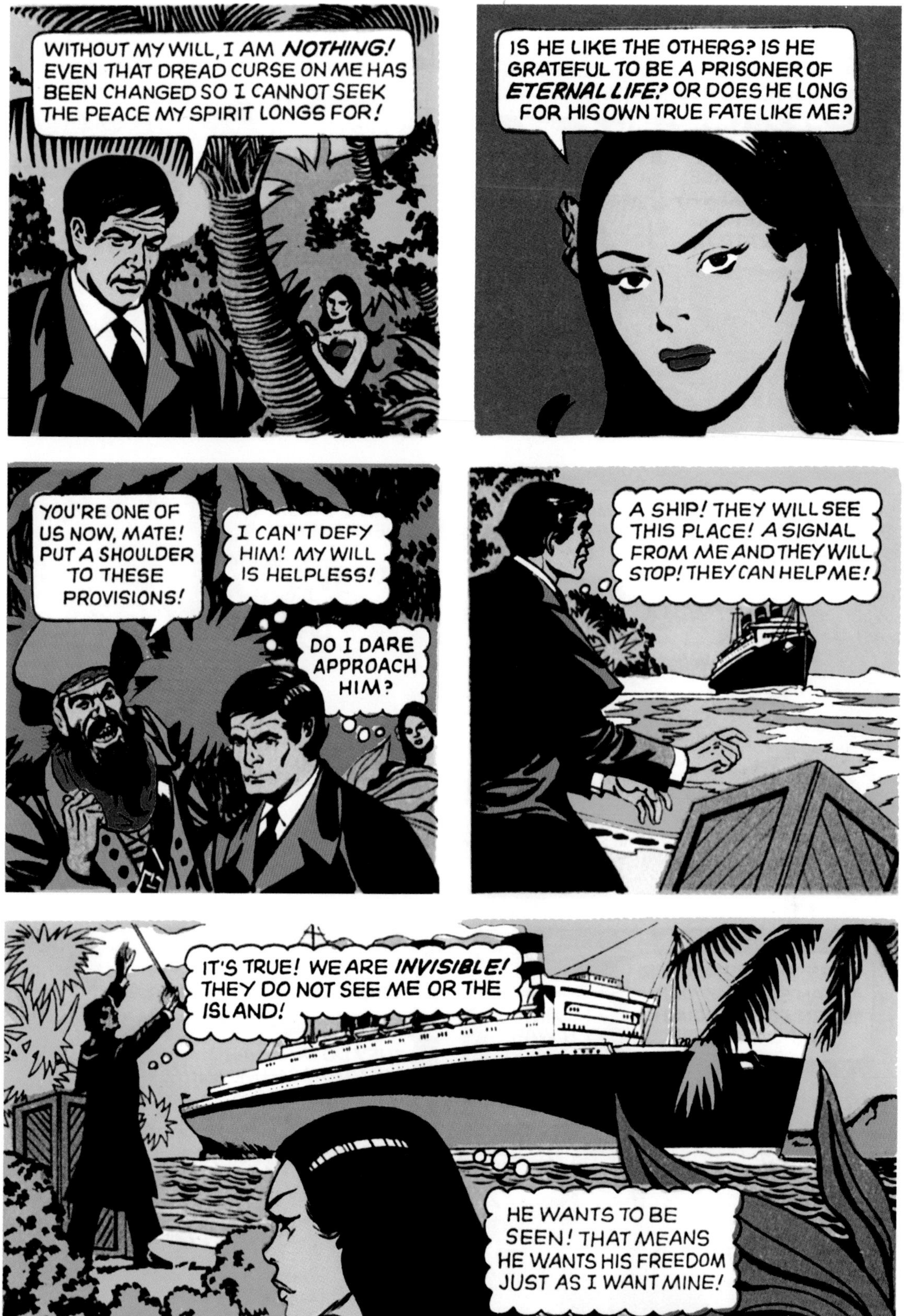
WITHOUT MY WILL, I AM NOTHING! EVEN THAT DREAD CURSE ON ME HAS BEEN CHANGED SO I CANNOT SEEK THE PEACE MY SPIRIT LONGS FOR!
IS HE LIKE THE OTHERS? IS HE GRATEFUL TO BE A PRISONER OF ETERNAL LIFE? OR DOES HE LONG FOR HIS OWN TRUE FATE LIKE ME?
YOU'RE ONE OF US NOW, MATE! PUT A SHOULDER TO THESE PROVISIONS!
I CAN'T DEFY HIM! MY WILL IS HELPLESS!
DO I DARE APPROACH HIM?
A SHIP! THEY WILL SEE THIS PLACE! A SIGNAL FROM ME AND THEY WILL STOP! THEY CAN HELP ME!
IT'S TRUE! WE ARE INVISIBLE! THEY DO NOT SEE ME OR THE ISLAND!
HE WANTS TO BE SEEN! THAT MEANS HE WANTS HIS FREEDOM JUST AS I WANT MINE!

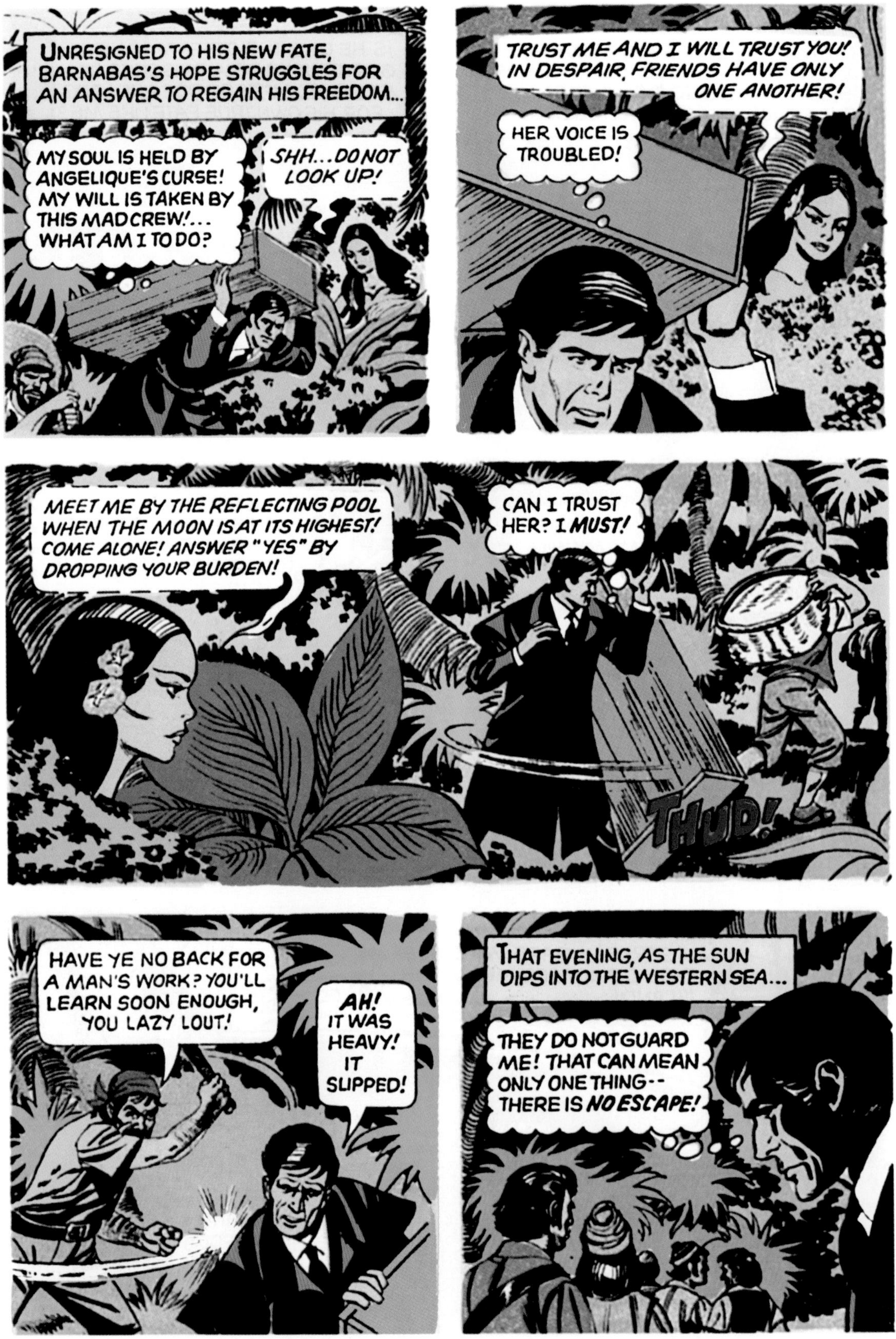

UNRESIGNED TO HIS NEW FATE, BARNABAS'S HOPE STRUGGLES FOR AN ANSWER TO REGAIN HIS FREEDOM...
MY SOUL IS HELD BY ANGELIQUE'S CURSE! MY WILL IS TAKEN BY THIS MAD CREW!... WHAT AM I TO DO?
SHH... DO NOT LOOK UP!
TRUST ME AND I WILL TRUST YOU! IN DESPAIR, FRIENDS HAVE ONLY ONE ANOTHER!
HER VOICE IS TROUBLED!
MEET ME BY THE REFLECTING POOL WHEN THE MOON IS AT ITS HIGHEST! COME ALONE! ANSWER "YES" BY DROPPING YOUR BURDEN!
CAN I TRUST HER? I MUST!
THUD!
HAVE YE NO BACK FOR A MAN'S WORK? YOU'LL LEARN SOON ENOUGH, YOU LAZY LOUT!
AH! IT WAS HEAVY! IT SLIPPED!
THAT EVENING, AS THE SUN DIPS INTO THE WESTERN SEA...
THEY DO NOT GUARD ME! THAT CAN MEAN ONLY ONE THING-- THERE IS NO ESCAPE!

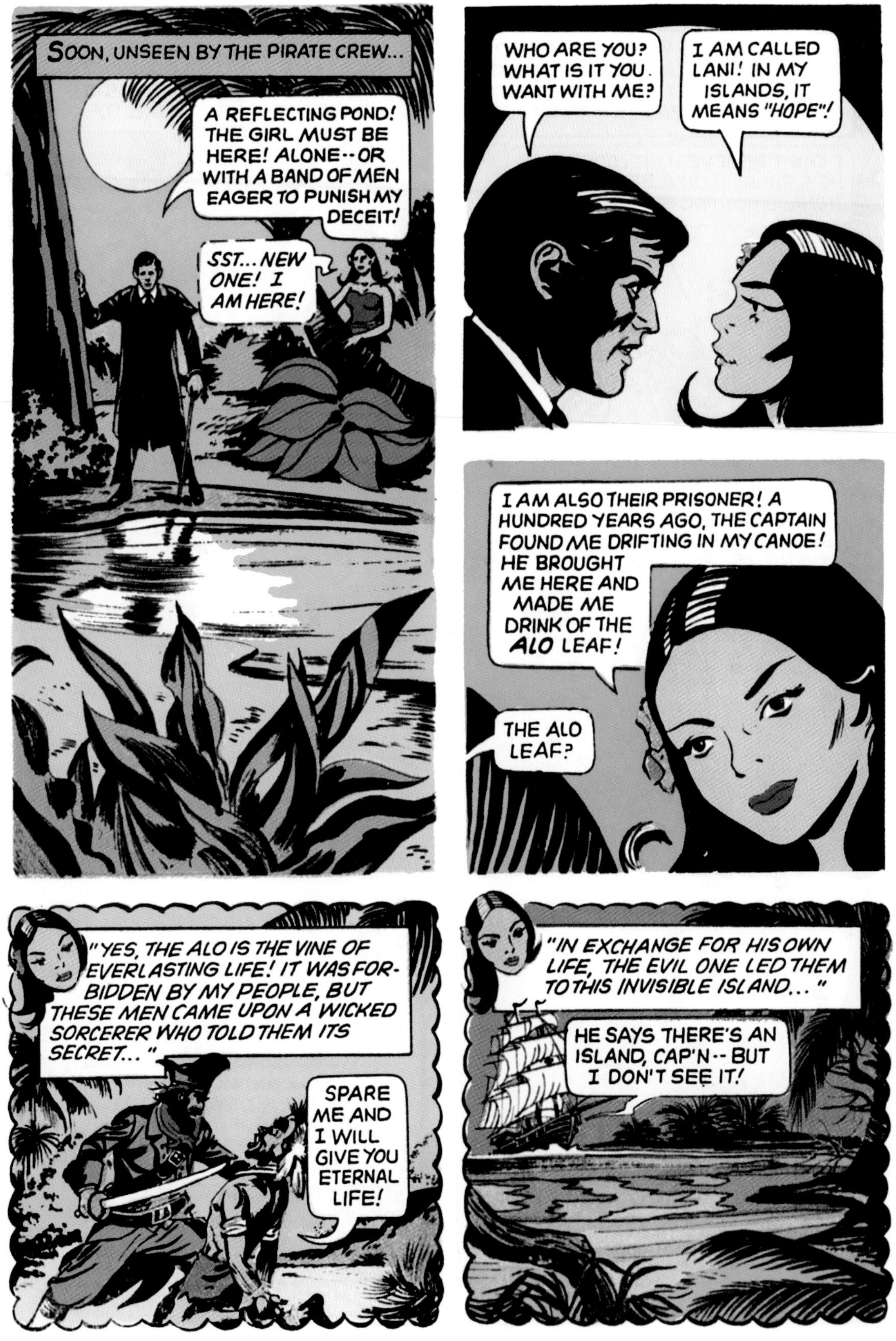

SOON, UNSEEN BY THE PIRATE CREW...
A REFLECTING POND! THE GIRL MUST BE HERE! ALONE--OR WITH A BAND OF MEN EAGER TO PUNISH MY DECEIT!
SST... NEW ONE! I AM HERE!
WHO ARE YOU? WHAT IS IT YOU WANT WITH ME?
I AM CALLED LANI! IN MY ISLANDS, IT MEANS "HOPE"!
I AM ALSO THEIR PRISONER! A HUNDRED YEARS AGO, THE CAPTAIN FOUND ME DRIFTING IN MY CANOE! HE BROUGHT ME HERE AND MADE ME DRINK OF THE ALO LEAF!
THE ALO LEAF?
"YES, THE ALO IS THE VINE OF EVERLASTING LIFE! IT WAS FORBIDDEN BY MY PEOPLE, BUT THESE MEN CAME UPON A WICKED SORCERER WHO TOLD THEM ITS SECRET..."
SPARE ME AND I WILL GIVE YOU ETERNAL LIFE!
"IN EXCHANGE FOR HIS OWN LIFE, THE EVIL ONE LED THEM TO THIS INVISIBLE ISLAND..."
HE SAYS THERE'S AN ISLAND, CAP'N--BUT I DON'T SEE IT!

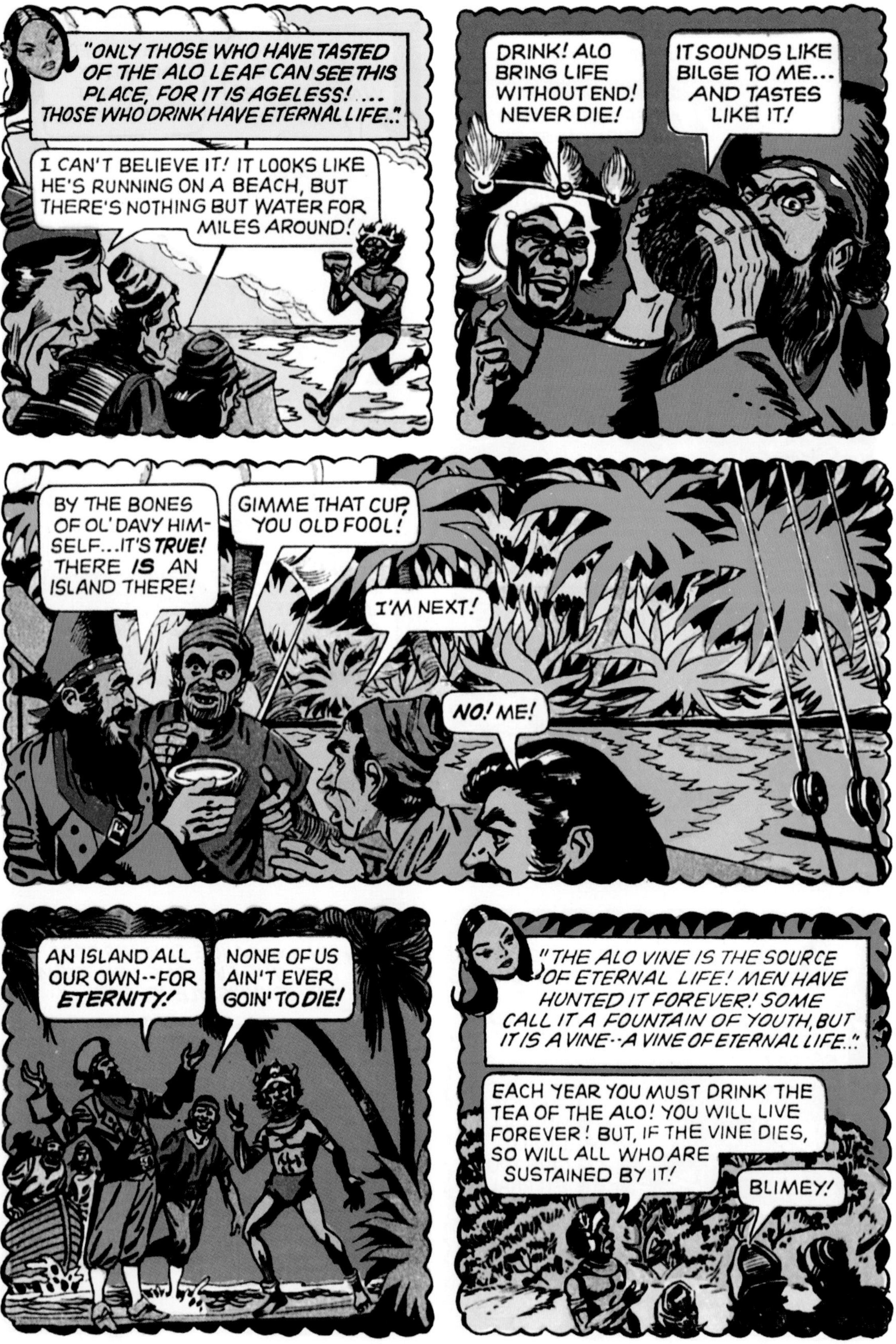
"ONLY THOSE WHO HAVE TASTED OF THE ALO LEAF CAN SEE THIS PLACE, FOR IT IS AGELESS! ... THOSE WHO DRINK HAVE ETERNAL LIFE..."
I CAN'T BELIEVE IT! IT LOOKS LIKE HE'S RUNNING ON A BEACH, BUT THERE'S NOTHING BUT WATER FOR MILES AROUND!
DRINK! ALO BRING LIFE WITHOUT END! NEVER DIE!
IT SOUNDS LIKE BILGE TO ME... AND TASTES LIKE IT!
BY THE BONES OF OL' DAVY HIM-SELF...IT'S TRUE! THERE IS AN ISLAND THERE!
GIMME THAT CUP, YOU OLD FOOL!
I'M NEXT!
NO! ME!
AN ISLAND ALL OUR OWN--FOR ETERNITY!
NONE OF US AIN'T EVER GOIN' TO DIE!
"THE ALO VINE IS THE SOURCE OF ETERNAL LIFE! MEN HAVE HUNTED IT FOREVER! SOME CALL IT A FOUNTAIN OF YOUTH, BUT IT IS A VINE--A VINE OF ETERNAL LIFE..."
EACH YEAR YOU MUST DRINK THE TEA OF THE ALO! YOU WILL LIVE FOREVER! BUT, IF THE VINE DIES, SO WILL ALL WHO ARE SUSTAINED BY IT!
BLIMEY!

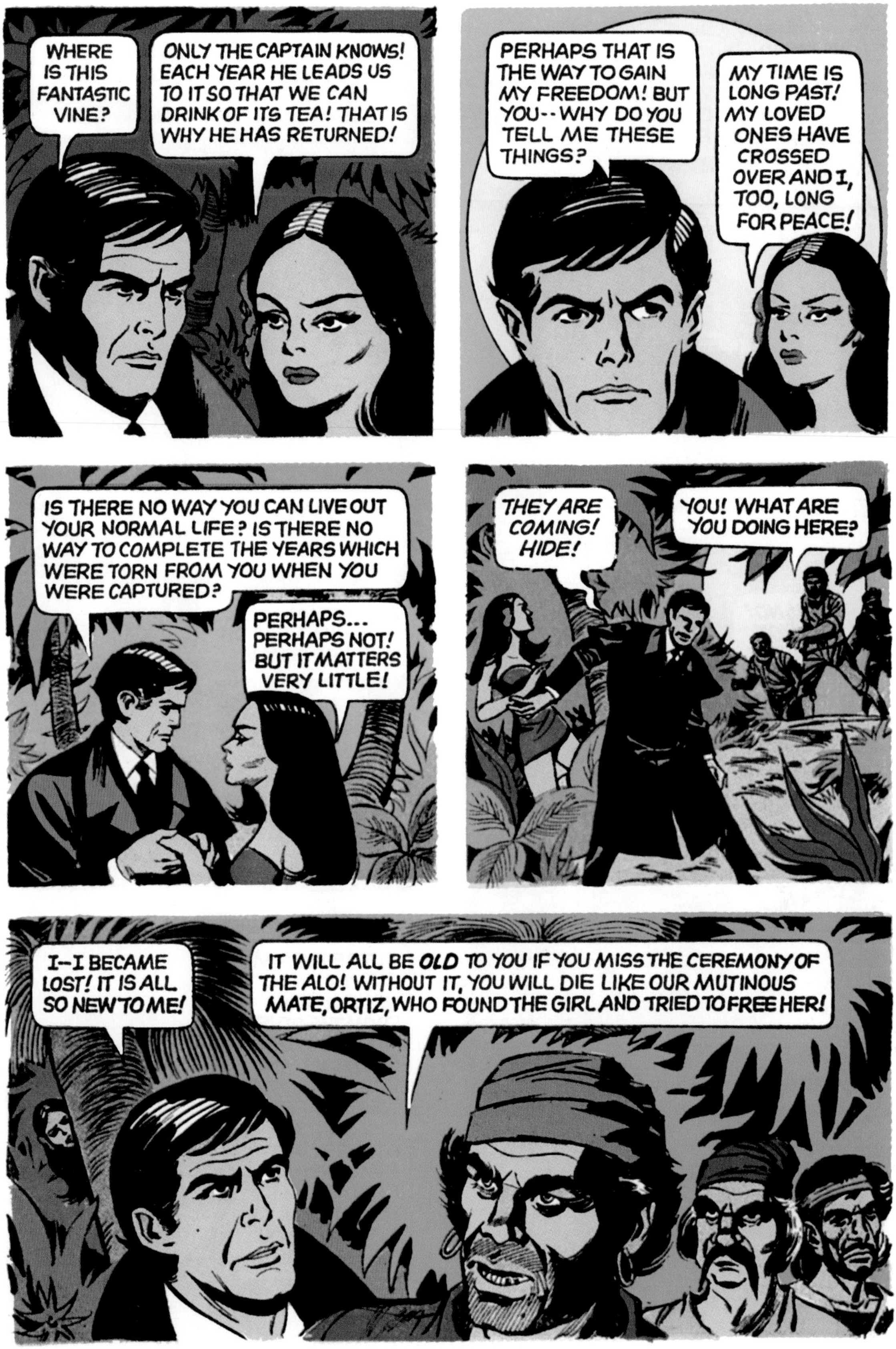
WHERE IS THIS FANTASTIC VINE?
ONLY THE CAPTAIN KNOWS! EACH YEAR HE LEADS US TO IT SO THAT WE CAN DRINK OF ITS TEA! THAT IS WHY HE HAS RETURNED!
PERHAPS THAT IS THE WAY TO GAIN MY FREEDOM! BUT YOU--WHY DO YOU TELL ME THESE THINGS?
MY TIME IS LONG PAST! MY LOVED ONES HAVE CROSSED OVER AND I, TOO, LONG FOR PEACE!
IS THERE NO WAY YOU CAN LIVE OUT YOUR NORMAL LIFE? IS THERE NO WAY TO COMPLETE THE YEARS WHICH WERE TORN FROM YOU WHEN YOU WERE CAPTURED?
PERHAPS... PERHAPS NOT! BUT IT MATTERS VERY LITTLE!
THEY ARE COMING! HIDE!
YOU! WHAT ARE YOU DOING HERE?
I--I BECAME LOST! IT IS ALL SO NEW TO ME!
IT WILL ALL BE OLD TO YOU IF YOU MISS THE CEREMONY OF THE ALO! WITHOUT IT, YOU WILL DIE LIKE OUR MUTINOUS MATE, ORTIZ, WHO FOUND THE GIRL AND TRIED TO FREE HER!

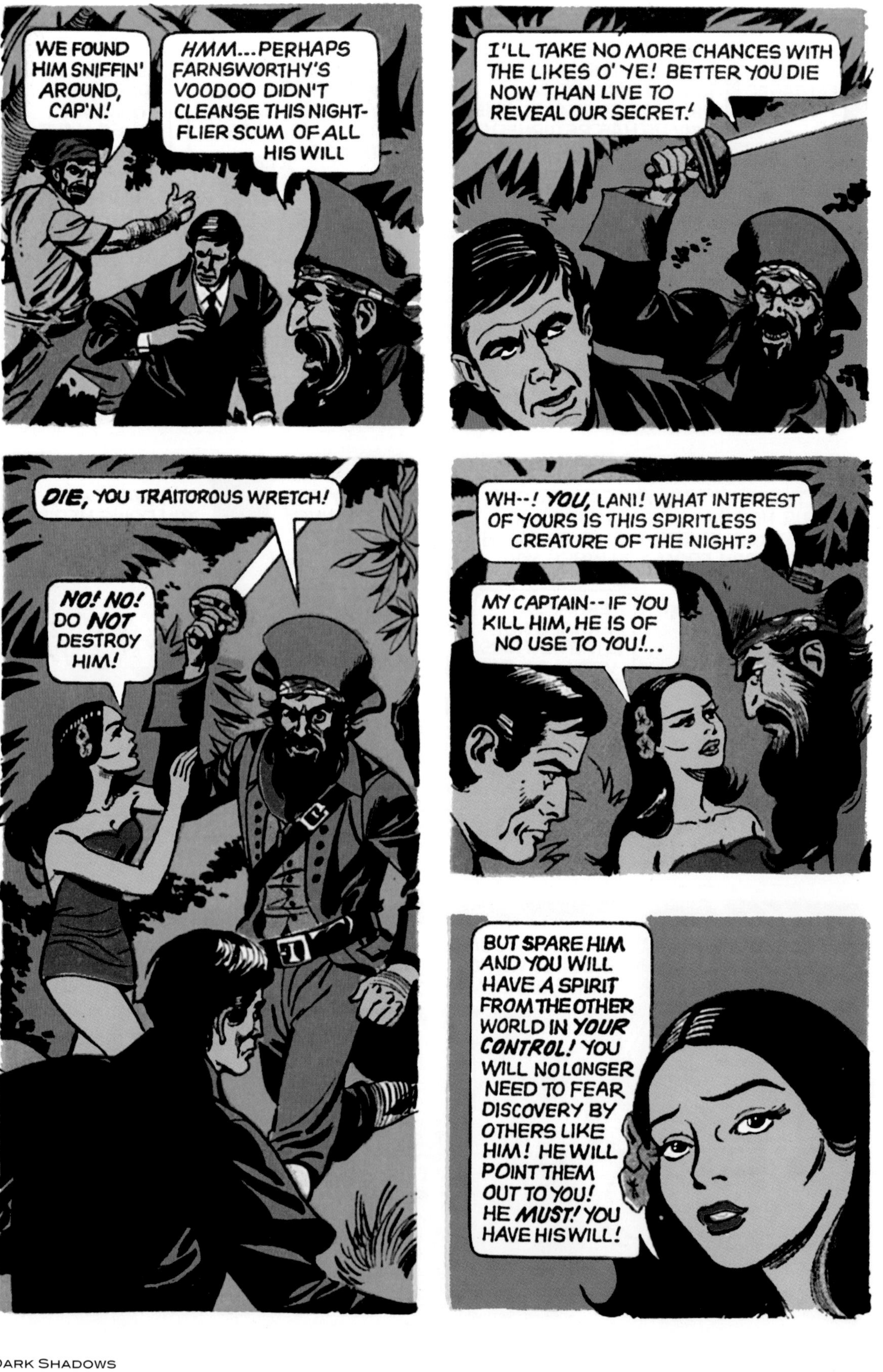

WE FOUND HIM SNIFFIN' AROUND, CAP'N!
HMM... PERHAPS FARNSWORTHY'S VOODOO DIDN'T CLEANSE THIS NIGHT-FLIER SCUM OF ALL HIS WILL
I'LL TAKE NO MORE CHANCES WITH THE LIKES O' YE! BETTER YOU DIE NOW THAN LIVE TO REVEAL OUR SECRET!
DIE, YOU TRAITOROUS WRETCH!
NO! NO! DO NOT DESTROY HIM!
WH--! YOU, LANI! WHAT INTEREST OF YOURS IS THIS SPIRITLESS CREATURE OF THE NIGHT?
MY CAPTAIN--IF YOU KILL HIM, HE IS OF NO USE TO YOU!...
BUT SPARE HIM AND YOU WILL HAVE A SPIRIT FROM THE OTHER WORLD IN YOUR CONTROL! YOU WILL NO LONGER NEED TO FEAR DISCOVERY BY OTHERS LIKE HIM! HE WILL POINT THEM OUT TO YOU! HE MUST! YOU HAVE HIS WILL!

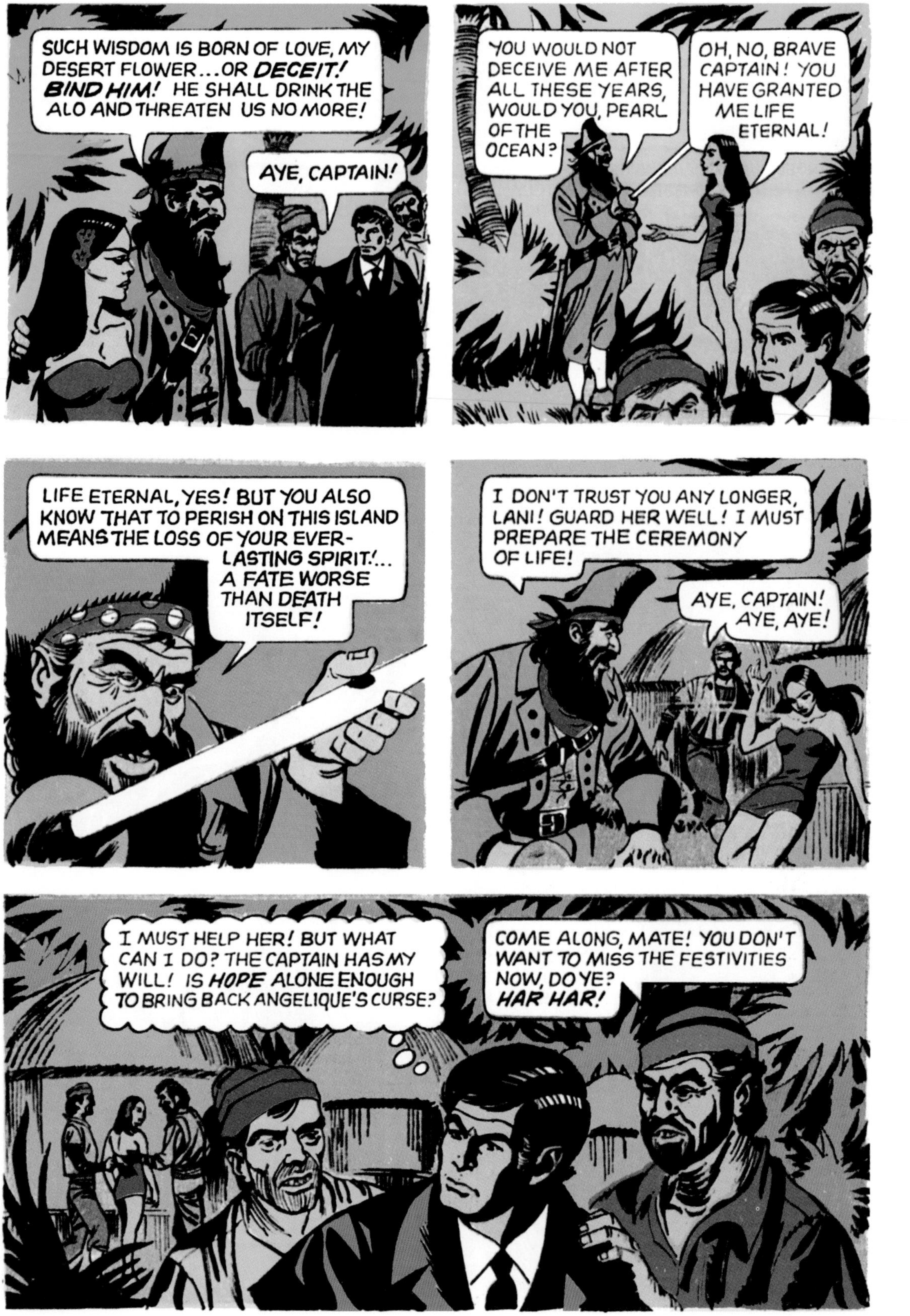
SUCH WISDOM IS BORN OF LOVE, MY DESERT FLOWER...OR DECEIT! BIND HIM! HE SHALL DRINK THE ALO AND THREATEN US NO MORE!
AYE, CAPTAIN!
YOU WOULD NOT DECEIVE ME AFTER ALL THESE YEARS, WOULD YOU, PEARL OF THE OCEAN?
OH, NO, BRAVE CAPTAIN! YOU HAVE GRANTED ME LIFE ETERNAL!
LIFE ETERNAL, YES! BUT YOU ALSO KNOW THAT TO PERISH ON THIS ISLAND MEANS THE LOSS OF YOUR EVER-LASTING SPIRIT!... A FATE WORSE THAN DEATH ITSELF!
I DON'T TRUST YOU ANY LONGER, LANI! GUARD HER WELL! I MUST PREPARE THE CEREMONY OF LIFE!
AYE, CAPTAIN! AYE, AYE!
I MUST HELP HER! BUT WHAT CAN I DO? THE CAPTAIN HAS MY WILL! IS HOPE ALONE ENOUGH TO BRING BACK ANGELIQUE'S CURSE?
COME ALONG, MATE! YOU DON'T WANT TO MISS THE FESTIVITIES NOW, DO YE? HAR HAR!

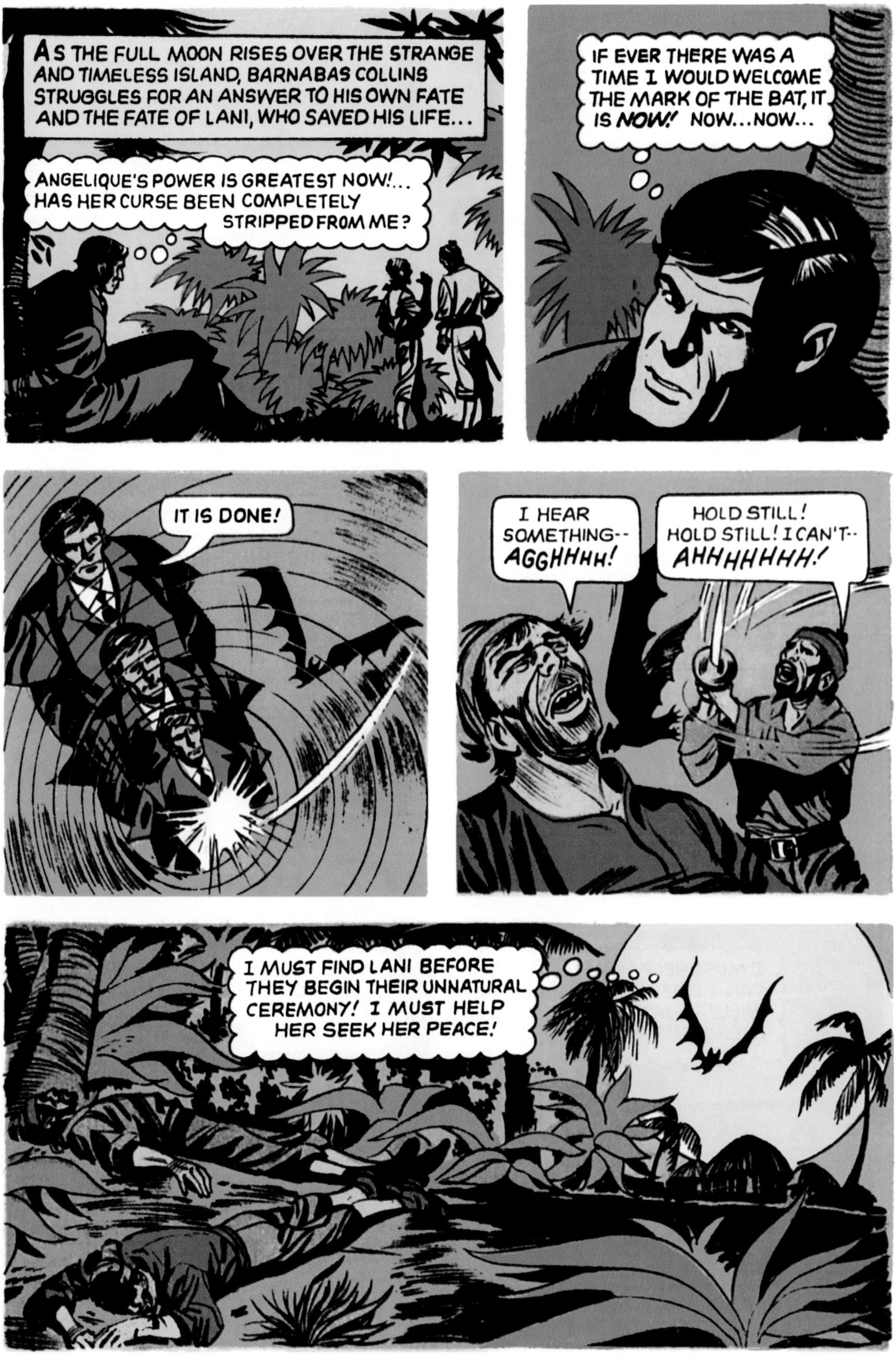
AS THE FULL MOON RISES OVER THE STRANGE AND TIMELESS ISLAND, BARNABAS COLLINS STRUGGLES FOR AN ANSWER TO HIS OWN FATE AND THE FATE OF LANI, WHO SAVED HIS LIFE...
ANGELIQUE'S POWER IS GREATEST NOW!... HAS HER CURSE BEEN COMPLETELY STRIPPED FROM ME?
IF EVER THERE WAS A TIME I WOULD WELCOME THE MARK OF THE BAT, IT IS NOW! NOW...NOW...
IT IS DONE!
I HEAR SOMETHING-- AGGHHHH!
HOLD STILL! HOLD STILL! I CAN'T-- AHHHHHHH!
I MUST FIND LANI BEFORE THEY BEGIN THEIR UNNATURAL CEREMONY! I MUST HELP HER SEEK HER PEACE!

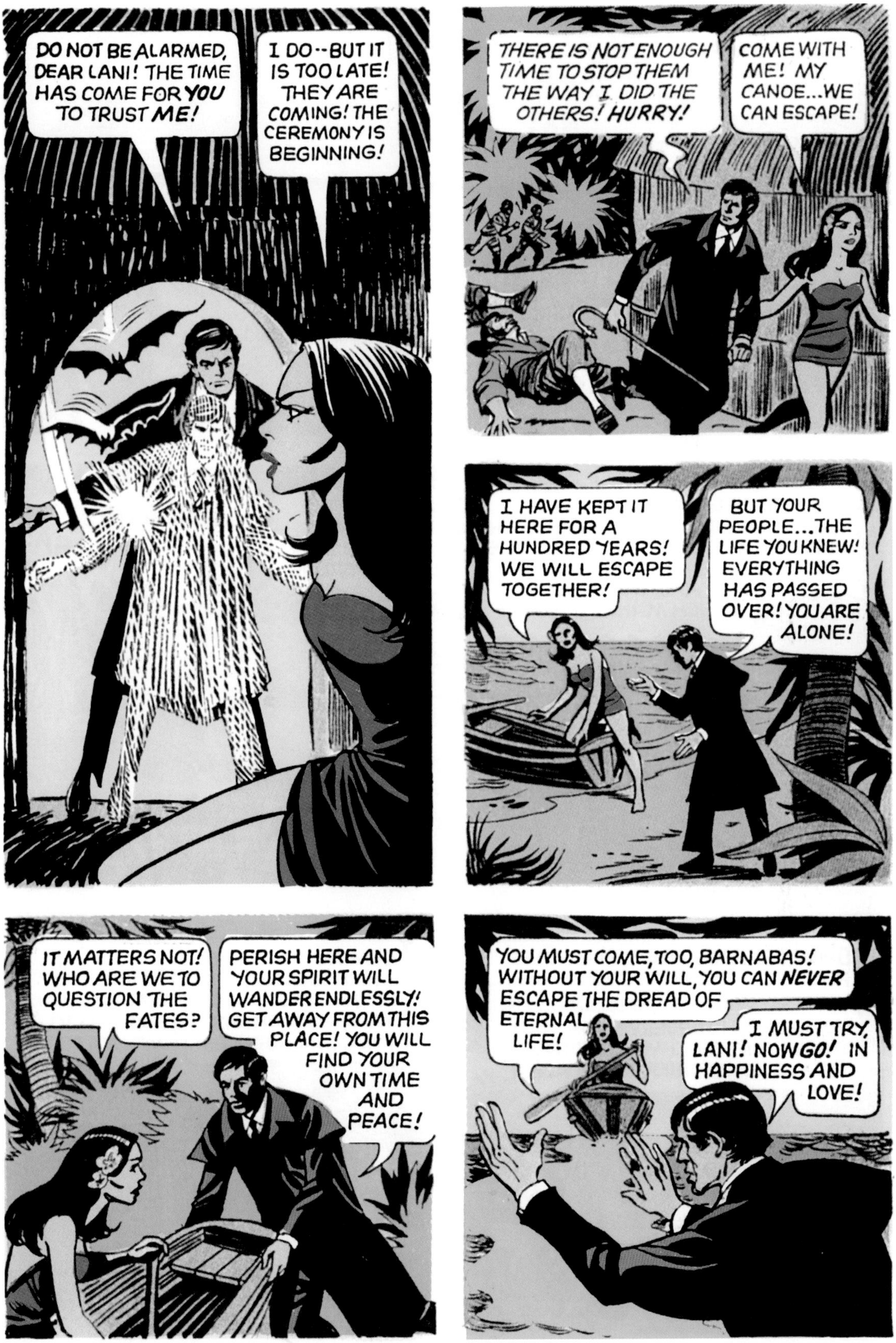
DO NOT BE ALARMED, DEAR LANI! THE TIME HAS COME FOR YOU TO TRUST ME!
I DO--BUT IT IS TOO LATE! THEY ARE COMING! THE CEREMONY IS BEGINNING!
THERE IS NOT ENOUGH TIME TO STOP THEM THE WAY I DID THE OTHERS! HURRY!
COME WITH ME! MY CANOE...WE CAN ESCAPE!
I HAVE KEPT IT HERE FOR A HUNDRED YEARS! WE WILL ESCAPE TOGETHER!
BUT YOUR PEOPLE...THE LIFE YOU KNEW! EVERYTHING HAS PASSED OVER! YOU ARE ALONE!
IT MATTERS NOT! WHO ARE WE TO QUESTION THE FATES?
PERISH HERE AND YOUR SPIRIT WILL WANDER ENDLESSLY! GET AWAY FROM THIS PLACE! YOU WILL FIND YOUR OWN TIME AND PEACE!
YOU MUST COME, TOO, BARNABAS! WITHOUT YOUR WILL, YOU CAN NEVER ESCAPE THE DREAD OF ETERNAL LIFE!
I MUST TRY, LANI! NOW GO! IN HAPPINESS AND LOVE!

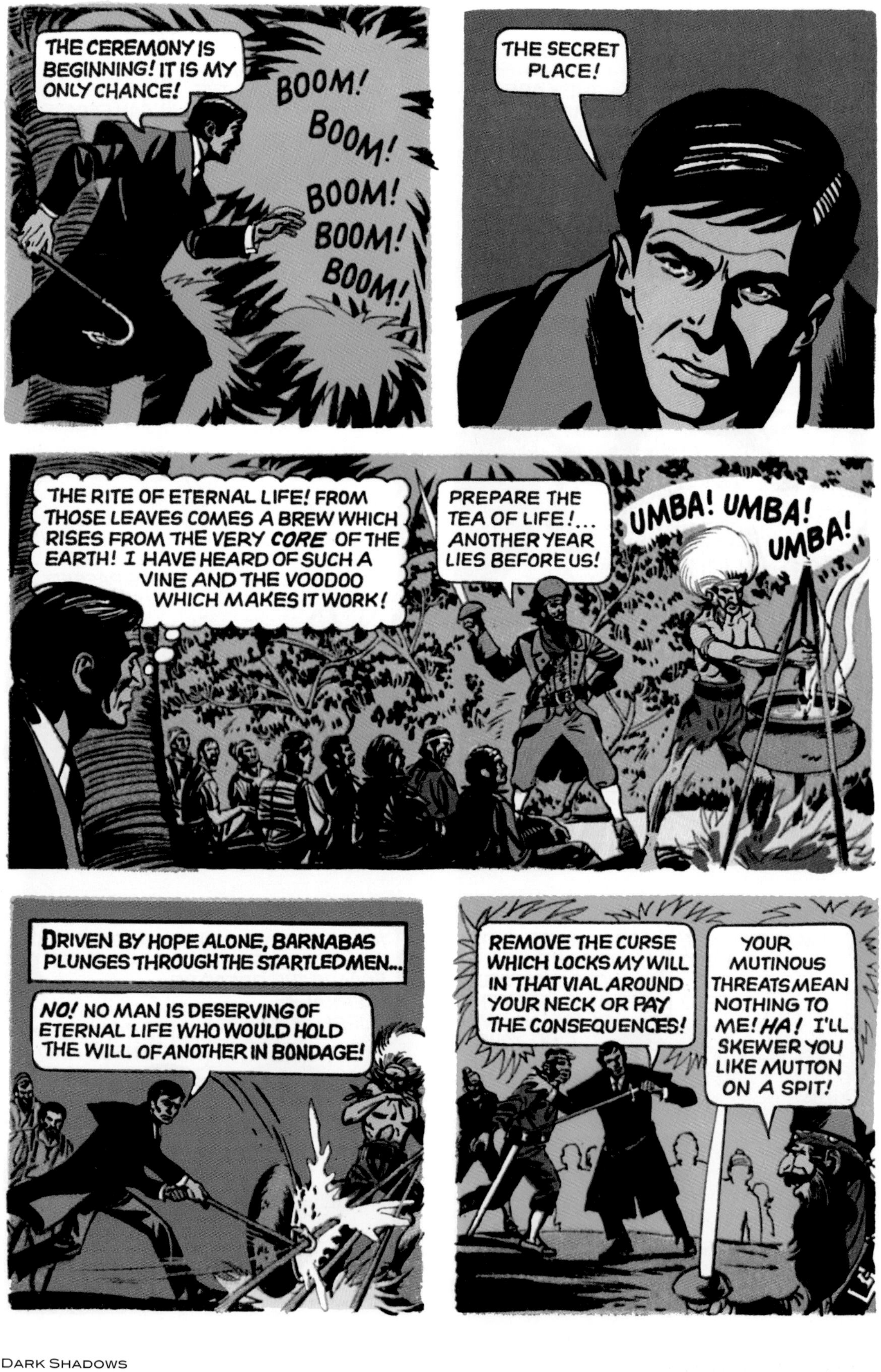
THE CEREMONY IS BEGINNING! IT IS MY ONLY CHANCE!
BOOM! BOOM! BOOM! BOOM! BOOM!
THE SECRET PLACE!
THE RITE OF ETERNAL LIFE! FROM THOSE LEAVES COMES A BREW WHICH RISES FROM THE VERY CORE OF THE EARTH! I HAVE HEARD OF SUCH A VINE AND THE VOODOO WHICH MAKES IT WORK!
PREPARE THE TEA OF LIFE!... ANOTHER YEAR LIES BEFORE US!
UMBA! UMBA! UMBA!
DRIVEN BY HOPE ALONE, BARNABAS PLUNGES THROUGH THE STARTLED MEN...
NO! NO MAN IS DESERVING OF ETERNAL LIFE WHO WOULD HOLD THE WILL OF ANOTHER IN BONDAGE!
REMOVE THE CURSE WHICH LOCKS MY WILL IN THAT VIAL AROUND YOUR NECK OR PAY THE CONSEQUENCES!
YOUR MUTINOUS THREATS MEAN NOTHING TO ME! HA! I'LL SKEWER YOU LIKE MUTTON ON A SPIT!

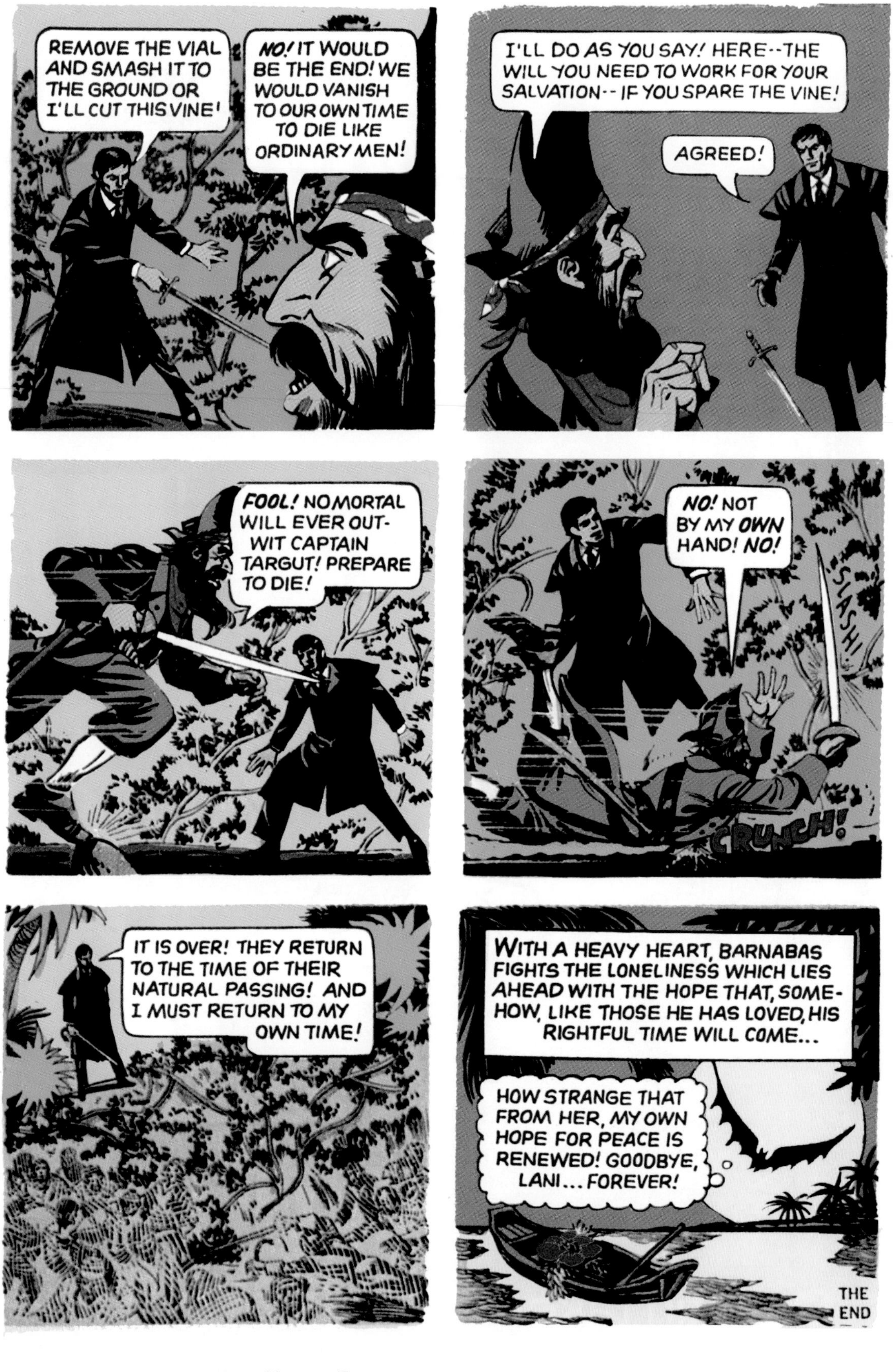
REMOVE THE VIAL AND SMASH IT TO THE GROUND OR I'LL CUT THIS VINE!
NO! IT WOULD BE THE END! WE WOULD VANISH TO OUR OWN TIME TO DIE LIKE ORDINARY MEN!
I'LL DO AS YOU SAY! HERE--THE WILL YOU NEED TO WORK FOR YOUR SALVATION--IF YOU SPARE THE VINE!
AGREED!
FOOL! NO MORTAL WILL EVER OUT-WIT CAPTAIN TARGUT! PREPARE TO DIE!
NO! NOT BY MY OWN HAND! NO!
SLASH!
CRUNCH!
IT IS OVER! THEY RETURN TO THE TIME OF THEIR NATURAL PASSING! AND I MUST RETURN TO MY OWN TIME!
WITH A HEAVY HEART, BARNABAS FIGHTS THE LONELINESS WHICH LIES AHEAD WITH THE HOPE THAT, SOME-HOW, LIKE THOSE HE HAS LOVED, HIS RIGHTFUL TIME WILL COME...
HOW STRANGE THAT FROM HER, MY OWN HOPE FOR PEACE IS RENEWED! GOODBYE, LANI... FOREVER!
THE END

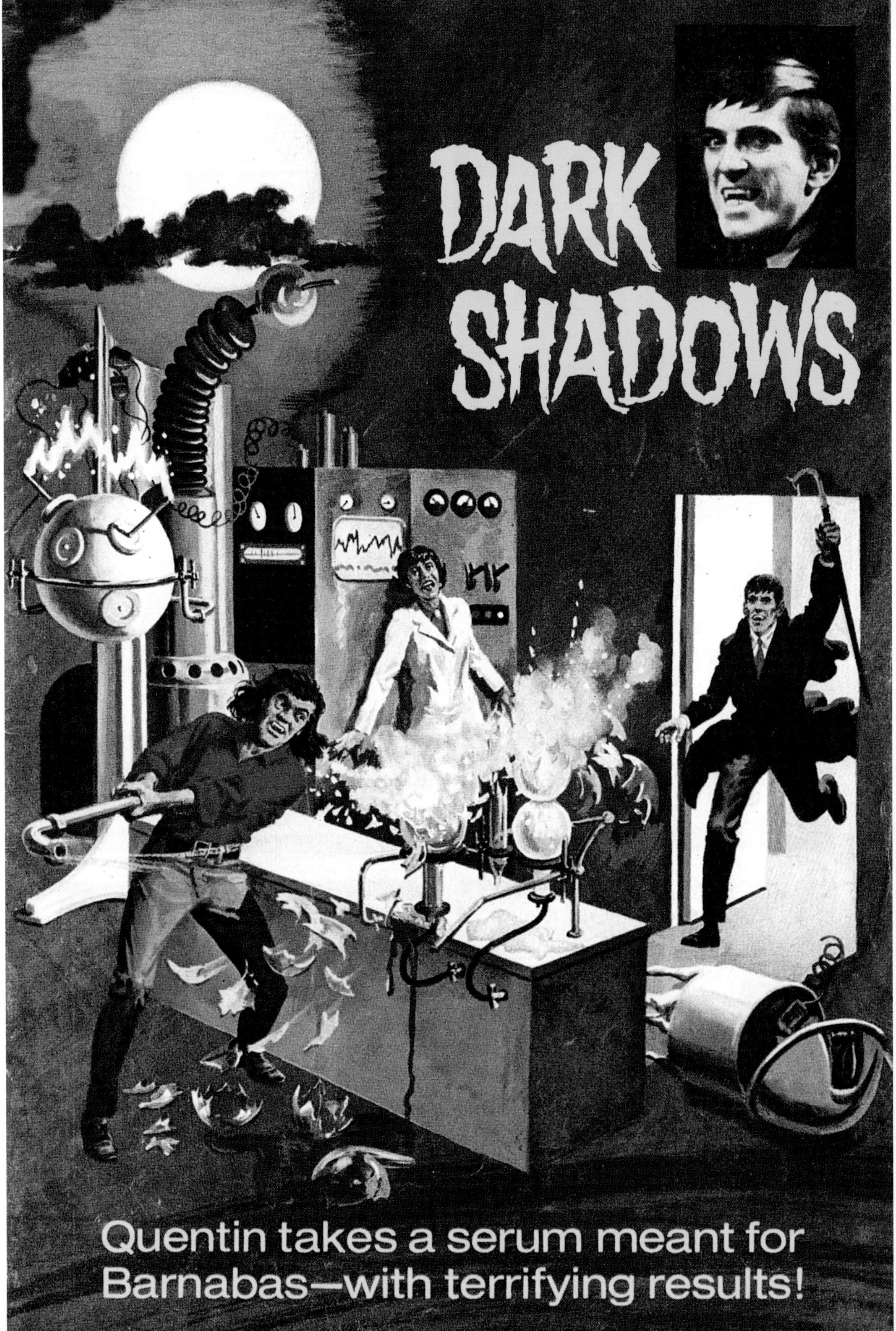
DARK SHADOWS
Quentin takes a serum meant for Barnabas—with terrifying results!

DARK SHADOWS

QUENTIN THE VAMPIRE

PART 1: The CHANGING CURSE

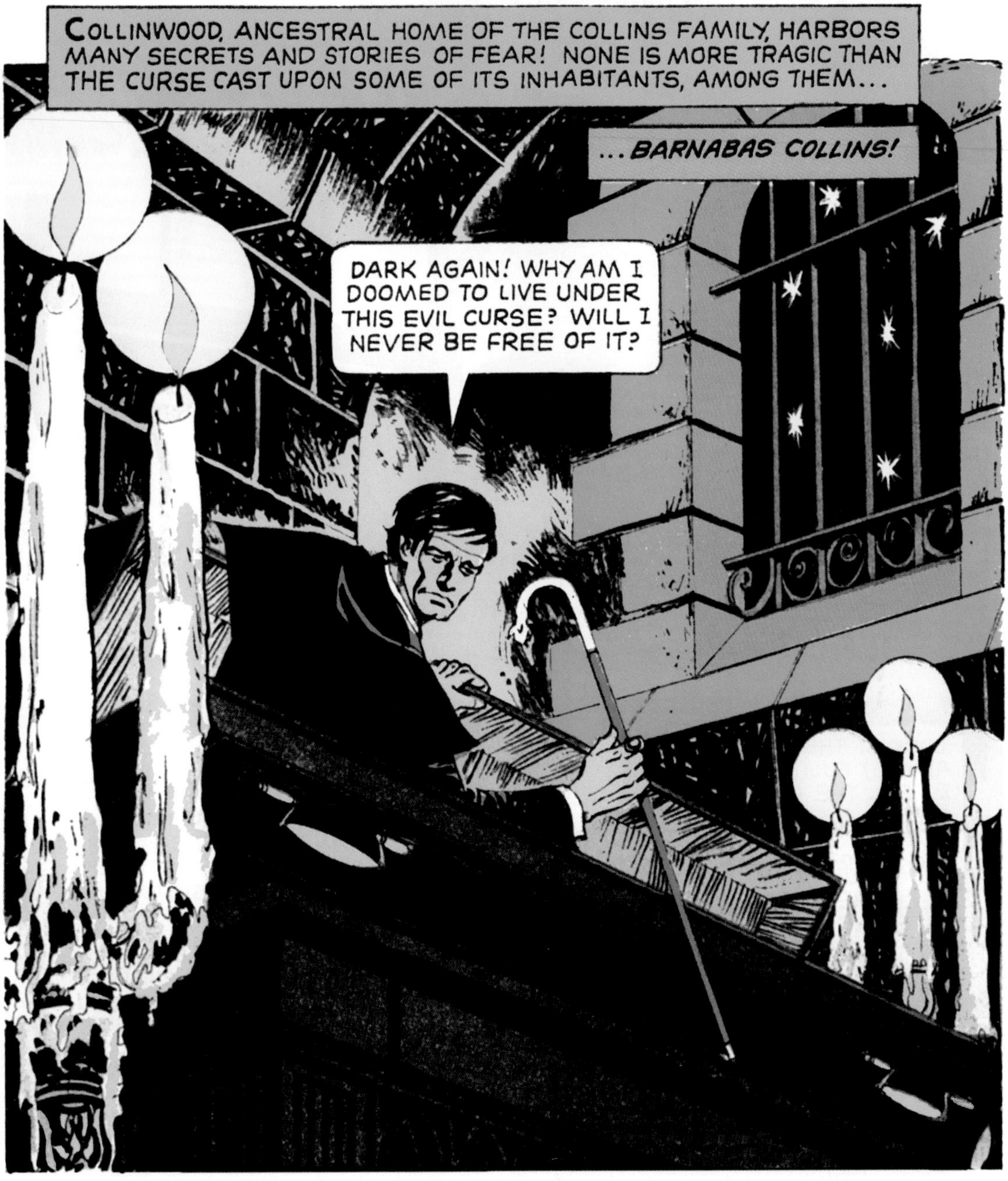
COLLINWOOD, ANCESTRAL HOME OF THE COLLINS FAMILY, HARBORS MANY SECRETS AND STORIES OF FEAR! NONE IS MORE TRAGIC THAN THE CURSE CAST UPON SOME OF ITS INHABITANTS, AMONG THEM...
...BARNABAS COLLINS!
DARK AGAIN! WHY AM I DOOMED TO LIVE UNDER THIS EVIL CURSE? WILL I NEVER BE FREE OF IT?

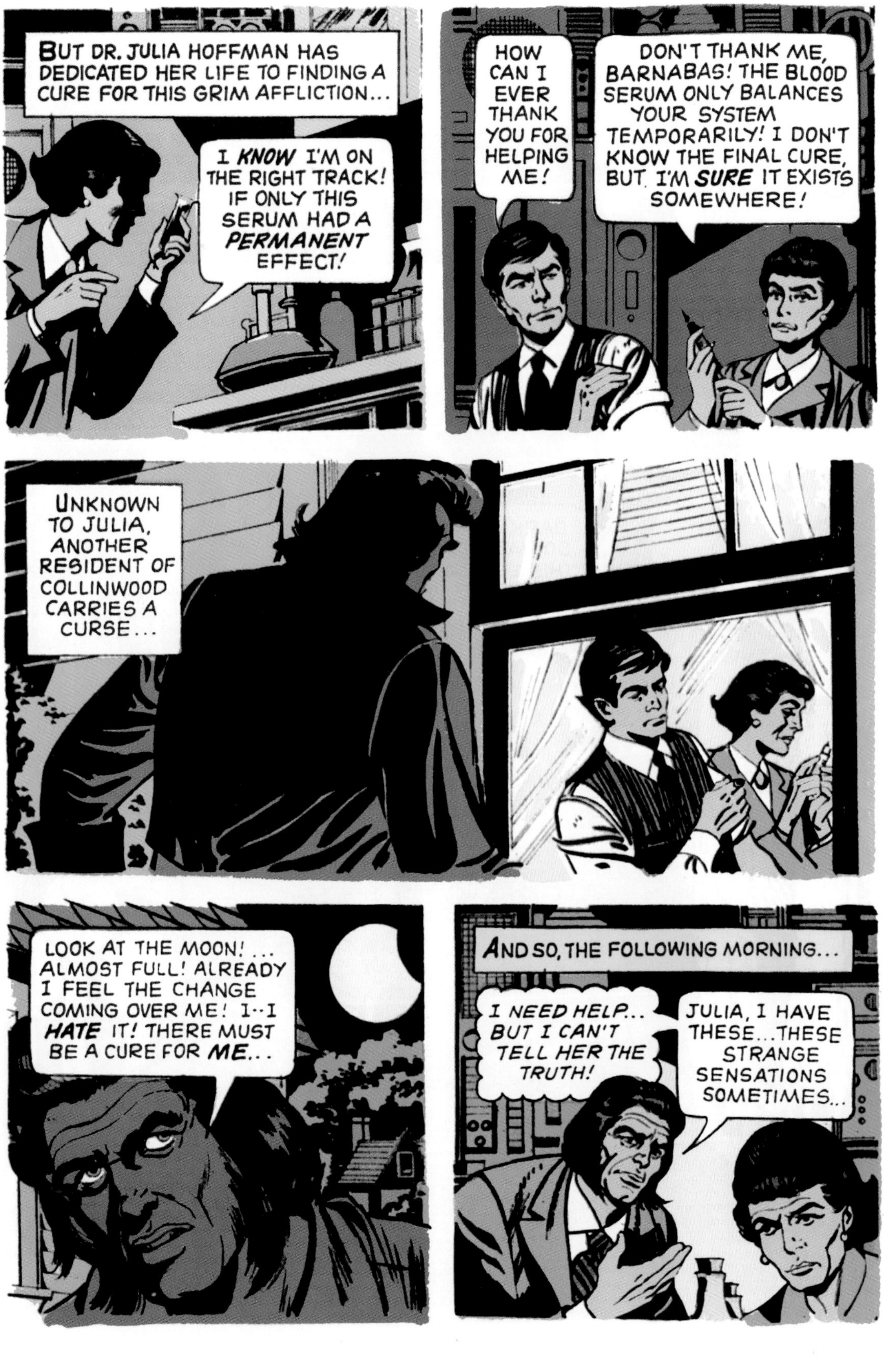
BUT DR. JULIA HOFFMAN HAS DEDICATED HER LIFE TO FINDING A CURE FOR THIS GRIM AFFLICTION...
I KNOW I'M ON THE RIGHT TRACK! IF ONLY THIS SERUM HAD A PERMANENT EFFECT!
HOW CAN I EVER THANK YOU FOR HELPING ME!
DON'T THANK ME, BARNABAS! THE BLOOD SERUM ONLY BALANCES YOUR SYSTEM TEMPORARILY! I DON'T KNOW THE FINAL CURE, BUT I'M SURE IT EXISTS SOMEWHERE!
UNKNOWN TO JULIA, ANOTHER RESIDENT OF COLLINWOOD CARRIES A CURSE...
LOOK AT THE MOON! ... ALMOST FULL! ALREADY I FEEL THE CHANGE COMING OVER ME! I--I HATE IT! THERE MUST BE A CURE FOR ME...
AND SO, THE FOLLOWING MORNING...
I NEED HELP... BUT I CAN'T TELL HER THE TRUTH!
JULIA, I HAVE THESE...THESE STRANGE SENSATIONS SOMETIMES...

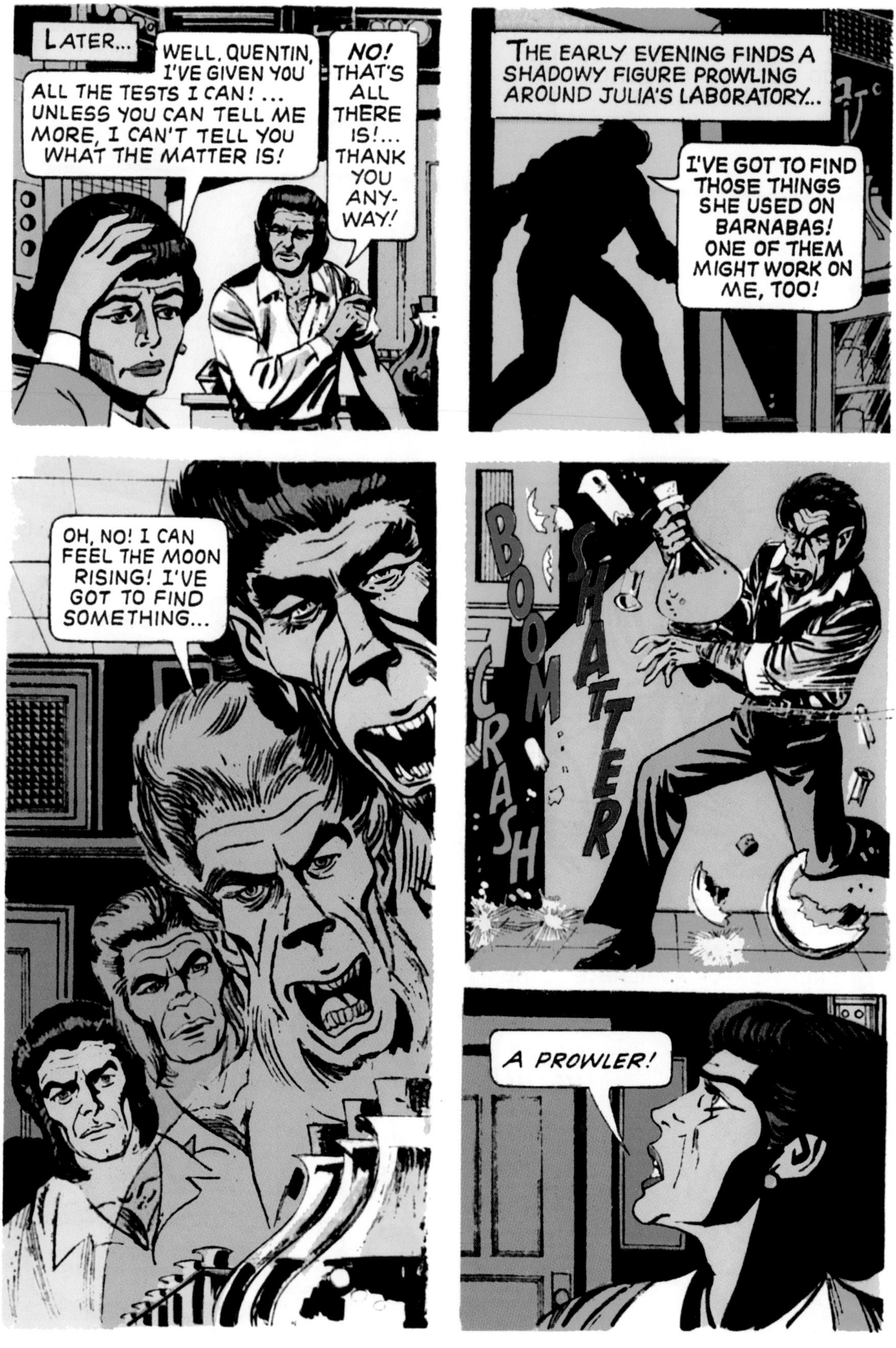
LATER...
WELL, QUENTIN, I'VE GIVEN YOU ALL THE TESTS I CAN! ... UNLESS YOU CAN TELL ME MORE, I CAN'T TELL YOU WHAT THE MATTER IS!
NO! THAT'S ALL THERE IS!... THANK YOU ANY-WAY!
THE EARLY EVENING FINDS A SHADOWY FIGURE PROWLING AROUND JULIA'S LABORATORY...
I'VE GOT TO FIND THOSE THINGS SHE USED ON BARNABAS! ONE OF THEM MIGHT WORK ON ME, TOO!
OH, NO! I CAN FEEL THE MOON RISING! I'VE GOT TO FIND SOMETHING...
BOOM
SHATTER
CRASH
A PROWLER!

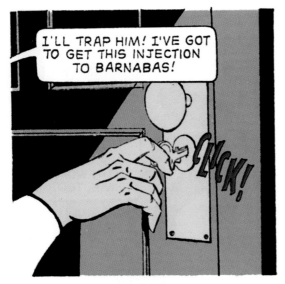

I'LL TRAP HIM! I'VE GOT TO GET THIS INJECTION TO BARNABAS!

CLICK!

BUT THE ENORMOUS STRENGTH OF THE WEREWOLF RIPS DOWN THE DOOR LIKE PAPER...

SLAM!

EEEE!! A MONSTER! HELP!!

TERRIFIED, SHE REACHES FOR THE ONLY WEAPON AVAILABLE...THE SERUM INJECTION FOR BARNABAS...

HELP! HELP!

ERGH! AHH...

WHAT'S HAPPENING TO THIS CREATURE?

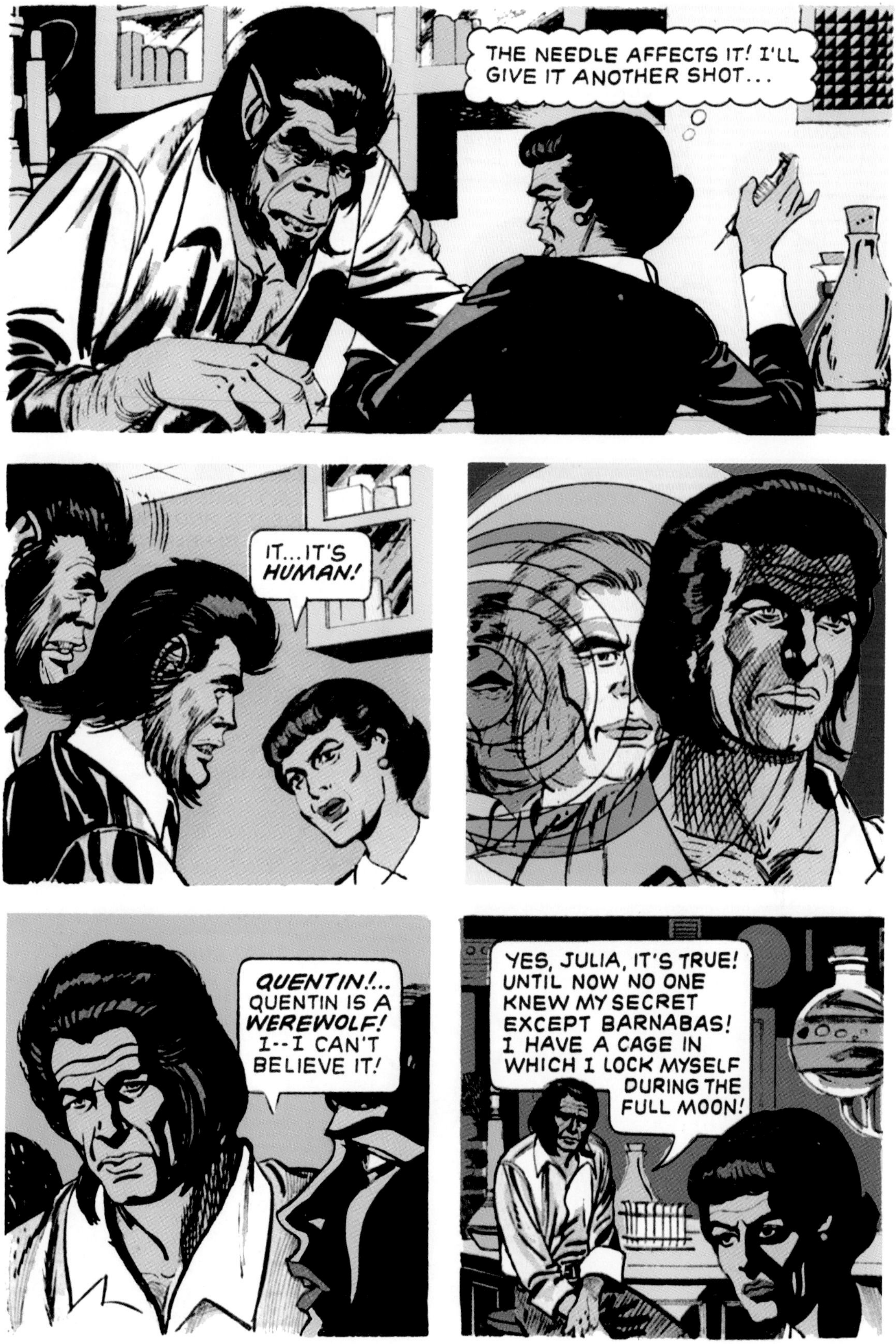
THE NEEDLE AFFECTS IT! I'LL GIVE IT ANOTHER SHOT...
IT...IT'S HUMAN!
QUENTIN!... QUENTIN IS A WEREWOLF! I--I CAN'T BELIEVE IT!
YES, JULIA, IT'S TRUE! UNTIL NOW NO ONE KNEW MY SECRET EXCEPT BARNABAS! I HAVE A CAGE IN WHICH I LOCK MYSELF DURING THE FULL MOON!

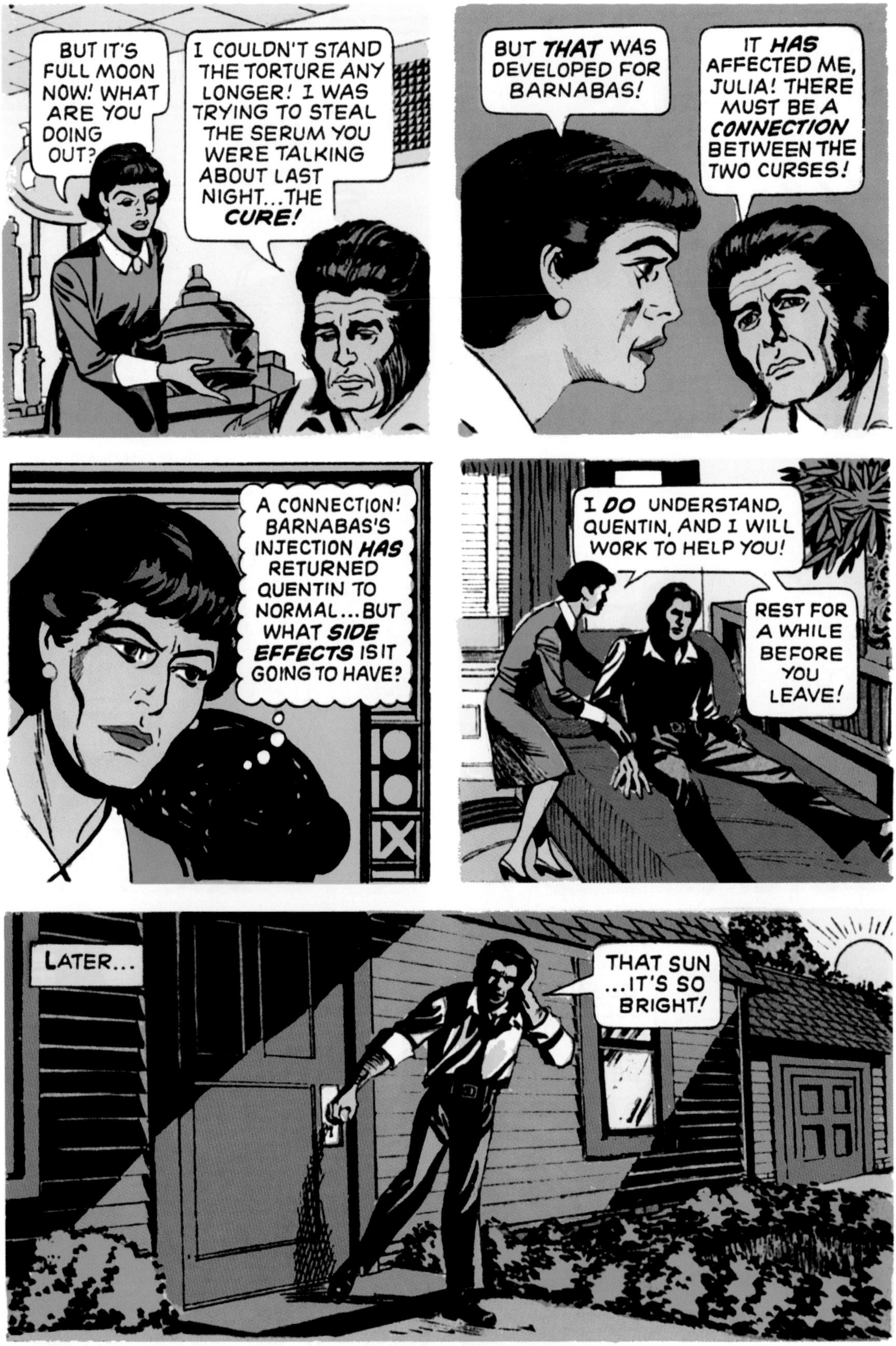
BUT IT'S FULL MOON NOW! WHAT ARE YOU DOING OUT?
I COULDN'T STAND THE TORTURE ANY LONGER! I WAS TRYING TO STEAL THE SERUM YOU WERE TALKING ABOUT LAST NIGHT... THE CURE!
BUT THAT WAS DEVELOPED FOR BARNABAS!
IT HAS AFFECTED ME, JULIA! THERE MUST BE A CONNECTION BETWEEN THE TWO CURSES!
A CONNECTION! BARNABAS'S INJECTION HAS RETURNED QUENTIN TO NORMAL... BUT WHAT SIDE EFFECTS IS IT GOING TO HAVE?
I DO UNDERSTAND, QUENTIN, AND I WILL WORK TO HELP YOU!
REST FOR A WHILE BEFORE YOU LEAVE!
LATER...
THAT SUN ...IT'S SO BRIGHT!

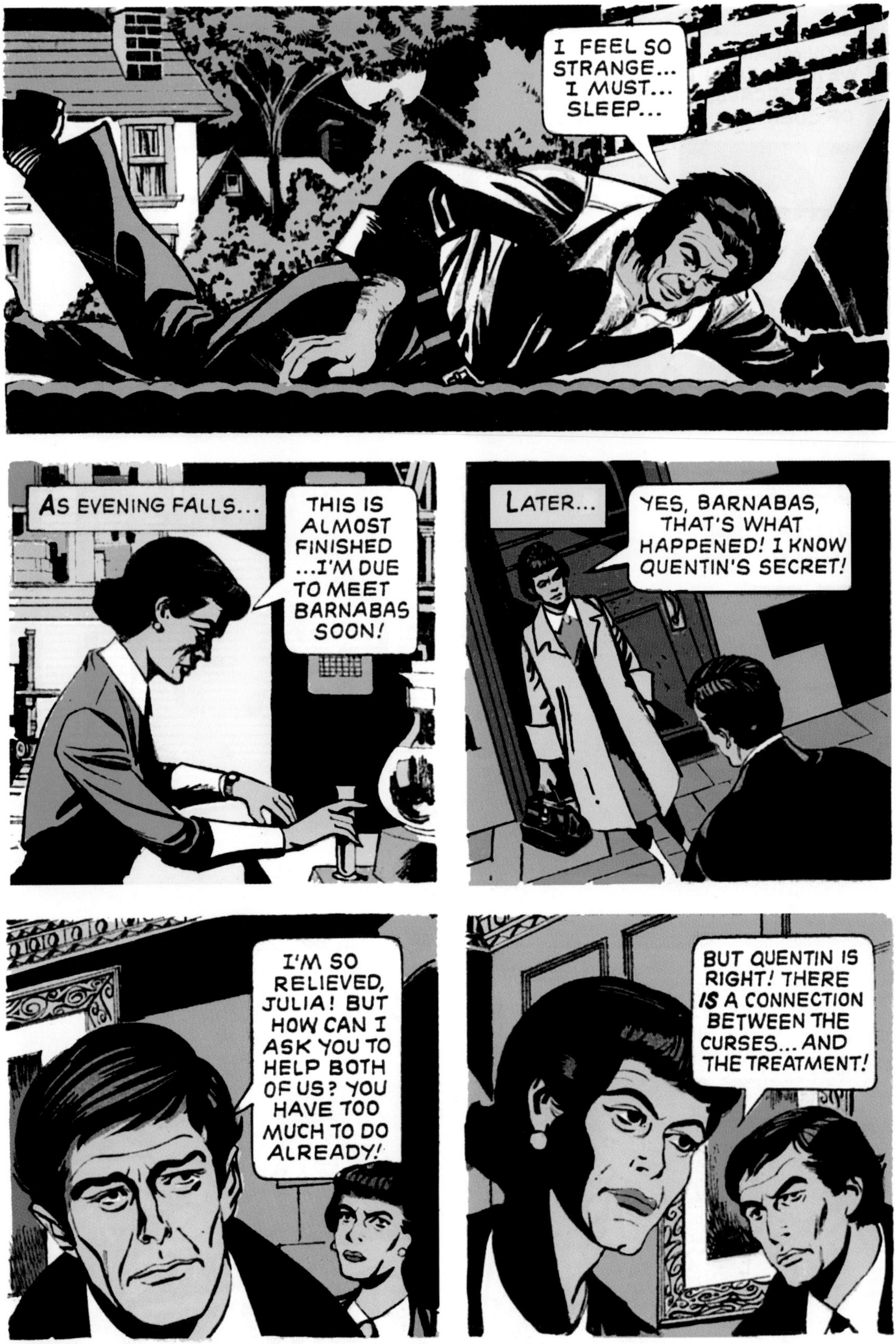
I FEEL SO STRANGE... I MUST... SLEEP...
AS EVENING FALLS...
THIS IS ALMOST FINISHED ...I'M DUE TO MEET BARNABAS SOON!
LATER...
YES, BARNABAS, THAT'S WHAT HAPPENED! I KNOW QUENTIN'S SECRET!
I'M SO RELIEVED, JULIA! BUT HOW CAN I ASK YOU TO HELP BOTH OF US? YOU HAVE TOO MUCH TO DO ALREADY!
BUT QUENTIN IS RIGHT! THERE *IS* A CONNECTION BETWEEN THE CURSES... AND THE TREATMENT!

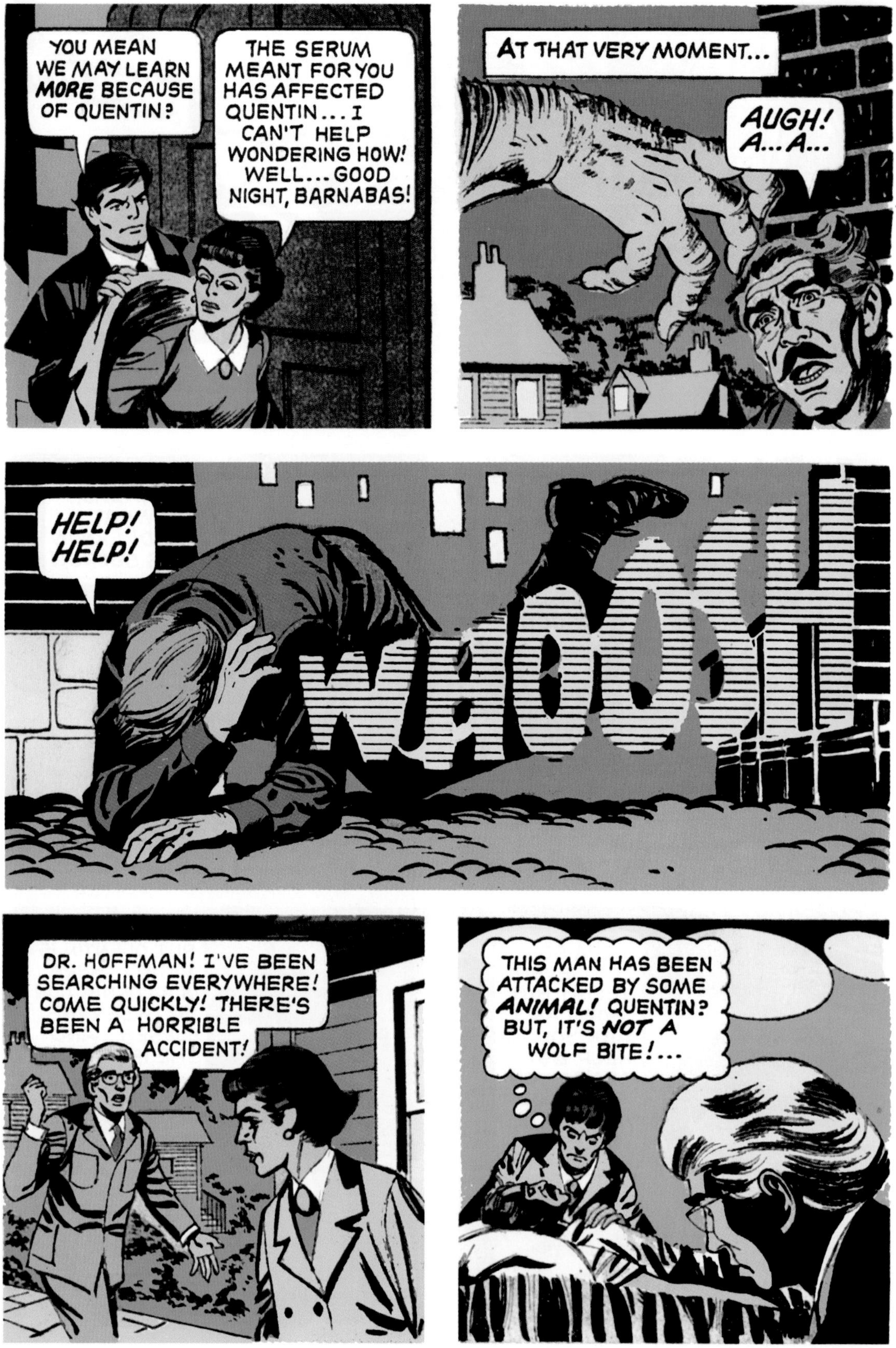
YOU MEAN WE MAY LEARN MORE BECAUSE OF QUENTIN?
THE SERUM MEANT FOR YOU HAS AFFECTED QUENTIN... I CAN'T HELP WONDERING HOW! WELL... GOOD NIGHT, BARNABAS!
AT THAT VERY MOMENT...
AUGH! A... A...
HELP! HELP!
WHOOSH
DR. HOFFMAN! I'VE BEEN SEARCHING EVERYWHERE! COME QUICKLY! THERE'S BEEN A HORRIBLE ACCIDENT!
THIS MAN HAS BEEN ATTACKED BY SOME ANIMAL! QUENTIN? BUT, IT'S NOT A WOLF BITE!...

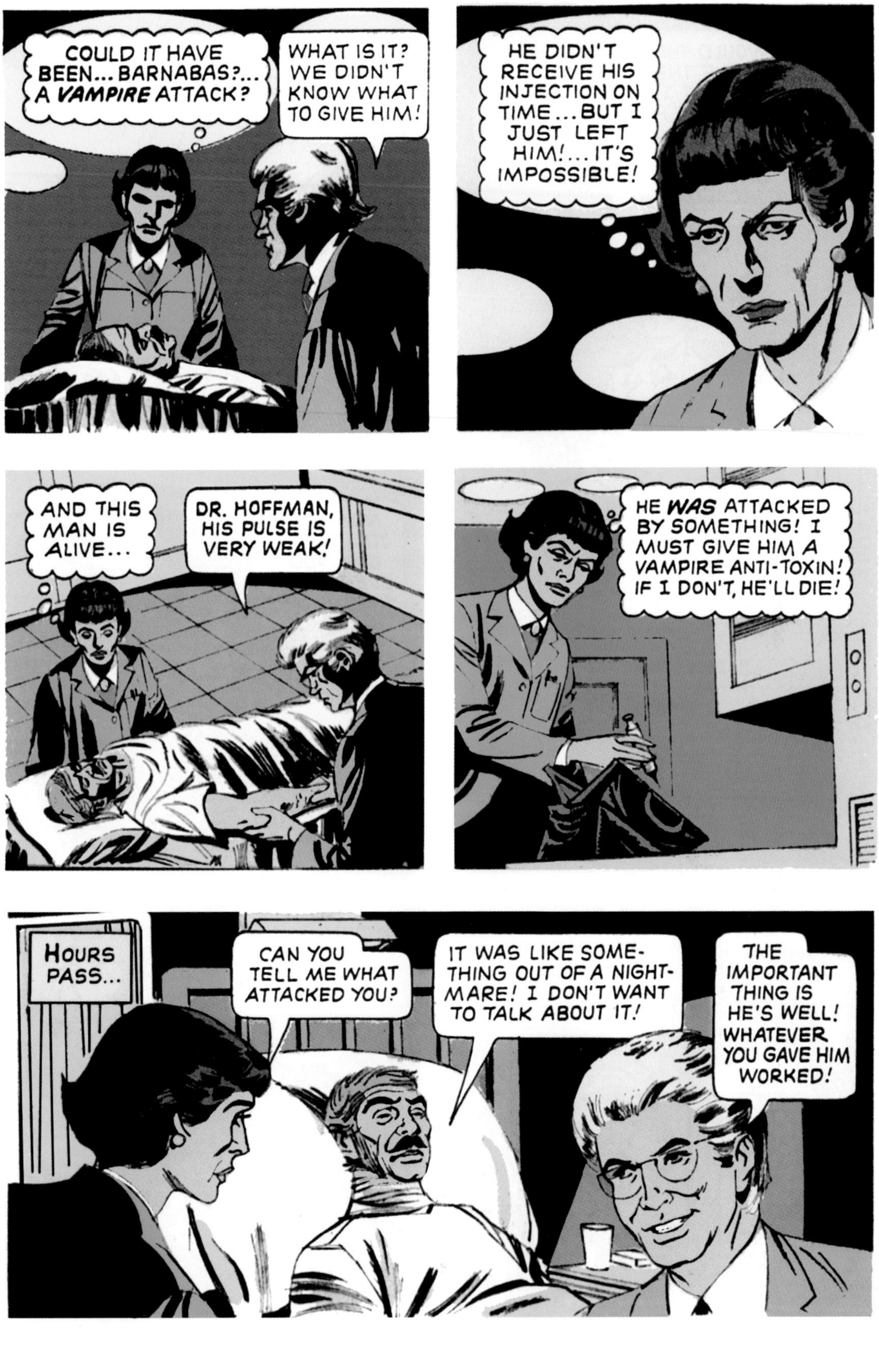
COULD IT HAVE BEEN... BARNABAS?... A VAMPIRE ATTACK?
WHAT IS IT? WE DIDN'T KNOW WHAT TO GIVE HIM!
HE DIDN'T RECEIVE HIS INJECTION ON TIME... BUT I JUST LEFT HIM!... IT'S IMPOSSIBLE!
AND THIS MAN IS ALIVE...
DR. HOFFMAN, HIS PULSE IS VERY WEAK!
HE WAS ATTACKED BY SOMETHING! I MUST GIVE HIM A VAMPIRE ANTI-TOXIN! IF I DON'T, HE'LL DIE!
HOURS PASS...
CAN YOU TELL ME WHAT ATTACKED YOU?
IT WAS LIKE SOME-THING OUT OF A NIGHT-MARE! I DON'T WANT TO TALK ABOUT IT!
THE IMPORTANT THING IS HE'S WELL! WHATEVER YOU GAVE HIM WORKED!

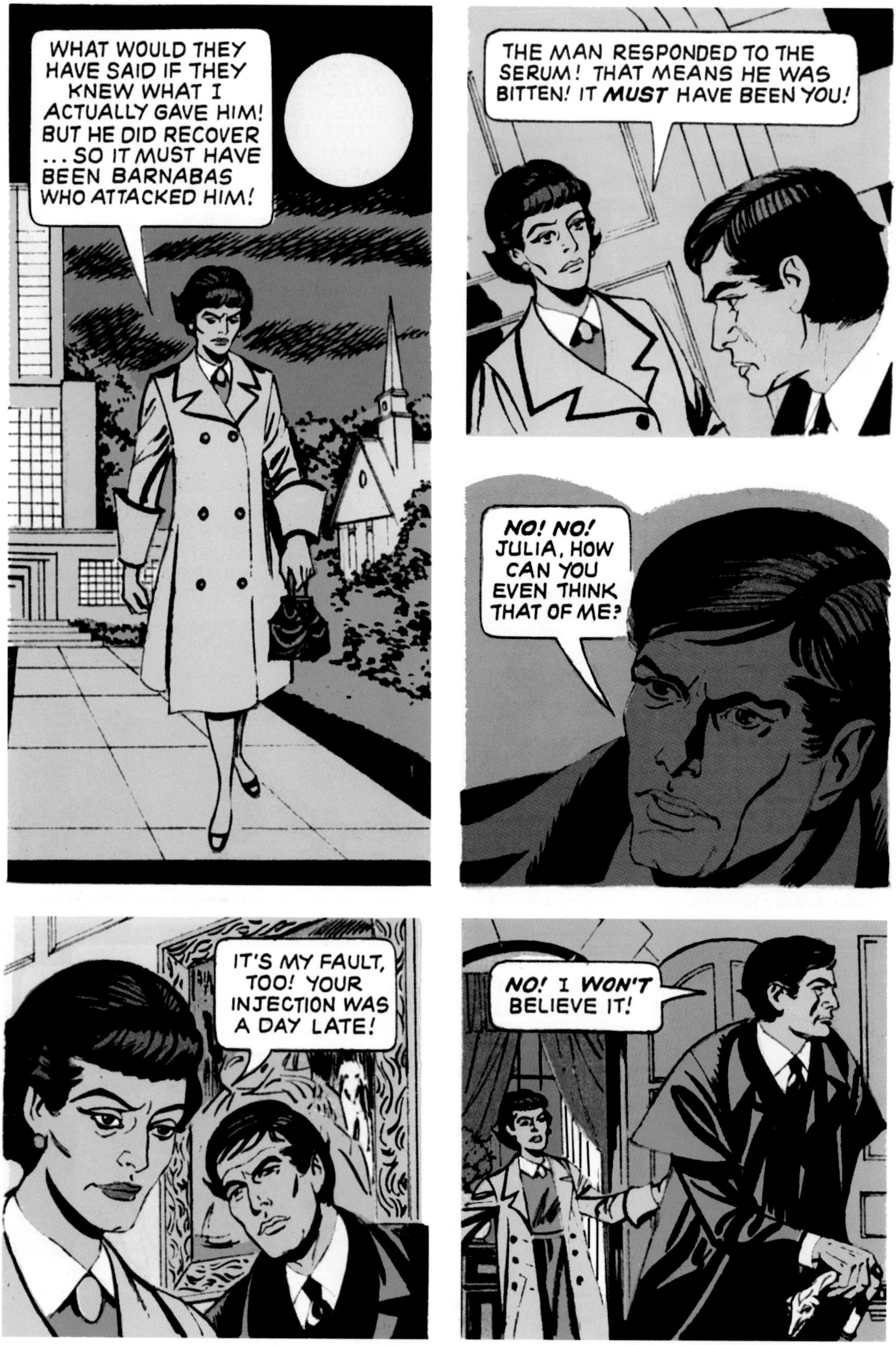
WHAT WOULD THEY HAVE SAID IF THEY KNEW WHAT I ACTUALLY GAVE HIM! BUT HE DID RECOVER ... SO IT MUST HAVE BEEN BARNABAS WHO ATTACKED HIM!
THE MAN RESPONDED TO THE SERUM! THAT MEANS HE WAS BITTEN! IT MUST HAVE BEEN YOU!
NO! NO! JULIA, HOW CAN YOU EVEN THINK THAT OF ME?
IT'S MY FAULT, TOO! YOUR INJECTION WAS A DAY LATE!
NO! I WON'T BELIEVE IT!

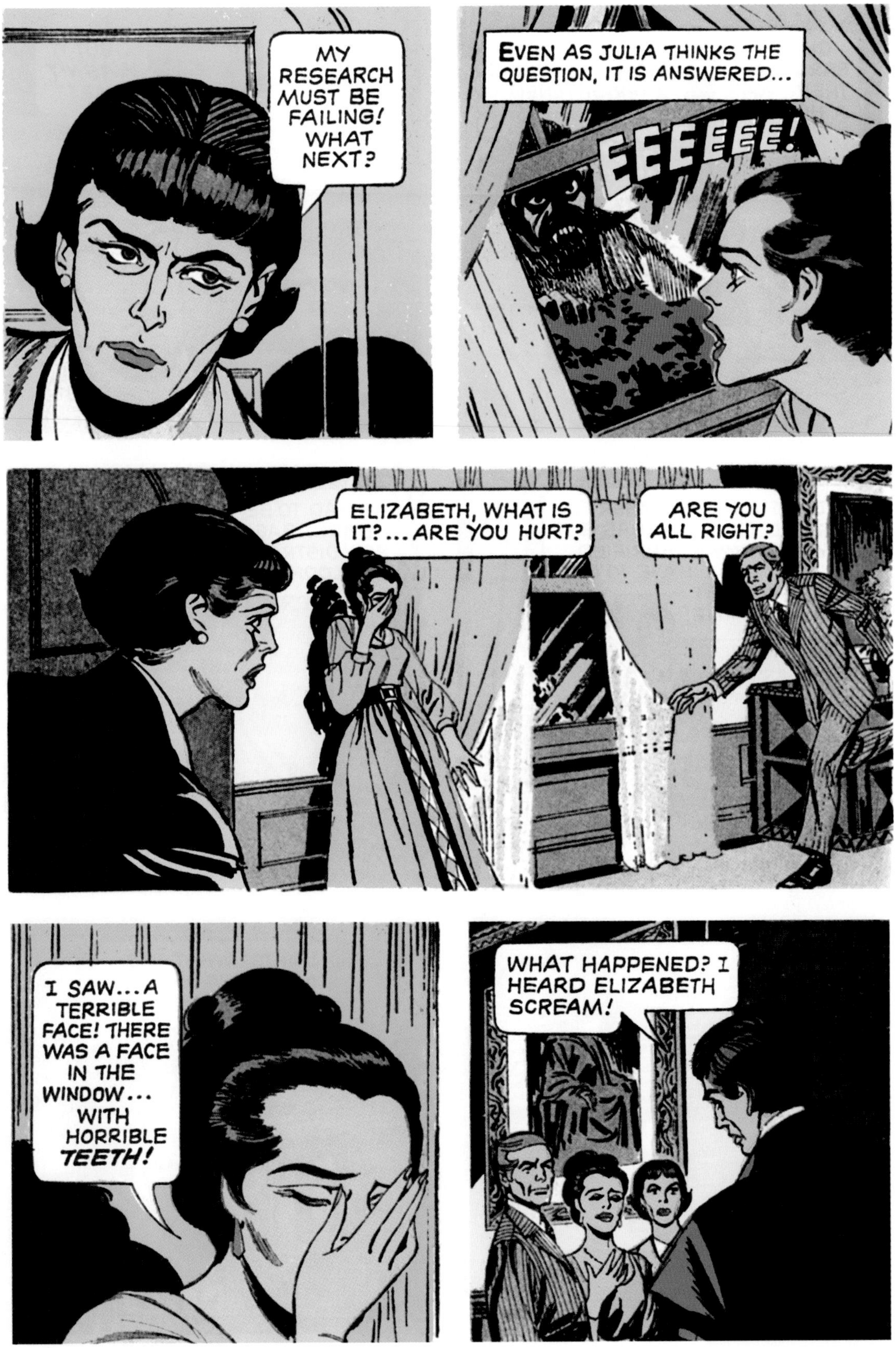
MY RESEARCH MUST BE FAILING! WHAT NEXT?
EVEN AS JULIA THINKS THE QUESTION, IT IS ANSWERED...
EEEEEE!
ELIZABETH, WHAT IS IT?... ARE YOU HURT?
ARE YOU ALL RIGHT?
I SAW... A TERRIBLE FACE! THERE WAS A FACE IN THE WINDOW... WITH HORRIBLE TEETH!
WHAT HAPPENED? I HEARD ELIZABETH SCREAM!

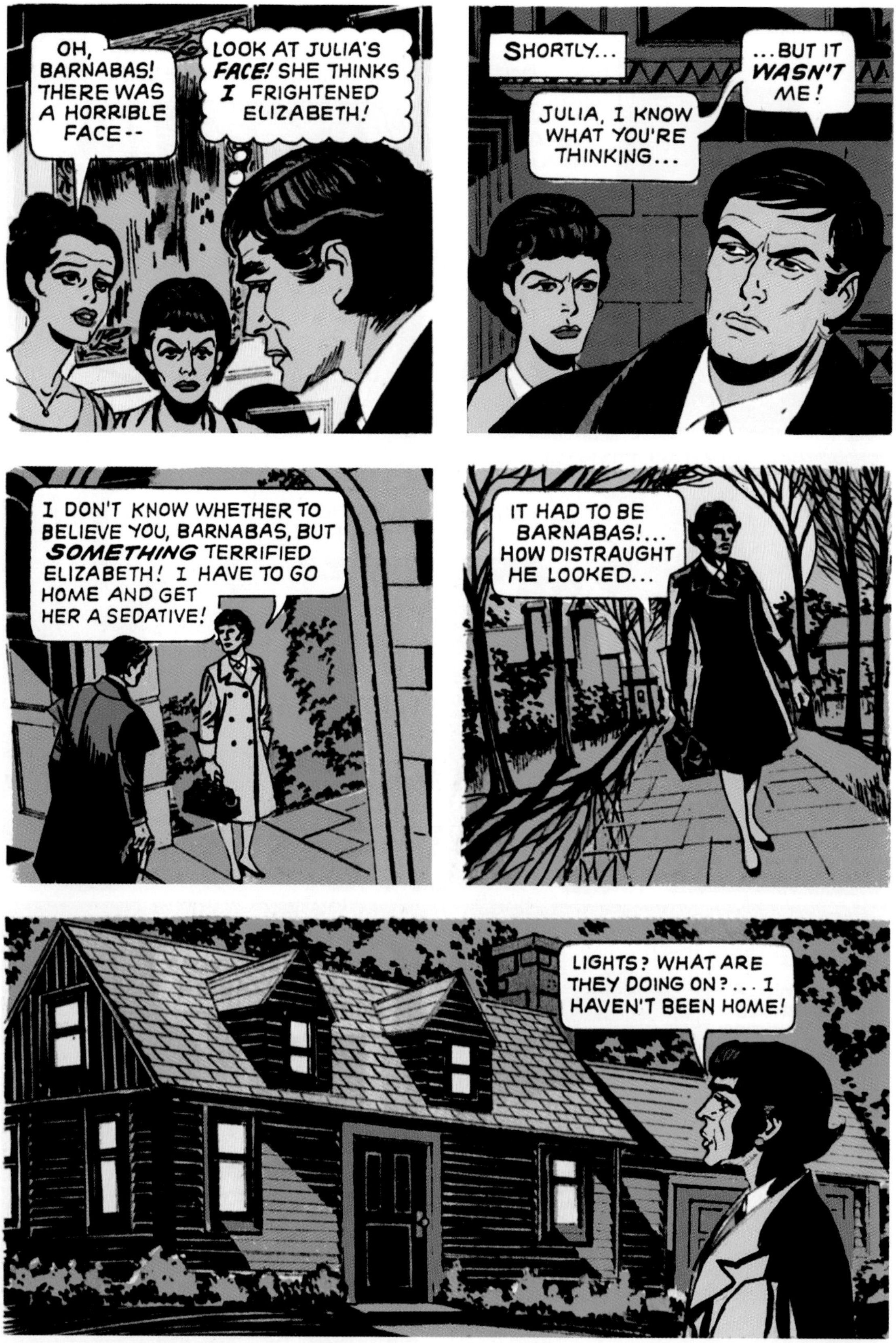

OH, BARNABAS! THERE WAS A HORRIBLE FACE--
LOOK AT JULIA'S FACE! SHE THINKS I FRIGHTENED ELIZABETH!
SHORTLY...
JULIA, I KNOW WHAT YOU'RE THINKING...
...BUT IT WASN'T ME!
I DON'T KNOW WHETHER TO BELIEVE YOU, BARNABAS, BUT SOMETHING TERRIFIED ELIZABETH! I HAVE TO GO HOME AND GET HER A SEDATIVE!
IT HAD TO BE BARNABAS!... HOW DISTRAUGHT HE LOOKED...
LIGHTS? WHAT ARE THEY DOING ON?... I HAVEN'T BEEN HOME!

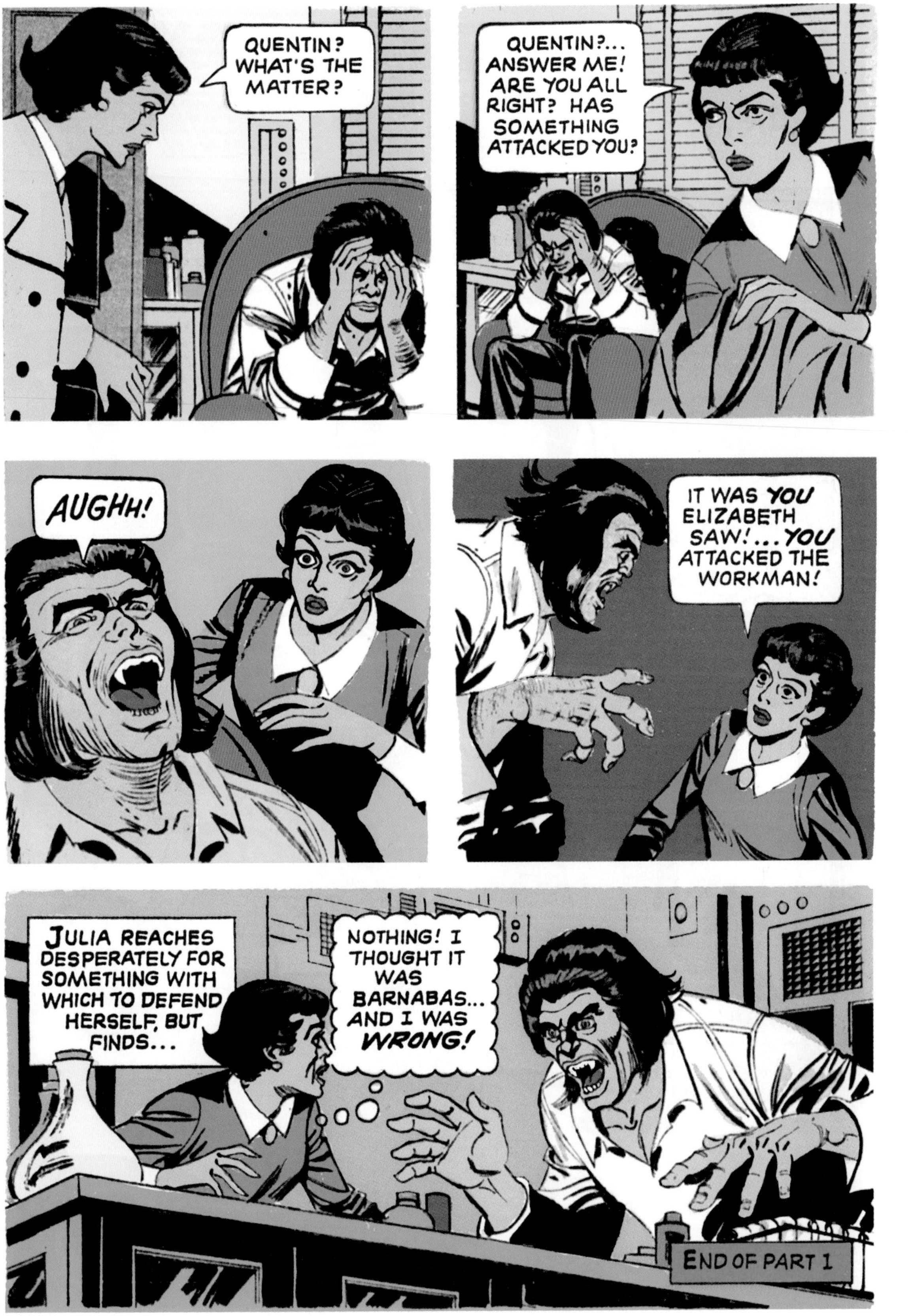
QUENTIN? WHAT'S THE MATTER?
QUENTIN?... ANSWER ME! ARE YOU ALL RIGHT? HAS SOMETHING ATTACKED YOU?
AUGHH!
IT WAS YOU ELIZABETH SAW!... YOU ATTACKED THE WORKMAN!
JULIA REACHES DESPERATELY FOR SOMETHING WITH WHICH TO DEFEND HERSELF, BUT FINDS...
NOTHING! I THOUGHT IT WAS BARNABAS... AND I WAS WRONG!
END OF PART 1

DARK SHADOWS
QUENTIN THE VAMPIRE
PART 2: The Search

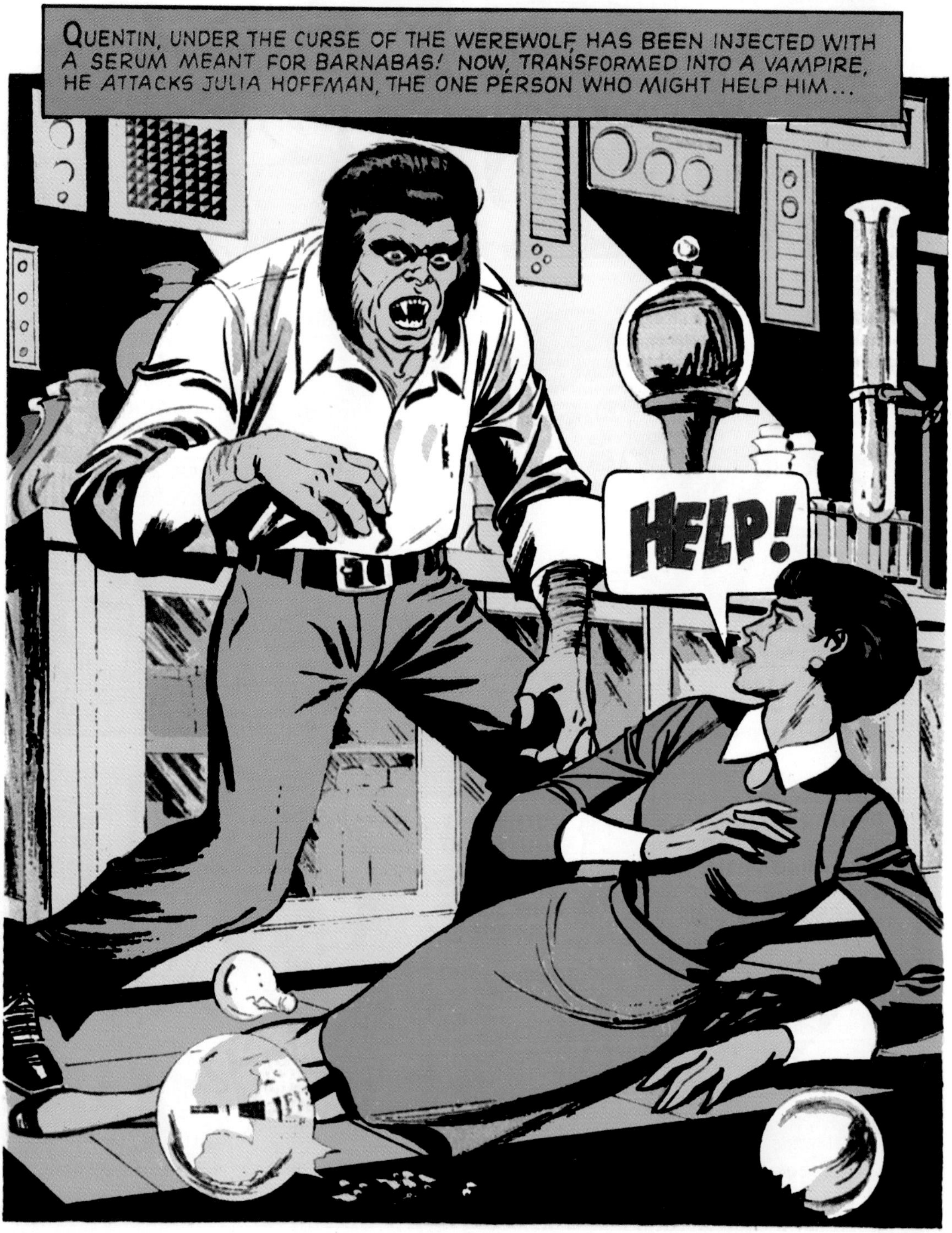
QUENTIN, UNDER THE CURSE OF THE WEREWOLF, HAS BEEN INJECTED WITH A SERUM MEANT FOR BARNABAS! NOW, TRANSFORMED INTO A VAMPIRE, HE ATTACKS JULIA HOFFMAN, THE ONE PERSON WHO MIGHT HELP HIM...
HELP!

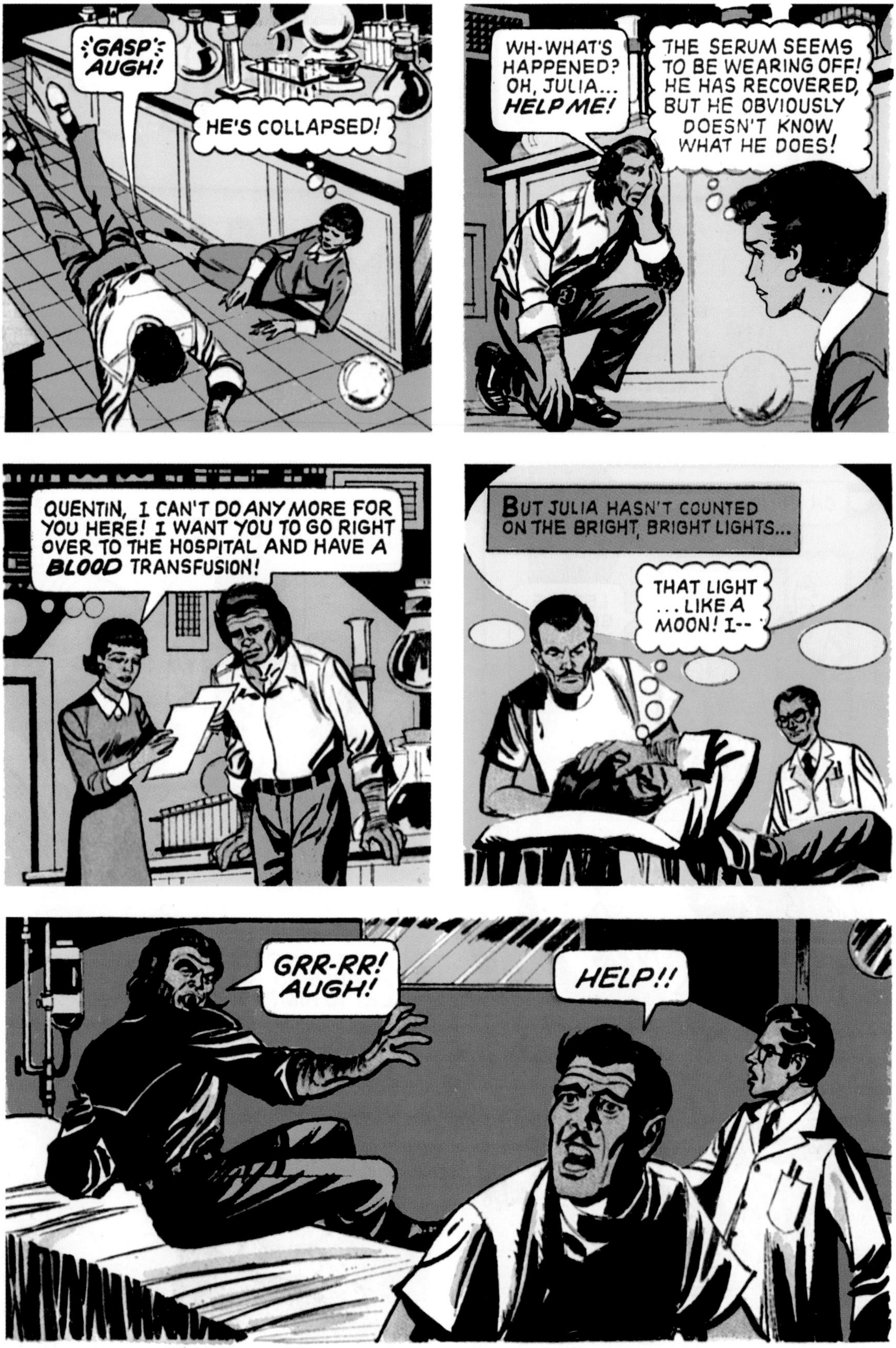
GASP AUGH!
HE'S COLLAPSED!
WH-WHAT'S HAPPENED? OH, JULIA... HELP ME!
THE SERUM SEEMS TO BE WEARING OFF! HE HAS RECOVERED, BUT HE OBVIOUSLY DOESN'T KNOW WHAT HE DOES!
QUENTIN, I CAN'T DO ANY MORE FOR YOU HERE! I WANT YOU TO GO RIGHT OVER TO THE HOSPITAL AND HAVE A BLOOD TRANSFUSION!
BUT JULIA HASN'T COUNTED ON THE BRIGHT, BRIGHT LIGHTS...
THAT LIGHT ... LIKE A MOON! I--
GRR-RR! AUGH!
HELP!!

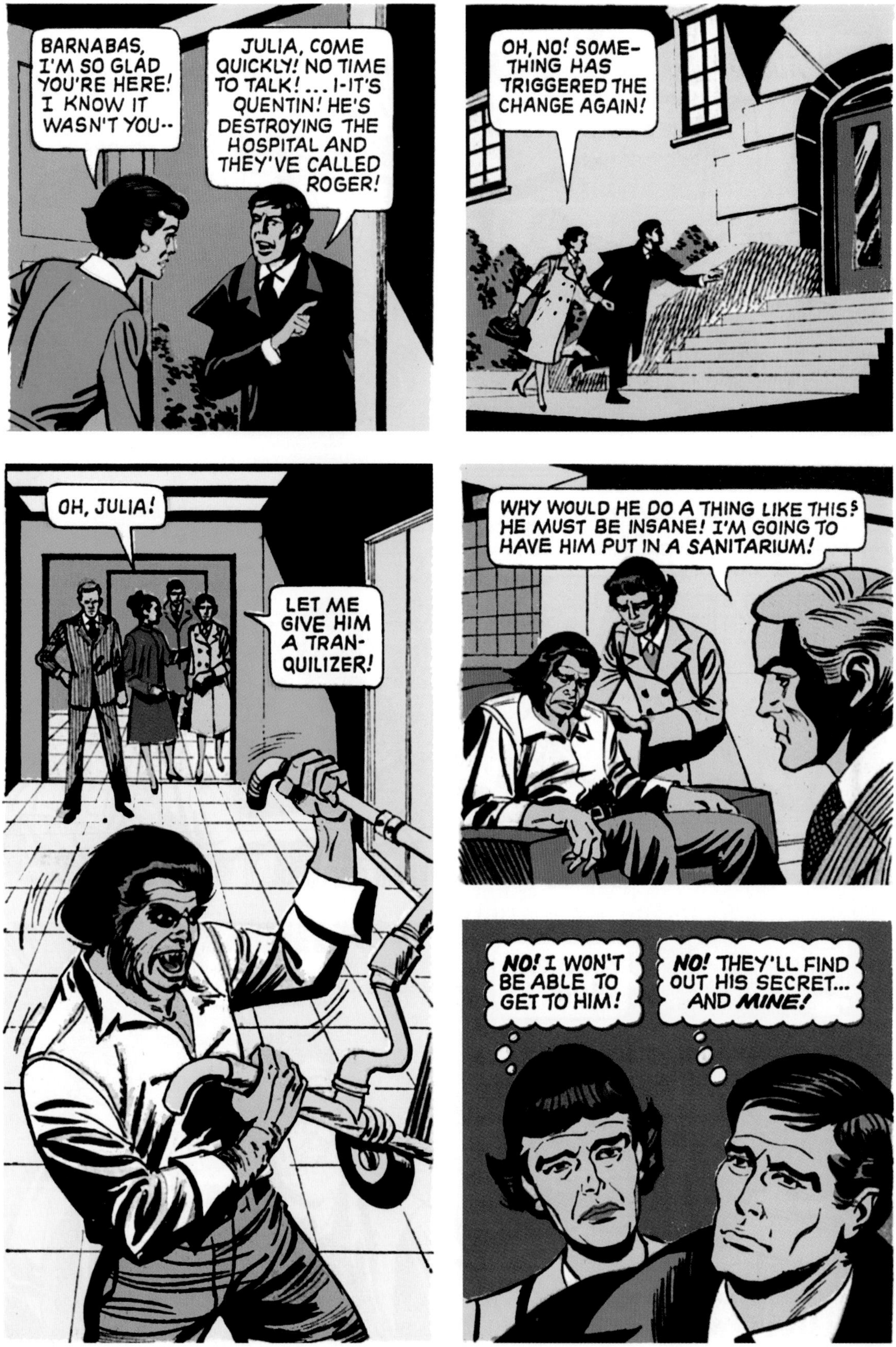
BARNABAS, I'M SO GLAD YOU'RE HERE! I KNOW IT WASN'T YOU--
JULIA, COME QUICKLY! NO TIME TO TALK! ... I-IT'S QUENTIN! HE'S DESTROYING THE HOSPITAL AND THEY'VE CALLED ROGER!
OH, NO! SOME-THING HAS TRIGGERED THE CHANGE AGAIN!
OH, JULIA!
LET ME GIVE HIM A TRAN-QUILIZER!
WHY WOULD HE DO A THING LIKE THIS? HE MUST BE INSANE! I'M GOING TO HAVE HIM PUT IN A SANITARIUM!
NO! I WON'T BE ABLE TO GET TO HIM!
NO! THEY'LL FIND OUT HIS SECRET... AND MINE!

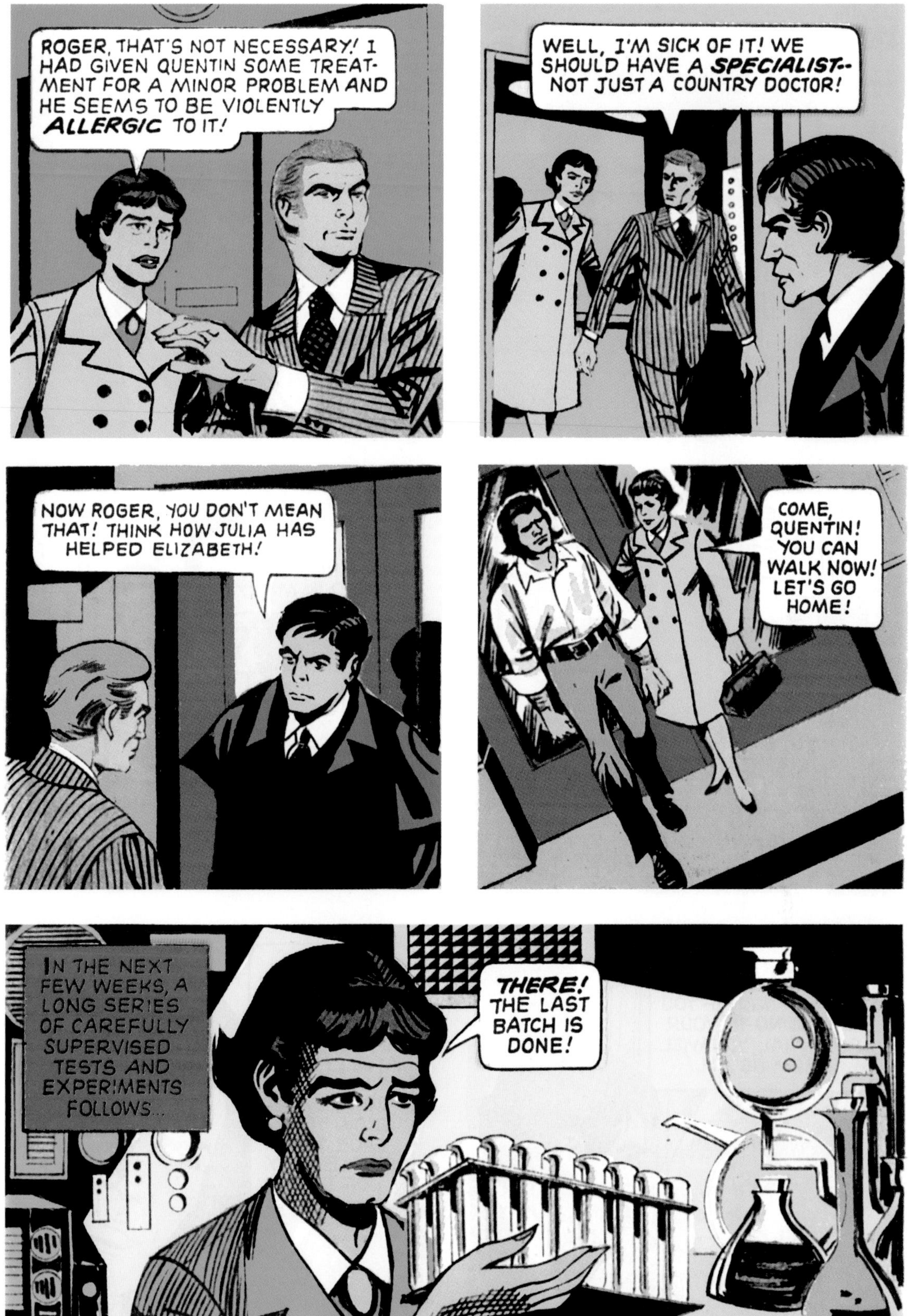
ROGER, THAT'S NOT NECESSARY! I HAD GIVEN QUENTIN SOME TREATMENT FOR A MINOR PROBLEM AND HE SEEMS TO BE VIOLENTLY ALLERGIC TO IT!
WELL, I'M SICK OF IT! WE SHOULD HAVE A SPECIALIST-- NOT JUST A COUNTRY DOCTOR!
NOW ROGER, YOU DON'T MEAN THAT! THINK HOW JULIA HAS HELPED ELIZABETH!
COME, QUENTIN! YOU CAN WALK NOW! LET'S GO HOME!
IN THE NEXT FEW WEEKS, A LONG SERIES OF CAREFULLY SUPERVISED TESTS AND EXPERIMENTS FOLLOWS...
THERE! THE LAST BATCH IS DONE!

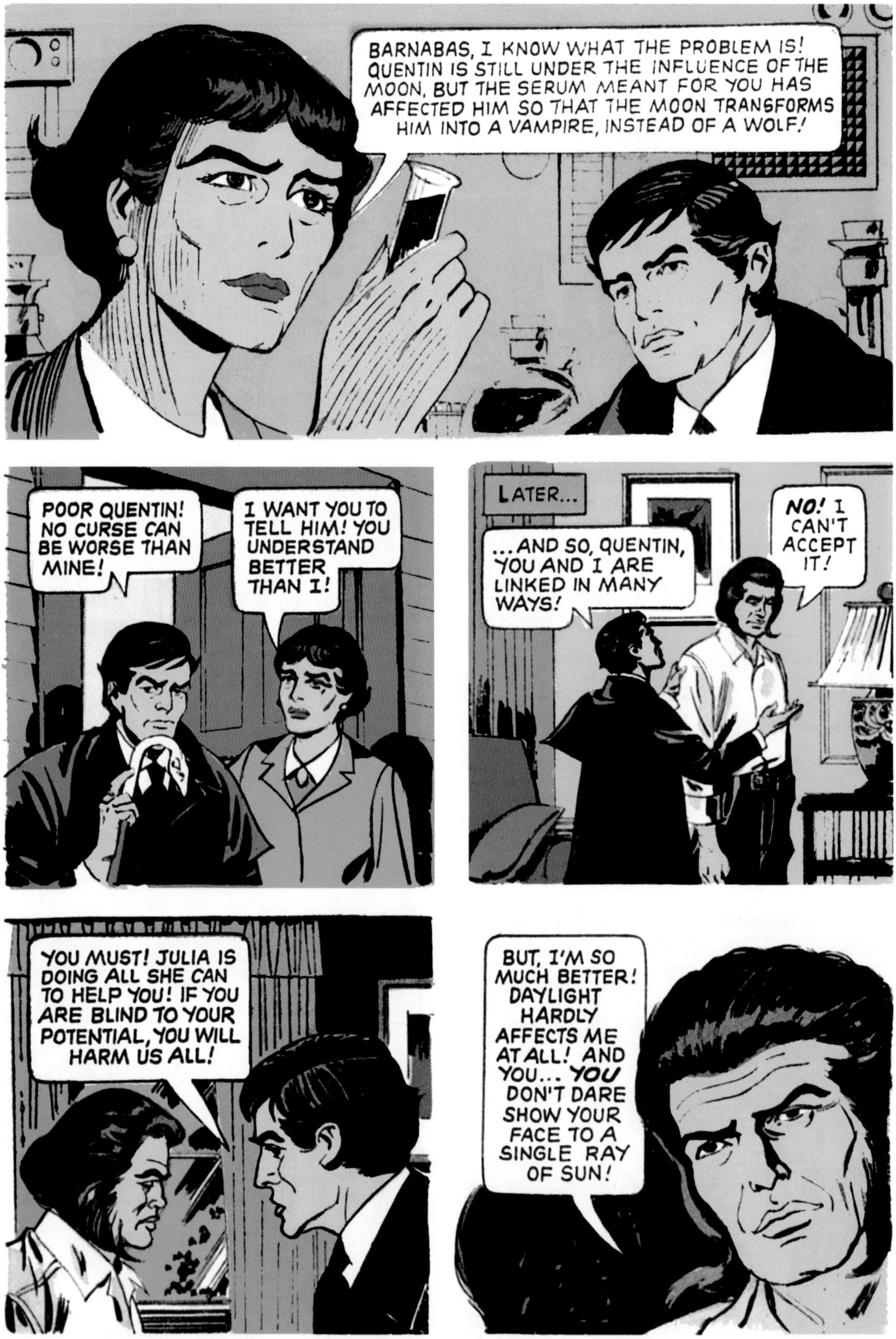
BARNABAS, I KNOW WHAT THE PROBLEM IS! QUENTIN IS STILL UNDER THE INFLUENCE OF THE MOON, BUT THE SERUM MEANT FOR YOU HAS AFFECTED HIM SO THAT THE MOON TRANSFORMS HIM INTO A VAMPIRE, INSTEAD OF A WOLF!
POOR QUENTIN! NO CURSE CAN BE WORSE THAN MINE!
I WANT YOU TO TELL HIM! YOU UNDERSTAND BETTER THAN I!
LATER...
...AND SO, QUENTIN, YOU AND I ARE LINKED IN MANY WAYS!
NO! I CAN'T ACCEPT IT!
YOU MUST! JULIA IS DOING ALL SHE CAN TO HELP YOU! IF YOU ARE BLIND TO YOUR POTENTIAL, YOU WILL HARM US ALL!
BUT, I'M SO MUCH BETTER! DAYLIGHT HARDLY AFFECTS ME AT ALL! AND YOU... YOU DON'T DARE SHOW YOUR FACE TO A SINGLE RAY OF SUN!

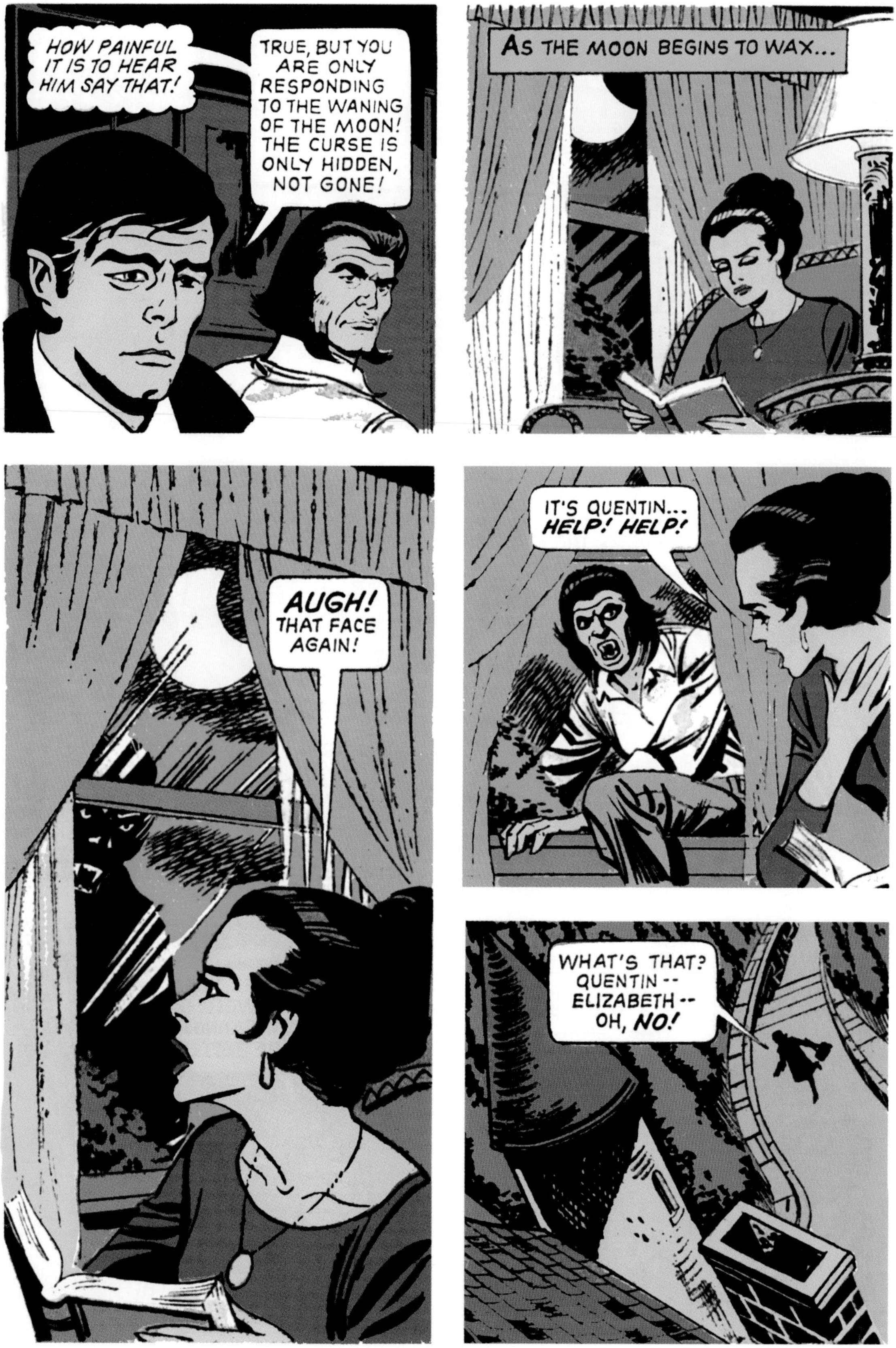
HOW PAINFUL IT IS TO HEAR HIM SAY THAT!
TRUE, BUT YOU ARE ONLY RESPONDING TO THE WANING OF THE MOON! THE CURSE IS ONLY HIDDEN, NOT GONE!
AS THE MOON BEGINS TO WAX...
AUGH! THAT FACE AGAIN!
IT'S QUENTIN... HELP! HELP!
WHAT'S THAT? QUENTIN -- ELIZABETH -- OH, NO!

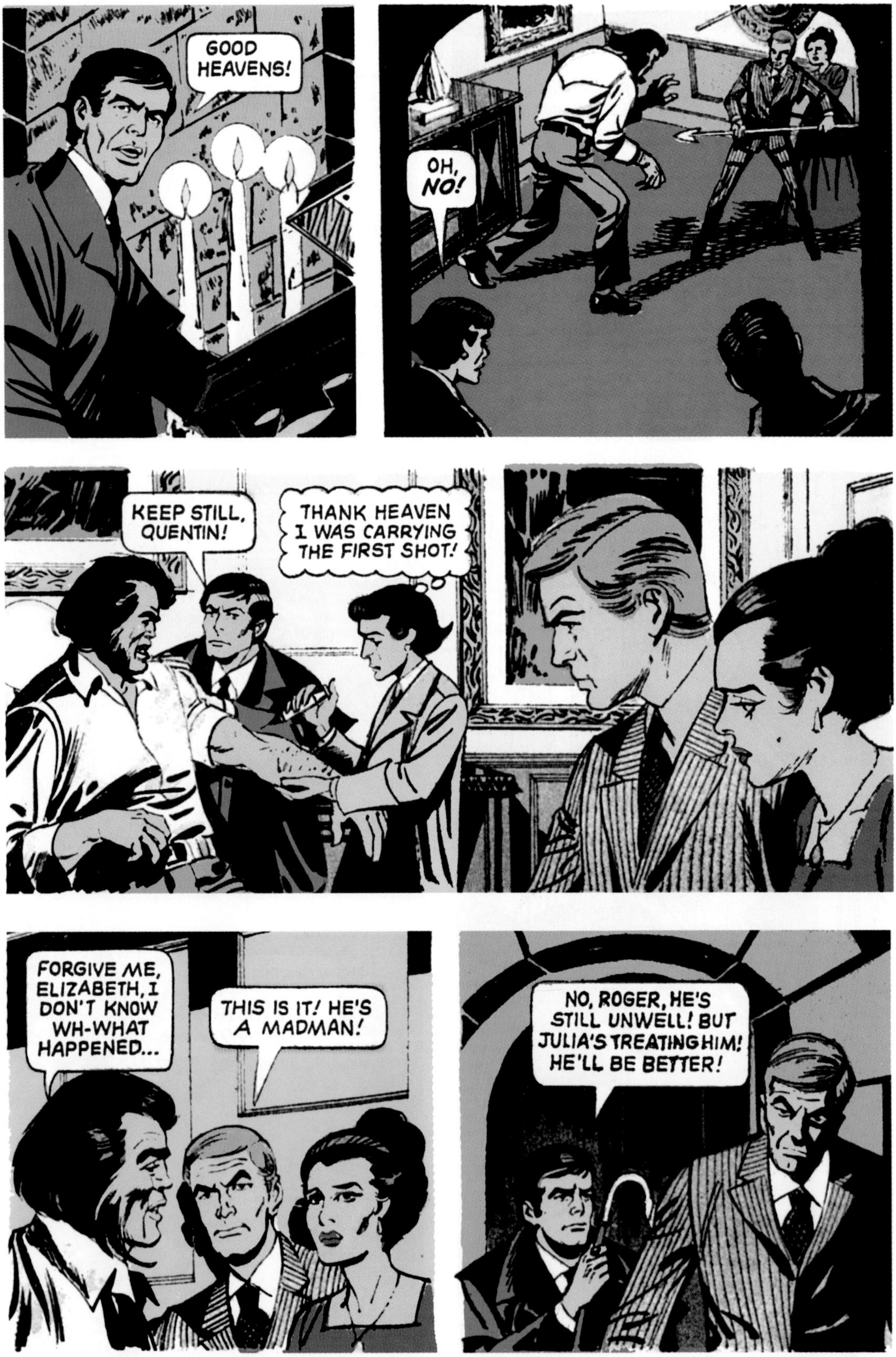
GOOD HEAVENS!
OH, NO!
KEEP STILL, QUENTIN!
THANK HEAVEN I WAS CARRYING THE FIRST SHOT!
FORGIVE ME, ELIZABETH, I DON'T KNOW WH-WHAT HAPPENED...
THIS IS IT! HE'S A MADMAN!
NO, ROGER, HE'S STILL UNWELL! BUT JULIA'S TREATING HIM! HE'LL BE BETTER!

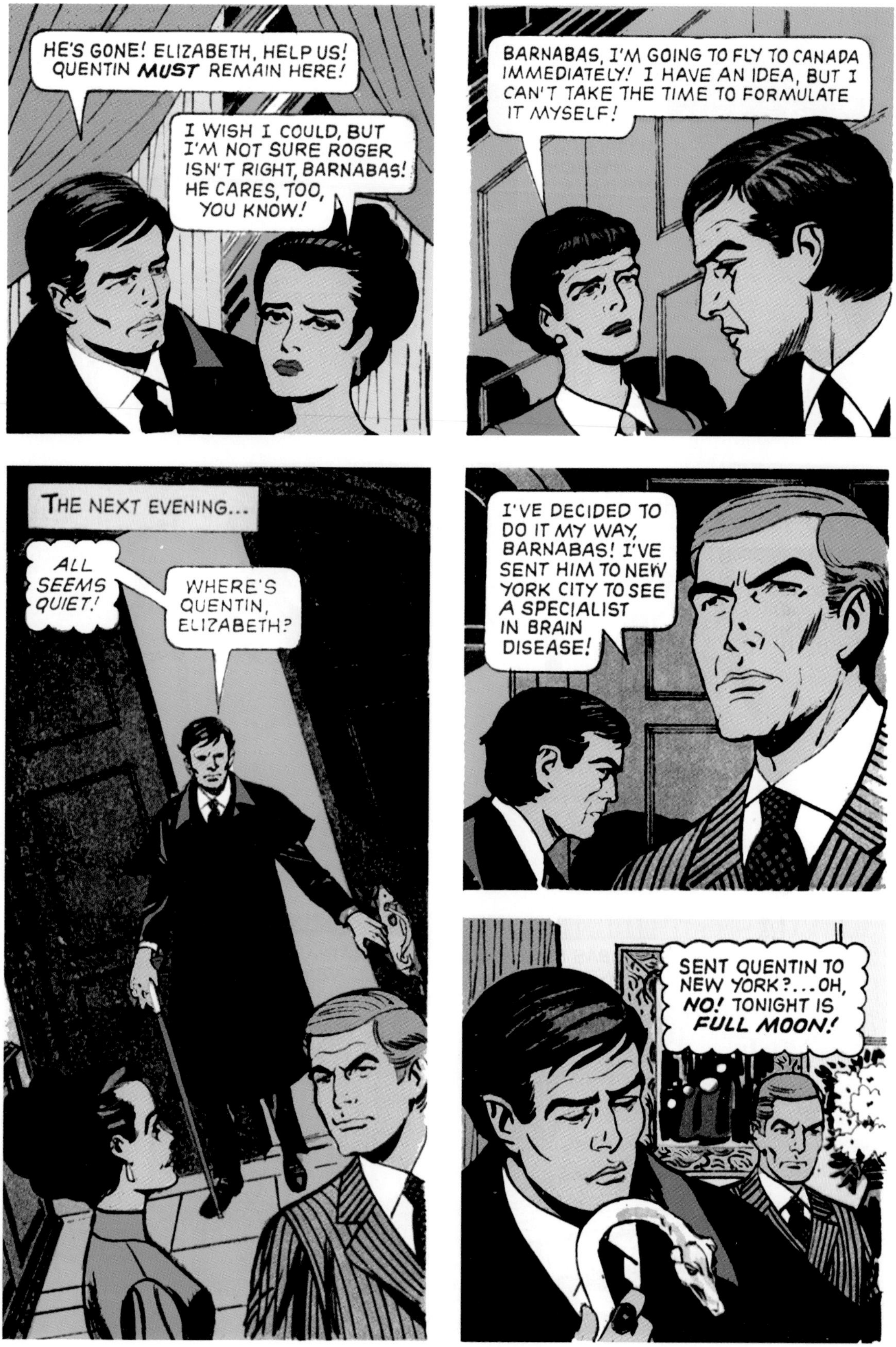

HE'S GONE! ELIZABETH, HELP US! QUENTIN MUST REMAIN HERE!
I WISH I COULD, BUT I'M NOT SURE ROGER ISN'T RIGHT, BARNABAS! HE CARES, TOO, YOU KNOW!
BARNABAS, I'M GOING TO FLY TO CANADA IMMEDIATELY! I HAVE AN IDEA, BUT I CAN'T TAKE THE TIME TO FORMULATE IT MYSELF!
THE NEXT EVENING...
ALL SEEMS QUIET!
WHERE'S QUENTIN, ELIZABETH?
I'VE DECIDED TO DO IT MY WAY, BARNABAS! I'VE SENT HIM TO NEW YORK CITY TO SEE A SPECIALIST IN BRAIN DISEASE!
SENT QUENTIN TO NEW YORK?...OH, NO! TONIGHT IS FULL MOON!

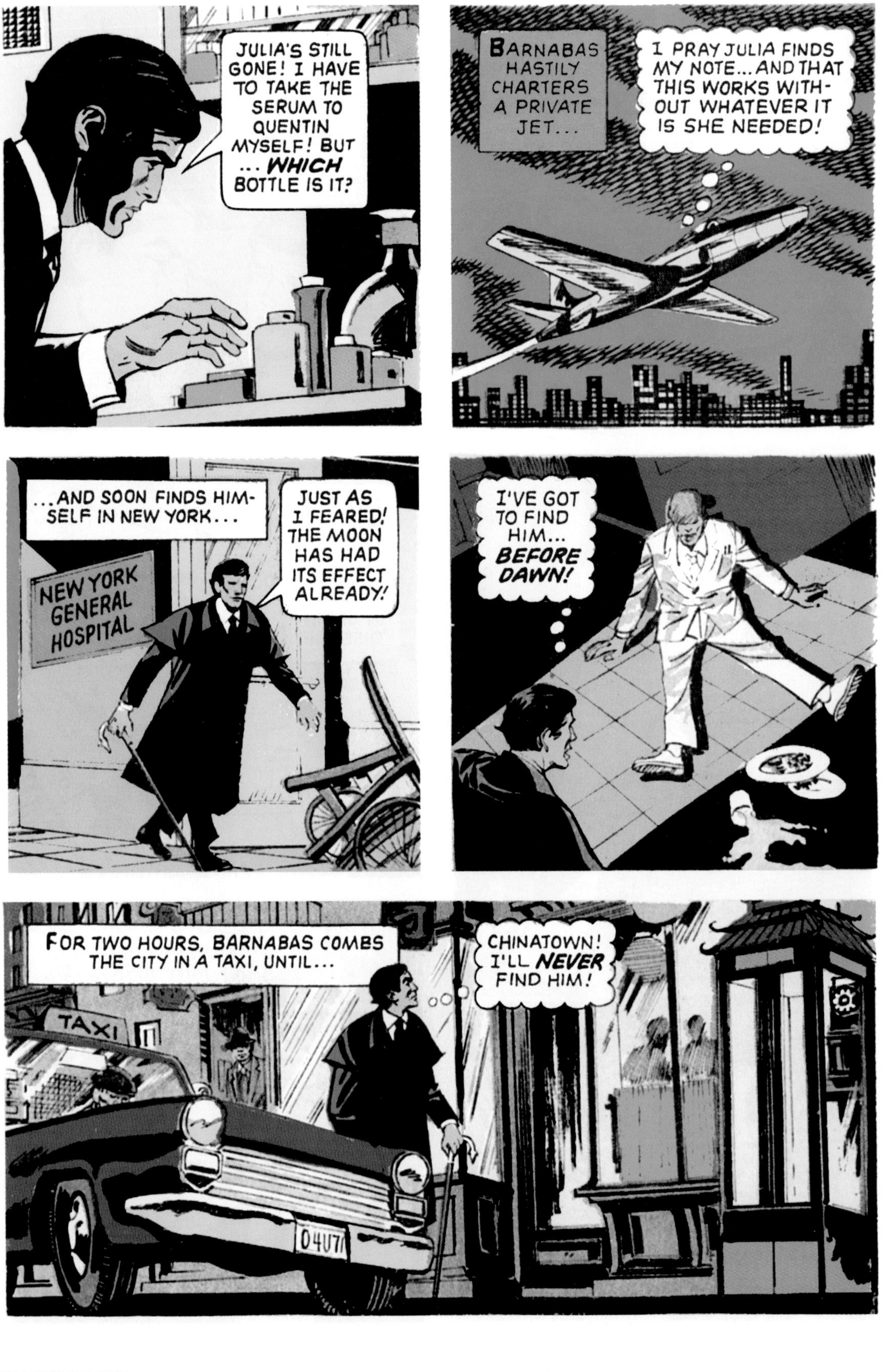
JULIA'S STILL GONE! I HAVE TO TAKE THE SERUM TO QUENTIN MYSELF! BUT ... WHICH BOTTLE IS IT?
BARNABAS HASTILY CHARTERS A PRIVATE JET...
I PRAY JULIA FINDS MY NOTE... AND THAT THIS WORKS WITH-OUT WHATEVER IT IS SHE NEEDED!
...AND SOON FINDS HIM-SELF IN NEW YORK...
JUST AS I FEARED! THE MOON HAS HAD ITS EFFECT ALREADY!
NEW YORK GENERAL HOSPITAL
I'VE GOT TO FIND HIM... BEFORE DAWN!
FOR TWO HOURS, BARNABAS COMBS THE CITY IN A TAXI, UNTIL...
CHINATOWN! I'LL NEVER FIND HIM!
TAXI
04U71

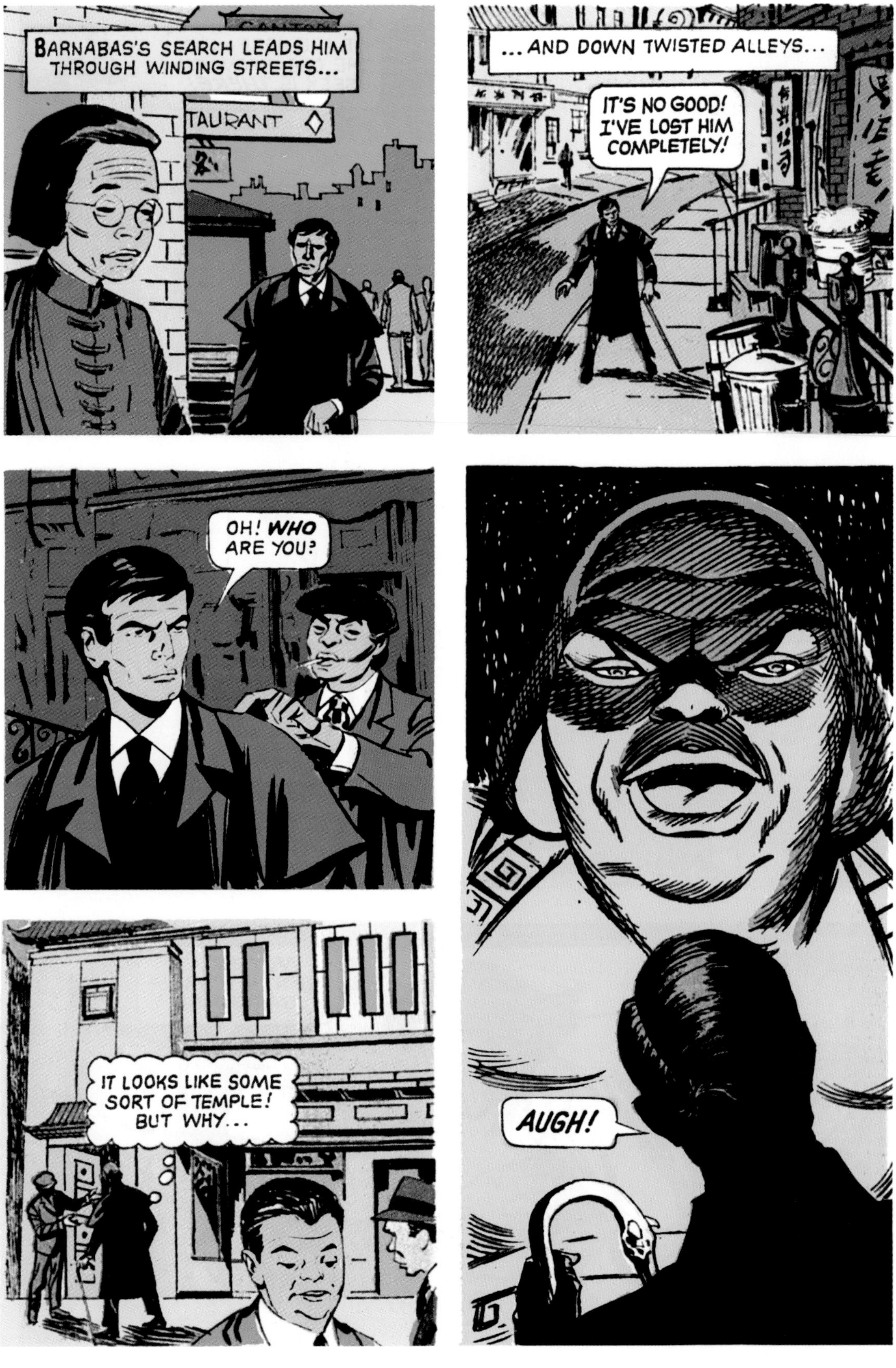
BARNABAS'S SEARCH LEADS HIM THROUGH WINDING STREETS...
TAURANT
...AND DOWN TWISTED ALLEYS...
IT'S NO GOOD! I'VE LOST HIM COMPLETELY!
OH! WHO ARE YOU?
AUGH!
IT LOOKS LIKE SOME SORT OF TEMPLE! BUT WHY...

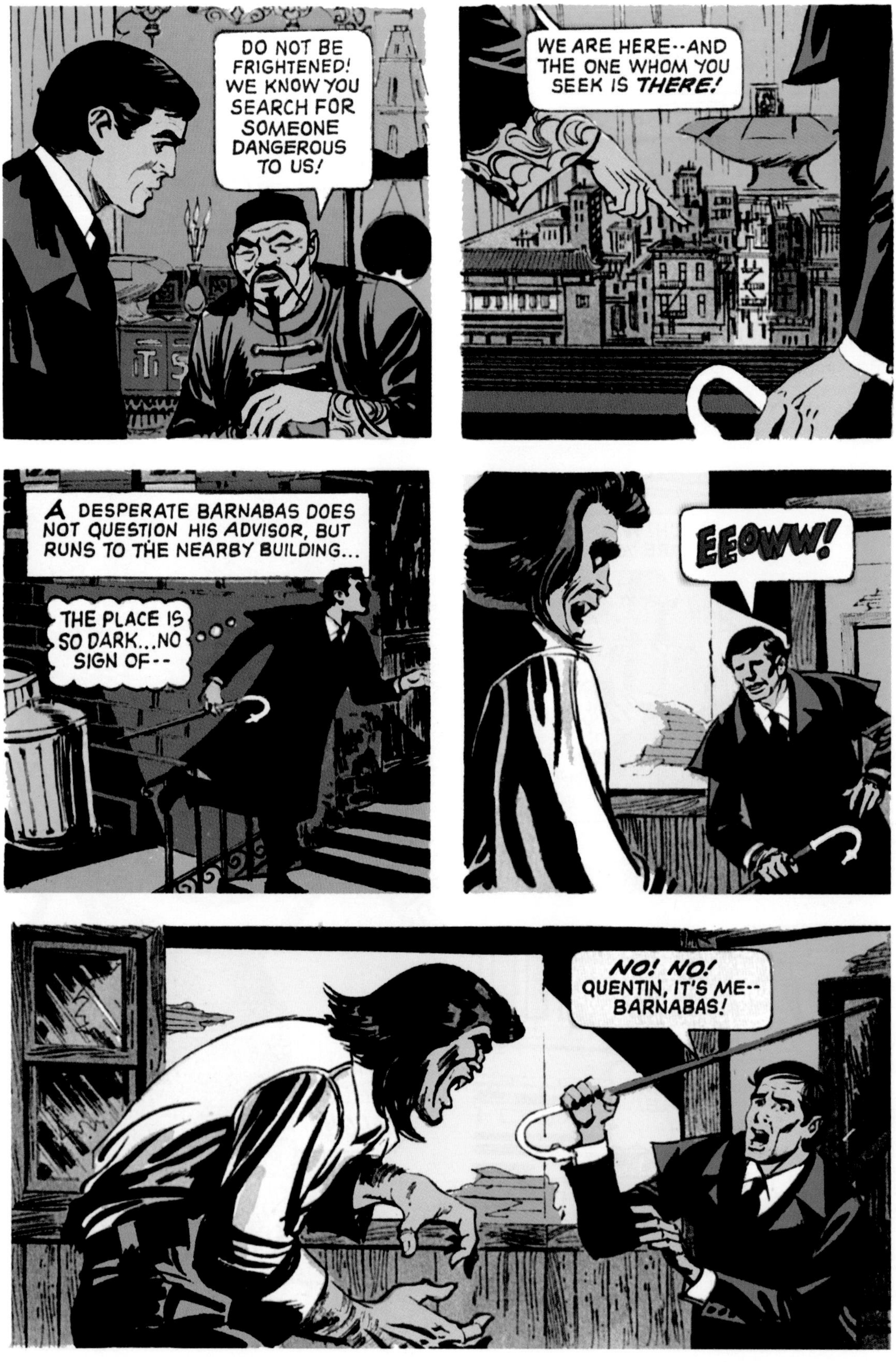
DO NOT BE FRIGHTENED! WE KNOW YOU SEARCH FOR SOMEONE DANGEROUS TO US!
WE ARE HERE--AND THE ONE WHOM YOU SEEK IS THERE!
A DESPERATE BARNABAS DOES NOT QUESTION HIS ADVISOR, BUT RUNS TO THE NEARBY BUILDING...
THE PLACE IS SO DARK...NO SIGN OF--
EEOWW!
NO! NO! QUENTIN, IT'S ME--BARNABAS!

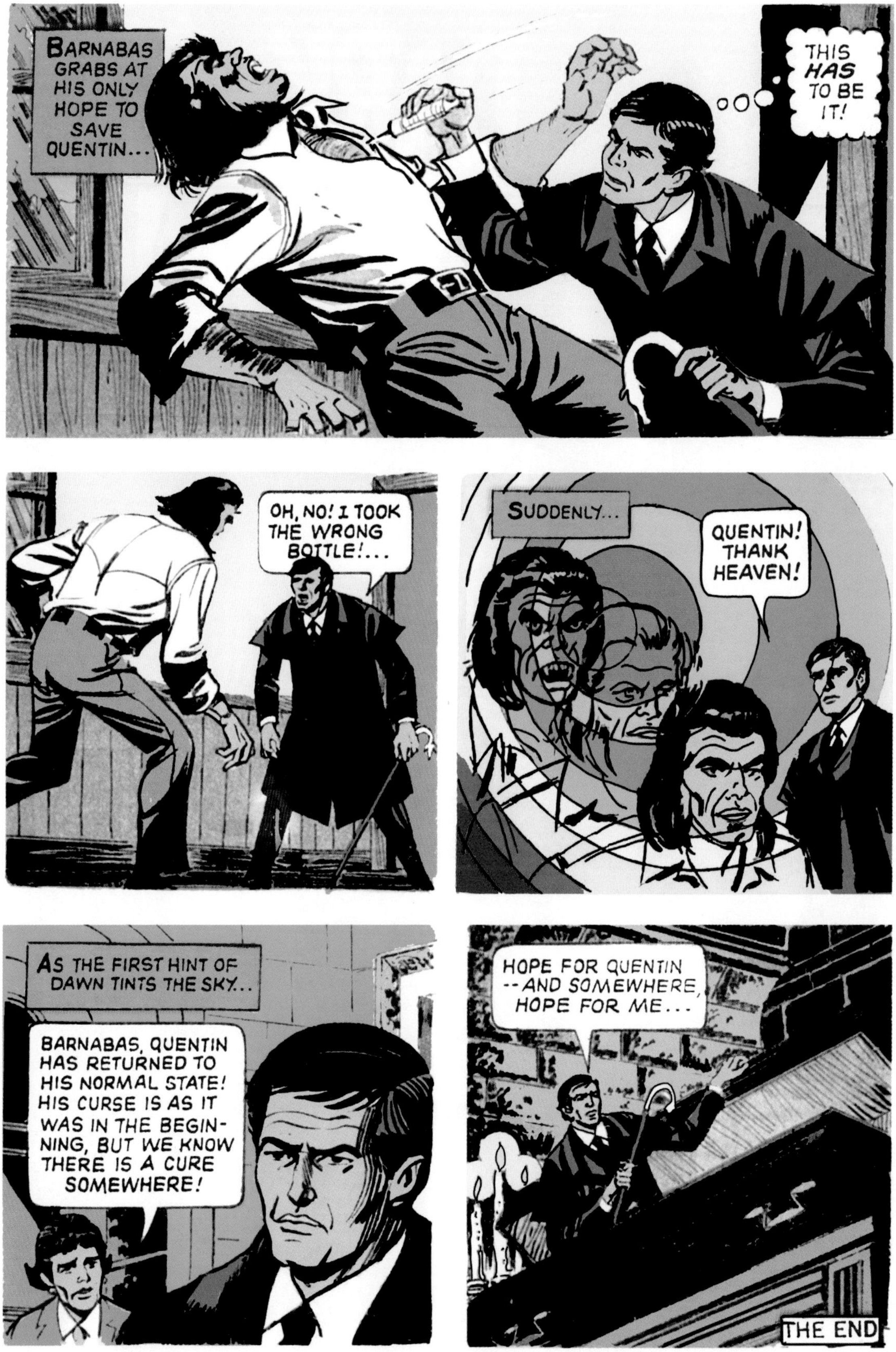
BARNABAS GRABS AT HIS ONLY HOPE TO SAVE QUENTIN...
THIS HAS TO BE IT!
OH, NO! I TOOK THE WRONG BOTTLE!...
SUDDENLY...
QUENTIN! THANK HEAVEN!
AS THE FIRST HINT OF DAWN TINTS THE SKY...
BARNABAS, QUENTIN HAS RETURNED TO HIS NORMAL STATE! HIS CURSE IS AS IT WAS IN THE BEGINNING, BUT WE KNOW THERE IS A CURE SOMEWHERE!
HOPE FOR QUENTIN --AND SOMEWHERE, HOPE FOR ME...
THE END

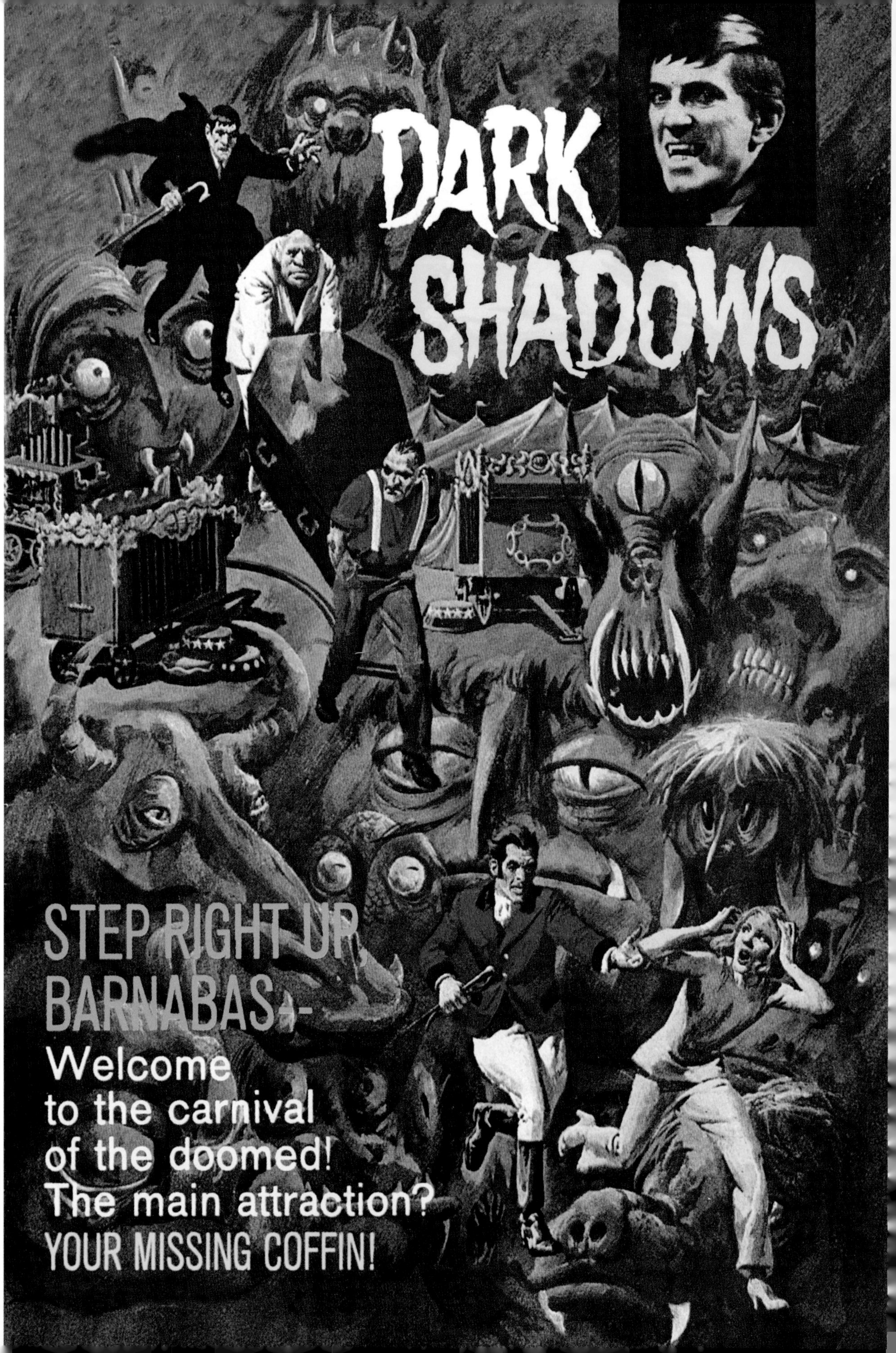
DARK SHADOWS
STEP RIGHT UP BARNABAS--
Welcome to the carnival of the doomed!
The main attraction?
YOUR MISSING COFFIN!

DARK SHADOWS The Crimson Carnival

PART 1: CIRCUS OF EVIL

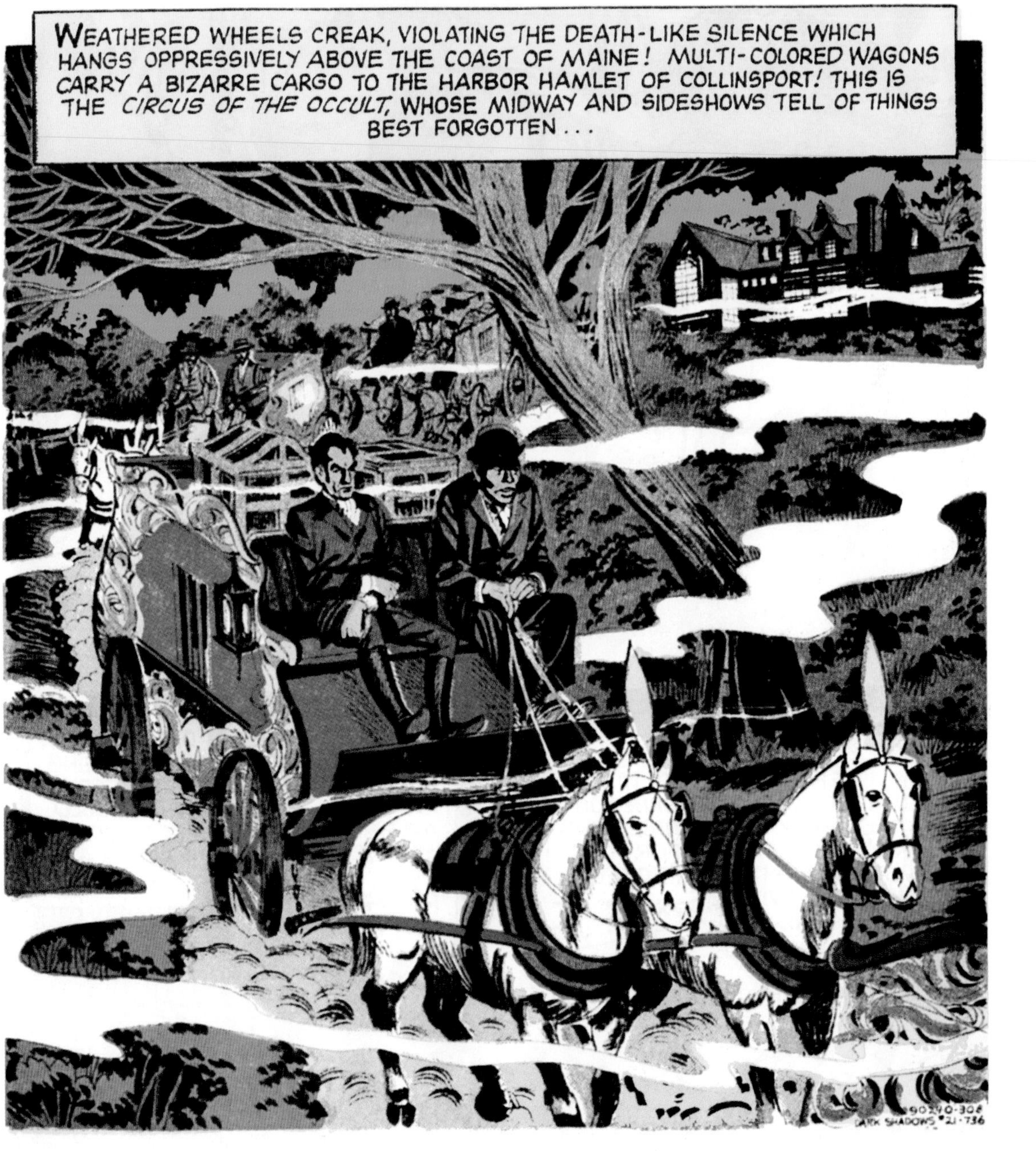
WEATHERED WHEELS CREAK, VIOLATING THE DEATH-LIKE SILENCE WHICH HANGS OPPRESSIVELY ABOVE THE COAST OF MAINE! MULTI-COLORED WAGONS CARRY A BIZARRE CARGO TO THE HARBOR HAMLET OF COLLINSPORT! THIS IS THE *CIRCUS OF THE OCCULT,* WHOSE MIDWAY AND SIDESHOWS TELL OF THINGS BEST FORGOTTEN . . .
DARK SHADOWS #21-736

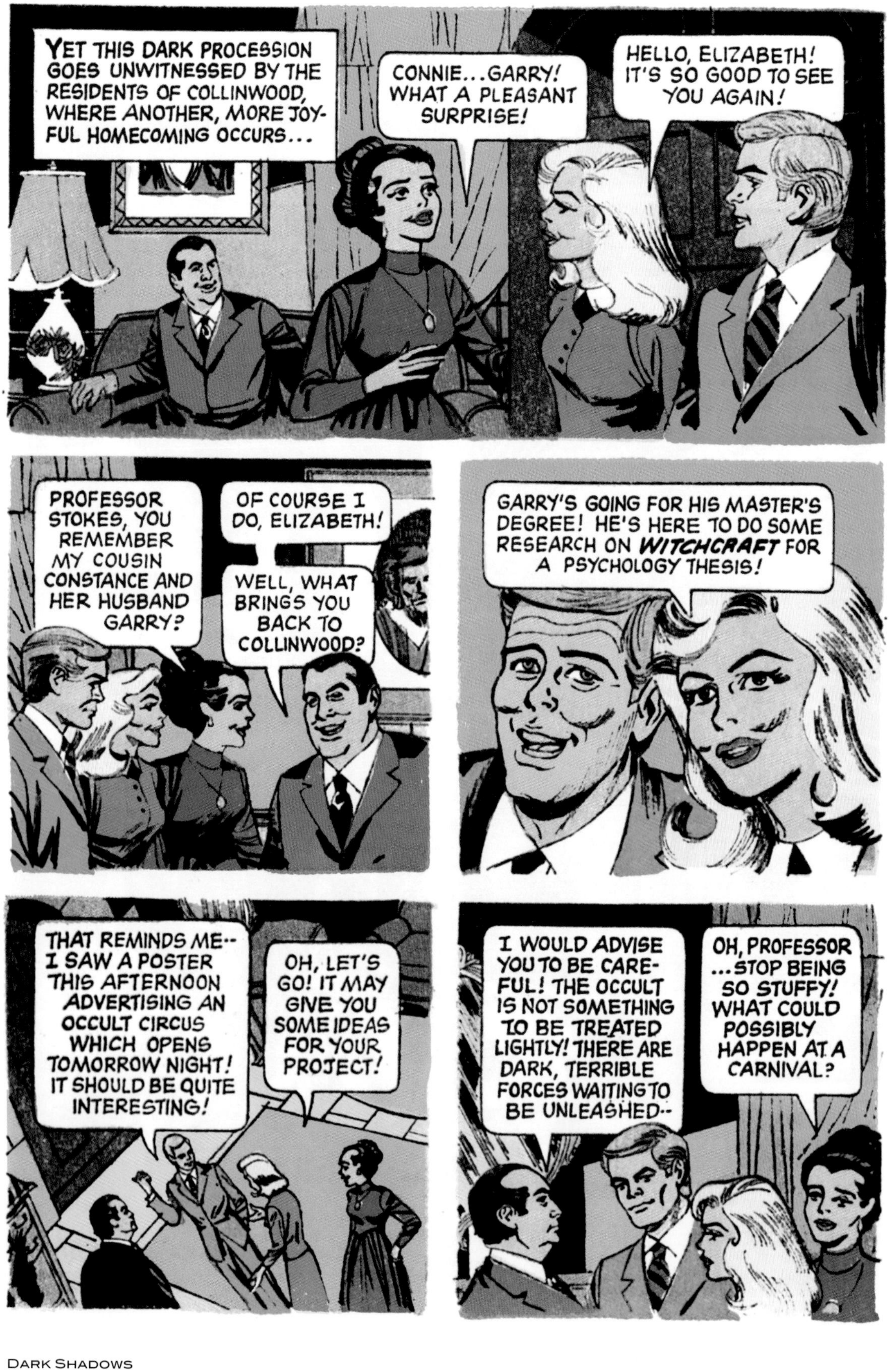
YET THIS DARK PROCESSION GOES UNWITNESSED BY THE RESIDENTS OF COLLINWOOD, WHERE ANOTHER, MORE JOY-FUL HOMECOMING OCCURS...
CONNIE...GARRY! WHAT A PLEASANT SURPRISE!
HELLO, ELIZABETH! IT'S SO GOOD TO SEE YOU AGAIN!
PROFESSOR STOKES, YOU REMEMBER MY COUSIN CONSTANCE AND HER HUSBAND GARRY?
OF COURSE I DO, ELIZABETH!
WELL, WHAT BRINGS YOU BACK TO COLLINWOOD?
GARRY'S GOING FOR HIS MASTER'S DEGREE! HE'S HERE TO DO SOME RESEARCH ON WITCHCRAFT FOR A PSYCHOLOGY THESIS!
THAT REMINDS ME-- I SAW A POSTER THIS AFTERNOON ADVERTISING AN OCCULT CIRCUS WHICH OPENS TOMORROW NIGHT! IT SHOULD BE QUITE INTERESTING!
OH, LET'S GO! IT MAY GIVE YOU SOME IDEAS FOR YOUR PROJECT!
I WOULD ADVISE YOU TO BE CARE-FUL! THE OCCULT IS NOT SOMETHING TO BE TREATED LIGHTLY! THERE ARE DARK, TERRIBLE FORCES WAITING TO BE UNLEASHED--
OH, PROFESSOR ...STOP BEING SO STUFFY! WHAT COULD POSSIBLY HAPPEN AT A CARNIVAL?

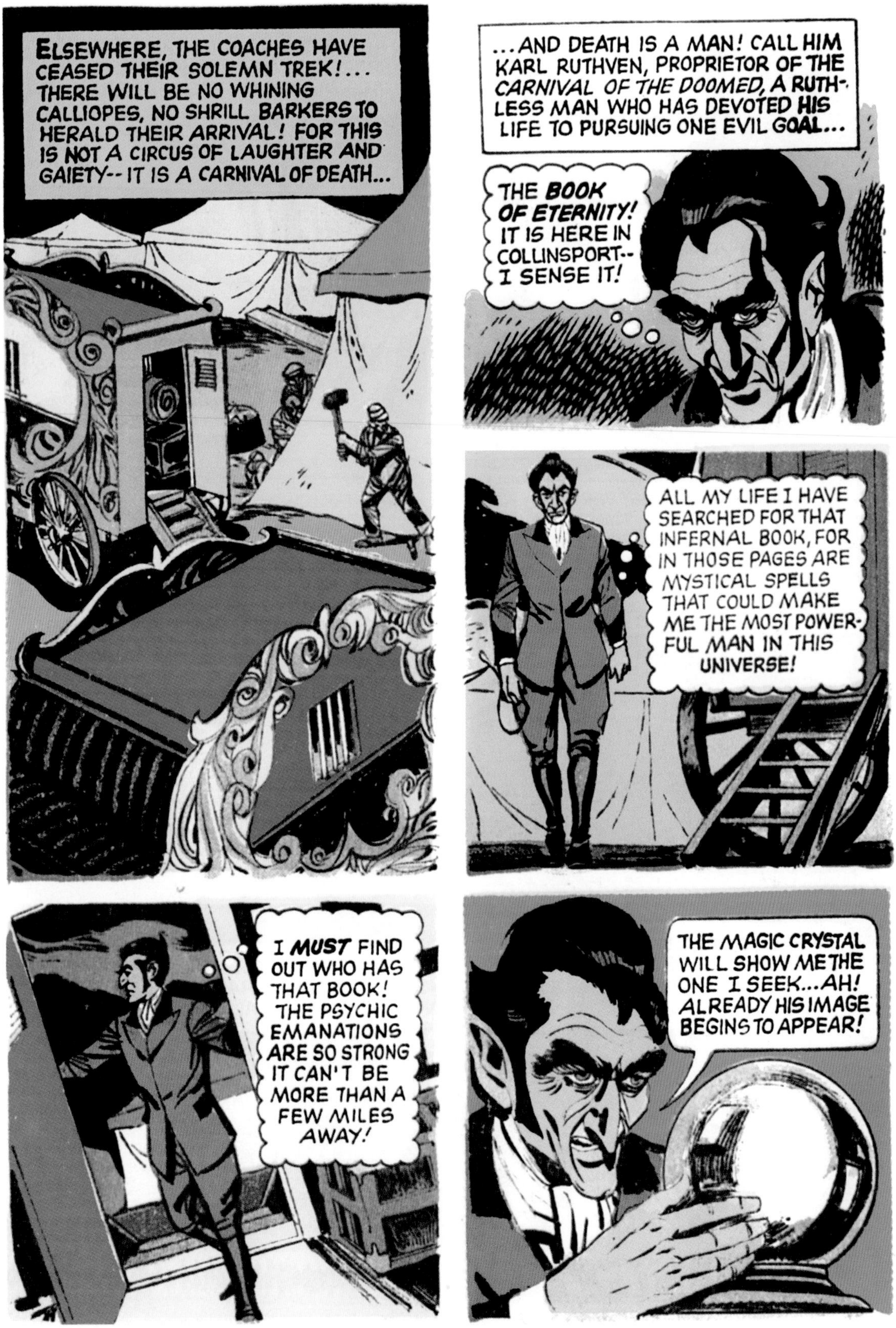
ELSEWHERE, THE COACHES HAVE CEASED THEIR SOLEMN TREK!... THERE WILL BE NO WHINING CALLIOPES, NO SHRILL BARKERS TO HERALD THEIR ARRIVAL! FOR THIS IS NOT A CIRCUS OF LAUGHTER AND GAIETY-- IT IS A CARNIVAL OF DEATH...
...AND DEATH IS A MAN! CALL HIM KARL RUTHVEN, PROPRIETOR OF THE CARNIVAL OF THE DOOMED, A RUTHLESS MAN WHO HAS DEVOTED HIS LIFE TO PURSUING ONE EVIL GOAL...
THE BOOK OF ETERNITY! IT IS HERE IN COLLINSPORT-- I SENSE IT!
ALL MY LIFE I HAVE SEARCHED FOR THAT INFERNAL BOOK, FOR IN THOSE PAGES ARE MYSTICAL SPELLS THAT COULD MAKE ME THE MOST POWERFUL MAN IN THIS UNIVERSE!
I MUST FIND OUT WHO HAS THAT BOOK! THE PSYCHIC EMANATIONS ARE SO STRONG IT CAN'T BE MORE THAN A FEW MILES AWAY!
THE MAGIC CRYSTAL WILL SHOW ME THE ONE I SEEK...AH! ALREADY HIS IMAGE BEGINS TO APPEAR!

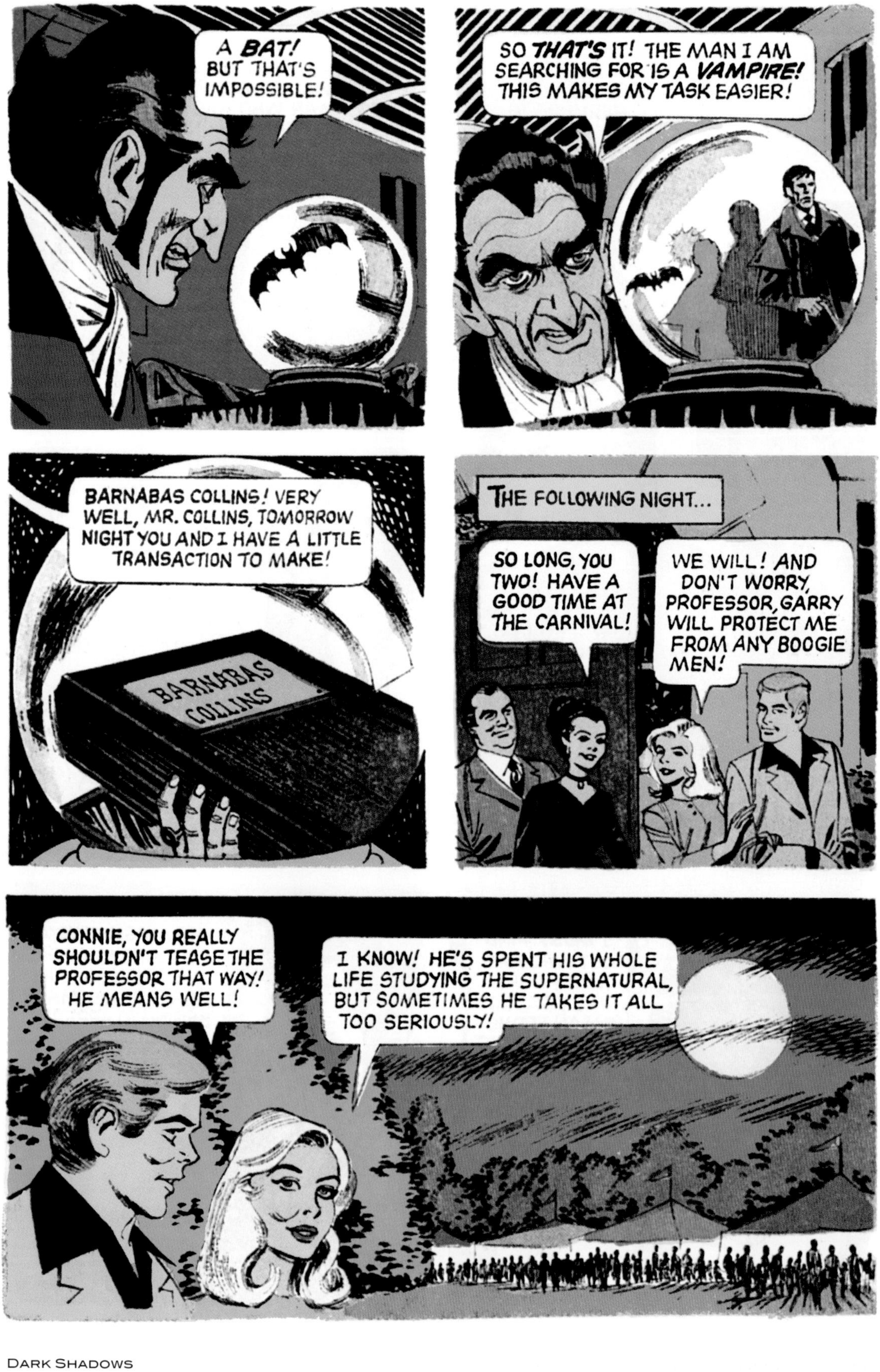
A BAT! BUT THAT'S IMPOSSIBLE!
SO THAT'S IT! THE MAN I AM SEARCHING FOR IS A VAMPIRE! THIS MAKES MY TASK EASIER!
BARNABAS COLLINS! VERY WELL, MR. COLLINS, TOMORROW NIGHT YOU AND I HAVE A LITTLE TRANSACTION TO MAKE!
BARNABAS COLLINS
THE FOLLOWING NIGHT...
SO LONG, YOU TWO! HAVE A GOOD TIME AT THE CARNIVAL!
WE WILL! AND DON'T WORRY, PROFESSOR, GARRY WILL PROTECT ME FROM ANY BOOGIE MEN!
CONNIE, YOU REALLY SHOULDN'T TEASE THE PROFESSOR THAT WAY! HE MEANS WELL!
I KNOW! HE'S SPENT HIS WHOLE LIFE STUDYING THE SUPERNATURAL, BUT SOMETIMES HE TAKES IT ALL TOO SERIOUSLY!

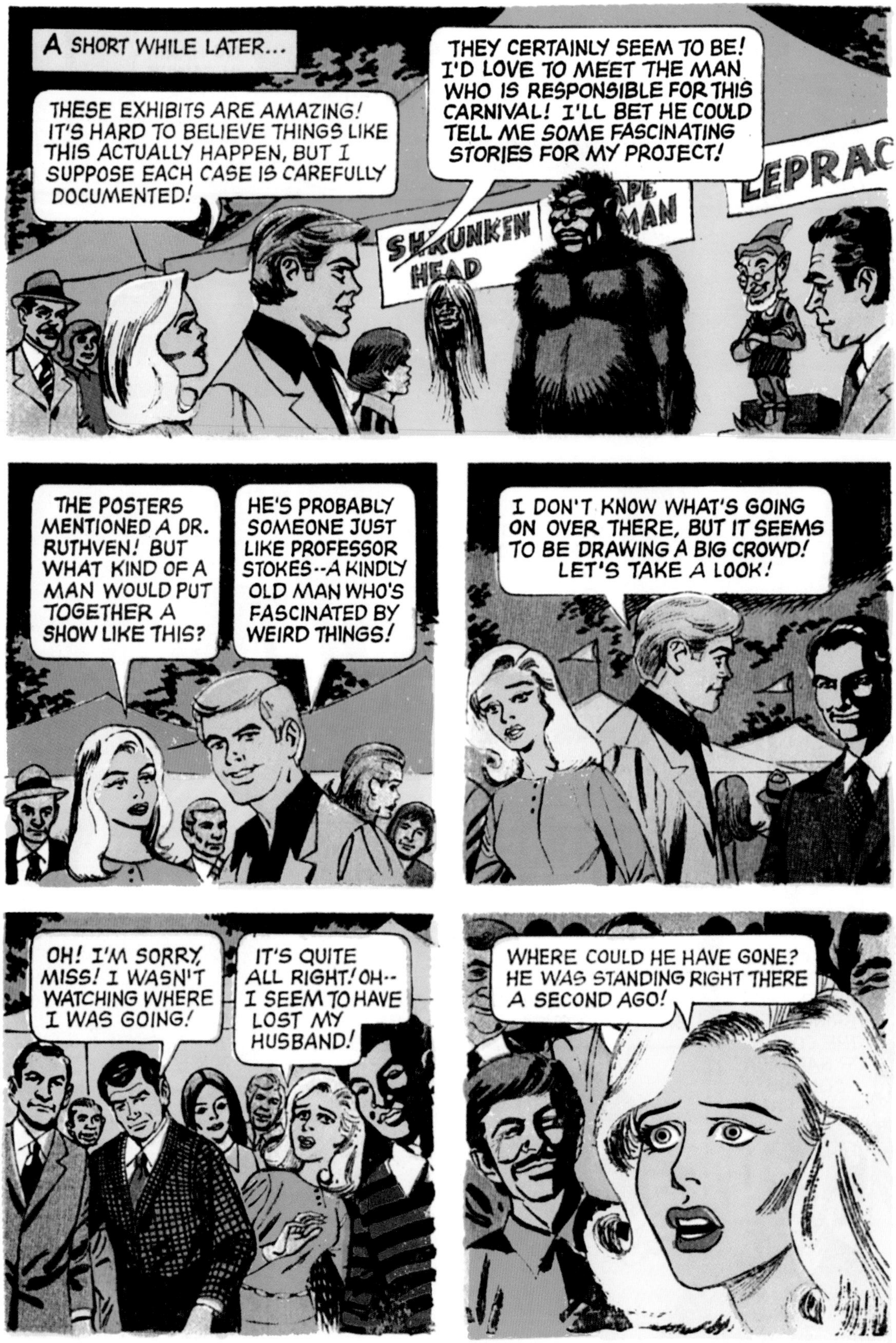
A SHORT WHILE LATER...
THESE EXHIBITS ARE AMAZING! IT'S HARD TO BELIEVE THINGS LIKE THIS ACTUALLY HAPPEN, BUT I SUPPOSE EACH CASE IS CAREFULLY DOCUMENTED!
THEY CERTAINLY SEEM TO BE! I'D LOVE TO MEET THE MAN WHO IS RESPONSIBLE FOR THIS CARNIVAL! I'LL BET HE COULD TELL ME SOME FASCINATING STORIES FOR MY PROJECT!
SHRUNKEN HEAD
APE MAN
LEPRAC
THE POSTERS MENTIONED A DR. RUTHVEN! BUT WHAT KIND OF A MAN WOULD PUT TOGETHER A SHOW LIKE THIS?
HE'S PROBABLY SOMEONE JUST LIKE PROFESSOR STOKES--A KINDLY OLD MAN WHO'S FASCINATED BY WEIRD THINGS!
I DON'T KNOW WHAT'S GOING ON OVER THERE, BUT IT SEEMS TO BE DRAWING A BIG CROWD! LET'S TAKE A LOOK!
OH! I'M SORRY, MISS! I WASN'T WATCHING WHERE I WAS GOING!
IT'S QUITE ALL RIGHT! OH-- I SEEM TO HAVE LOST MY HUSBAND!
WHERE COULD HE HAVE GONE? HE WAS STANDING RIGHT THERE A SECOND AGO!

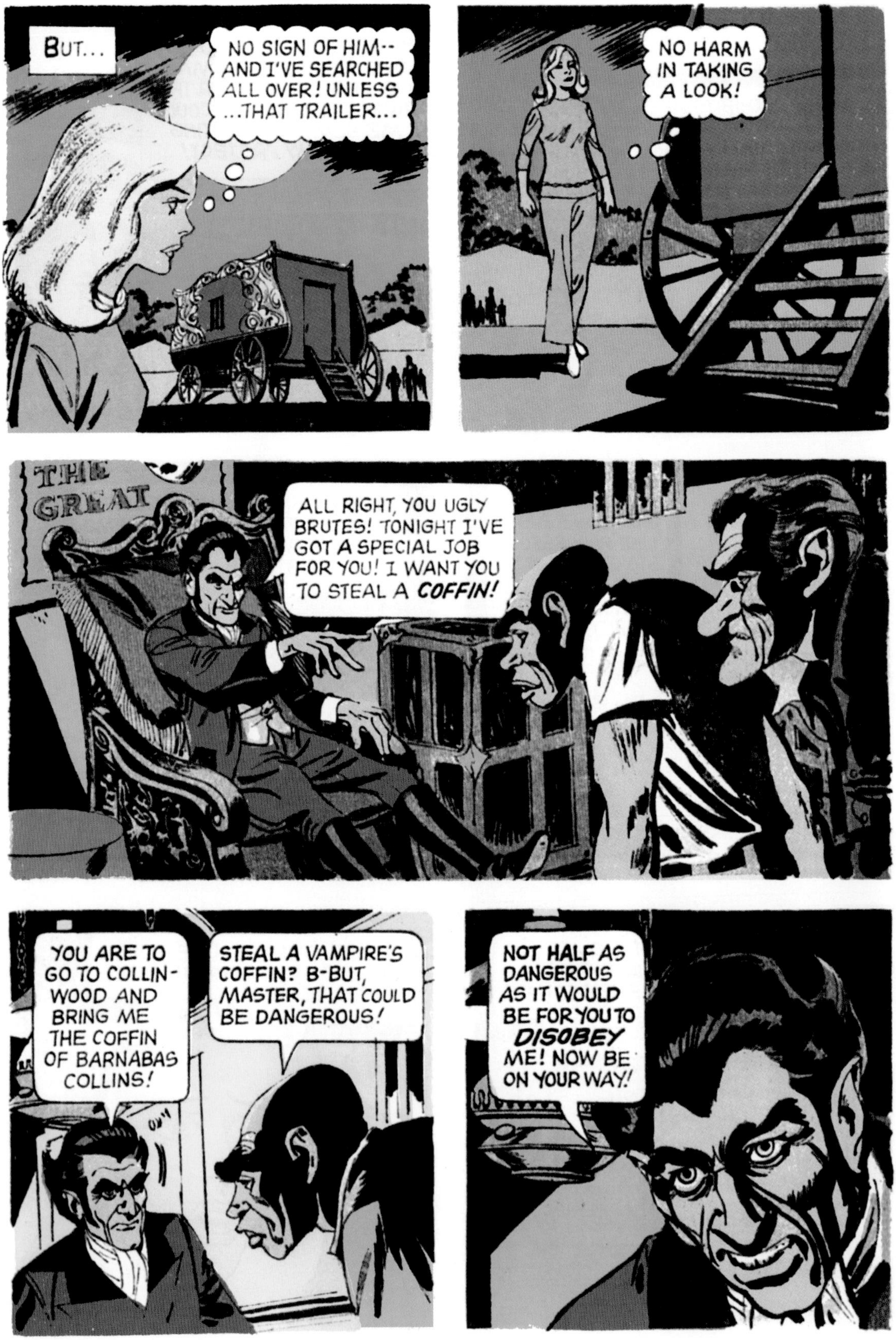
BUT...
NO SIGN OF HIM-- AND I'VE SEARCHED ALL OVER! UNLESS ...THAT TRAILER...
NO HARM IN TAKING A LOOK!
THE GREAT
ALL RIGHT, YOU UGLY BRUTES! TONIGHT I'VE GOT A SPECIAL JOB FOR YOU! I WANT YOU TO STEAL A COFFIN!
YOU ARE TO GO TO COLLIN-WOOD AND BRING ME THE COFFIN OF BARNABAS COLLINS!
STEAL A VAMPIRE'S COFFIN? B-BUT, MASTER, THAT COULD BE DANGEROUS!
NOT HALF AS DANGEROUS AS IT WOULD BE FOR YOU TO DISOBEY ME! NOW BE ON YOUR WAY!

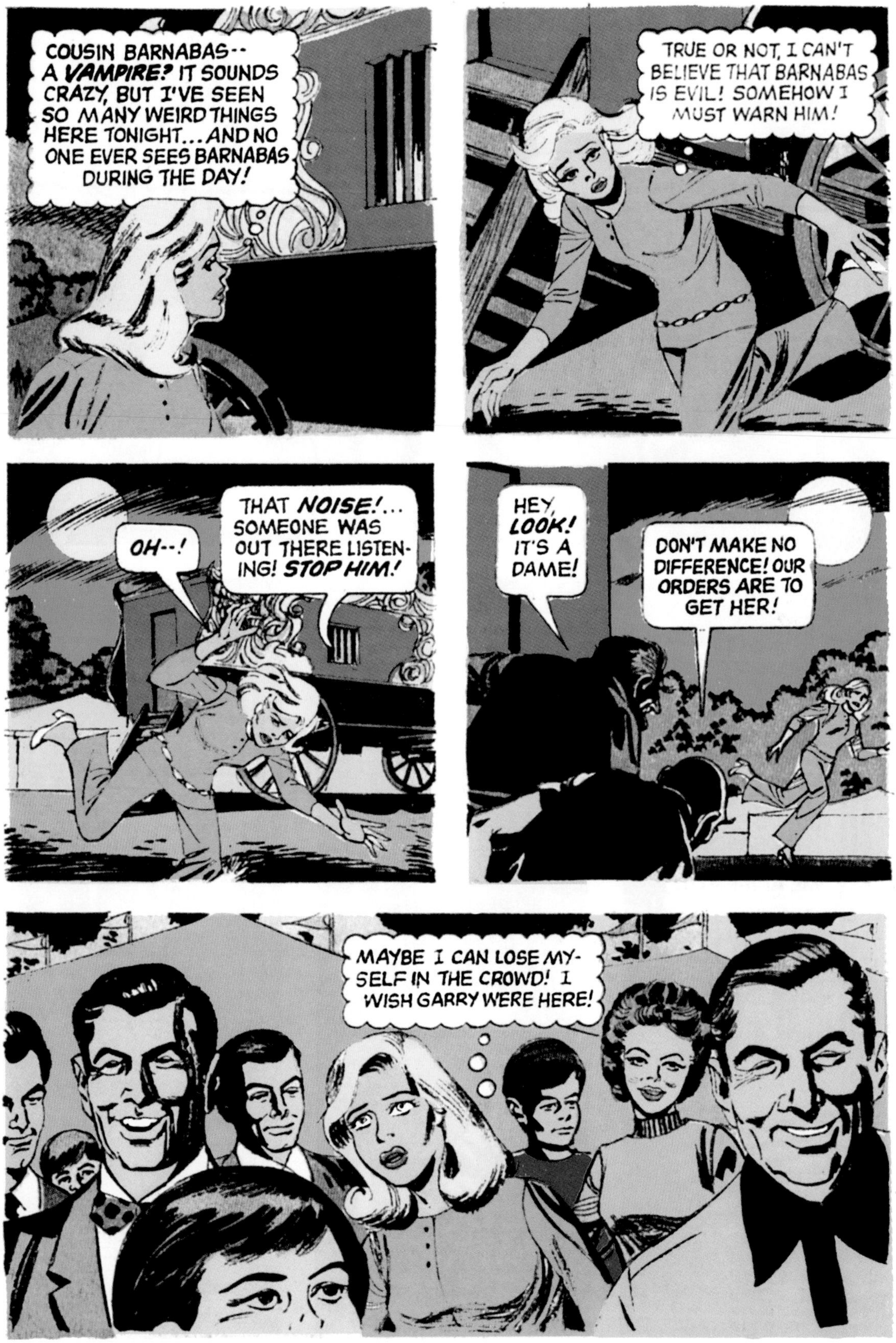
COUSIN BARNABAS-- A VAMPIRE? IT SOUNDS CRAZY, BUT I'VE SEEN SO MANY WEIRD THINGS HERE TONIGHT...AND NO ONE EVER SEES BARNABAS DURING THE DAY!
TRUE OR NOT, I CAN'T BELIEVE THAT BARNABAS IS EVIL! SOMEHOW I MUST WARN HIM!
OH--!
THAT NOISE!... SOMEONE WAS OUT THERE LISTENING! STOP HIM!
HEY, LOOK! IT'S A DAME!
DON'T MAKE NO DIFFERENCE! OUR ORDERS ARE TO GET HER!
MAYBE I CAN LOSE MYSELF IN THE CROWD! I WISH GARRY WERE HERE!

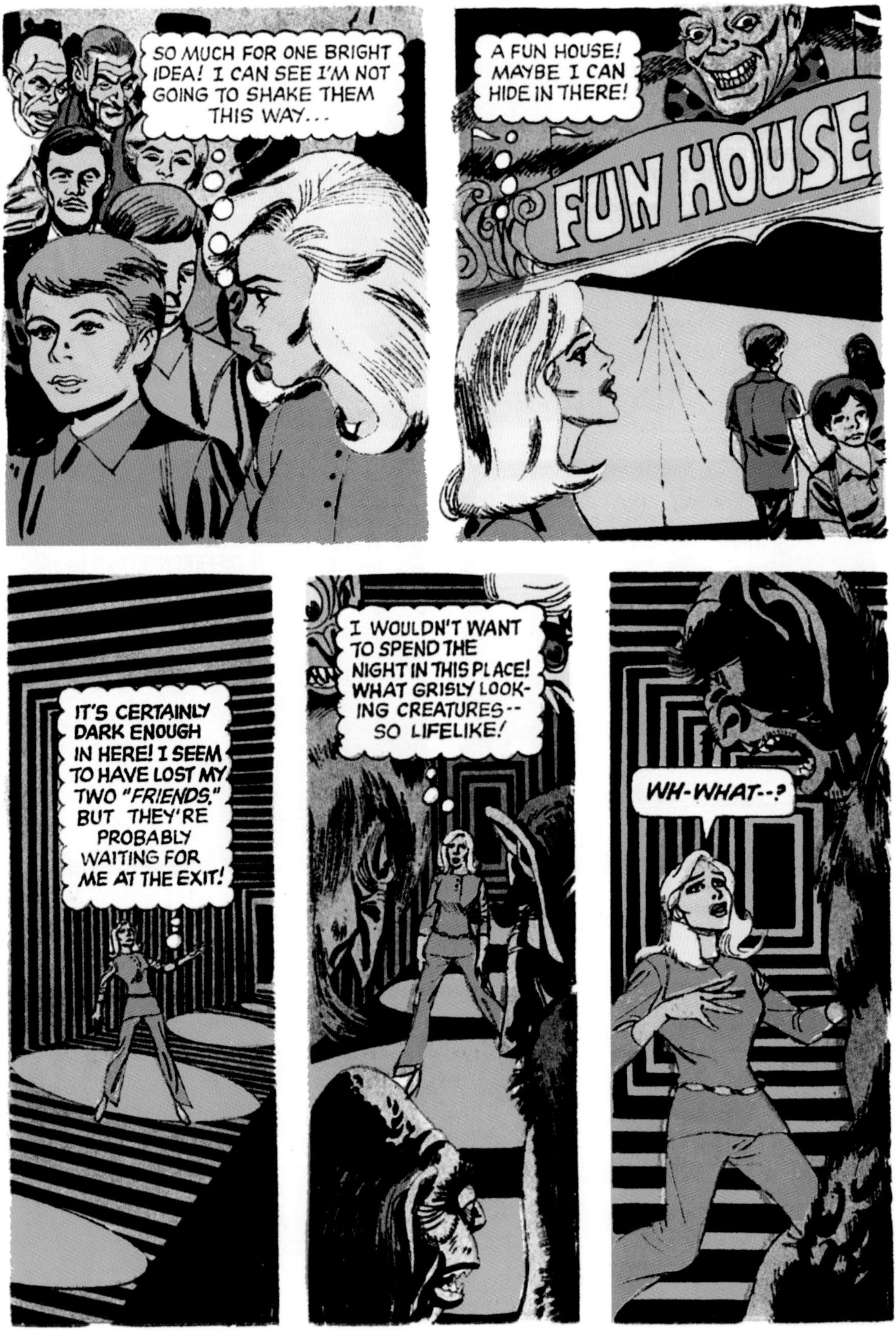
SO MUCH FOR ONE BRIGHT IDEA! I CAN SEE I'M NOT GOING TO SHAKE THEM THIS WAY...
A FUN HOUSE! MAYBE I CAN HIDE IN THERE!
FUN HOUSE
IT'S CERTAINLY DARK ENOUGH IN HERE! I SEEM TO HAVE LOST MY TWO "FRIENDS," BUT THEY'RE PROBABLY WAITING FOR ME AT THE EXIT!
I WOULDN'T WANT TO SPEND THE NIGHT IN THIS PLACE! WHAT GRISLY LOOKING CREATURES-- SO LIFELIKE!
WH-WHAT--?

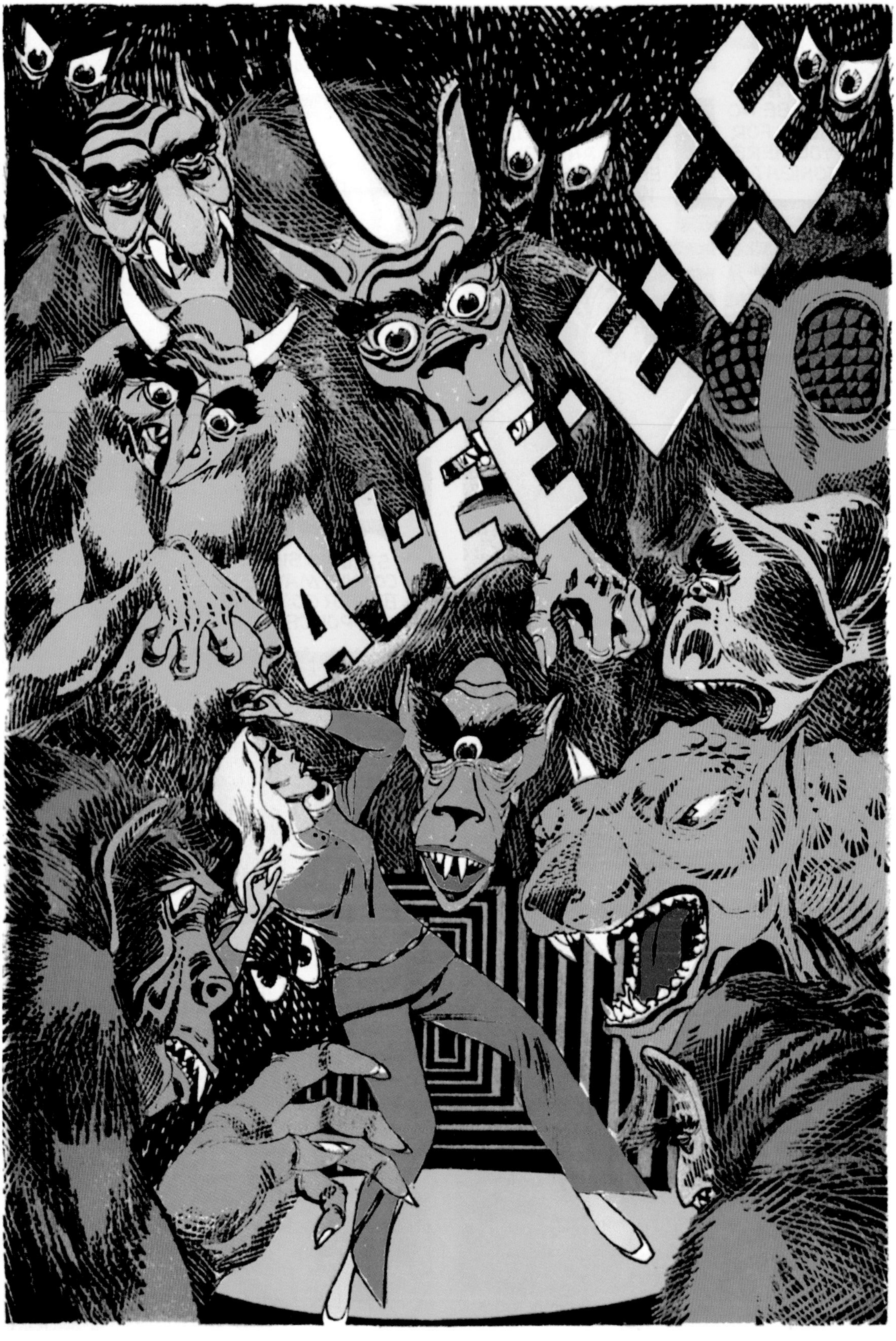
A-I-E-E-E-E-E

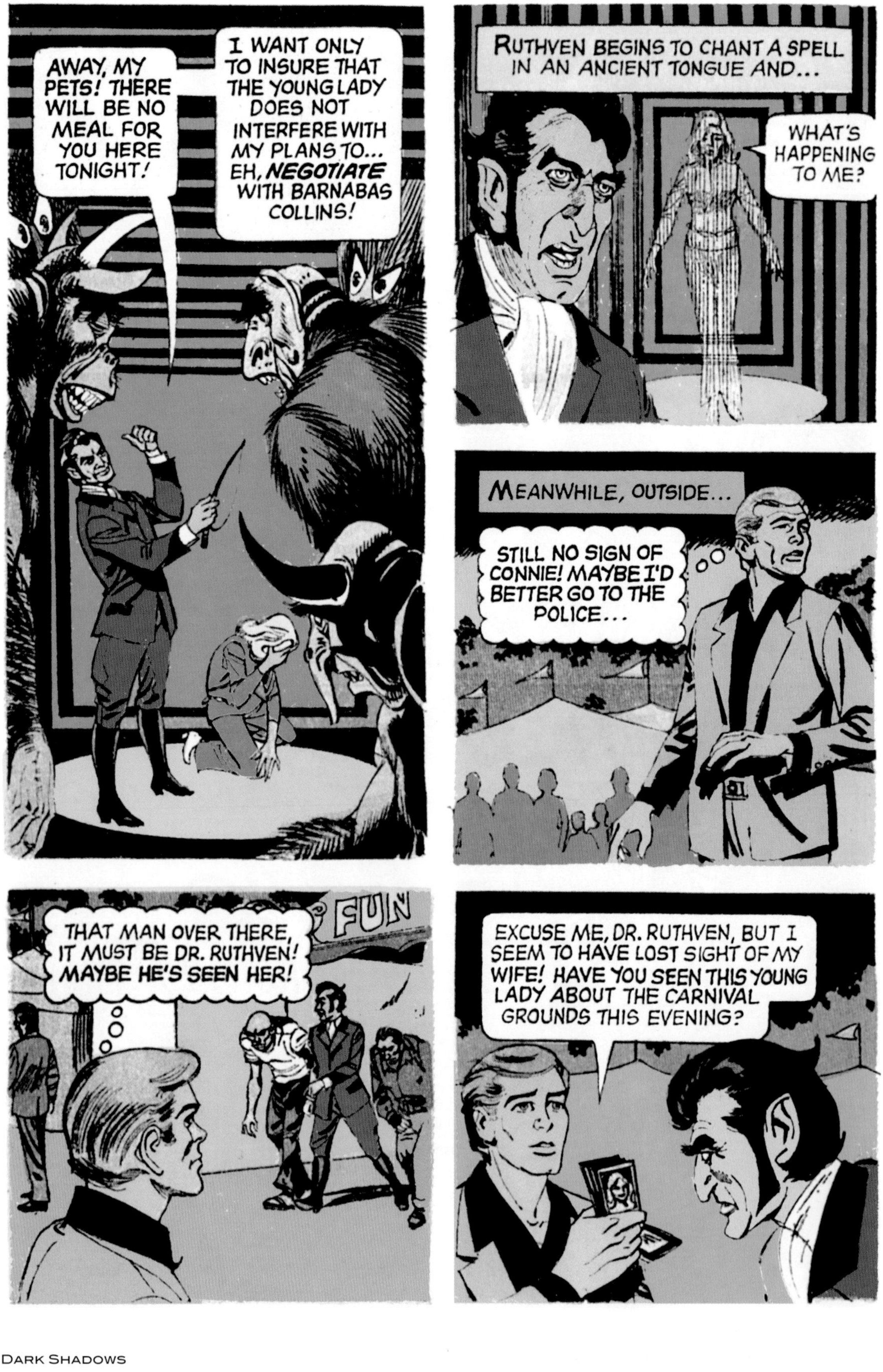
AWAY, MY PETS! THERE WILL BE NO MEAL FOR YOU HERE TONIGHT!
I WANT ONLY TO INSURE THAT THE YOUNG LADY DOES NOT INTERFERE WITH MY PLANS TO... EH, NEGOTIATE WITH BARNABAS COLLINS!
RUTHVEN BEGINS TO CHANT A SPELL IN AN ANCIENT TONGUE AND...
WHAT'S HAPPENING TO ME?
MEANWHILE, OUTSIDE...
STILL NO SIGN OF CONNIE! MAYBE I'D BETTER GO TO THE POLICE...
FUN
THAT MAN OVER THERE, IT MUST BE DR. RUTHVEN! MAYBE HE'S SEEN HER!
EXCUSE ME, DR. RUTHVEN, BUT I SEEM TO HAVE LOST SIGHT OF MY WIFE! HAVE YOU SEEN THIS YOUNG LADY ABOUT THE CARNIVAL GROUNDS THIS EVENING?

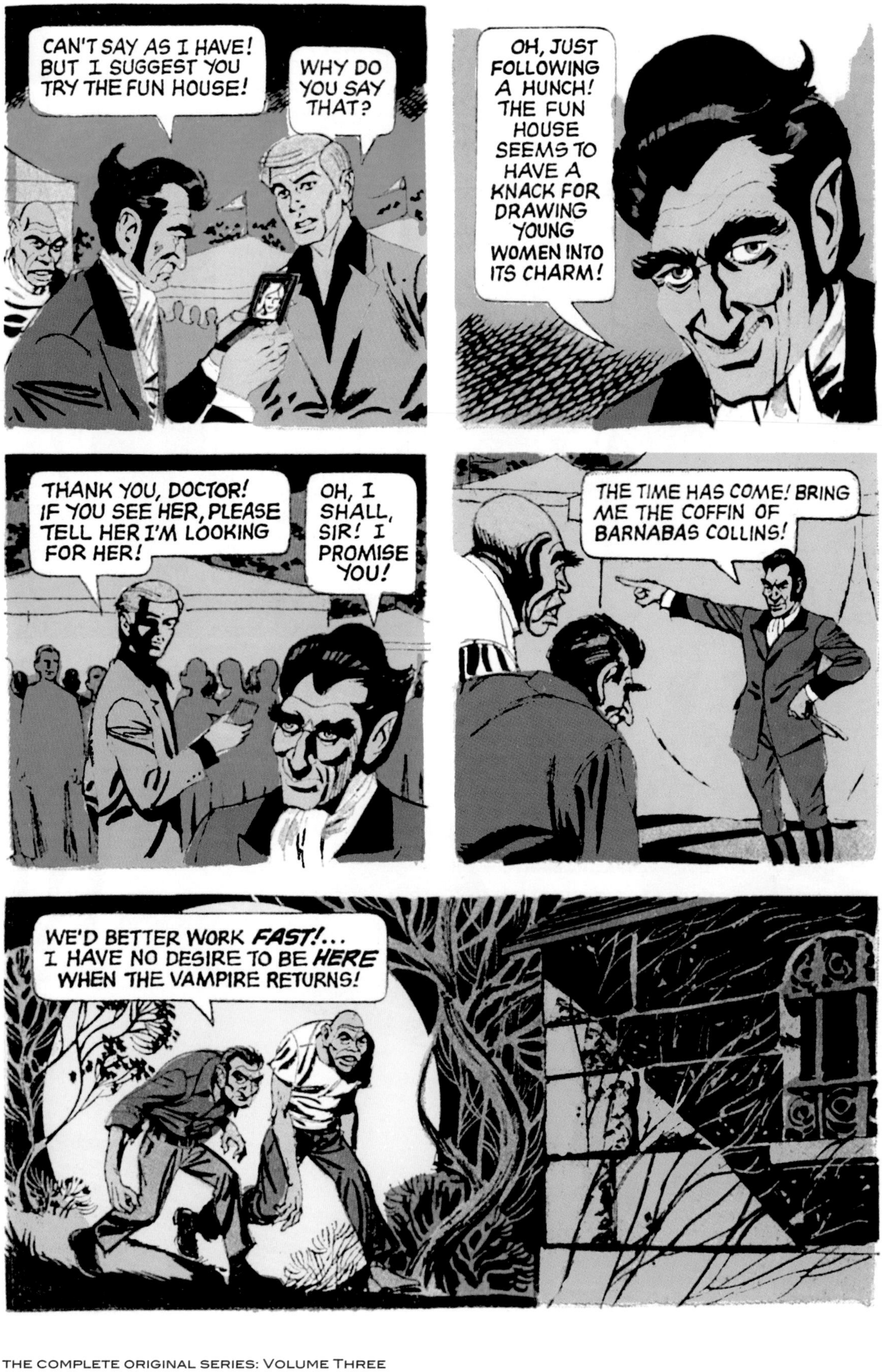

CAN'T SAY AS I HAVE! BUT I SUGGEST YOU TRY THE FUN HOUSE!
WHY DO YOU SAY THAT?
OH, JUST FOLLOWING A HUNCH! THE FUN HOUSE SEEMS TO HAVE A KNACK FOR DRAWING YOUNG WOMEN INTO ITS CHARM!
THANK YOU, DOCTOR! IF YOU SEE HER, PLEASE TELL HER I'M LOOKING FOR HER!
OH, I SHALL, SIR! I PROMISE YOU!
THE TIME HAS COME! BRING ME THE COFFIN OF BARNABAS COLLINS!
WE'D BETTER WORK FAST!... I HAVE NO DESIRE TO BE HERE WHEN THE VAMPIRE RETURNS!

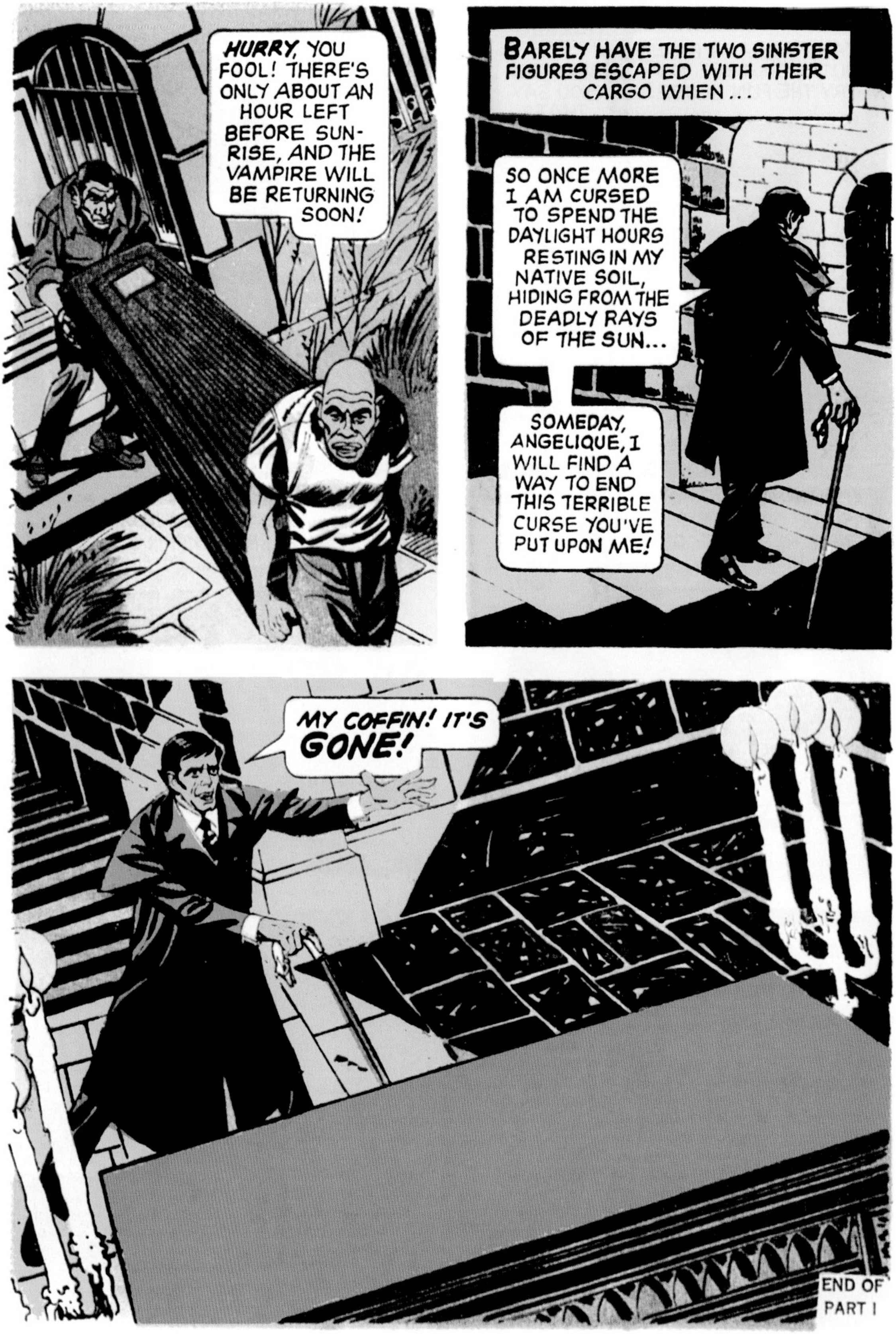
HURRY, YOU FOOL! THERE'S ONLY ABOUT AN HOUR LEFT BEFORE SUN-RISE, AND THE VAMPIRE WILL BE RETURNING SOON!
BARELY HAVE THE TWO SINISTER FIGURES ESCAPED WITH THEIR CARGO WHEN...
SO ONCE MORE I AM CURSED TO SPEND THE DAYLIGHT HOURS RESTING IN MY NATIVE SOIL, HIDING FROM THE DEADLY RAYS OF THE SUN...
SOMEDAY, ANGELIQUE, I WILL FIND A WAY TO END THIS TERRIBLE CURSE YOU'VE PUT UPON ME!
MY COFFIN! IT'S GONE!
END OF PART I

DARK SHADOWS

THE CRIMSON CARNIVAL

PART 2: WAR OF THE WILLS

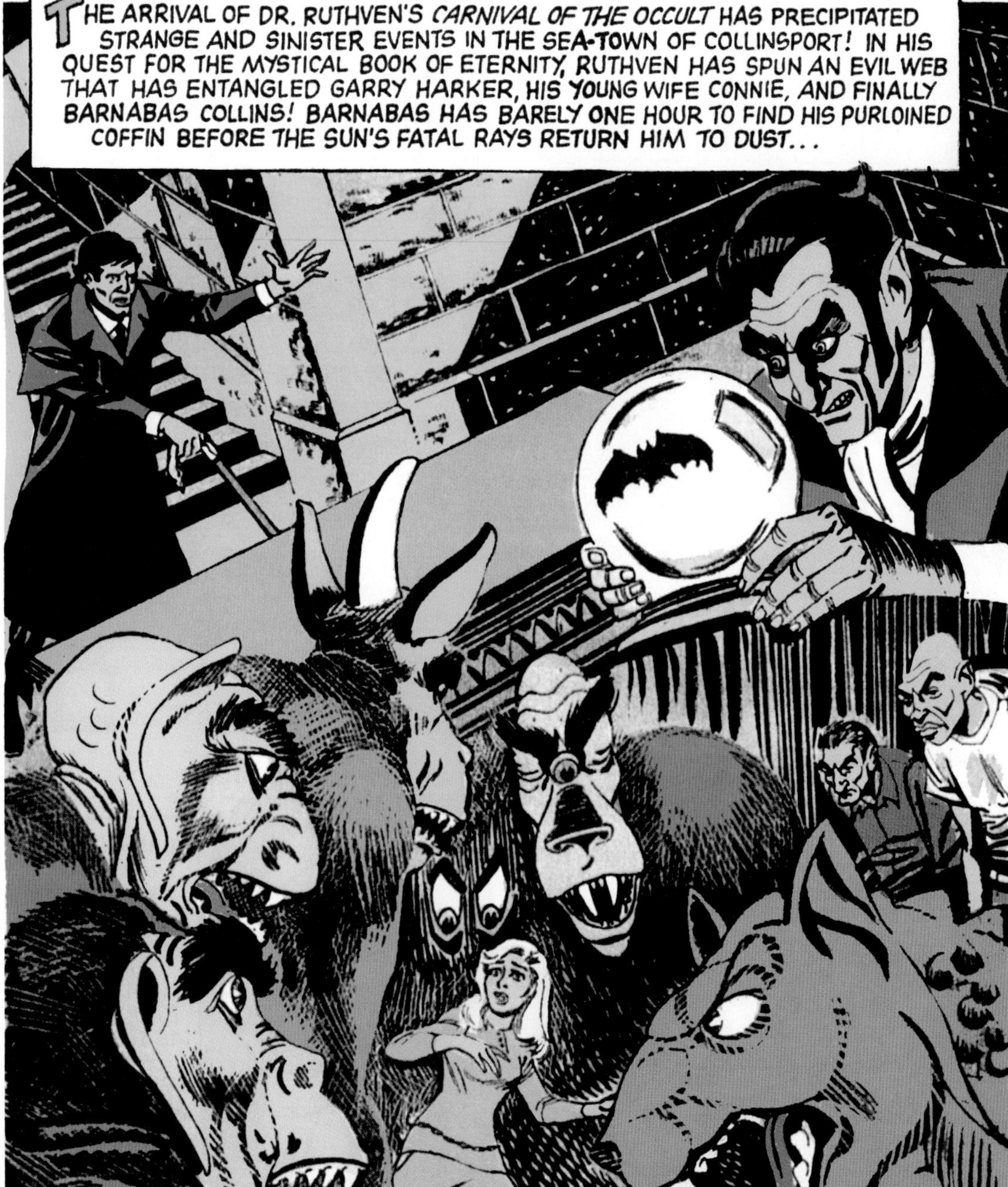
THE ARRIVAL OF DR. RUTHVEN'S CARNIVAL OF THE OCCULT HAS PRECIPITATED STRANGE AND SINISTER EVENTS IN THE SEA-TOWN OF COLLINSPORT! IN HIS QUEST FOR THE MYSTICAL BOOK OF ETERNITY, RUTHVEN HAS SPUN AN EVIL WEB THAT HAS ENTANGLED GARRY HARKER, HIS YOUNG WIFE CONNIE, AND FINALLY BARNABAS COLLINS! BARNABAS HAS BARELY ONE HOUR TO FIND HIS PURLOINED COFFIN BEFORE THE SUN'S FATAL RAYS RETURN HIM TO DUST...

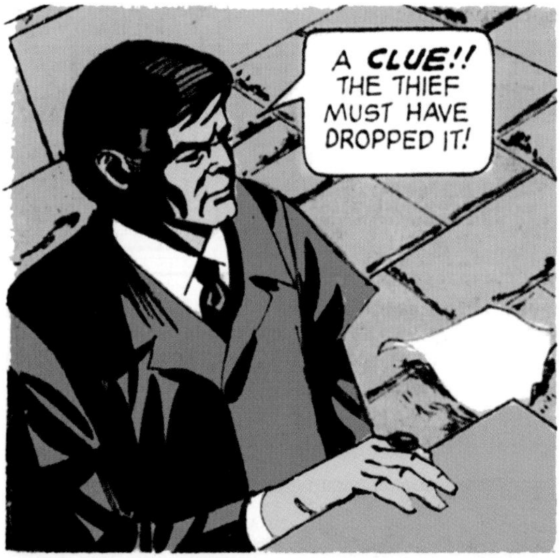
A CLUE!! THE THIEF MUST HAVE DROPPED IT!

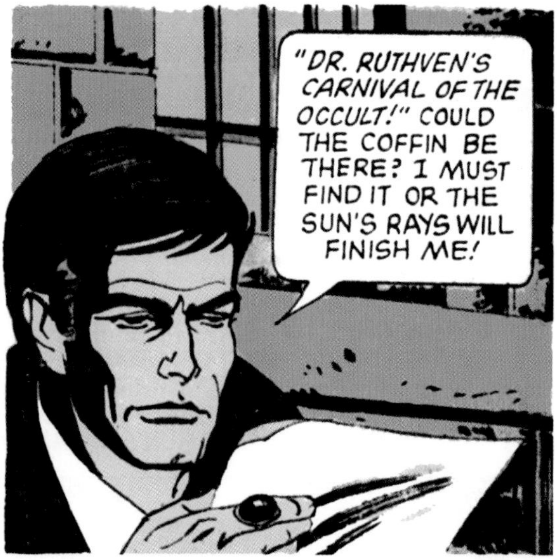
"DR. RUTHVEN'S CARNIVAL OF THE OCCULT!" COULD THE COFFIN BE THERE? I MUST FIND IT OR THE SUN'S RAYS WILL FINISH ME!

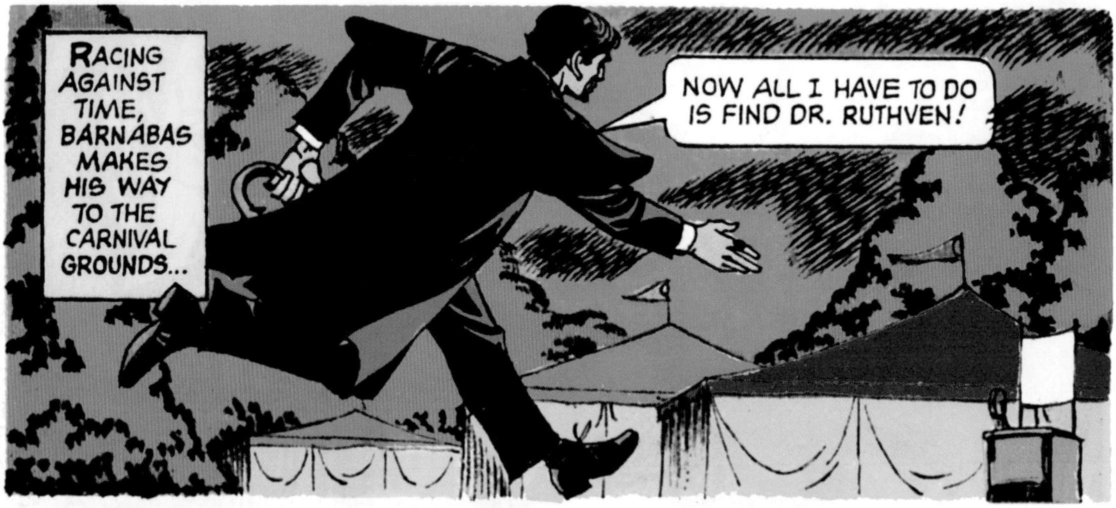
RACING AGAINST TIME, BARNABAS MAKES HIS WAY TO THE CARNIVAL GROUNDS...
NOW ALL I HAVE TO DO IS FIND DR. RUTHVEN!

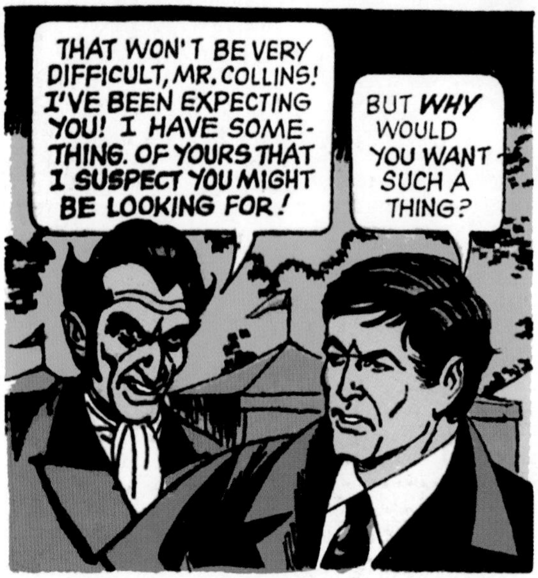
THAT WON'T BE VERY DIFFICULT, MR. COLLINS! I'VE BEEN EXPECTING YOU! I HAVE SOMETHING. OF YOURS THAT I SUSPECT YOU MIGHT BE LOOKING FOR!
BUT WHY WOULD YOU WANT SUCH A THING?

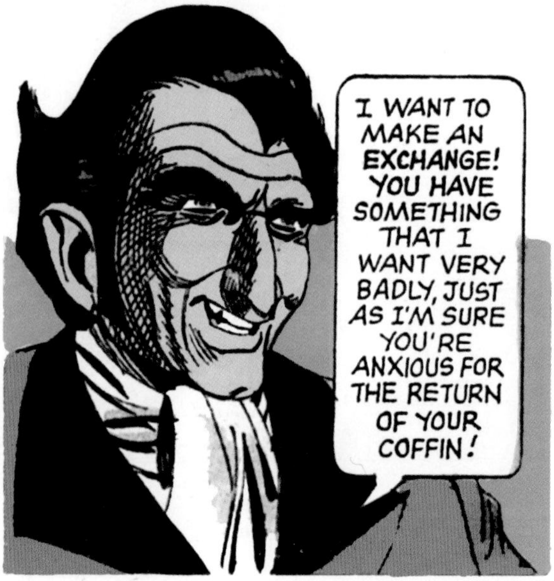
I WANT TO MAKE AN EXCHANGE! YOU HAVE SOMETHING THAT I WANT VERY BADLY, JUST AS I'M SURE YOU'RE ANXIOUS FOR THE RETURN OF YOUR COFFIN!

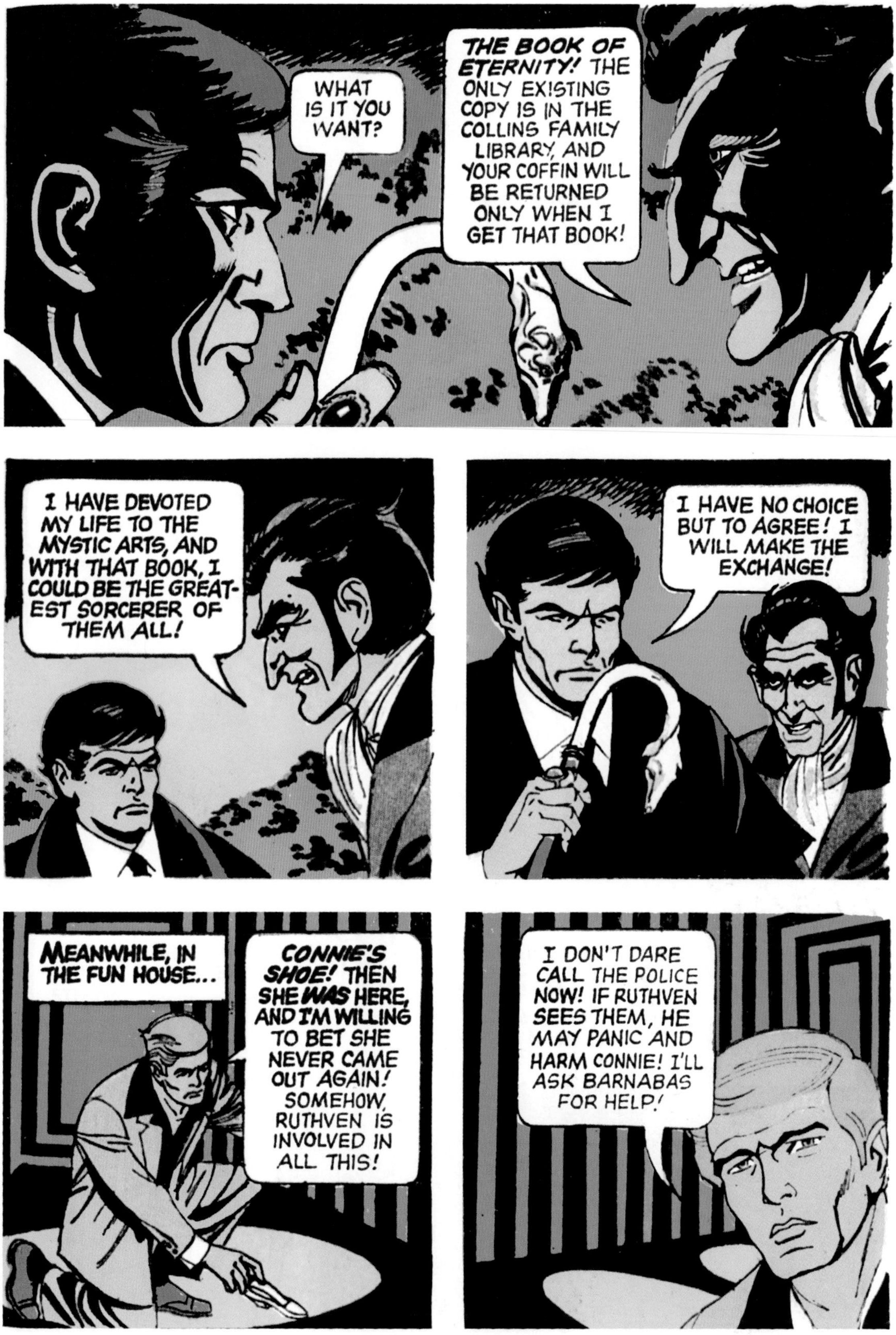
WHAT IS IT YOU WANT?
THE BOOK OF ETERNITY! THE ONLY EXISTING COPY IS IN THE COLLINS FAMILY LIBRARY, AND YOUR COFFIN WILL BE RETURNED ONLY WHEN I GET THAT BOOK!
I HAVE DEVOTED MY LIFE TO THE MYSTIC ARTS, AND WITH THAT BOOK, I COULD BE THE GREATEST SORCERER OF THEM ALL!
I HAVE NO CHOICE BUT TO AGREE! I WILL MAKE THE EXCHANGE!
MEANWHILE, IN THE FUN HOUSE...
CONNIE'S SHOE! THEN SHE WAS HERE, AND I'M WILLING TO BET SHE NEVER CAME OUT AGAIN! SOMEHOW, RUTHVEN IS INVOLVED IN ALL THIS!
I DON'T DARE CALL THE POLICE NOW! IF RUTHVEN SEES THEM, HE MAY PANIC AND HARM CONNIE! I'LL ASK BARNABAS FOR HELP!

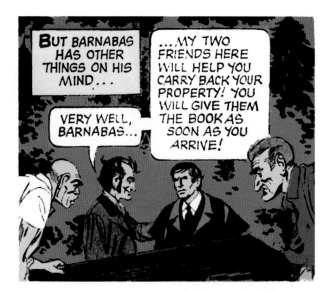

BUT BARNABAS HAS OTHER THINGS ON HIS MIND...

VERY WELL, BARNABAS...

...MY TWO FRIENDS HERE WILL HELP YOU CARRY BACK YOUR PROPERTY! YOU WILL GIVE THEM THE BOOK AS SOON AS YOU ARRIVE!

AND IF I DON'T?

WE NEEDN'T DISCUSS THAT! I JUDGE YOU TO BE AN HONORABLE MAN, MR. COLLINS!

AND SO, A FEW MINUTES LATER...

HARRY, LOOK-- A COFFIN!

IT'S ALL RIGHT, MADAM! WE'RE ADDING A NEW EXHIBIT TO THE FUN HOUSE! THIS IS JUST ONE OF THE PROPS!

AT COLLINWOOD, GARRY SEARCHES FOR BARNABAS...

BARNABAS! BARNABAS!

THAT'S ODD... HE DOESN'T SEEM TO BE AROUND!

WHERE COULD HE POSSIBLY HAVE GONE AT THIS TIME OF NIGHT?

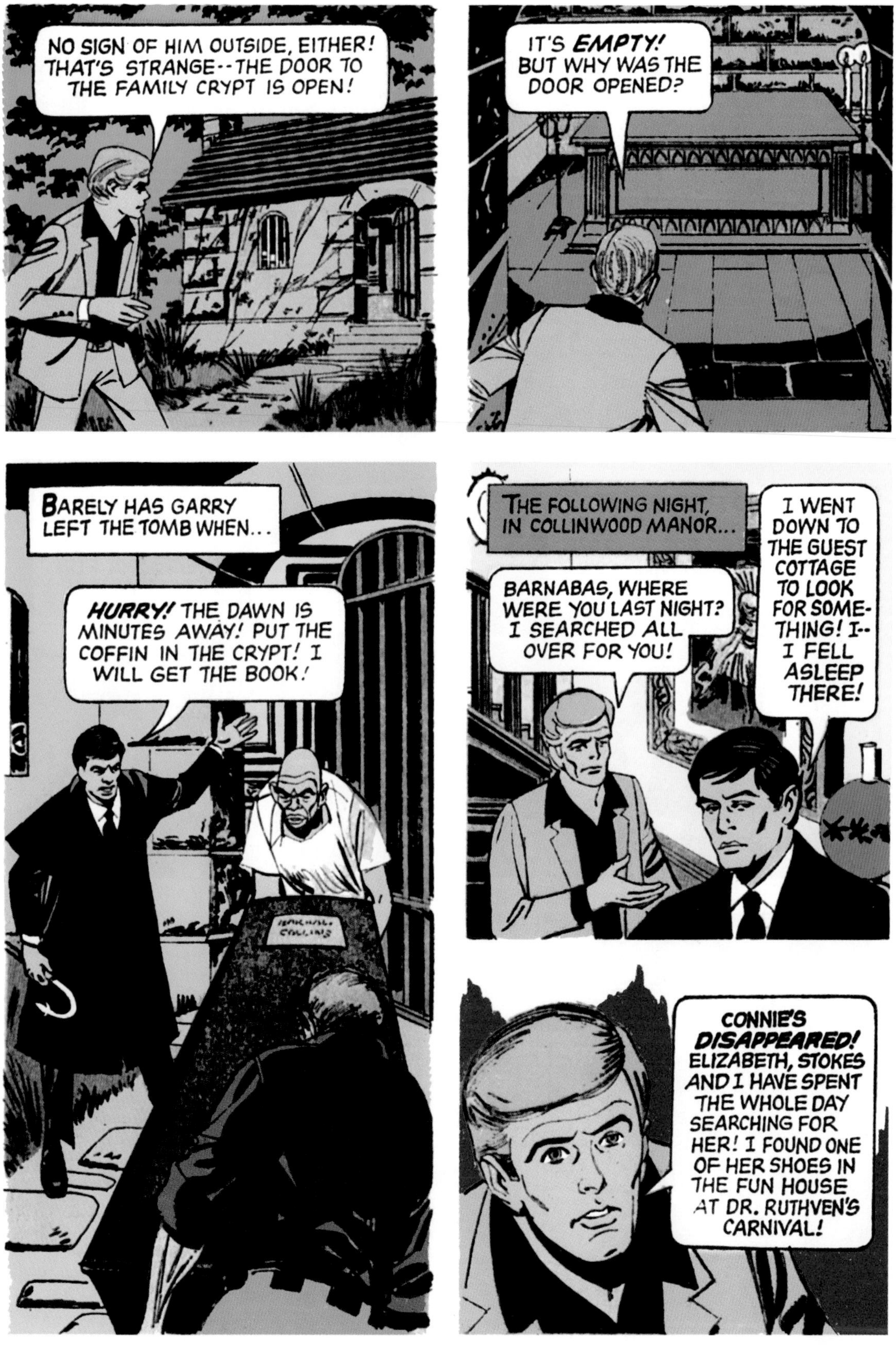
NO SIGN OF HIM OUTSIDE, EITHER! THAT'S STRANGE--THE DOOR TO THE FAMILY CRYPT IS OPEN!
IT'S EMPTY! BUT WHY WAS THE DOOR OPENED?
BARELY HAS GARRY LEFT THE TOMB WHEN...
HURRY! THE DAWN IS MINUTES AWAY! PUT THE COFFIN IN THE CRYPT! I WILL GET THE BOOK!
THE FOLLOWING NIGHT, IN COLLINWOOD MANOR...
BARNABAS, WHERE WERE YOU LAST NIGHT? I SEARCHED ALL OVER FOR YOU!
I WENT DOWN TO THE GUEST COTTAGE TO LOOK FOR SOMETHING! I-- I FELL ASLEEP THERE!
CONNIE'S DISAPPEARED! ELIZABETH, STOKES AND I HAVE SPENT THE WHOLE DAY SEARCHING FOR HER! I FOUND ONE OF HER SHOES IN THE FUN HOUSE AT DR. RUTHVEN'S CARNIVAL!

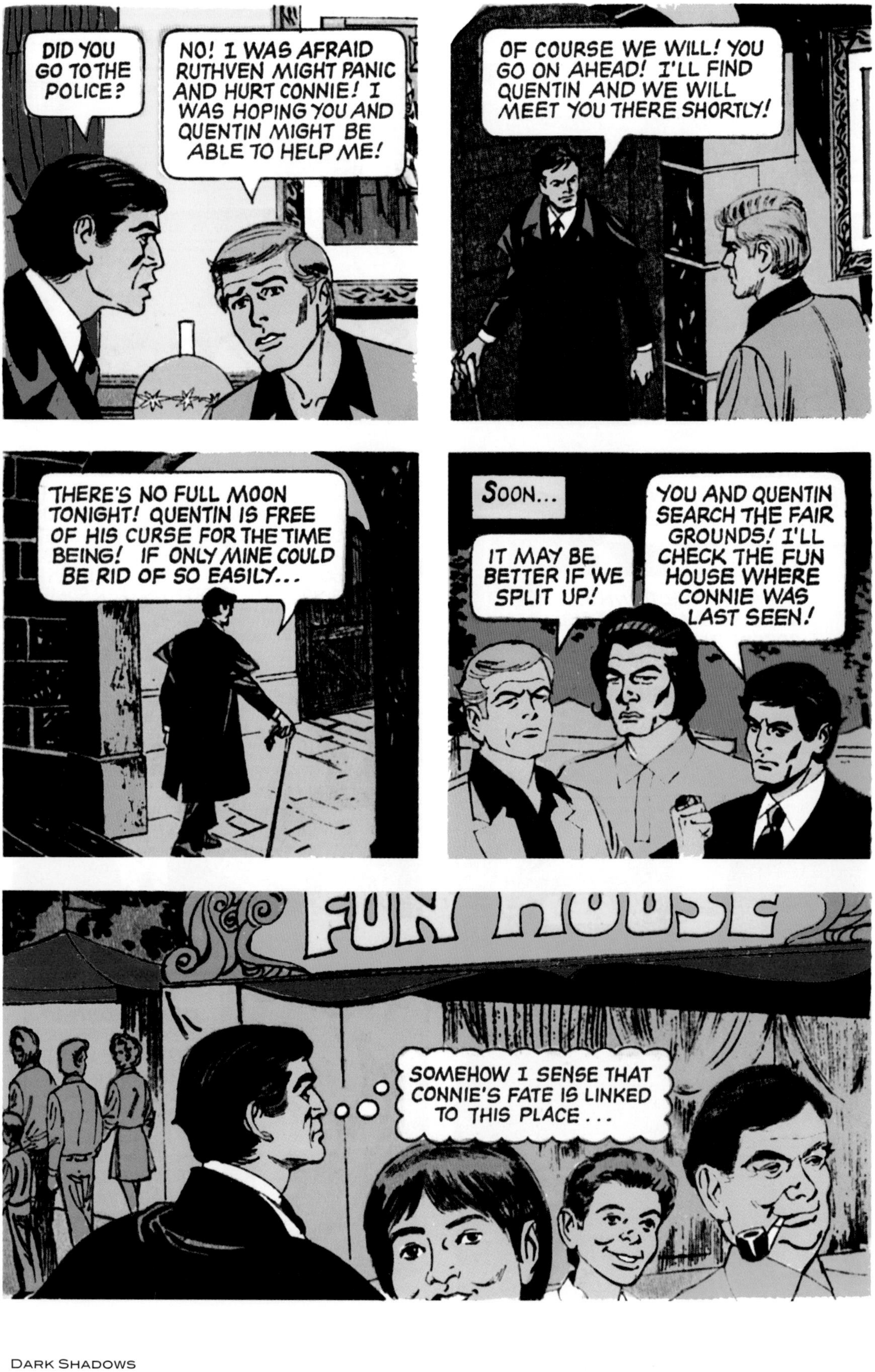
DID YOU GO TO THE POLICE?
NO! I WAS AFRAID RUTHVEN MIGHT PANIC AND HURT CONNIE! I WAS HOPING YOU AND QUENTIN MIGHT BE ABLE TO HELP ME!
OF COURSE WE WILL! YOU GO ON AHEAD! I'LL FIND QUENTIN AND WE WILL MEET YOU THERE SHORTLY!
THERE'S NO FULL MOON TONIGHT! QUENTIN IS FREE OF HIS CURSE FOR THE TIME BEING! IF ONLY MINE COULD BE RID OF SO EASILY...
SOON...
IT MAY BE BETTER IF WE SPLIT UP!
YOU AND QUENTIN SEARCH THE FAIR GROUNDS! I'LL CHECK THE FUN HOUSE WHERE CONNIE WAS LAST SEEN!
FUN HOUSE
SOMEHOW I SENSE THAT CONNIE'S FATE IS LINKED TO THIS PLACE...

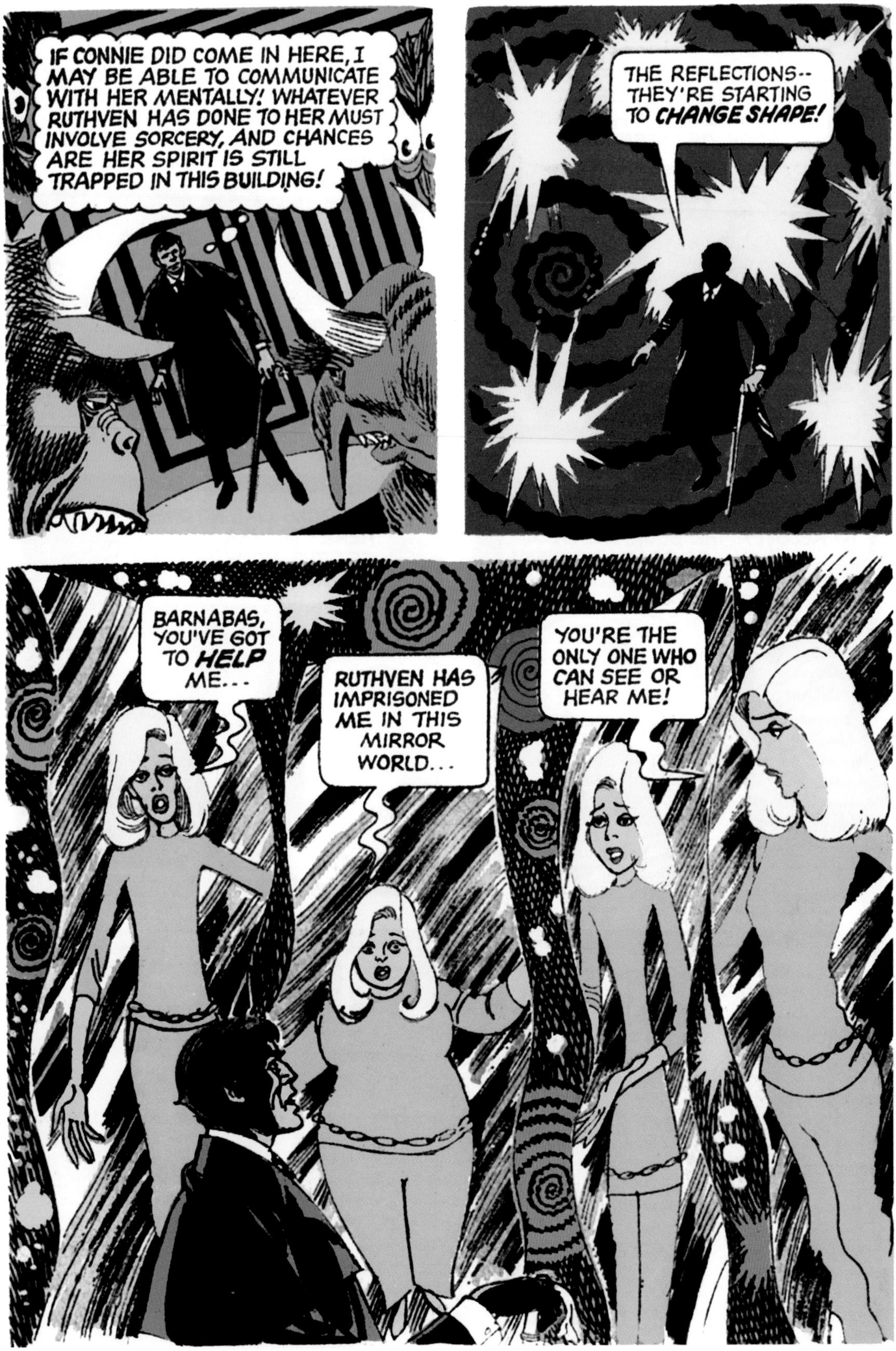
IF CONNIE DID COME IN HERE, I MAY BE ABLE TO COMMUNICATE WITH HER MENTALLY! WHATEVER RUTHVEN HAS DONE TO HER MUST INVOLVE SORCERY, AND CHANCES ARE HER SPIRIT IS STILL TRAPPED IN THIS BUILDING!
THE REFLECTIONS-- THEY'RE STARTING TO CHANGE SHAPE!
BARNABAS, YOU'VE GOT TO HELP ME...
RUTHVEN HAS IMPRISONED ME IN THIS MIRROR WORLD...
YOU'RE THE ONLY ONE WHO CAN SEE OR HEAR ME!

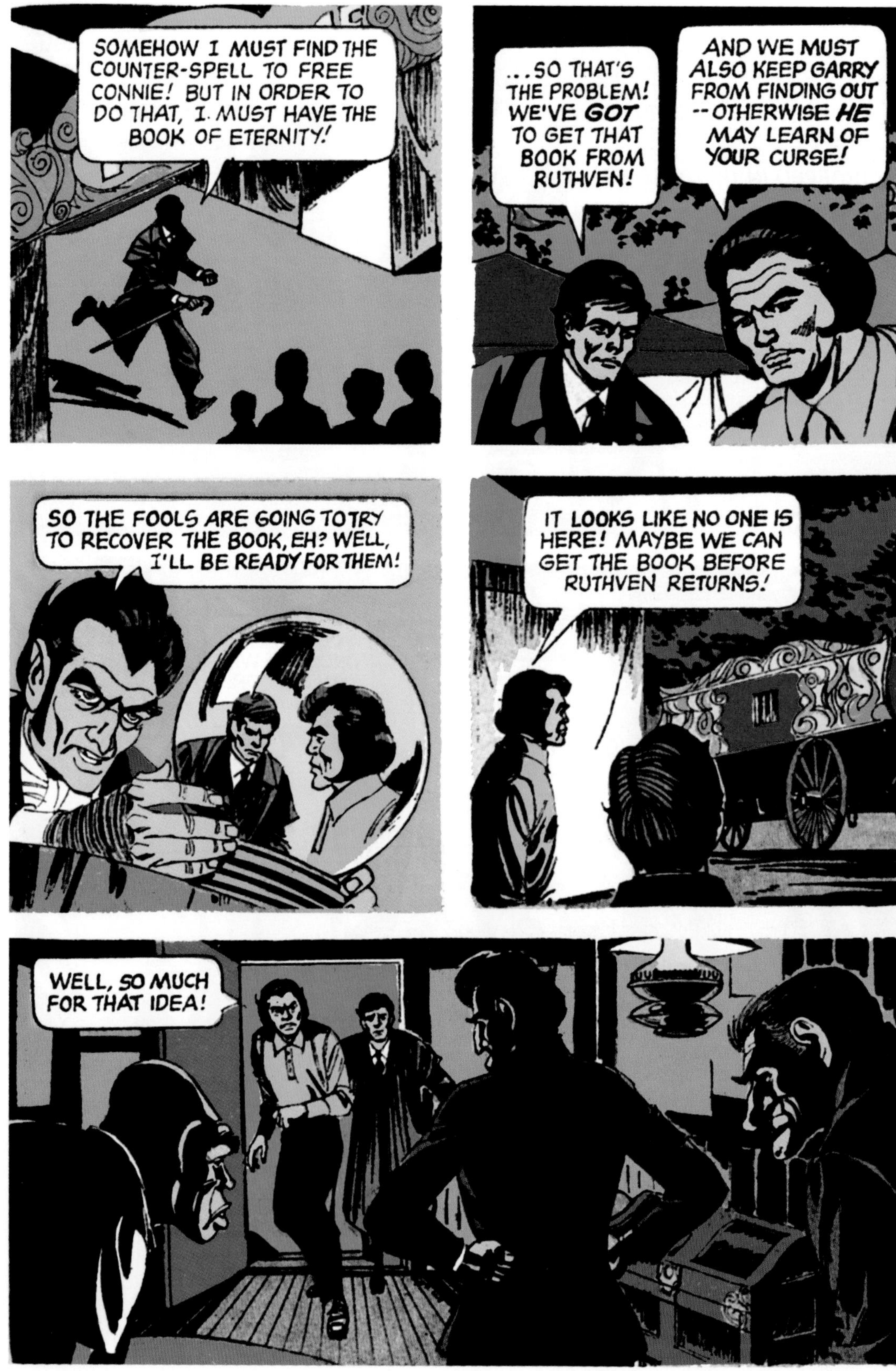
SOMEHOW I MUST FIND THE COUNTER-SPELL TO FREE CONNIE! BUT IN ORDER TO DO THAT, I MUST HAVE THE BOOK OF ETERNITY!
...SO THAT'S THE PROBLEM! WE'VE GOT TO GET THAT BOOK FROM RUTHVEN!
AND WE MUST ALSO KEEP GARRY FROM FINDING OUT --OTHERWISE HE MAY LEARN OF YOUR CURSE!
SO THE FOOLS ARE GOING TO TRY TO RECOVER THE BOOK, EH? WELL, I'LL BE READY FOR THEM!
IT LOOKS LIKE NO ONE IS HERE! MAYBE WE CAN GET THE BOOK BEFORE RUTHVEN RETURNS!
WELL, SO MUCH FOR THAT IDEA!

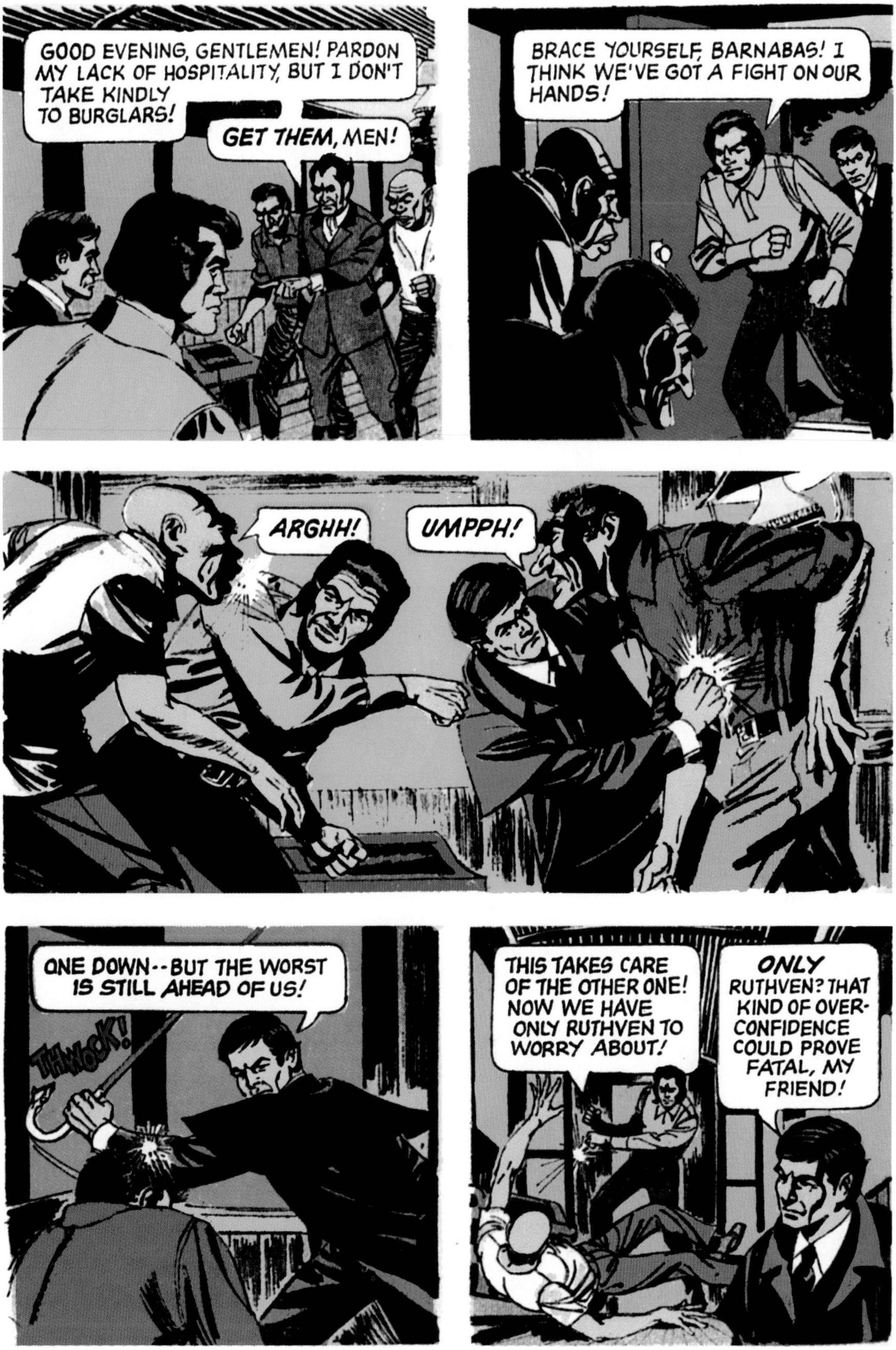
GOOD EVENING, GENTLEMEN! PARDON MY LACK OF HOSPITALITY, BUT I DON'T TAKE KINDLY TO BURGLARS!
GET THEM, MEN!
BRACE YOURSELF, BARNABAS! I THINK WE'VE GOT A FIGHT ON OUR HANDS!
ARGHH!
UMPPH!
ONE DOWN--BUT THE WORST IS STILL AHEAD OF US!
THWOCK!
THIS TAKES CARE OF THE OTHER ONE! NOW WE HAVE ONLY RUTHVEN TO WORRY ABOUT!
ONLY RUTHVEN? THAT KIND OF OVER-CONFIDENCE COULD PROVE FATAL, MY FRIEND!

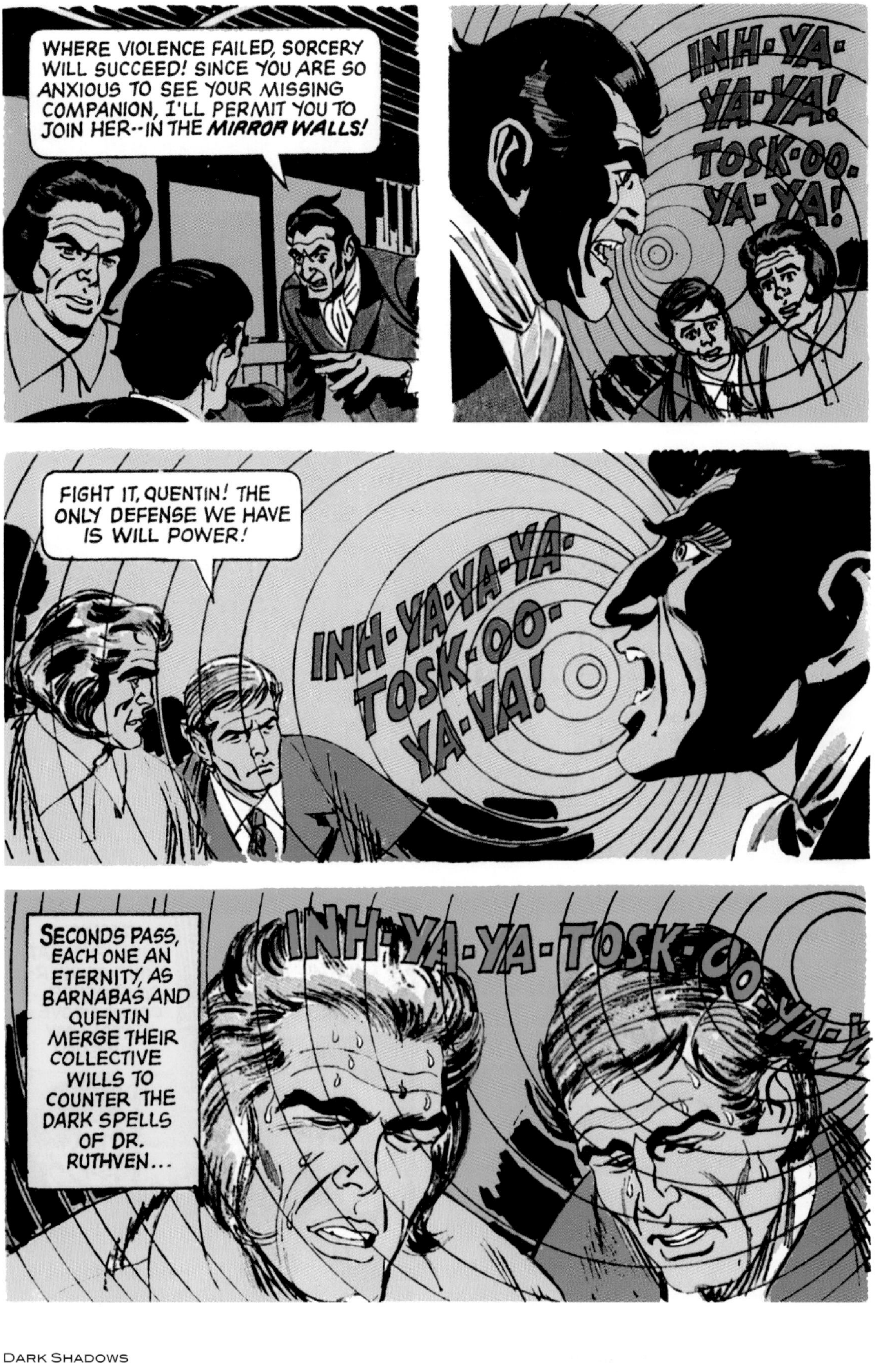
WHERE VIOLENCE FAILED, SORCERY WILL SUCCEED! SINCE YOU ARE SO ANXIOUS TO SEE YOUR MISSING COMPANION, I'LL PERMIT YOU TO JOIN HER--IN THE MIRROR WALLS!
INH-YA-YA-YA! TOSK-OO-YA-YA!
FIGHT IT, QUENTIN! THE ONLY DEFENSE WE HAVE IS WILL POWER!
INH-YA-YA-YA-TOSK-OO-YA-YA!
SECONDS PASS, EACH ONE AN ETERNITY, AS BARNABAS AND QUENTIN MERGE THEIR COLLECTIVE WILLS TO COUNTER THE DARK SPELLS OF DR. RUTHVEN...
INH-YA-YA-TOSK-OO-YA-

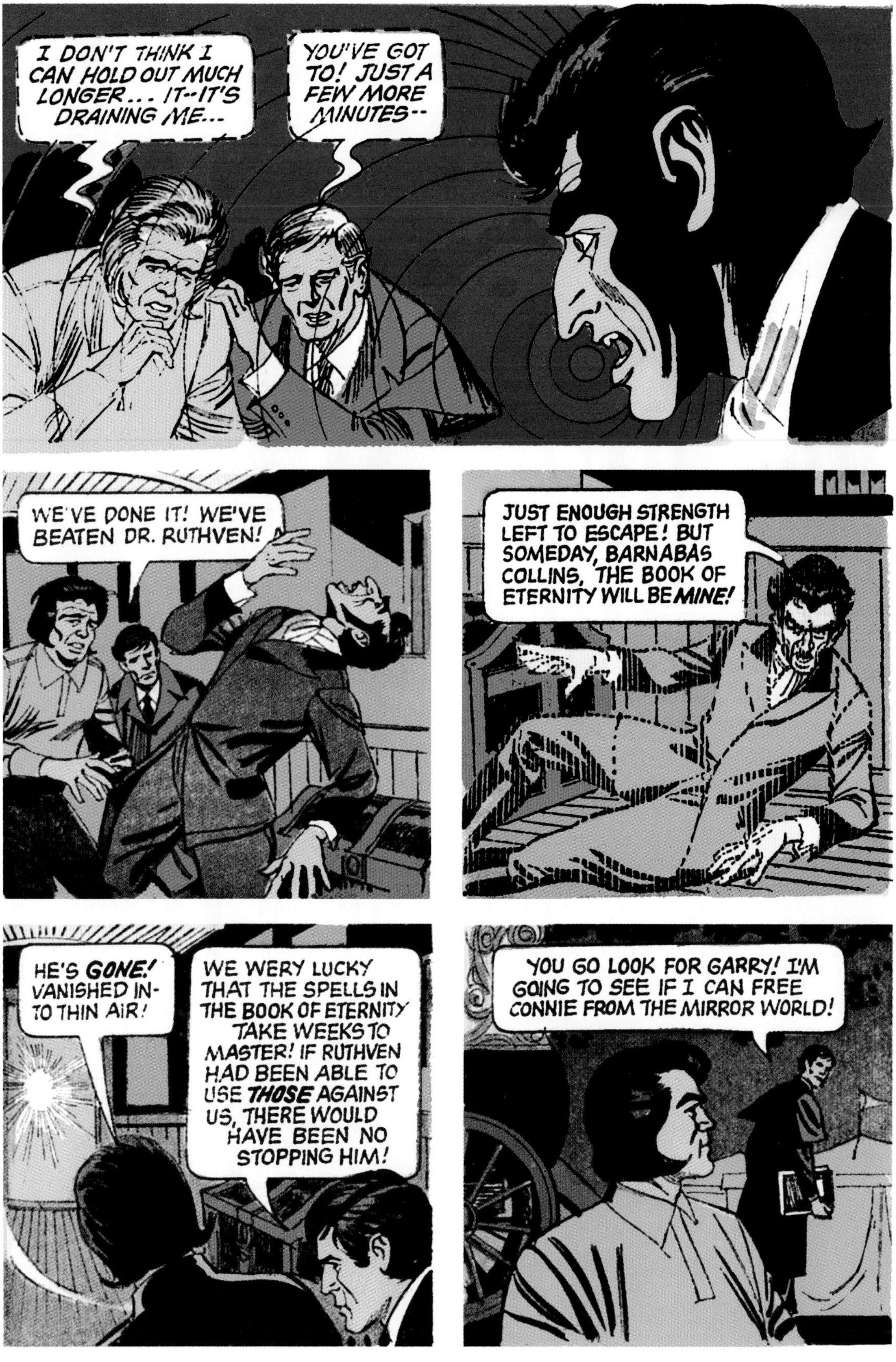
I DON'T THINK I CAN HOLD OUT MUCH LONGER... IT--IT'S DRAINING ME...
YOU'VE GOT TO! JUST A FEW MORE MINUTES--
WE'VE DONE IT! WE'VE BEATEN DR. RUTHVEN!
JUST ENOUGH STRENGTH LEFT TO ESCAPE! BUT SOMEDAY, BARNABAS COLLINS, THE BOOK OF ETERNITY WILL BE MINE!
HE'S GONE! VANISHED INTO THIN AIR!
WE WERY LUCKY THAT THE SPELLS IN THE BOOK OF ETERNITY TAKE WEEKS TO MASTER! IF RUTHVEN HAD BEEN ABLE TO USE THOSE AGAINST US, THERE WOULD HAVE BEEN NO STOPPING HIM!
YOU GO LOOK FOR GARRY! I'M GOING TO SEE IF I CAN FREE CONNIE FROM THE MIRROR WORLD!

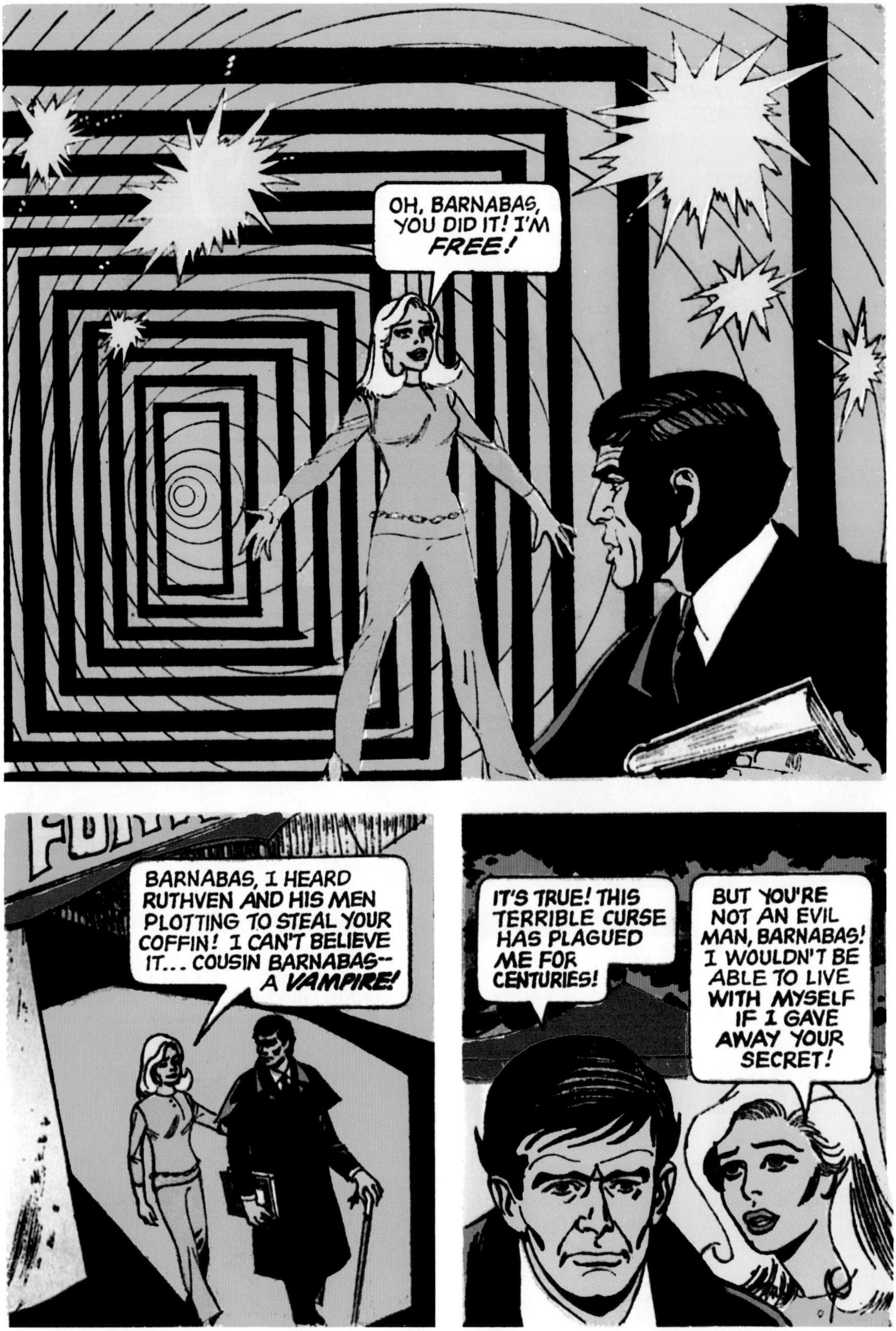
OH, BARNABAS, YOU DID IT! I'M FREE!
BARNABAS, I HEARD RUTHVEN AND HIS MEN PLOTTING TO STEAL YOUR COFFIN! I CAN'T BELIEVE IT... COUSIN BARNABAS-- A VAMPIRE!
IT'S TRUE! THIS TERRIBLE CURSE HAS PLAGUED ME FOR CENTURIES!
BUT YOU'RE NOT AN EVIL MAN, BARNABAS! I WOULDN'T BE ABLE TO LIVE WITH MYSELF IF I GAVE AWAY YOUR SECRET!

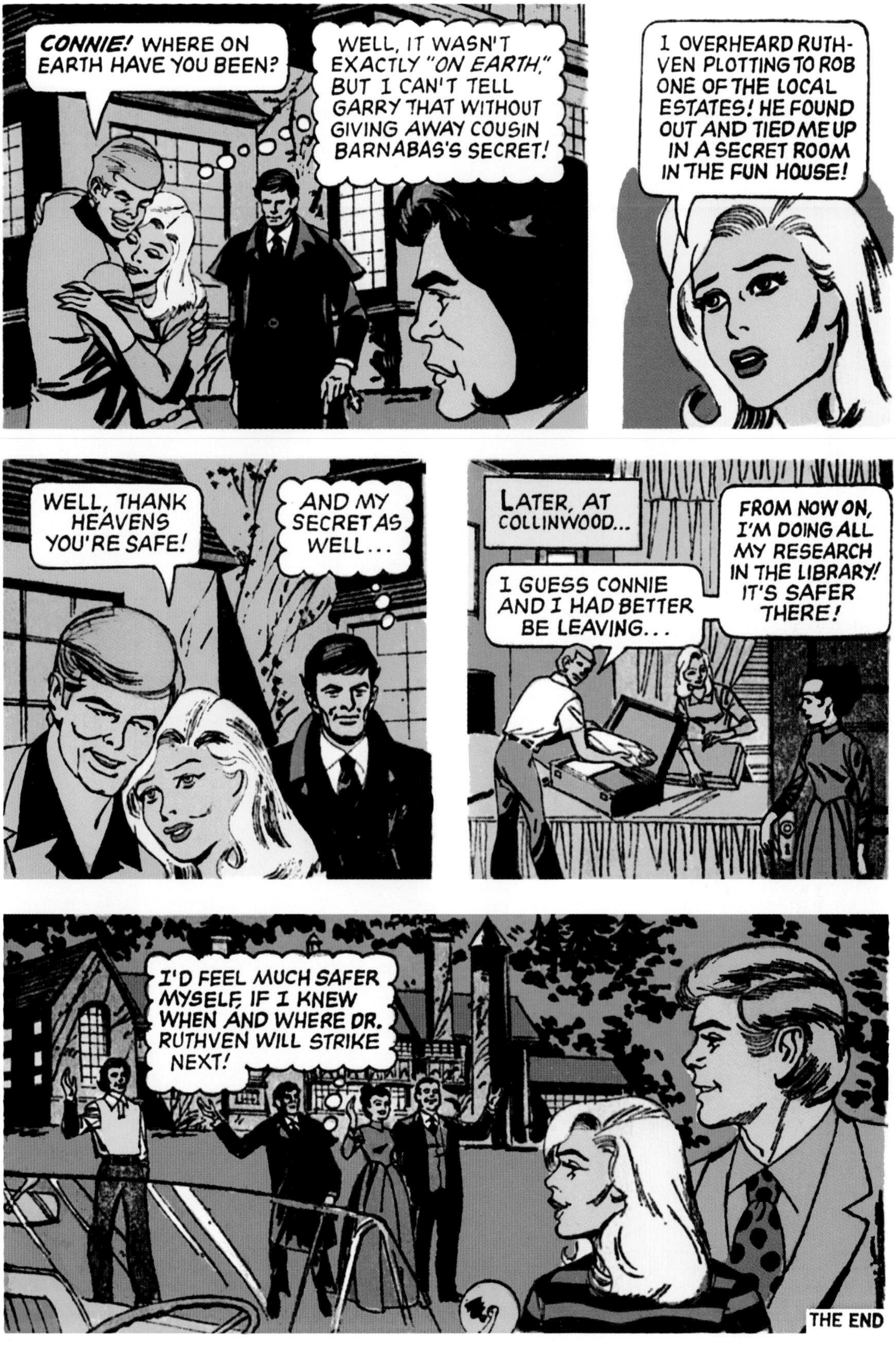
CONNIE! WHERE ON EARTH HAVE YOU BEEN?
WELL, IT WASN'T EXACTLY "ON EARTH," BUT I CAN'T TELL GARRY THAT WITHOUT GIVING AWAY COUSIN BARNABAS'S SECRET!
I OVERHEARD RUTHVEN PLOTTING TO ROB ONE OF THE LOCAL ESTATES! HE FOUND OUT AND TIED ME UP IN A SECRET ROOM IN THE FUN HOUSE!
WELL, THANK HEAVENS YOU'RE SAFE!
AND MY SECRET AS WELL...
LATER, AT COLLINWOOD...
I GUESS CONNIE AND I HAD BETTER BE LEAVING...
FROM NOW ON, I'M DOING ALL MY RESEARCH IN THE LIBRARY! IT'S SAFER THERE!
I'D FEEL MUCH SAFER MYSELF, IF I KNEW WHEN AND WHERE DR. RUTHVEN WILL STRIKE NEXT!
THE END

Photos from the Original Series

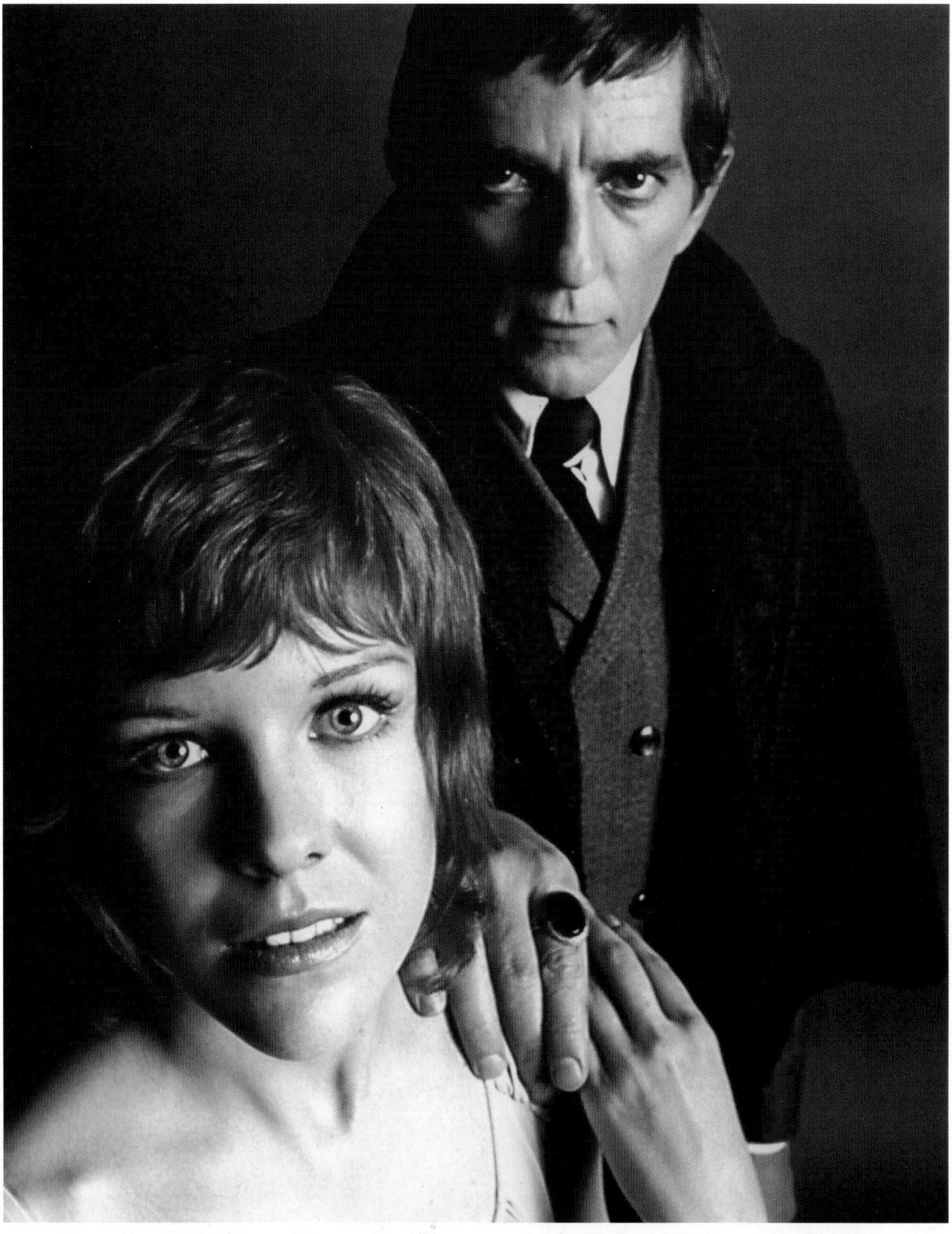

Above: 1970 ABC-TV publicity photo of Jonathan Frid as Barnabas Collins and Donna Wandrey as Roxanne Drew. Opposite page: David Selby as Quentin Collins in 1970.

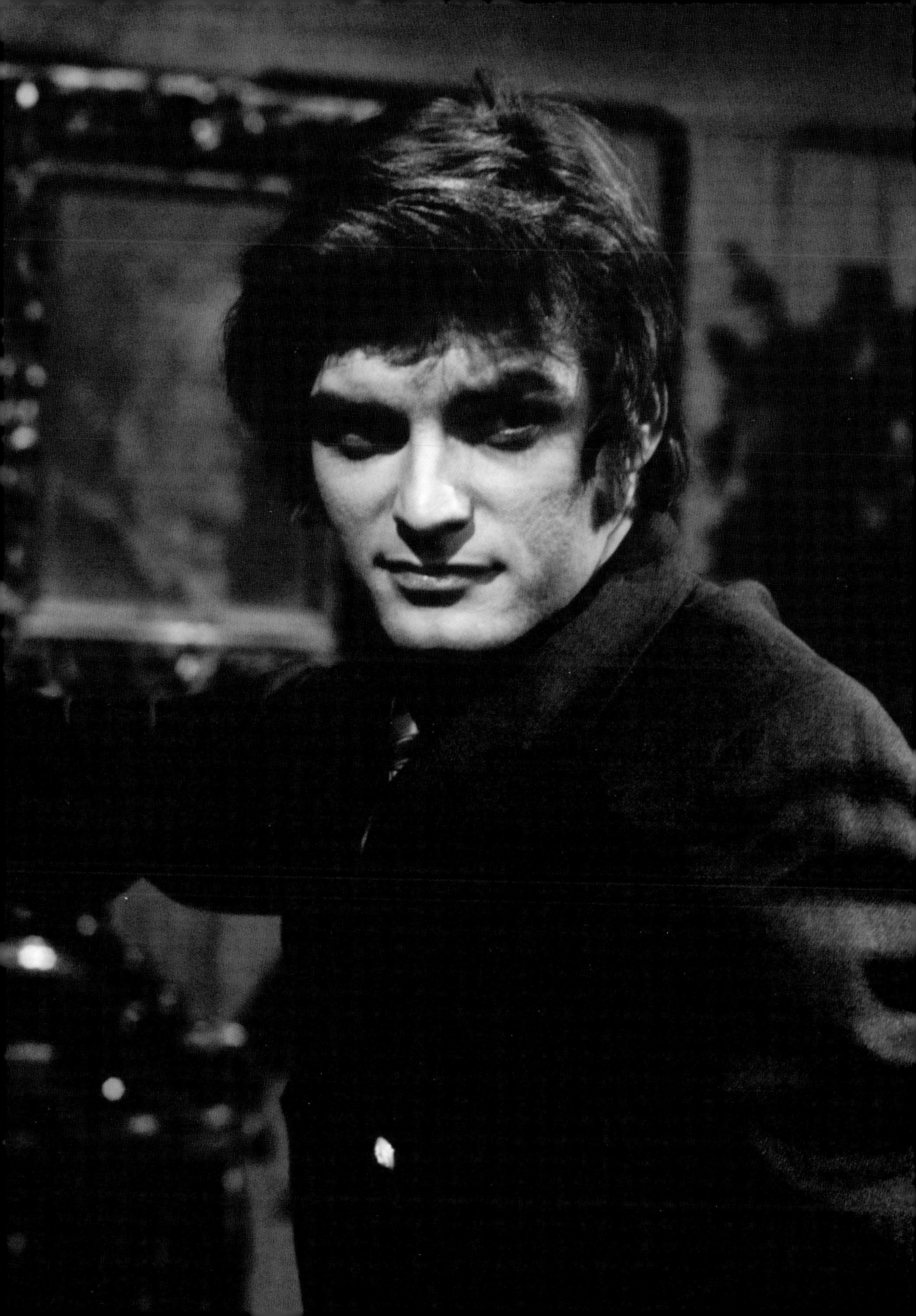

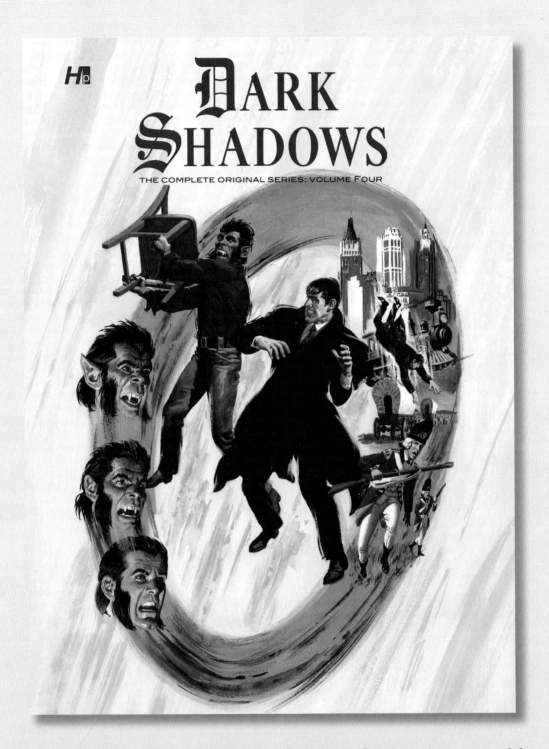